Sophie Pembroke has been dreaming, reading and writing romance ever since she read her first Mills & Boon as part of her English Literature degree at Lancaster University, so getting to write romantic fiction for a living really is a dream come true! Born in Abu Dhabi, Sophie grew up in Wales and now lives in a little Hertfordshire market town with her scientist husband, her incredibly imaginative and creative daughter and her adventurous, adorable little boy. In Sophie's world, happy *is* for ever after, everything stops for tea, and there's always time for one more page...

Award-winning romance author **Kerri Carpenter** writes contemporary romances that are sweet, sexy and sparkly. When she's not writing, Kerri enjoys reading, cooking, watching movies, taking Zumba classes, rooting for Pittsburgh sports teams and anything sparkly. Kerri lives in northern Virginia with her adorable (and mischievous) rescued poodle mix, Harry. Visit Kerri at her website, kerricarpenter.com, on Facebook (Facebook.com/authorkerri), Twitter and Instagram (@authorkerri), or subscribe to her newsletter.

Also by Sophie Pembroke

The Unexpected Holiday Gift
Newborn Under the Christmas Tree
Island Fling to Forever
Road Trip with the Best Man
CEO's Marriage Miracle
Carrying the Millionaire's Baby
Slow Dance with the Best Man
Proposal for the Wedding Planner

Also by Kerri Carpenter

Falling for the Right Brother
Bidding on the Bachelor
Bayside's Most Unexpected Bride

Discover more at millsandboon.co.uk

PREGNANT ON THE EARL'S DOORSTEP

SOPHIE PEMBROKE

THE DATING ARRANGEMENT

KERRI CARPENTER

MILLS & BOON

First Published in Great Britain 2019
by Mills & Boon, an imprint of HarperCollinsPublishers,
1 London Bridge Street, London, SE1 9GF

Pregnant on the Earl's Doorstep © 2019 Sophie Pembroke
The Dating Arrangement © 2019 Kerri Carpenter

ISBN: 978-0-263-27254-3

0719

MIX
Paper from
responsible sources
FSC C007454
FSC
www.fsc.org

This book is produced from independently certified FSC™
paper to ensure responsible forest management.

For more information visit: www.harpercollins.co.uk/green

Printed and bound in Spain
by CPI, Barcelona

PREGNANT ON THE EARL'S DOORSTEP

SOPHIE PEMBROKE

For Carolyn

CHAPTER ONE

LENGROTH CASTLE LOOKED bigger than it had on the website. More imposing.

On the slick, professional website of the Earl of Lengroth the castle had been bathed in sunlight, with impossibly blue skies shining behind its corner towers, the stone walls almost white in the sunshine. In reality, even on a dry July day in Scotland, the skies were more white with cloud than blue, and the stone was a heavy, dark and imposing grey. The seventeen stone steps up to the dark wooden front door seemed designed to put visitors off altogether—they were narrow, steep, and they looked slippery with moss encouraged by the moat they rose across.

In fact, the whole scene was enough to make Heather Reid want to jump on the first train back to Hertfordshire and never return.

Except she couldn't. Not until she'd done what she'd come to do. After that…? Well, what happened next was anybody's guess. By then the ball would be firmly in the court of Ross Bryce, Earl of Lengroth.

Steeling herself, Heather crossed the gravelled courtyard from the open front gate and carefully made her way up those seventeen slippery steps. Halfway up, she risked a glance down at the moat. The water was black and bottomless. Much like her fear.

Heather swallowed and took another step.

A splash beside her made her jump and almost lose her footing. Grappling for purchase on one of the higher steps, Heather darted her gaze around, looking for the cause of the sound. A fish? Duck? Crocodile? She wouldn't put it past the Earls of Lengroth to have installed the Loch Ness Monster in their moat.

Then she spotted the rubber duck, bobbing happily on the dark water.

'Not a monster,' she whispered to herself. 'That's a start.'

But that duck definitely hadn't been there when she'd started climbing the steps. Risking letting go of her step, Heather looked up at the windows overhead, trying to see who might have thrown the rubber duck.

Nothing.

Ross Bryce had kids, she remembered uncomfortably. Two of them, perfectly turned out in a party dress and a sailor suit respectively, featured on the home page of the website, standing and smiling sweetly next to their handsome father, the Earl, and their beautiful mother, Lady Jane Bryce, Countess of Lengroth.

She'd been physically sick when she'd seen that photo and realised how monumentally she'd screwed up. Of course, she'd been throwing up a lot lately anyway. But seeing that photo had marked the moment she'd realised just how much trouble she was in, and the magnitude of the consequences she had to face.

There was still no sign of the duck's owner, but Heather had been a teacher long enough to know that when a child threw a duck at you it meant you weren't wanted. In fact, she was pretty sure she'd have been able to figure that much out even *without* her teaching qualification.

Carefully, she reached down to the water and retrieved the duck as it bobbed past, tucking it under her arm.

'I don't want to be here, either, kid, believe me,' she muttered.

And then she took the next step anyway—because what choice did she have?

She'd made a mistake and now she needed to own up to it, deal with it and face it head-on. She knew only too well what happened when people ducked their own guilt and tried to cover up their actions with lies.

The big brass knocker on the castle door echoed around the courtyard as she lifted it and let it fall against the wood. At least she'd survived the steps and the duck missile. As long as the door didn't open outwards and send her flying into the moat she was almost there.

And then would come the really hard part.

She'd practised what she would say to Ross— it was hard to think of him as the Earl of Lengroth at this point— all the way up on the train. She'd thought of different ways to break the news, but it all came down to the one basic fact.

I'm pregnant. With your child.

She really hoped his wife wasn't in the room when she saw him again.

Not that he'd mentioned his wife, of course, when they'd met that night in London. Or his kids. He'd told her about the castle, and about lonely dark Scottish nights— even in early June, apparently. He'd talked about the countryside and his responsibilities and the parties he went to.

But he'd failed to mention his family. And he hadn't been wearing the wedding ring she'd seen on his finger later, in the most prominent website photo of them all—a large family portrait.

'You must have all the aristocratic ladies after you,' she'd joked, when he'd told her where he lived and shown her a snapshot on his phone. *'How do you know they're interested in you and not your castle?'*

'Trust me,' he'd replied with a wicked grin. *'My castle is the least impressive thing about me.'*

Heather groaned, just remembering the line. How had she fallen for that? She blamed the cocktails her friend Lacey had insisted on them drinking.

Was anybody *ever* going to open this door? She really wasn't enjoying reliving the worst mistake of her life in her head while she waited. She'd done enough of that over the last month as it was.

Now she was there, at Castle Lengroth, she just wanted to get this over with. She wanted to see Ross Bryce and tell him everything. She wanted this to be someone else's problem, too, even if just for a few minutes before he inevitably threw her out.

Heather didn't have high hopes for this meeting. But she knew it was something she had to do. Ross deserved to know about the baby—even if he didn't want anything to do with it, or her, after this. At least she'd have done the right thing.

Because, apart from one stupid night in London almost two months ago, Heather Reid *always* did the right thing. Her mother had taught her that much—if only by being a stunning example of what happened when a person didn't.

Finally the door creaked open to reveal an elegant, polished older lady in a navy skirt suit and a cream blouse, with a string of pearls around her neck and sensible navy shoes on her feet.

'I'm here to see the Earl of Lengroth,' Heather said as

confidently as she could, as if it were the sort of thing she said every day.

'You're late,' the woman told Heather sternly. 'Come on. He's waiting.'

Heather blinked twice, then followed. She got the feeling that this woman wasn't used to being disobeyed.

'Um…how am I late, exactly?'

Well, she *was* late—six weeks late at this point— but she was pretty sure the woman wasn't talking about Heather's period.

'I didn't have an appointment…' Maybe she should have made one. Except she couldn't imagine that Ross was going to be happy to see her again.

The woman didn't answer—in fact, Heather wasn't even sure if she heard her over the sound of her own heavy footsteps on the polished stone floors of the hallway. On either side the walls were painted dark shades of green, in between bare stone columns, and every now and again they'd pass a chair with tartan cushions, as if there to give people a chance to recover from the unrelenting hard darkness of the place.

Finally, after several more hallways, eight chairs and two staircases, the woman stopped in front of another heavy wooden door and rapped her knuckles sharply against it.

'Come in,' a male voice called, and as the woman opened the door Heather thought she heard him mutter, 'Finally…' under his breath.

Heather stepped inside just as the woman said, 'The new nanny is here, sir.'

Nanny? Okay, someone had got something *seriously* confused here.

But as Heather stared at the darkly handsome man behind the mahogany desk she realised that a case of mistaken identity was the least of her problems. Because the man sitting at the desk belonging to the Earl of Lengroth wasn't the man she'd slept with in London almost two months earlier.

Cal Bryce had never harboured any ambitions to be the Earl of Lengroth. He didn't want the title, the castle, the requirement to provide an heir, the responsibility, or to have to uphold the reputation expected of a sterling member of the aristocracy.

And in fairness, he still didn't have most of those things. He wasn't the Earl—he remained the Hon Calvin Bryce, as he'd always been as the Earl's younger brother. The castle *wasn't* his—it belonged to his nephew Ryan, the eight-year-old newly minted Earl. He *didn't* have to provide an heir—and he didn't think anyone was expecting Ryan to do so for quite some years yet.

Since his brother Ross's death, however, the responsibility *was* all his—at least until Ryan turned eighteen. And the reputation... Well, it seemed that was Cal's to fix, too.

What on earth made you take that corner so fast, brother? Cal thought, not for the first time since he'd got that middle-of-the-night call and heard Mrs Peterson, the castle housekeeper, shrieking incomprehensibly down the phone at him from thousands of miles away in Scotland.

'They're dead! They're both dead, Cal!' she'd finally managed to say.

And the bottom had fallen out of Cal's world.

His whole life Ross had been a constant. And he'd needed that so badly—especially when they were growing up. While the world around them might have believed that the Bryce family were a perfect example of modern aristocracy done right, Ross and Cal had known the truth.

The family weren't above scandal and outrageous behaviour—they'd just grown very, very good at covering it up.

As a child, all Cal had known was tha[...] out of the way when his father started shouti[...] he was drinking it was better not to be in the [...] Ross, three years older, had taught him all the [...] places—and the signs to look out for telling him [...] was time to run. And when Cal got it wrong Ross had stood between him and the Earl to give his little brother a head start.

Cal had idolised Ross. Until six weeks ago.

Even as he'd grown up into a teen, and then a young man, it had taken Cal some time to realise the true nature of his genetic inheritance. The Bryces hid their scandals well—even from their own flesh and blood. But once he'd seen his first evidence—walking in on his father in bed with the barmaid from the village pub was a scene sadly seared into his memory—he'd started to notice it everywhere. Especially as his parents had become less careful of their words around him.

There was the affair his mother had been having with the family lawyer for most of Cal's life. The endless parade of barmaids and local girls he'd seen letting themselves out of the castle kitchens in the mornings. The bruises on Ross's face and arms after a shouting match with their big bear of a father—red-faced and fuming so much of the time.

Hell, there was even the legend of the Lengroth ghost, which was currently causing him issues in ways the woman couldn't possibly have imagined a hundred years ago when she'd died. The story went that a century earlier one of the local village girls had got pregnant and claimed the father was the Earl. Shunned by the local village people, and with her reputation ruined, she'd come to the castle to ask for his help. The Earl had denied her and sent her away, and she'd fallen down the castle steps and died—although some still whispered to this day that she'd been pushed.

Cal wished he didn't know the truth about that one, if he was honest. His ancestors were enough of a disappointment to him already.

But not Ross. Ross had married the beautiful and lovely Janey and had two beautiful and lovely children. Ross had bucked the family trend.

Cal couldn't even look at the battlements of Lengroth Castle without remembering all the awfulness that had happened inside it. But Ross had moved the family in—made the castle a home, even if it *was* still stone-walled and imposing. Ross had found a way to overcome their genetic disposition towards scandal and bad behaviour.

At least so Cal had believed, until he'd returned home to take over the reins after Ross's death.

Now he was starting to think that Ross had just been better than all of them at hiding his true self.

Cal had thought that the world of business was hard—building up and running a company with a multiple seven-figure turnover took time, energy and commitment. He'd thought he understood about responsibility and challenges.

But that had been before he'd had to deal with the gambling debts, the lies and promises Ross had left behind him.

And before he'd had to hire a nanny for two grieving and uncontrollable children.

He eyed the latest one—the ninth in six weeks—as Mrs Peterson showed her in. In addition to being a full forty minutes late, she looked a little casual for a job interview, dressed in a flowery sundress and sandals—with a jumper on top because this *was* summer in Scotland, after all. Her copper-coloured hair flowed loose in waves over her shoulders, and she carried a rucksack on her back, as if she were a gap year student going travelling. Which she might be, he supposed. She looked young enough.

She also had a rubber duck tucked under her arm, but Cal decided he wasn't even going to ask about that.

The bottom line was that desperate guardians couldn't be choosers, and the agency must be running out of nannies to send him by now.

Mrs Peterson was also looking unimpressed with her. *She*, Cal noticed, was wearing her best suit and heels—the way she always did when there was a potential new member of staff on-site or an important visitor of some sort. She must have got more wear out of it in the last six weeks than in the decade beforehand. But Cal knew she'd have her fluffy slipper boots back on the moment she made it back to the kitchen. The stone floors of Castle Lengroth were hard on the feet.

He turned his attention back to the nanny. Part of him wanted to dismiss her out of hand, but another, larger part, knew that he needed her. He wasn't capable of being the parental figure his niece and nephew so desperately required. He just wasn't father material—he'd always known that.

Which meant he needed someone who would stick it out and look after Daisy and Ryan for the next six weeks—and he'd got the impression from his most recent call to the agency that this was his last shot.

Which meant he had to be persuasive. And he had to follow the plan he and Mrs Peterson had cooked up the night before.

1. Offer her more than she can get anywhere else
2. Make it completely conditional on her finishing the six weeks
3. Don't mention the ghost

Easy.

'Okay, Miss...' he consulted the notes from his call with the agency '...Thomas. Here's the deal. My niece and nephew need a reliable, effective and capable nanny for the next six weeks of the school holidays, until they leave for boarding school in England. Your agency says that you're up to the job, and I have to believe them. So I'm going to make you an offer you won't get anywhere else. If you stick out six weeks here at Castle Lengroth, and get the children prepared physically, mentally and emotionally for boarding school, I'll pay you for a full year's work at your agency base rate. But if you quit before the six weeks are up you get nothing.'

The redheaded nanny opened her mouth, then closed it again. Then she said, 'I think there's been some sort of misunderstanding—'

Cal cut her off before she could get any further. That was another thing he and Mrs Peterson had agreed on— not giving her too much time to overthink things. He knew that the agency nannies talked to each other—they probably had their own message group on social media or something—so she almost certainly already knew the situation here.

The last nanny had quit before she'd even made it into the castle, when ten-year-old Daisy had thrown a bucket of soapy water over her from the nursery window above the front steps. Cal wasn't risking losing this one before she even met the devil children.

'I know what you must have heard from your predecessors, Miss Thomas,' he said, smiling as charmingly as he could, given what was on the line here. 'I can't imagine it's many families that go through eight nannies before they find the right one. But I have an excellent feeling about you,' he lied.

'Eight nannies?' she echoed faintly, and Cal cursed himself for mentioning it. It sounded so much worse spelt out like that.

'The children have been through a lot since their parents died nearly two months ago,' he said, defensively. 'It's natural that they're acting out a bit. And, in fairness, seven of the eight said it wasn't the children that drove them away, it was the ghost.'

Dammit. I wasn't supposed to mention the ghost.

In the doorway, Cal saw Mrs Peterson throw up her hands in despair and turn to leave, closing the door behind her. Obviously she knew a lost cause when she saw one.

But the new nanny didn't even seem to register his mention of a supposed supernatural being haunting the castle. Probably because she was a sensible person who didn't believe in ghosts and was going to accept his offer. He hoped.

'Eight nannies in less than two months?' she said incredulously.

Then her pale face turned somehow even whiter. Cal resisted the impulse to check over his shoulder for the ghost.

'Wait, their parents…? The Earl of Lengroth, Ross Bryce, and his wife…?'

'Yes. My brother, Ross, and my sister-in-law, Janey,' Cal confirmed, confused.

She sank into the chair opposite him without being invited to do so. Since she looked as if she might fall over otherwise, Cal didn't object. He probably should have asked her to sit before he'd hit her with the terms of the job, actually.

'They died? When?'

She placed the rubber duck on the desk absently. Really—*who* brought a rubber duck to a job interview?

'Almost two months ago,' Cal repeated, since the information clearly wasn't going in.

She couldn't be a local girl if she didn't know that already, although he'd guessed that from her accent anyway. It had been a mere blip of a mention in the national news—a blink-and-you'd-miss-it piece. But locally it had dominated the newspapers for weeks.

'June,' she said softly, and bit down on her lip. 'It must have been just after I—' She broke off and shook her head, copper curls rustling.

'Miss Thomas. Tragic though my brother's passing is...' Cal swallowed hard at the memory, hearing Mrs Peterson's panicked voice all over again '...I really think we should get back to the matter in hand. Your position as nanny to my niece and nephew.'

She looked up, her green eyes bright. 'And *I* think, Mr Bryce, that we need to start over. You see, I'm not Miss Thomas from the agency, and I'm not here for the nanny position. I'm here about your brother.'

And suddenly Cal knew that his faith in his perfect older brother was about to take another hit.

One it might not be able to recover from.

CHAPTER TWO

THE YOUNGER, EVEN more handsome Bryce brother stared at her across the desk—some sort of family heirloom, Heather supposed, given the weight and colour of it. The rubber duck clashed horribly with the surroundings, bringing a sense of surrealism to the whole scene.

As if it wasn't absurd enough already.

Don't get distracted by the desk. Or the duck. Focus on what you're here to do.

Except mentally debating the provenance of furniture was far easier than telling the man sitting behind it that she'd had a one-night stand with his dead brother. Before he was dead. Obviously.

Oh, this was going to go badly.

'You're not from the agency?' Mr Bryce repeated. 'Then who exactly are you? And, more importantly, who were you to my brother?'

Did he already know? Maybe Ross had done this sort of thing all the time. Maybe she was just the latest in a line of women his brother had taken 'meetings' with over the last couple of months.

Heather took a deep breath, and began. 'My name is Heather Reid,' she said, forcing herself to meet his gaze. 'About two months ago I met your brother, Ross, in a nightclub in London and spent the night with him. And now I'm pregnant with his child.'

A child who would never know their father. Heather clutched at the arm of the chair as reality hit home now the words were out in the open. Ross was dead. The vibrant, laughing, charming man she'd spent the night with was gone. More importantly, her child's father was dead.

He might have been an adulterous liar, but she wouldn't wish death on *anybody*. Especially since it meant she was all alone in this now.

Even if Ross had thrown her out of the castle she'd have always known that her child had a father he or she could go to later, if they needed to. That there was someone else in the world that they belonged to.

And now there was only her. And her baby's uncle, sitting on the other side of that damn desk, staring at the rubber duck she'd placed between them.

His expression had hardly changed, she realised. Whatever he was feeling about her revelation, it wasn't shock. Which told her a lot more about Ross's general behaviour than she liked.

'Mr Bryce?' she said, when he didn't answer.

'Cal,' he said tiredly, rubbing a hand over his forehead. 'My name is Cal Bryce.'

'Right. Um… Cal, then.' She waited. Still no response. 'Do you want to…I don't know…see some ID or something?'

Cal's eyebrows rose slowly as he turned his gaze back on her. 'For you or for the baby?'

Heat flushed to her cheeks. 'Right. Obviously you'll want some sort of DNA test at some point—which is fine. I mean, for all you know I'm some random woman who read about your brother's death and came here to try it on and get some money out of you. Except I'm not.'

Cal was looking at her as if that was *exactly* what he

thought she was, now she came to mention it. Heather couldn't really blame him. She was *not* good at this.

'Oh! I have one thing that might help...' She pulled her phone from the pocket of her dress and scrolled back through the photos to find the one she wanted before holding it out over the desk to show him.

His eyes darkened as he stared at the photo of her and Ross, surrounded by the dim lights and noise of that London bar, both grinning into the lens as he'd held the phone out to snap the picture. Something to remember him by, he'd said.

Turned out she really didn't need the photo.

Cal sat back, looking up again, over her shoulder, and Heather took the phone back. This couldn't be pleasant for him, either.

Although, *he* wasn't the one who might throw up the sandwich she'd eaten on the train any second now, because of a load of stupid hormones, so her sympathy only went so far.

'Do you believe me?' she asked quietly, when he still said nothing.

'Yes,' Cal replied. 'The lawyers will want the test, of course, but, yes. I believe you. I'm just trying to figure out what to do next.'

Heather gave him a small, lopsided smile. 'You and me both.'

He wasn't that much like Ross, now she'd got past the looks, Heather decided. Ross hadn't stopped talking the whole time they were together—about himself, about her, about places he'd been or wanted to go—yet he still hadn't managed to say any of the things that really mattered.

Cal, after his initial pitch for the nanny job, had been practically silent ever since she'd broken the news.

But he believed her. That was a big thing. She was clinging on to that.

'What did you hope to get from coming here today?' Cal asked finally.

Heather shrugged one shoulder. 'I'm not sure. Mostly I just wanted to tell Ross about the baby. I knew...' She swallowed. 'After I took the test, and he didn't answer his phone, I looked up the castle he'd talked about online. I saw the photos of him and his family on the website. He didn't... When we met he wasn't wearing a wedding ring, and he didn't say anything to lead me to believe he was in a relationship, let alone married with kids.'

Cal's eyes fluttered shut for a second. 'No. I suppose he wouldn't have.'

'So I wasn't coming here for a happy-ever-after, or to demand that he marry me, or anything. I was sort of expecting him to throw me out, to be honest, so in some ways this is already going better than that.'

Apart from the bit where his brother was dead, of course. Oh, she was *really* screwing this up.

'Basically, I knew the right thing to do would be to tell Ross that he was going to be a father. Again. That's all I wanted. After that... Well, it would have been up to him. I just wanted to do the right thing.'

Because that mattered. She needed to be able to look her reflection in the eye when she caught sight of it in the mornings. She needed to know she'd done the right thing for her child.

The way her own mother hadn't.

And now she'd done that.

Which meant she had to figure out what the hell happened next on her own.

'The right thing?' Cal repeated the words with an ironic smile. As if there *was* such a thing in a woeful situation like this one.

He pitied that baby, being born into the Bryce family, with its legacy of screw-ups, scandals and sadness. What chance did it have?

Or perhaps he or she would be luckier than the rest of them. After all, this baby wouldn't have to grow up in Lengroth Castle, surrounded by reminders of the expectations the world placed upon it and knowing that if he or she didn't want to meet them, they'd have to learn how to hide the truth.

And, most of all, this baby would have Heather Reid, which was more than Ross's other two kids had. They were stuck with Uncle Cal, screwing them up for the rest of their childhoods.

Cal knew what Ross had been thinking when he'd named him as guardian—he'd been assuming it would never be needed. And who else was there, really? Who else would be able to understand the legacy of the Bryce family well enough to try and fix things for them all—or at least hide the truth a little longer?

Heather Reid wouldn't understand that, he'd bet. She was probably an honest, good girl, out of her depth in the pool of Lengroth scandals.

Of course, he could be overestimating her. Because, really, who travelled all the way from London to the wilds of Scotland just to 'do the right thing'? Nobody in Cal's family, that was for certain.

He wasn't sure any of his ancestors or relatives would even know what the right thing *was*, if it came calling. Not even Ross.

So, as trustworthy as Heather seemed, Cal knew better than to take those wide, innocent eyes at face value.

'Did you hope he'd support you financially?' he asked. That had to be it, right? Ross had told her he lived in a damn castle—of course she was after money. 'Or buy you off, so he didn't have to tell Janey?'

The worst part was that was probably exactly what Ross *would* have done. What Bryce men had been doing for generations to cover up their misdemeanours and betrayals. Hiding their scandals away under a blanket of hush money.

It was just that Cal had been so sure that Ross was different. And that if Ross could be different maybe he could, too. Maybe the scandal gene had skipped a generation, or something.

But here it was, fresh and revitalised for a whole new era of Bryces, ready to bring the Earldom of Lengroth into disrepute once and for all. Hiding bad behaviour had been a lot easier before the advent of social media.

Across the desk, he saw Heather's eyes had widened with shock. 'I didn't… *No.* Like I said—I have a job of my own. Supply teaching might not pay brilliantly, but I like working with the kids and it'll pay enough to support me *and* this baby, just. So, no, I wasn't expecting money. As I told you—if anything, I was expecting him to throw me out.'

'But you came anyway?'

'But I came anyway.'

Cal eyed her across the desk. She seemed genuine. Sincere. But then, people always did—until they screwed you over.

Then his gaze landed on the duck again. 'I have to ask…' He gestured towards it.

Spots of pink appeared on Heather's cheeks. 'Oh! It sort of…appeared in the moat as I was approaching the door. It seemed wrong to leave it there so I brought it in with me.'

Daisy, Cal was willing to bet. After tossing a bucket

of water out of that nursery window a rubber duck was nothing. Practically a step down, in fact.

Cal thought wistfully of the time when he'd honestly believed that his niece and nephew were delightful, well-behaved children. When he'd lived thousands of miles away and only seen them for an afternoon at a time.

'How do you imagine the duck got there?' he asked Heather. 'In the moat, I mean?' An idea was starting to form somewhere in the back of his brain. It was entirely possible that it was a terrible idea, but it wasn't as if he had any better ones to go with. Especially since it seemed that the latest nanny from the agency hadn't even made it as far as the castle gates.

'Oh, I couldn't possibly say.'

There was a wry smile on Heather's face that told Cal everything he needed to know. Firstly, that she knew *exactly* who must be responsible for the duck, but wasn't going to drop the kids in it. And, secondly, that Heather Reid was an open book, with her every thought and feeling shown on her face for him to read—as long as he could see it.

It was the second of those two facts that convinced him to follow the hare-brained plan that had evolved in his mind. After all, if he could see Heather's face he'd know when she was about to do something stupid. Like sell her story about her night with the Earl to the local papers. Or try to blackmail him for financial support. Or whatever.

And maybe, just maybe, what Daisy and Ryan really needed was someone on their side—the way Cal had always had Ross. And Cal had a feeling that Heather could be that person.

If she said yes.

Well, he'd never know if he didn't ask.

'So. You're pregnant with my niece or nephew. I am

guardian to your baby's half-brother and half-sister. Clearly whatever happens next we're all in each other's lives now.'

Heather frowned. 'I...I suppose.'

Her lack of enthusiasm was, Cal supposed, understandable. He wouldn't want to be a part of this family either if he hadn't been born into it. Even then, actually. But he didn't have any choice. All he could do now was try and make growing up as a Bryce less awful for Daisy and Ryan than it had been for him and Ross. And he sure as hell couldn't do that on his own.

He took a breath and tried to smile as he said, 'In which case I have a proposition for you. If you'll hear it?'

He had no idea what to do next if she wouldn't.

A proposition? Heather remembered all too well what had happened *last* time a guy with the surname Bryce had propositioned her. But Cal didn't seem like the sort.

She'd come all this way. The least she could do was hear him out. After all, it wasn't as if she had any clear idea of her path forward. All she knew was that she needed to figure out a way to handle her situation without bringing scandal and shame down on her father. *Again.* He'd had enough of that for one lifetime, and last time... Well, the bottom line was she couldn't risk that happening again.

She needed to manage this carefully. Maybe Cal could help her do that.

'I'm listening,' she said neutrally, watching his expression.

Cal leaned forward in his chair, folded his hands on the desk next to the rubber duck and gazed straight into her eyes. 'I want you to stay here for the summer as nanny to Daisy and Ryan—Ross's children.'

Heather blinked. 'What?' She might have been less

surprised if he'd suggested he ravish her over the desk, or that they set up a rubber duck factory together. 'I'm… I'm not a nanny.'

'No, you're a teacher. Which means you know kids a hell of a lot better than I do, for sure. Daisy and Ryan…they're ten and eight and they're struggling. They need someone who knows what they're doing and I think that person is you. Plus, teachers get great summer holidays, right?'

Six weeks. Six weeks in which she'd normally be planning for the next school year, sorting out her classroom, preparing supplies and resources… Except she'd been on a maternity leave cover contract for a year and, despite the promise of another position when the teacher she was covering for returned, last-minute budget cuts meant she didn't *actually* have a new job for September yet. No class to prepare for. And, given all the upheaval in her life, she'd figured some supply work might be best for the next term or so anyway. Until she figured out what she was doing.

All of which meant she really *didn't* have anything to do this summer.

She thought back to Cal's rambled job description when he'd thought she was Miss Thomas.

'If you stick out six weeks here at Castle Lengroth, and get the children prepared physically, mentally and emotionally for boarding school, I'll pay you for a full year's work at your agency base rate. But if you quit before the six weeks are up you get nothing.'

Did that offer still stand? A year's wages, even at nanny agency rates, would go an awful long way towards providing her with the cushion she needed to take care of this baby—and herself—until she got a new job. She could break the news of her pregnancy to her father in her own time and, while she'd have to tell *him* about the whole sleeping with a married earl thing, maybe no one else would need to know. It didn't seem that Cal was desperate to shout it from the rafters.

There'd be talk at home, of course. But an unmarried mother was a totally different thing to an aristocratic homewrecker. And very different again from last time, with her mother. Maybe it would be okay...

Besides, if things got bad she'd have money, and if she had money she had options. She could go and stay somewhere else for a while, until everything blew over. Take Dad with her, even. Maybe Wales, where they'd used to go on family holidays before.

Heather ran her tongue across her suddenly dry lips. 'What are the terms?'

She didn't *want* to spend the summer in Scotland. Not that she had anything against the country particularly, but it wasn't where she belonged. Especially not in this dark and foreboding castle with duck-wielding children.

But if *she* didn't want to be in this scary, imposing place, how must the kids feel about it? They'd grown up here, of course. But given what she knew of their father, and what she could therefore guess about their parents' marriage and family relationships, would that be a good thing or a bad thing?

'Same as if you really were the nanny from the agency,' Cal said. 'In fact, no one but us two need to know that you aren't. I think that would be better for now, don't you?'

Heather gave a slow nod. But *would* it be better? She wasn't good at secrets. She knew the harm they could do. But under the circumstances...what option did she have?

'So, you'd stay a full six weeks and get the children ready for boarding school—I have a folder with the details somewhere...' He looked around his immaculate desk, empty except for the rubber duck, then back at Heather. 'Or perhaps Mrs Peterson does. Anyway. You do that and I'll pay you a year's wages—not as a bribe, or because my brother got you into trouble, but because you'll have earned it.'

He'd anticipated her issues with the arrangement, Heather realised. As much as she could use the money, it *did* feel like a bribe—and that wasn't what she'd come here for. But he'd offered the money before he'd even known who she was, so it was a genuine payment for services rendered.

God, how bad *were* these kids?

At least there's only two of them. That can't be harder to handle than a class of thirty-four, right? And I manage them well enough.

Besides, teaching was one thing. Living with and supporting kids through important life changes was something else entirely. Something she needed to learn to do now she was going to become a mother.

'I don't suppose I can take some time to think about it?' she asked.

Cal shrugged. 'Honestly…? You might as well say yes now. Even if you leave in the next day or two nobody will be surprised. In fact, forty-eight hours will be more than the last nanny managed.'

'You're not selling this, you know.'

'I know.' Cal sighed. 'I'm not going to lie to you. The kids are hard work. I don't understand them, and I don't think they even *want* to be understood. Plus, the castle might actually be haunted—but you'll be long gone by Halloween, so hopefully that won't be an issue.'

'I don't believe in ghosts.' There were enough things in the real world to be terrified of, Heather had found, without adding a whole new fictional layer of fear.

'Even better.' Cal gave her a small smile—maybe the first she'd seen from him. It made him look younger, lighter. And even more handsome. 'The bottom line is, if you stay you can get to know your baby's family. And we can get to know you. You might decide you want nothing to do with us afterwards, but at least you'll have the information to make that decision with. And I'll get to help you financially without it being underhand or dodgy.'

'No one else will know why I'm really here?' Heather asked. That was important. 'I haven't... You're the only person who knows about the baby.'

He looked a little surprised at that. 'No one else will hear about it from me,' he promised.

And against her better judgement Heather believed him.

Six weeks. Six weeks to figure out what she wanted to do next and earn the money to pay for it. Six weeks to figure out how to admit to her father how badly she'd screwed up. To steel herself against his disappointment and upset.

Nannies were practically servants, right? And servants were prized for being invisible. Heather liked being invisible. If people didn't see you they were less likely to talk about you, taunt you or humiliate you.

She'd spent her childhood being part of the most talked about family in her small village. Here she could be completely anonymous—despite the scandal she carried inside her.

Six weeks.

How hard could that be?

She nodded. 'Okay.'

CHAPTER THREE

CAL HARDLY LET her get the word out before he pressed a button on the phone on his desk and called Mrs Peterson.

'Is she staying?' his housekeeper asked bluntly through the speakerphone. 'Or do I need to call another taxi? Only you know how much Harris hates driving all the way up here every time you lose another nanny. He'll be on his lunch break now, anyway.'

She made it sound as if he was misplacing them somewhere, in the nooks and crannies of the cavernous castle. As if they weren't actually running out through the front door without looking back.

The last one hadn't even waited for Harris—the driver of Lengroth village's only taxi—to show up. She'd walked the three miles to the station instead.

'Miss Reid is staying with us,' Cal said smugly.

'Reid?' He could almost hear Mrs Peterson's eyebrows rising. 'I thought the agency said her name was Thomas?'

Damn. He wasn't good at subterfuge. But he'd have to get better quickly if he was going to disguise his brother's pregnant mistress as a nanny for the next month and a half.

'A mix-up at the agency, it seems. Our new nanny is Miss Heather Reid.'

'I've stopped bothering to learn their names,' Mrs Peterson replied. 'Did the agency get the time of the interview wrong, too?'

'Yes. Yes, they did.' Mrs Peterson valued promptness highly, and what was one more little white lie if it smoothed the relationship between the nanny and the housekeeper of Lengroth Castle? 'In fact, Miss Reid was technically fifteen minutes early.'

'Hmph.'

Across the desk, Heather was looking most amused by his attempts to pacify his housekeeper. He resisted the urge to toss the rubber duck at her to stop her silent laughter.

'So if you could please come up to the office and take Miss Reid for a tour of the castle, and to meet the children…?'

There was a loud sigh on the speakerphone. 'I suppose,' she said, and then the line went dead.

'Mrs Peterson is not a big fan of nannies?' Heather asked.

'To be honest, the last few we've had haven't really tried to endear themselves to her.' Cal tried to smile reassuringly. 'Mrs Peterson is a sweetheart when you get to know her, I promise.'

Heather looked sceptical.

But when Mrs Peterson arrived a few minutes later—Cal suspected she hadn't wasted time going all the way back down to the kitchen…she'd probably figured she'd be needed to show the nanny out before she even got that far—Heather smiled sweetly at her and talked about how excited she was to get to know the children and the castle.

'We'll see how long *that* lasts,' Mrs Peterson muttered ominously.

As they shut the door behind them Cal let out a long breath and sank down into his chair to process the last half an hour. Much as he'd far rather take a nap, there were still so many things to deal with.

So, taking stock…

Pluses: he had someone to look after Daisy and Ryan, hopefully for the rest of the summer, so he could get on with fixing everything their father, his brother, had screwed up before his death.

Minuses: that person was pregnant with Ross's child, and was basically another scandal waiting to happen.

Cal didn't think Heather was about to go running to the papers, seeking a pay-out for the headline *Adulterous Earl Fathers Baby from the Grave* or anything, but he knew better than most that appearances could be deceiving. At least this way he'd be keeping the scandal close to home, until he was sure of Heather's character. And the baby *was* a Bryce—he definitely believed that much.

Another nephew or niece for him to not know how to love. After all, it wasn't as if he'd ever been given any examples of loving parenthood, or even a loving relationship.

'Your heart's as cold as a Scottish winter,' his latest ex-girlfriend had told him as she'd walked out. *'The view might be nice, but you wouldn't want to live there.'*

She might have had a point, he had to admit. But *his* life wasn't the problem here. Ross's was. And not just because of Heather.

With a sigh, Cal pulled over the folder sitting on the corner of his desk, sending the rubber duck toppling over as he did so. The folder's cover was blank—purposely. Cal didn't need a reminder to know what was inside it.

Another of his big brother's follies.

Living the lives they did, the Earls of Lengroth had never been particularly good at holding on to their money. Fortunately the estate was still reasonably lucrative—

with most of it rented out to farmers or tenants in the linked village. But the castle took a lot of upkeep, which required all that money.

At least it did when there was someone sensible at the reins—usually an estate manager or the current Countess of Lengroth.

Ross, however, seemed to have believed he could do it all himself. Or maybe he'd felt he *needed* to, in order to keep his secrets. Because what Ross mostly seemed to have done with the estate finances was gamble it away.

Cal's eyes fluttered closed as he tried, for an unsavoury moment, to imagine his perfect big brother at the gambling tables, throwing away his children's inheritance. Or in a London bar, seducing Heather Reid.

The latter was alarmingly easy. With that river of copper hair, and those soft green eyes, Cal could easily imagine any man's attention being drawn to her, even across a darkened bar.

He opened his eyes again. *Not helping, Cal.* Especially since he liked to think—in his better moments—that he might actually be able to resist the kind of scandalous fall from grace that seemed to afflict all the Earls of Lengroth sooner or later.

'But I'm *not* the Earl,' he muttered to himself.

He was going to do everything in his power to stop Ryan from following that same path. But first he had to finish fixing Ross's mistakes.

He flipped open the folder, ready to start again.

Most of the basic gambling debts he'd dealt with up front, the moment he'd found them. He should have used the estate money, he knew, but that was Ryan's, and Cal didn't want his nephew to be saddled with money troubles from the outset. Fortunately Cal's own property business in the States was lucrative enough that he'd had enough personal wealth to fill the hole. His accountant hadn't been happy about it, but then neither was Cal, really.

More problematic to deal with were the times when Ross had clearly tried to use his title and minor celebrity in place of money. Or to impress, Cal supposed. He wasn't sure what else would explain the obligation sitting on top of the pile, waiting for him to fix it. An email from a magazine editor, confirming plans made with Ross for later in the summer.

'Why on earth would Ross have invited a reporter to come and stay at the castle?' he wondered aloud, rubbing a hand over his eyes as if that would change the contents of the printout in front of him.

It didn't.

Only one way to find out, Cal supposed.

He picked up the phone to try and explain to this editor that, with Ross dead, there was no way in hell he was letting a journalist anywhere near Lengroth Castle this summer.

She'd left the rubber duck in Cal's office, Heather realised as Mrs Peterson showed her yet another identical green and grey room in the cold, dead castle. She should have brought it with her—either as a peace offering or a sign that she couldn't be intimidated by flying bath toys.

Except she was, of course—intimidated. And not just by ducks.

Thirty-four children in a classroom were one thing. Two children alone in a castle, with a ghost and a revolving door for nannies, were something completely different.

Heather felt sick again. Didn't this castle have *any* bathrooms? She wasn't sure that Mrs Peterson had shown her one.

'And this will be your room,' Mrs Peterson said finally, opening the door on a grey room with a grey metal bed and a green and grey tartan bedspread. There was a chair by the window, looking out over the front of the castle all the way to the grey gates. Heather wondered if this was where Daisy had thrown the duck from.

'Is there a bathroom?' Heather entered the room cautiously, looking for a bathroom door and possibly a ghost, or a child waiting to jump out at her and pelt her with bath toys. She saw neither.

'Down the hall,' Mrs Peterson answered. 'Lengroth Castle was built before the advent of your modern en suite bathrooms, you realise.'

Lengroth Castle had clearly been built before indoor plumbing, central heating, electricity and Wi-Fi technology, too, but Heather sincerely hoped *they'd* all been included in any subsequent remodelling.

'Down the hall? Right...'

Feeling she'd taken in enough of the room, Heather dumped her rucksack beside the bed, turned to Mrs Peterson and said, 'So, shall we go and meet the children?' in her best Mary Poppins voice.

Mrs Peterson looked suspicious.

'I mean, that *is* what I'm here for,' Heather went on, knowing she was babbling and unable to stop herself. 'To be a nanny, I mean.' And definitely not the bearer of the children's illegitimate half-sibling or anything. *No, sir.*

Oh, she was *terrible* at lying. Clearly she took after her father and not her mother there. Why had she ever thought she could pull this off?

But after a long moment Mrs Peterson stepped back, out of the doorway. 'The nursery is this way.'

She click-clacked off down the corridor, her heels

echoing off the stone walls, and stopped at the next door, a good ten metres away.

Heather steeled herself, and followed.

'Children,' Mrs Peterson said as she opened the nursery door, 'this is Miss Reid, your new nanny.' She sounded almost...*fond*, Heather realised. Which, given what she knew of the children so far, didn't make much sense.

Unless they were in it together, determined to drive away any newcomers to the castle.

Heather was so engaged in a sudden daydream of Mrs Peterson dressing up in a white sheet pretending to be a ghost, while Daisy and Ryan stood behind her hurling rubber ducks at an invading army of nannies, that she almost forgot to greet the children.

'Hello! You can call me Heather. And you two must be Daisy and Ryan!' She was still channelling Mary Poppins, she realised. If she wasn't careful she might burst into song at any moment.

'She doesn't look like the other nannies,' Ryan said, eyeing her with suspicion.

His dark hair was curled over his forehead, so like his father's and his uncle's that Heather felt a pang of sympathy all over again.

Mrs Peterson looked at Heather and sighed. 'No. No, she doesn't.'

'Maybe that means I'll last longer than they did,' Heather replied, a little archly.

Mrs Peterson's mouth flickered into something that might almost, *almost* be considered a smile. If she squinted. The almost smile was gone so quickly that Heather wasn't entirely sure she hadn't imagined it.

'Daisy. Come and say hello to Miss Reid.'

Over at the window, looking out over the very steps

Heather had climbed to get into the castle, sat Daisy. She must take after her mother, Heather decided, given the pale mousy hair, braided into thin plaits that hung over her thinner shoulders. There was nothing about Daisy that spoke of the broad-shouldered confidence the Bryce men seemed to be born with.

Then she turned away from the window to face Heather and pierced her with sharp, intelligent amber eyes that were all her Uncle Cal.

'Nannies don't wear baggy jumpers,' she said, looking Heather up and down. 'Or trainers.'

'Well, this one does,' Heather said cheerfully.

These kids had better get used to her wardrobe, since she hadn't brought anything smart in her small rucksack. In fact, she hadn't brought much of anything. A single change of clothing, her phone charger, that sort of thing. She hadn't been planning on staying, after all. She'd have to find out if Cal's generous employment deal included an advance for suitable work wear.

'I'll leave you to it, then, Miss Reid,' Mrs Peterson said, as if she were saying, *I hope the lions don't eat you, but they probably will.*

'Heather, please,' she tried one last time, but Mrs Peterson ignored her.

'Dinner is at six in the dining hall,' she added, closing the door behind her.

Heather looked at the children. The children looked at Heather, clearly waiting for her to break first.

They'd broken eight different nannies, Heather remembered uncomfortably. But they wouldn't break her. Because Heather knew something that they didn't.

They were family. Or they would be once this baby was born. And if Heather had learned one thing from her taunting, scandal-ridden childhood, it was this: you never ran out on family.

'Right,' she said, clapping her hands together *à la* Mary Poppins. 'Mrs Peterson has shown me all around the inside of the castle—how about you two show me around outside?'

Daisy and Ryan exchanged a look that Heather couldn't read.

'Outside?' Daisy asked suspiciously, as if there had to be a catch somewhere.

'Yep. I saw some great-looking woodland on my way in—I bet that's fun to explore.' She shot a sideways look at Daisy, who was trying to communicate something to her brother using only her eyebrows. 'Plus, I understand that the castle moat has some very unusual ducks in it.'

Ryan stifled a snigger at that, while Daisy glared at him so hard that Heather thought lasers might shoot out of her eyes.

'Come on! It's summer. You two should be outside, enjoying the glorious sunshine.' Heather glanced out of the window. 'But grab your wellies on the way, yeah?'

They *were* in Scotland, after all.

The dining hall at Lengroth Castle was large, cold, prone to damp and currently mostly empty.

From the head of the oversized table Cal stared down at the vacant seats arranged around him. Alone, it was almost too easy for him to remember them occupied by Ross, or their parents. Even society's brightest and best, in the castle's heyday, before his father's rages had taken greater hold and entertaining had become just too risky.

Right now, though, all that was missing was his niece, his nephew and his new nanny.

'Dinner will be cold,' Mrs Peterson said, speaking volumes with her tone.

With just those four innocent words, Cal knew exactly what she was *really* asking.

Who is this Miss Reid? Why is she here? Do you re-ally expect me to believe that the local agency sent her, with an accent like that? And, most importantly, *What has she done with the children?*

'I'm sure they'll be here soon,' Cal said, as mildly as he could. 'Miss Reid seems like a very responsible person.' Apart from sleeping with strange, married earls she met in London bars. 'And her references are impeccable.'

She was practically family, after all. And if Cal's parents had taught him anything about family it was that they knew where the bodies were buried, so you had to keep them close.

'Hmm…' Mrs Peterson said, speaking volumes once more with just one noise.

Suddenly the huge, wooden door of the castle crashed open.

'Sorry we're late!'

Heather's English tones rang through the castle corridors, probably reaching them a good thirty seconds after she spoke, due to the distance from the door to the dining room. Clearly she had some lungs on her.

'Where's the damn…? I mean, Daisy, where's the dining room?'

The last was quieter, but sound carried well in the castle. Something Cal had had reason to curse plenty of times in his life.

'I think they're here,' Cal said redundantly, and Mrs Peterson gave him a look that suggested that, given their joint ability to state the obvious, he and Miss Reid deserved each other.

'I'm so sorry!' Heather gasped as she and the children barrelled through the big double doors at one end of the dining hall. Not the end nearest to the front door, Cal noticed, which meant that Ryan had been playing his usual trick of trying to get the new nanny disorientated and lost.

He blinked as he took in the full impact of their appearance. Behind him Mrs Peterson made a faint noise of either astonishment, disgust, or both.

Mud was dripping from Heather's nose. And her hair. And her sodden jumper. The skirt of her sundress was caked in mud, and there were twigs in her cascading copper hair.

Daisy and Ryan were suspiciously clean by comparison.

Cal surveyed his niece and nephew, both of whom appeared to be working hard at maintaining an air of innocence. Then he met Heather's gaze and saw there a determination and steeliness that surprised him with its depth.

It's going to take more than a fall in the river to scare this one off, kids.

At least, that was what he assumed had happened. It was what they'd done to nanny number three, anyway. There was a stretch where the bridge didn't *quite* reach the far bank—not since the river had swelled and burst its banks the winter before. It was simple enough to jump to safety via the stepping stones on the other side, but only if you knew to look for them. If you weren't paying proper attention when you reached the end of the bridge—say if an evil child was distracting you by dangling from a tree, or something—it was easy to miss the fact that the bridge basically gave way to a river of mud.

'Miss Reid, perhaps you would like to freshen up before dinner?' Mrs Peterson said, as if Heather had merely a smudge of dust on her nose or something.

Ryan snorted. Daisy, as ever, remained implacable. The girl was definitely her mother's daughter, Cal decided. Janey must have known what Ross was really like—what was going on behind her back. But he'd never seen a glimpse of it in her calm, serene expression.

Heather gave a grateful smile. 'I won't be long. Children, why don't you come with me? We can all change for dinner.'

'But *we're* not muddy,' Ryan protested.

They hadn't eaten since lunch, what with the impromptu nature ramble Heather had taken them on, so Cal assumed the boy must be starving. He knew *he* was.

'The great outdoors is full of all sorts of germs, though,' Heather said airily. 'You definitely need to wash before you eat. Maybe even have a bath...'

There was a wicked twinkle in her eye. One Cal approved of mightily.

'But our dinner will get cold,' Daisy said, perfectly reasonably.

Heather pulled an expression of regretful sorrow Cal was *almost* sure was fake.

'I know—I'm *so* sorry. So *clumsy* of me to slip in the mud on the bridge. If only I'd known that the bridge ended short of the riverbank I wouldn't have spent so long flailing around in the mud, waiting for you two to come down from the trees and help me up. And then we wouldn't have been late for dinner.'

She flashed a quick smile at Cal and Mrs Peterson.

'All my fault, you see. But the children and I really *must* clean ourselves up before dinner. Please, don't wait for us, though.'

She ushered the children out of the dining room, Ryan

still grumbling as they went. Cal watched them go, smiling. This might all work out a lot better than even he had planned.

'I make that one to Miss Reid and nil to Daisy and Ryan,' Mrs Peterson murmured softly.

Cal glanced up to see that the older woman had a small smile on her face. One he didn't think he'd seen since he'd returned for Ross's funeral.

'I think you're right,' he replied. 'Now, do you think we can reheat dinner?'

CHAPTER FOUR

THE ENFORCED PRE-DINNER baths hadn't made Heather any more popular with the children—or with Cal and Mrs Peterson, she imagined, since they'd both waited to eat with them. But then falling in a muddy riverbank hadn't really endeared Daisy, Ryan or Lengroth Castle itself to Heather, so she didn't feel too bad about it.

If nothing else, she'd shown the children that their actions had consequences.

It seemed to be working—for now, anyway. And by the time Heather was showered and changed—and thank heaven for whoever had upgraded the castle plumbing, even if they *hadn't* given her an en suite bathroom—the children were also scrubbed and dressed.

'Great!' she said, eyeing the bathroom that linked the children's bedrooms—which she was almost certain classified as en suite, whatever Mrs Peterson said. 'Now, if you just pick up those wet towels and put your dirty clothes in the washing basket we can all get some dinner.'

Her stomach rumbled and she hoped the kids didn't hear it. Hunger was a sign of weakness. She couldn't afford to show any more weakness in front of them now they'd seen her flailing around in the mud, helpless.

There were mutters and glares, but the towels were

picked up. Heather held in a smile. They were getting somewhere.

Back down in the dining room Heather had expected to find Cal gone, sure that he'd have already eaten. But instead he and Mrs Peterson were waiting for them, and as they appeared in the doorway, pink from scrubbing, hair sleek and still wet, she disappeared to the kitchen to get the food.

Cal raised an eyebrow at her and Heather was suddenly very aware that she probably didn't look much older than Daisy, with her copper hair in two heavy, wet plaits that hung over her shoulders. There hadn't been time to dry it, even though the castle still held a chill, despite it being the middle of summer.

She slipped into the chair at the place setting furthest away from him, and watched to make sure that the children took their seats nicely, too.

Perhaps they were worn out from fighting her all afternoon, because they sat down without any fuss at all. Or perhaps they were just saving their energy for a renewed resistance tomorrow.

Mrs Peterson returned with hot plates and a dinner of pie and vegetables, which Heather devoured happily. Across the table she could see Daisy passing Ryan her meat and taking his vegetables in return, but since they both ate plenty she decided to pick her battles.

They ate mostly in silence. Heather had many questions she wanted to ask, but not in front of the children. Besides, she got the impression that Mrs Peterson would be scandalised by most of the things she wanted to know.

She wanted to know more about the father of her child. Was that so unusual?

There was pudding after the pie—some sort of sloppy custard thing that the children and Cal ate happily but that renewed Heather's pregnancy sickness with a vengeance. She pushed the bowl away and hoped she didn't look too green. Mrs Peterson pulled an offended face, but Heather was pretty sure she'd have been more offended if she'd eaten it and then thrown it up again.

God, she was tired. This day had already been so much longer than she'd anticipated, and she'd barely had any time alone to process the events of it. It didn't look as if she was going to get any time to herself just yet, either. After all, there was still bedtime to get through, and she couldn't see Daisy and Ryan going quietly to sleep.

Cal was watching her, she realised as she looked up from the bowl of pudding. No, not watching. *Studying.* She tried to sit up straighter, and even contemplated taking an actual mouthful of dessert until a strong wave of nausea told her not even to think about it.

'Mrs Peterson,' Cal said suddenly. 'As Miss Reid has already bathed and changed the children into their pyjamas, perhaps you could supervise bedtime tonight? I have some contract issues to discuss with Miss Reid.'

Heather shot him a grateful smile as Mrs Peterson agreed and ushered the children out of the dining room, making them pause in the doorway to say a dutiful but insincere goodnight.

And then it was just the two of them.

'You look dead on your feet,' Cal said.

Heather didn't bother to deny it.

'Come on. We'll go through to my sitting room. I need a brandy. And you can have…something else,' he said, vaguely, obviously remembering that alcohol was not on the menu for her for the next seven months. Longer, if she breastfed.

In fact, given what had happened the last time she'd

drunk alcohol, Heather rather thought she might give it up all together. Just to be on the safe side.

Cal's sitting room was warm, cosy and welcoming in a way that nowhere else in the castle Heather had seen so far had managed. She curled up in the armchair near the unlit fireplace, and pulled a blanket over her knees more for comfort than warmth.

Cal handed her a glass of something frosty and misty before pouring himself a brandy.

Heather cautiously took a sip. It was delicious.

'Home-made elderflower cordial and sparkling water,' Cal said, taking his own seat opposite her. 'Mrs Peterson makes it.'

'It's lovely.' Heather took another sip.

'Better with champagne,' Cal replied. 'But under the circumstances... Speaking of which—what happened by the river? You didn't hurt yourself or the baby? I should have asked before... Do you want me to take you to the hospital to get checked? I'll be honest, I don't really know how these things work.'

Heather smiled at his concern. 'Neither do I, really. But I didn't fall hard or anything. Just slipped into the mud at the end of the bridge. More embarrassing than painful—which I imagine was just what the children intended.'

'Probably,' Cal admitted. 'So you don't need the hospital?'

Heather shook her head. 'I'm fine.' Then a thought occurred to her and she frowned. 'But I do need to transfer my medical care up here if I'm staying. To keep up my midwife appointments and scans and what have you.' She hadn't even thought about that side of things when she'd agreed to Cal's deal.

'And are you?' he asked, pausing with his glass halfway to his lips as he waited for her answer.

Heather frowned. 'Am I what?'

'Staying.'

Cal had no idea what he was going to do if she said no now. Of course she'd been happy to take his deal before she'd met the kids. But an afternoon with Daisy and Ryan—not to mention Mrs Peterson's disapproving gaze—might well have changed her mind.

But if she could put up with a mud dunking from his niece and nephew, maybe she'd be strong enough to stick it out. To be honest, she already seemed to have more control over them after one afternoon than some of the previous nannies had had after a week or more.

Heather was the right person for this job—Cal could feel it. And not just because she was a scandalous time bomb waiting to explode.

She still hadn't answered. That was a bad sign, right? Or maybe she was just making very sure of her answer. She didn't seem like the impulsive type—her encounter with Ross notwithstanding.

Finally she nodded, and Cal let out the breath he'd been holding and took a celebratory sip of his brandy.

'I'm staying,' Heather confirmed. 'Which means there's a lot of things we need to sort out.'

'I can give you the details of our family doctor. He's been looking after the Bryces for decades.' *And keeping their secrets.* 'He'll look after you. It's only for six weeks, after all.'

How many appointments would she need in that time anyway?

'I suppose… But my twelve-week scan is due soon.

I'll need to get that moved to the nearest hospital with a maternity unit. Which is…?'

'Edinburgh, I imagine,' Cal replied, thankful possibly for the first time for the remote location and lack of facilities at Lengroth. At least in Edinburgh he was unlikely to be recognised and asked a lot of awkward questions. 'We'll get Dr Harvey to book it for you, and I'll take you down to the city for it.'

She looked surprised at his offer. 'Thank you.'

Cal shifted uncomfortably under her grateful gaze. 'Of course. It's only right. Now, what else do you need now you're staying?'

'Clothes,' Heather said, pulling a face. 'Probably maternity ones before too long, I suppose. Um…teaching materials for the children? Do they have laptops? I didn't bring mine, and it would be good to get them to do some online tests and figure out where they're at with their learning.'

'Can online quizzes test cunning and guile?' Cal asked. 'Because they'd probably ace those.'

Heather shook her head, a small smile on her face. 'I get the feeling that they're so used to acting up to get attention from people they've forgotten how to be any other way.'

'And you're going to remind them?' Cal asked.

Heather nodded. 'Well, me *and* you.'

Wait. What?

Cal put down his glass and frowned at her. 'You *do* remember our deal here, Miss Reid, right?'

Heather rolled her eyes. 'You really don't have to call me that, you know. Especially when Mrs Peterson isn't listening.'

'Fine. Heather, then. Our deal…?'

'I spend the next six weeks getting the children ready

for whichever awful boarding school you're shipping them off to, and you pay me lots of money and give me whatever I need to make it happen.'

'I think you added the last bit yourself, but fine.' Cal shook his head as her other words caught up with him. 'And the school isn't awful. In fact, Derryford Academy is one of the most highly regarded boarding schools in the country. Ross and I both went there.'

Heather muttered something that sounded suspiciously like, *Explains a lot...* under her breath. Cal ignored her.

'And the fact it's such a good school is why I need you here—to make sure their academics are up to scratch. They're coming in late as it is. Ross wanted to send them as soon as they were old enough, but Janey insisted on keeping them at home, so...' He shrugged.

There was a peculiar look on Heather's face. It took Cal a moment to realise what it was. Pain.

'Were you in love with my brother?' he asked softly.

If she had been... Well, he could only imagine how painful this whole situation was for her. She'd claimed it was only a one-night stand, but people lied—he knew that well enough. And maybe she hadn't wanted to admit to him, Ross's brother, about a long-term affair.

Heather shot him a surprised look. 'No! I told you, it was just one night. I barely even knew him.'

She sounded convincing, but liars often did. 'You looked in actual agony when I mentioned his wife,' he pointed out.

Another flash of pain spread across her face, contradicting her words. Cal was just starting to feel smug about his ability to see through her lies when she spoke again.

'I wasn't in love with Ross, Cal. I barely knew him. In fact, if I *had* known him I never would have gone back to his hotel room with him that night. If I'd known he was married…that he had children…'

She shuddered, and Cal realised he'd read her all wrong after all. He kept doing that with this woman. Normally he prided himself on being able to see through the lies and the covers people put up to mask their real feelings and actions. What made Heather so different?

Then he realised.

She wasn't lying to him.

'If I feel pain, it's for his wife. For his kids. For the mistakes I made,' Heather went on. 'I should have asked more questions, been more certain, before I went back with him. That's a mistake that's going to haunt me for a long time.'

'Because of the baby?' Cal guessed.

He *wanted* to understand her, he realised. To figure out how she could be so open and honest about her feelings and actions when it seemed like no one else he'd ever known could.

Heather shook her head and a bright smile spread across her face, transforming the atmosphere in the room. 'This baby is the best thing to come from that night. And, however many mistakes *I* made to get to this point, I know that a baby is never a mistake. He or she is a new life, a new chance for happiness—for them, and maybe even for me.'

Cal sat back in his chair, amazed. 'You're really not like other people, are you?'

Heather pulled a face. 'I don't know what you mean.'

And she didn't, he realised. Because this was just who she was—open and honest and without guile or lies. No wonder he hadn't got a clue what to make of her.

'It doesn't matter,' he said, shaking his head. 'What

matters is that you're staying and that you'll get the kids ready for school in time.'

He needed to focus on the important stuff, the big picture—not get carried away trying to make sense of his brother's one-night stand. Like getting the kids out of the castle. And keeping that damn reporter from *Elite* magazine away from Lengroth altogether.

His conversation with the editor had not been encouraging; apparently she was sending over a copy of the contract for Cal's lawyers to look at. And she'd made it very clear that he did *not* want to be found in breach of it…

He shook away that concern for another time and turned his attention back to Heather. But she just added another layer to the issue. The last thing he needed was a reporter staying at the castle alongside the woman who was carrying the late Earl's illegitimate child.

'Are you okay?' Heather asked, with genuine concern in her voice. 'You're kind of…staring.'

He looked away. Quickly. 'Sorry. Just…lots on my mind. Picking up all the loose threads after Ross… You know…'

'Of course.' Heather got quickly and neatly to her feet. 'I'll leave you to it. I need to get to bed if I'm going to start teaching the children tomorrow.'

She smoothed down the sundress she was wearing under a chunky knitted cardigan. She wasn't showing at all yet, Cal realised. Would she be by the end of the summer? He didn't know. If she was nearly twelve weeks, as she said, then she'd be four and half months by September.

Halfway through, he thought. Hopefully by then he'd have some idea of what to do about her and the baby. But for now…

'I'll arrange for laptops for all three of you. And I'll

get a credit card for you, linked to the castle account. You'll be able to order whatever clothes you need, teaching supplies…that sort of thing.'

'Thank you.' Heather's wide smile was grateful. 'That would be wonderful.'

He'd set a generous limit on the card, Cal decided as she left the room. See how close she came to reaching it. If she did—well, who *wouldn't* make the most of that opportunity? And if she didn't…maybe she really was different from the other people in his life.

Either way, the children would be out of his hair and someone else's problem. That was what really mattered.

Heather was awoken early the next morning, before the sun had even crept over the hills, by the sound of shrieking. High-pitched, ear-ringing, brain-hurting, shrieking.

She blinked, trying to remember where she was, what was happening, who could be screaming…

Daisy.

Throwing the covers aside, she raced to the doorway that led to the hall, then down the short distance to the children's rooms.

The stone floors of the castle were freezing under her bare feet, even in summer. Heather didn't care. She burst into Daisy's room and found Ryan already there, huddled in a heap at the end of her bed, his hands over his ears.

'Daisy. *Daisy.*'

It wasn't good to wake a dreamer. Or was that a sleepwalker? Either way, Heather knew she had to do it. She gave the girl a small shake on her shoulder. Then a harder one.

Daisy's eyes popped open. 'You shouldn't be in my room after lights out,' she said, for all the world as if she'd just awoken from a restful nap.

Heather shared a quick glance with Ryan, who just shrugged. 'She always does this.'

Does what? Heather wondered. Scream, dream or pretend it never happened?

'You were screaming,' Heather said soothingly. 'Did you have a bad dream?'

'No,' Daisy said sharply, but Heather would have known it was a lie even without the shrieking. Her eyes were wide and terrified, red and raw around the edges.

'Do you want to talk about it?' Heather asked.

Daisy rolled over to face the wall, pulled the blanket up to her chin and stubbornly shut her eyes. 'I want to go back to sleep. Alone.'

Heather waited a few minutes, but Daisy showed no signs of moving or talking. Her breathing was too shallow for her to be asleep, but Heather knew she was stubborn enough to pretend all the way until morning.

Time to try a different approach.

Getting quietly to her feet, as if she really did believe Daisy was sleeping and didn't want to wake her, Heather motioned to Ryan to follow her back through the linked bathroom to his room. Once the connecting doors were closed behind them, Heather smiled and spoke at a more normal volume.

'Come on, let's get you tucked in again, too.'

It was the first time she'd been alone with Ryan, she realised—without Daisy's glares and nudges to control his reactions. She planned to take advantage of it.

'Does she often have nightmares?' Heather asked as she shook out his duvet.

Ryan nodded sleepily. 'Most nights. But she doesn't always scream. Sometimes she just whimpers, and then she calms down again when I go in and lie down with her.'

These poor children. Stuck in this castle, grieving for

their parents, and now their uncle wants to send them away to boarding school.

Cal was concerned that their academic learning should be up to the standard required at Derryford Academy. Heather was far more worried about ensuring that their mental and emotional well-being was up to living there.

And right now she wasn't at all sure it was.

'Do you have nightmares, too?' Heather asked softly.

Ryan's eyes were already drifting closed again, proving more than his words that this really was an everyday occurrence for him.

'Sometimes,' he murmured, his voice heavy with sleep. 'But not like Daisy.'

His breathing evened out and Heather knew he was asleep again. She'd have to save her questions for another time.

In the meantime… *I need to do more reading. Learn about grieving children…how to help them.*

But one thing she already knew. Whatever these children had been through, they needed the same thing all children needed. Love, understanding and someone to listen. They needed to feel secure and safe.

And, judging by Daisy's nightmares—not to mention the mud incident and the flying rubber duck—they didn't.

Heather knew what it was like to grow up without one parent. She couldn't imagine how she'd have coped if she'd lost her father as well as her mother. But she could identify a little with Daisy and Ryan.

The children were playing defence—attacking anyone who came near before they could *be* attacked. Heather wasn't sure what form they expected that attack to come in, but they were definitely expecting it.

She needed to find a way to show them that they were

safe and loved. But she was only staying until September. She wasn't a long-term solution here.

But she knew a man who was.

These children needed family. And right now that family consisted of their uncle Cal—a man who planned to ship them off to boarding school so he didn't have to deal with them.

Not if she could help it.

Tucking Ryan in one last time, she left the children sleeping to head back to her own room, already planning how best to approach Cal with her ideas.

She shut the bedroom door quietly, turned—and screamed.

CHAPTER FIVE

CAL CLAPPED A hand over Heather's mouth to stop her screaming. The last thing they needed after all this was Daisy waking up and starting to shriek again. There was only so much night-time noise his ears could take.

'It's me. Cal. Not a ghost, or whatever.'

He'd never even seen a hint of the damn thing, but every other nanny seemed convinced that the castle was haunted, so why would Heather be any different. *Of course* she'd screamed.

He'd automatically pulled her into his arms, he realised belatedly, and the soft curves under her pyjamas were pressed up against his bare chest and boxers. *Not* the most professional start to their working relationship. But, God, it felt good.

The strange feeling that had made him stare at her earlier that evening swept over him again—half-amazement, half-disbelief that she was even real.

One thing was definitely real, though, and that was the way she felt in his arms. If this were any other woman he'd definitely be thinking about kissing her right now. About keeping her this close the whole night long...

Except she was his employee, *and* she was carrying his brother's child, so this was the most inappropriate line of thought ever.

Oh, who was he kidding? He was thinking it anyway.

'I'm not screaming any more,' Heather said, sounding far more calm and rational than he felt, with her copper curls tickling his neck and the scent of her filling his lungs.

Cal let go. Quickly.

'Sorry,' he said, stepping away. 'I just didn't want you to wake the kids again.'

'I kind of got that.'

Why was she looking at him that way? She couldn't *know* all the things he'd been thinking about doing to her as her body touched his, right? At least she'd brought him to his senses before his lower body had *really* started to react to the situation.

Cal thought many calming thoughts and hoped the corridor was dark enough to hide his blushes. And other things.

'So...uh... Daisy had another nightmare?' he asked redundantly.

Heather nodded. 'Ryan says she has them a lot. Sorry, I probably should have waited for you to go in—'

'No!' Cal said, sharply. 'No. You're the nanny—it's your place.'

Her expression turned curious, and then disapproving in turn, with the pale, wan light from the lamp on the wall highlighting the planes and shadows of her face.

'You're their uncle,' she said. 'It's more your place than mine.'

Cal shook his head. 'I tried once. She threw pillows at me and screeched even louder than she did when she was dreaming. Trust me, it's better for everyone that you do it.'

Heather was still staring at him. Assessing him. He didn't like it. Even if her scrutiny had finally got his body back on board with their strictly professional relationship terms.

'You want the children to be ready to go to boarding school in six weeks?' she said slowly, as if she were just catching up to how difficult that would be.

'That's the idea.'

'Then you're going to have to show them that it's safe for them to leave. And come back again.'

Cal frowned. 'Is this something to do with the ghost? Have you been having some sort of séance when I wasn't looking?'

Maybe he should get an exorcist in, or something. Did they come for atheists? He wasn't sure.

'It's not the damn ghost they're afraid of,' Heather snapped. 'I told you—I don't even believe in them.'

'Then what is it?'

Heather's smile was small and sad. 'Everything else.'

'That makes no sense. They're rich, privileged kids.' Or they would be, once Cal had sorted out the castle's precarious financial situation. 'What do they have to be scared of?'

'They've lost their *parents*, Cal,' Heather snapped, clearly at the end of her patience with his lack of understanding. 'Their whole world has shifted, and nothing they placed their trust in before has held true. They don't know what or who to believe in, and they don't know what's going to happen next. Of course they're terrified.'

'Well, when you put it like that...' Cal rubbed the back of his neck tiredly, wishing he could go back to bed. No, wishing he could go back in time to when none of this had been his problem. When Ross had still been the perfect older brother who could be relied on to take care of all the family stuff.

But that had all been lies anyway.

'Did you honestly not think about how their parents' deaths must have affected them?' Heather asked, more softly now.

'No, I did. I just...'

How could he explain that when his own parents had died he'd felt nothing. That, growing up, he'd sometimes daydreamed about what would happen if his father *did* die. Would their mother suddenly realise she loved them after all? Realise that they were more than just an heir and a spare?

Even in his daydreams he hadn't really believed it.

But Ross and Janey had been different—or so he'd believed. He'd hoped they really *did* love their children, the way he and Ross had always wanted to be loved.

Now, with everything he'd learned about Ross and his marriage since their death, Cal realised he'd begun to see them as just like his parents.

'Of course I did. I knew they were grieving, that they missed them. But by the time I arrived here and took over, on the day of the funeral, they were both already so cold. Distant. I just assumed...'

First he'd assumed that they knew he couldn't give them what they needed. That he was no good at this family stuff and had no idea how to be a guardian. Then, later, he'd assumed they felt the same way about Ross and Janey as he had about his own parents' deaths.

But he had a feeling Heather wouldn't understand any of that.

'My first priority was to get the estate management and its finances under control,' he said instead. 'Ross... It turned out things weren't in as great a shape as I'd been led to believe. This is the kids' future security and livelihood. I was looking out for their futures.'

'They need security *now*, Cal. And not the financial type. They need love.'

Then they were out of luck. Because love was one thing Cal had no experience or knowledge of.

'Then love them,' he said, turning on his heel to head back to his cold, lonely bedroom.

Heather would have to learn to love them as their half-sibling's mother.

Because he knew that *he* couldn't.

Heather's eyes were gritty with sleep when she awoke late the next morning. After the pre-dawn antics with Daisy, and that disturbing conversation with Cal, it had taken her an age to get back to sleep again. And when she finally had her dreams had been restless—filled with a strange sense of longing, desperation and the remembrance of a body against hers. She'd assumed it to be Ross—until her eyes had flashed open and she'd realised it was Cal.

Added to her general pregnancy tiredness, the disturbed night meant that she was totally exhausted. And she still had to go into battle today—with and for Daisy and Ryan.

She showered quickly in the chilly bathroom down the corridor, then dressed in the same sundress and cardigan she'd worn for dinner. Until Cal came good on his clothes-shopping promise her wardrobe was severely limited. Thank goodness she always packed extra underwear in case of emergency.

Being properly prepared was important. Which was why she practised all her arguments and approaches towards Cal as she got ready to face the day.

The periodic nausea that had plagued her for weeks seemed to be abating at last, which was something. In every other way she felt totally unprepared for the day ahead.

She was missing something about Cal, she decided as she brushed her teeth, grateful that the toothpaste didn't make her gag for the first time in weeks. He seemed like a good guy, genuinely trying to help his niece and nephew—but in all the wrong ways. Could she show him the right ones in the next six weeks?

She hoped so.

'Ah, Miss Reid. So good of you to join us.'

Mrs Peterson nodded pointedly to the table, already laid with breakfast, as Heather entered the dining room. Daisy and Ryan were in their seats, and Cal was reading a newspaper on his tablet at the head of the table. A slight heat rose to Heather's cheeks as she remembered him as she'd seen him last—half-naked in the dark, his arms around her waist.

Damn her pregnancy hormones. They'd had her body in a spin just at the closeness of him—at least as soon as her initial terror had worn off and she'd realised who it was that held her.

Not that the 'who' made it any better. Next to Ross Bryce, the second most inappropriate person for her to be fantasising about had to be his brother.

With an apologetic smile Heather slipped into her seat as the others started to help themselves to toast, eggs, fruit and pastries.

First order of business, Heather decided as she poured herself a cup of tea, was to figure out the rules and traditions of Lengroth Castle. If she wanted to achieve anything here it would be a hundred times easier with Mrs Peterson on her side, and Mrs Peterson seemed to value things being done the right way.

Heather dreaded to think what Mrs Peterson would

say when she discovered the real reason she'd come to Lengroth…

Secondly, she needed to remind Cal about the laptops, and money for school supplies. And clothes—much as she hated to rely on him for those. It felt too much like being paid off after sleeping with Ross.

But he was her employer; he had a responsibility towards her that had nothing to do with his brother. Maybe she could think of it as him providing her with a uniform—that might help.

Before she could get to point three on her to-do list—or to the plate of pastries—Cal looked up and caught her eye briefly before looking away. Was he embarrassed about their middle-of-the-night conversation—argument, really?

'The laptops you asked for will be arriving this afternoon, Miss Reid. Sorry I couldn't get them here any sooner.'

So we're back to Miss Reid, then. That didn't bode well, even if the laptops did.

'That's much sooner than I expected. Thank you…' She trailed off, unsure of what to call him. Mr Bryce? Cal? My Lord—except he wasn't the Earl, was he? What was the etiquette here?

Something else to figure out, Heather supposed.

'And I've ordered a credit card for your use. In the meantime…' He reached into his pocket and pulled out his wallet. Removing a card from it, he handed it down the table to her. 'This should serve to get you started online.'

Mrs Peterson's eyebrows were so high Heather was half-afraid they might float off into the rafters of the dining hall. Apparently Cal didn't do this for all his nannies, then.

But she was different. Because he knew she had to stay. Or he was bribing her to stay, to stave off a scandal. Heather wasn't sure which one it was any more.

Confused, she took the card and tucked it securely into the pocket of her cardigan. Somehow she was going to have to figure all this out, save the children, and then sort out her own future and her baby's. But definitely not until after breakfast.

Helping herself to pastries, she turned to smile at the children, who stared sullenly back. The shadows under Daisy's eyes were grey smudges, and made her look paler and more gaunt than she already was. Ryan picked miserably at his bowl of cereal.

Start there, she decided. *Everything else can wait a few days at least. The kids need me now.*

Did they know about the sort of things their father had got up to? She hoped not. As she also hoped that Cal was right that the family were good at keeping their secrets. Daisy and Ryan didn't deserve the gossipy taunts and comments that she'd suffered as a child because of her mother's behaviour.

'So, kids… If the laptops aren't arriving until this afternoon we've got one last morning of freedom before lessons start. What would you like to spend it doing?'

Daisy and Ryan exchanged one of their secret looks, then turned to smile eerily identical smiles at Heather.

Heather swallowed. Suddenly she was regretting asking.

Cal looked up in amusement as Heather asked the fateful question. Really, as a teacher, surely she should know better than to give two devil children a *choice* in what they wanted to do next. Hell, he knew nothing about kids except how to avoid them—and even *he* knew that much.

At the far end of the table Mrs Peterson was watching, too, and Cal was sure he detected a hint of a smile around her thin lips. Old Peterson had been with the family since before Cal was born, but he could still count the number of times he'd seen her smile on both hands.

She knew all the family secrets, his mother used to say. Which was why she had a job for life. It was impossible to keep *anything* from Mrs Peterson.

Cal wondered if she'd known about Ross and the sort of man he really was. He almost hoped not. Mrs Peterson had doted on his brother, and he'd hate that to be tainted the way his own relationship with him had.

'We'd like to show you the village,' Daisy said, with total innocence in her voice. If a person didn't know her better, anyway.

But Cal knew. And he was already calculating the number of different ways the children could get into trouble.

He was up to twenty-four before Heather said, 'Lengroth village? Sure, if you like.' She sounded surprised. 'I came through it on my way here yesterday. There didn't seem to be a lot there, but maybe it'll look different with you two as my tour guides.'

She smiled warmly—a smile that only faltered slightly as Mrs Peterson said, 'I dare say it will.'

Well, whatever Daisy's cunning plan was, this would work wonderfully for Cal. With the children and Heather safely out of the castle and out of his way he could get on with the real work he still had to do. Like making another phone call to his lawyer to see what they'd made of Ross's contract with the magazine.

He was just contemplating a *pain au chocolat* to round off his breakfast before he got to work when Heather's face brightened even more, and Cal was filled with a strange sense of foreboding.

'I know! Uncle Cal can take us down to the village—it's too far to walk there *and* back, I think. Maybe we can all have some lunch together as a treat. What do you think?'

Daisy and Ryan looked as uncertain as he felt about Heather's suggestion, and Mrs Peterson was *definitely* smiling now.

But Heather ignored them all and clapped her hands together. 'Brilliant! It's a plan, then. Let's all meet at the front door in thirty minutes, ready to go.'

And with that she snatched up the last *pain au chocolat* and walked out with his breakfast, his credit card and his free morning.

Perfect.

'That's two to Miss Reid,' Mrs Peterson murmured as she cleared away his empty plate.

Cal ignored her, and went to get ready to drive down to the village.

Cal felt a strange sensation of lightening as he drove out through the front gates of Lengroth Castle, Heather in the passenger seat beside him and the children suspiciously quiet in the back seat. He was almost certain that Daisy and Ryan were plotting something, but since he had no idea what he decided to go with the flow and enjoy the day.

He was away from the castle, the sun was shining and he had a beautiful if untouchable woman at his side. Life could be much worse.

The village of Lengroth was small, mostly filled with grey stone terraced houses that echoed the castle's forbidding walls. The streets were narrow, winding up and down each side of the valley the village sat in. From every spot in the village the castle of Lengroth, up on the hill, was visible, looming over them.

Cal purposefully kept his back to it as they got out of the car.

'So, where shall we start?' Heather asked, sounding unreasonably excited about the outing, in Cal's opinion.

'The sweet shop?' Ryan suggested hopefully.

Heather smiled. 'Maybe let's save that until after lunch. But a stroll along the high street sounds like a great idea.'

'The high street?' Cal asked, with a hint of incredulity in his voice. 'I think that title is a little grand for what Lengroth has to offer.' At most, it was a low street. It barely even qualified as a road.

Still, Heather seemed charmed as they strolled past the Mountain Ram pub and across the road by the chip shop, the corner shop—and the long-suffering Mr Reynolds' sweet shop. In fact, for just a moment Cal could almost let himself believe that they were a real family, doing real family things—not a patchwork of relatives and strangers who hardly even knew each other.

But the kids were behaving, Heather seemed relaxed and happy, and no one was demanding anything much from him, so Cal decided to relax and enjoy the rare Scottish sunshine for a change.

At least until Ryan darted across the road—narrowly missing being hit by a passing cyclist—and ran away from them down an alley.

Cal froze, just for a moment, then moved to chase him—only to find that Heather had beaten him to it. She was already across the road, disappearing through the same gap in the buildings that Ryan had, leaving him with Daisy.

He wanted to follow them, but that would mean dragging Daisy along, too—he could hardly leave her behind.

'Where would your brother be running to?' he asked, still staring after Heather.

No reply.

Annoyed, Cal turned to face Daisy—only to find her gone, too.

'Dammit.' Cal bit back a stronger curse as he spun around to check the street for his wayward niece. Nothing.

Except… A flash of movement in the distance, past the pub and behind the trees, made Cal realise he knew *exactly* where Daisy had gone.

He didn't want to go *there*. He'd been avoiding it ever since he came back to Lengroth. But apparently his niece wasn't giving him that option.

With a sigh, Cal followed her.

CHAPTER SIX

HEATHER SLIPPED DOWN the narrow alleyway, her eyes constantly moving as she searched the shadows for Ryan. What kind of nanny was she, losing one of her charges on her second day? Cal must be fuming. Or probably grilling Daisy on what Ryan thought he was playing at.

What *did* Ryan think he was playing at? It wasn't as if there were a lot of places to run away to in Lengroth, and he'd run in the opposite direction to the sweet shop so it couldn't even be that. It didn't make any sense.

Maybe he was just one of those boys who needed to run. She'd had one of those in the last school she worked at—he'd needed to escape over the fence at least once a day. The caretaker would chase him down and he'd come back, docilely enough, and go to class. But the next day it would be exactly the same.

But Ryan hadn't run yesterday. And Cal hadn't mentioned his escaping act as one of the many problems he'd experienced with the children. Was this something new? Was he running away from *her*?

The alleyway took another turn, and Heather sighed as she rounded it—then stopped as she realised it led to a dead end.

A dead end with Ryan at the end of it, sitting calmly upon an upturned wooden crate.

He grinned impishly at her, then the smile faded. 'Where's Uncle Cal?'

'With Daisy, I hope.' Heather moved to sit on another crate opposite him, trying to make sense of exactly what was going on.

Ryan shook his head, his dark hair waving from side to side as he did so. 'No. No, no, *no*. Daisy is going to be so cross. I was supposed to lead *both* of you away. Why didn't he follow?' he asked plaintively. Then his face darkened and he answered his own question. 'It's because he can't be bothered with me and Daisy, isn't it?'

'That's not it, Ryan,' Heather said soothingly. 'One of us needed to stay with Daisy, and I was quicker than Uncle Cal, that's all.' At least she hoped that was what had happened. She hadn't dared look back to check for fear of losing Ryan's trail.

'He can't, though,' Ryan said, looking up at her with big eyes. 'He didn't want to come back to Lengroth in the first place—I heard him tell Mrs Peterson. And when you two were rowing outside our rooms last night—'

Heather winced. She'd thought he was asleep, but maybe they'd woken him up again. Sound carried surprisingly well in Lengroth Castle for a building of its size and with the thickness of its walls. 'We weren't rowing. And you weren't meant to hear that.'

'Well, I did. And I know he doesn't love us or want us. He just wants you to get us ready so he can send us away, doesn't he?'

The boy had a point, but Heather knew she couldn't concede it. 'Your uncle wants the best for your education and for your future. He's very busy with the estate right now—'

'Dad never spent so much time in his study when *he* ran the estate.'

Apparently not very well, Heather thought, but didn't say.

'Your uncle loves you,' she said firmly instead. After all, however much trouble they caused him, they were his own flesh and blood. How could he *not* love them? 'He's just not very good at showing it.' *At all. Ever.*

Ryan shook his head mulishly. 'He doesn't want us. That's okay. We don't want him, either. That's what Daisy says.'

Daisy. There was something else he'd said about Daisy, and in her relief at finding him safe she'd almost missed it. What was it…?

Heather blinked as it came to her. 'Ryan, what did you mean when you said Daisy would be cross because you were supposed to lead *both* of us away? Is this a plan you and Daisy made?'

'*Daisy's* plan,' Ryan corrected 'They're always Daisy's plans. She just tells me what to do.'

'And today it was to run away so Cal and I would follow. But why?'

That was the part that didn't make any sense. Unless Daisy wanted to be left alone… Heather's eyes widened. Had Daisy wanted the distraction so *she* could escape, too?

'Ryan, what did Daisy need to be alone to do?'

He wouldn't meet her eyes.

Heather took several deep breaths and tried again. 'Ryan, I promise I won't be cross. And neither will Daisy.'

'Yes, she will,' he muttered, and Heather didn't try to deny it again. The boy knew his sister better than she did.

Slipping off her crate, Heather crouched in front of Ryan, her hands either side of him, looking up until he couldn't help but meet her gaze. 'Ryan, I promise you I am only here to help you. And I'm not going anywhere until you want to leave, okay? So you can trust me.'

Ryan's eyes were red around the rims, she realised. With unshed tears or lack of sleep? Or just the stress of being an eight-year-old earl whose life didn't make sense any more?

Probably all three.

'Everyone goes away—that's what Daisy says,' he whispered. 'Our parents. The nannies. And Uncle Cal will go back to America as soon as he's sent us away, too.'

The worst part was she couldn't tell him he was wrong. Shifting to perch beside him on the box, Heather put an arm around Ryan's shoulders. 'Sometimes when people go they come back again, you know.'

'Not when they're dead,' Ryan said bluntly. 'Or when you throw things at them from the nursery window.'

'Daisy threw a rubber duck at me. I stayed,' Heather pointed out. 'Even after you let me fall in the muddy riverbank.'

Ryan sneaked a quick look at her at that, a small smile on his face.

'Yeah, I guess I must have looked pretty funny,' Heather said. 'The thing is, Ryan, I can't bring your parents back—no one can. And maybe those other nannies weren't meant to stay. But I will. Until September. I promise you that. And as for Uncle Cal—'

'Don't lie to me,' Ryan said quickly. 'Don't tell me he's staying if he isn't.'

Heather sighed. 'You're right. I can't promise you anything on Uncle Cal's behalf—only he can do that. But I *can* tell you that he's doing everything he can to make sure you and Daisy have a secure future, okay? He's looking out for you, even if it doesn't feel like it.'

It wasn't enough, though, Heather knew. These kids needed more than that. And they needed more than a detached Uncle Cal tagging along on day trips or new computers to do their schoolwork on.

Which meant she needed to have another conversation with Cal Bryce. And she was pretty sure he wasn't going to like it.

'Come on,' she said to Ryan. 'Let's go and find Daisy and Uncle Cal.'

The boy followed happily enough, apparently feeling a little better for getting some things off his chest.

It was only as they reached the high street again that Heather realised he'd never answered her question about what Daisy had wanted to be alone to do.

Cal approached the spot behind the trees slowly, quietly, not wanting to disturb Daisy as she knelt at the base of the tree stump.

Who had told her that this was where her parents had died? Had it been gossip in the town, or one of the local nannies?

Either way, she knew. And she'd wanted to come here so badly she'd sent her brother running off to cause a distraction—he was sure of it. Ryan always did do everything his big sister suggested.

Swallowing, Cal took another step forward, hating it that he was there—hating it even more that Daisy was.

The pub had fixed up the mess that had been made of their front wall, and Stan the landlord had planted some bedding plants along the new wall—green and purple, the Lengroth colours, in memory of Ross and Janey. Ross had been Stan's best customer, by all accounts.

The tree the car had hit, after it had come through the wall, had been too damaged to be saved. That had been sawn off, a foot or so from the grass, and sanded smooth.

Daisy had placed something on top of the stump, Cal realised as he got closer.

He stepped on a fallen twig, snapping it loudly underfoot, and Daisy spun around, jumping to her feet.

'You followed me,' she said, as if he were in the wrong. 'You were supposed to follow Ryan.'

He'd known it had to be a plan. 'Heather followed Ryan. He'll be fine.'

'He probably hasn't gone very far anyway.' Daisy turned back to face the tree stump again. 'He's always too much of a scaredy-cat to run far.'

'You've done this before, then?' Cal moved around to the other side of the stump so he could see her face.

'All the time,' she replied nonchalantly. 'The other nannies never told you because they didn't want to get into trouble for losing Ryan. And I was always back where they'd left me before they returned with him.'

It was just as well all those other nannies had quit. He'd have fired them anyway.

'I think Heather would have told me if I hadn't been here today.'

Daisy gave him a sceptical look. So young…so cynical.

'Yeah, I'm surprised, too,' he admitted, taking a seat on the bench next to the pub wall. He patted the wood beside him, motioning for Daisy to join him. She didn't. 'So why do you keep coming back here?' he asked.

'To talk to them.'

Right. 'But why here? Most people would go to the churchyard, you know. If you want to visit their graves Heather will take you.'

Not him. The last place he wanted to be was in that churchyard, with generation after generation of Bryces and their scandals haunting him, more real than the Lengroth ghost. No, scratch that. The churchyard was the second to last place he wanted to be.

Here was the absolute last. Looking at the spot where his brother had died.

'Because this is the last place that they were alive,' Daisy said, with the simplicity and bluntness of a child. 'It's just their bodies in the ground by the church. Here is where they were last really *them*.'

'That makes sense.' Or at least, he supposed it did if you were ten. 'What is it you want to say to them?'

Daisy's face closed up. 'That's private.'

'Right.' Cal looked over at the tree stump. Sitting on top of it was Ross's old teddy bear—the one he'd kept on the top shelf in the nursery. 'I'll tell you what, then. You have your conversation and I'll go and wait by the road for your brother and Heather. Okay?'

He'd still be able to see her from the road, but not to hear her words. It was about as much privacy as he was willing to give her, under the circumstances.

Daisy weighed the idea up, glancing between him and the road, then back to the tree stump. Finally she nodded. 'Okay.'

True to his word, Cal walked out of earshot and waited by the wall, scanning the streets for Heather and Ryan. No sign yet, but if Daisy wasn't worried neither was he. High above the village loomed Lengroth Castle, with all the worries he still had to deal with inside it. That was enough worrying to be going on with, anyway.

Then he frowned as his gaze followed the road down the hill from the castle to the wall he leaned against, moved past the memorial flowers and to Daisy, by the tree stump.

It's the wrong way round, he realised suddenly.

Mrs Peterson had told him that Ross and Janey had been

returning to the castle in the early hours of the morning, after some party or another, when they'd crashed. Ross had been over the limit, so Janey had been driving—and she had never liked to drive at night.

It had sounded plausible, so he'd never questioned it. And he'd never felt the need to return to the scene of the accident, as Daisy obviously did. But now he was here he saw what was wrong with the story.

For the car to have hit the wall, and then the tree, it must have been driving *away* from the castle—not towards it.

Where were you going, Ross? And why?

Cal shook his head. Another puzzle for him to try and make sense of.

A flash of movement across the road caught his eye and he saw Heather waving at him as she and Ryan walked towards him. He waved back, tucking away his questions about his brother to think about later, when he was alone.

First he needed to deal with his niece and nephew. Not to mention their nanny.

'You run to Daisy,' Heather whispered to Ryan as they got closer. 'Leave Uncle Cal to me.'

She'd been terrified for a moment when she'd seen Cal standing alone by the pub wall, but then Ryan had gasped and she'd seen Daisy, just beyond him, talking to a tree stump.

Why she'd needed to send her brother running off so she could do that, Heather had no idea. But she was sure she would find out soon enough.

Once they were safely across the road, Ryan dashed over to his sister and Heather moved more slowly to stand beside Cal.

'Don't shout at him for running off,' she said before he could speak. 'He already thinks you can't wait to get rid of him, so don't make things worse. I've already spoken to him on the walk back about not running away any more.'

Cal didn't even flinch at her words, which made it worse somehow. Ryan was right; he *didn't* want the responsibility of the children. But now he had it she was going to make damn sure he realised how lucky he was to have them—and how his responsibility stretched far beyond their financial futures.

She had no patience for people who walked out on their obligations to their children.

'He did it for Daisy,' he said, surprising her.

She hadn't expected him to realise that.

'It was a plan. She wanted to visit the place where their parents died, and Ryan distracted you so she could slip away here. Apparently they've done it to all the other nannies.'

Heather winced, looking over at the two children together by the tree stump. 'Those poor kids.'

'Yeah. Apparently none of the other nannies told me about Ryan's running away because they thought they'd get into trouble.'

He gave her a look she couldn't quite read.

'You'd have told me, right? If I hadn't been here?'

'Yes.' Because it would have been the right thing to do. He was their guardian, and he deserved to know what was happening in their lives. And because it might have prompted him to take slightly more interest in their emotional well-being.

'Good.' Cal glanced up towards the castle, frowning. Obviously he was still thinking about whatever paperwork or accounts he'd left undone that morning, rather than about the children in his care.

Heather opened her mouth to tell him what she thought of that, but then Daisy and Ryan appeared. Daisy was holding a teddy bear Heather hadn't noticed on their way into town. She must have been hiding it under her summer jacket.

'Can we go to the bakery and get sausage rolls for lunch?' Ryan asked, seemingly unaffected by their visit to the spot where his parents died.

Heather supposed that in the end it was just another place. Although it seemed that it meant more than that to Daisy.

She really needed to talk to Daisy.

After she'd straightened Cal's priorities out, anyway.

'Yes, we can get sausage rolls,' Heather agreed. 'And then go back to the castle. We've got work to be getting on with.'

Daisy was silent all through the sausage roll eating and the drive back to the castle. She was even silent through the discovery of the three laptops that had arrived for them while they were out.

Ryan, apparently more comfortable around Heather since their talk that morning, happily chatted and asked questions as she set the laptops up, plugging two of them in to charge at the desks in the playroom next to the kids' bedrooms. For now, it would have to double as a classroom, too.

Daisy, meanwhile, sat on the window seat pretending to read. Heather knew she was only pretending, because she'd forgotten to turn any pages for the last twenty minutes. Plus, she was staring at her and Ryan.

'Right—here we go,' Heather said eventually, as she

got the evaluation website she'd chosen up and running on both the kids' laptops.

Ryan leaned in closer, manoeuvring himself onto the seat at his desk without ever taking his eyes off the screen. Daisy ignored her.

Heather held in a sigh. 'Daisy? Would you come over here, please?'

With a considerable amount of eye-rolling, and slamming the book closed, Daisy crossed the room to join them at the two desks.

'Before I can start teaching you I need to know how much you've already learned,' Heather explained as Daisy took her seat. 'So, what I would like you to do this afternoon is work your way through the questions on the screens—I've started you off on the ones that are appropriate for your ages.'

A tiny fib; she'd actually started them both one stage lower. That way they wouldn't be intimidated if they found it a little tricky, and if they flew through them they'd feel better about themselves—and hopefully the idea of education in general.

'The questions will keep coming until you reach a point where the programme thinks it has fully assessed your levels, and then it will tell you you're done. And when it's finished we're done for the day, too. I figured we could play a game afterwards, or go for an early-evening walk before dinner. Just not by the river,' she added, and Ryan flashed her a grin.

She was definitely making progress with Ryan.

'So, basically, this is your way of teaching us without you having to do any work,' Daisy said. 'What are *you* going to be doing while we sit here doing tests?'

Daisy not so much.

'I am going to go and have a conversation with your

uncle about your programme of study.' Which sounded a lot better than *I'm going to yell at Cal until he at least tries to connect with you both, so you don't have to go visiting your dead parents for love and affection.*

'So you won't even be in the *room* while we're doing this!'

Daisy sounded incredulous at the unfairness of life. Heather would have thought she'd have been used to it by now.

'Aren't you afraid we're going to cheat?' Ryan asked curiously.

Heather got the impression that trust hadn't been a big factor in their education before now.

'I trust you both to take this seriously,' she said, and watched as Ryan's shoulders straightened with pride. Daisy, however, had a scheming gleam in her eye.

'Besides,' Heather went on with a shrug, 'these tests are to judge the level of work I'm going to set you from here on. If you cheat to do better then you'll get work that's too hard. If you pretend you're stupid to get easier work I guarantee you'll be bored stiff by the end of the week. So really it's up to you.'

Daisy's gleam faded.

'I'll wait until I'm certain you're both happy with the software. So, if you're both ready?' Heather asked. 'You can begin.'

And she could get to work on her real challenge—Cal Bryce.

CHAPTER SEVEN

CAL DIDN'T REALISE he'd been waiting for the knock on his study door until he heard it. His shoulders tensed as he called, 'Come in.'

Heather's copper curls appeared around the door first, followed by the rest of her.

'Miss Reid,' he said, and she scowled. 'Sorry—Heather.'

'I need to talk to you about the children.'

'I need to talk to you about them, too,' he countered, motioning to the seat on the other side of his desk.

There was no rubber duck on the desk between them this time. Cal had a strange feeling that it might have made things easier if there was.

'Where are they, for a start?' he asked as she sat.

'Taking some online quizzes to help me assess their level of learning,' Heather replied. 'And, no, that isn't just so I don't have to teach them anything this afternoon.'

That sounded like a Daisy accusation if ever he'd heard one. 'Aren't you afraid that they'll cheat with you out of the room?'

Heather gave him a curious look—one that didn't quite make sense in the context of his question. A look that made Cal feel decidedly uncomfortable.

'No, I'm not afraid they'll cheat,' she said.

Cal tore his gaze away from her inquisitive one and shuffled the papers in front of him back into their folder. He didn't want Heather to see the annotated copy of Ross's contract with the magazine his lawyer, Graham, had sent over. In fact, he wasn't even sure *he* wanted to see it. Graham hadn't sounded particularly happy about it when he'd called.

'So, what do you want to talk about?' he asked, pushing the whole magazine thing to the back of his mind. He had more important things to worry about right now, anyway. Like Heather and the children.

He frowned suddenly. When had *they* become more important than the business of Lengroth Castle? Because that definitely wasn't the natural order of things in the Bryce family.

The words burst out from Heather in a tirade, and he realised quickly how much she'd been holding back all morning.

'Here's the thing. I know you think you're looking after Ross's children by taking care of their financial futures and stability, and by making sure they get a good education. But that's not enough. And it's not what they need right now. They're grieving, they're struggling, and they need a hell of a lot more from you than a good investment portfolio.'

Since Cal was mostly aiming for not bankrupting the estate in paying off Ross's debts, Heather's assessment seemed a little optimistic, but he took the point. Well, mostly…

'This is what I can do for them,' he said. 'And this *does* matter.'

Heather rolled her eyes. 'Yes, fine—it matters. But what good is it going to do them if they're so screwed up by their childhood that they go off the rails before they're eighteen and blow through their inheritance in a fortnight the moment they get it?'

Cal froze at her words. Heather couldn't know it, but she was describing the life cycle of the average Bryce male right there. How had he never seen that before? Yes, their tendency towards scandal and self-destruction might be bred into the genes, but it wasn't *only* there. It was learned, too.

It was too late for Ross, and probably too late for Cal, too. But maybe it wasn't too late for Ryan and Daisy.

Obviously encouraged by his stunned silence, Heather went on. 'They need more than a nanny and a good boarding school, Cal. They've lost their parents—you saw what lengths they went to today just to feel close to them again. They've closed off until they only have each other. They don't believe anyone will stay—that's why they've been driving the nannies away. Well, them and the ghost, I suppose...'

'But *you'll* stay,' Cal said. 'Won't you?'

She met his gaze, her eyes a wonderful bright green against her pale skin. Like summer leaves, full of life and vibrancy.

'Yes, I'll stay.'

There was a promise in her words, a truth he could rely on, and Cal realised that he trusted her in a way he hadn't trusted anyone since Ross. Since he was a child who hadn't known any better.

Heather would stay.

If there were no other truths and hard facts in the world *that* at least he was sure of. Whatever happened to Lengroth and the estate finances, and the children and boarding school, and even that damn ghost, Heather was one of them now. Tied in through a baby no one had expected or wanted until it was growing inside her and Heather had decided to love it anyway.

Because that was the sort of person she was. He'd only known her two days but Cal knew that already. Heather was good and honest and true and faithful. She'd said she would stay, so she would.

And even if a large part of his brain was telling Cal that he should send her away…set her free from Lengroth before the Bryce family ruined her the way they ruined everything else…Cal knew he wouldn't do it.

Not because she looked beautiful when she was feeling righteous about something, or because she'd shown up with a rubber duck under her arm to tell him about her night with Ross because it was 'the right thing'. Not even because she was pregnant with Ross's child, and the only nanny who stood a chance of sticking it out with Daisy and Ryan.

But because Lengroth Castle—and more specifically his niece and nephew—needed an infusion of that goodness if they ever wanted to stand a chance of breaking the cycle of destruction and pain in the future.

'But if I'm staying, Cal—'

'Which you are,' he interrupted quickly, in case she'd changed her mind while he was ruminating.

'Then I need you to support me with the children.'

'I told you—laptops, books, whatever you need,' he said quickly. 'Money is no object.' He might have depleted his own personal funds significantly to pay off Ross's debts, but that didn't mean he was exactly hard up compared to the rest of the population. He could afford whatever it took to help Heather fix his niece and nephew. And there were always investments he could cash in if it proved necessary.

Soon Lengroth would be back on its feet and the estate would repay everything he'd invested. At least that was the plan.

But Heather shook her head. 'This isn't about money, Cal. It's about *you*.'

He stared blankly at her and she sighed.

'They need more than *things*,' she explained. 'They've lost their parents—they've lost love and faith and their trust in the world. They need their new guardian to step up and fill that gap. They need you to love them and show them that. Every single day.'

'Love?'

Money, he could do. Love… He had no idea how *that* would work.

'Love,' Heather said again, more firmly. 'You're their only parent now, Cal, like it or not. Which means you need to be mother and father to them. You need to show them that they're safe and loved and that they can come to you when they need help, or when they're scared or lonely, or just because they need a hug.'

Cal shook his head. Love was too abstract—too far removed from his experiences in this castle. But Heather was right—Daisy and Ryan were his responsibility now, and if this was what they needed he had to find a way to give that to them. As much as he'd like to hand the whole thing over to Heather to fix, that wouldn't work long-term. Yes, she was staying—but only until September. After that it would be boarding school and Lengroth Castle in the holidays for years to come.

He needed to find a way to make that work. And if he didn't want Daisy and Ryan to end up like the rest of them he had to do it fast.

Cal ran Heather's words back in his head. *'Show them that they're safe and loved.'* But how? How was he supposed to do that?

He caught Heather's steady green gaze across the desk and realised the answer was right in front of him.

He smiled. 'Fine. But if you want me to do those things the kids aren't the only ones you're going to have to teach.'

Heather blinked. When her eyes opened again Cal was still looking at her, a faint smirk on his lips.

'Teach?' Was this some sort of bizarre come-on? What was she missing here?

'I need kid lessons,' Cal clarified with a shrug. 'I've never had children—never spent much time with them before. I have literally no idea how to do what you're asking. So if you want me to do it you'll have to teach me how.'

'Teach you how to…*love*?' Who didn't know how to love another person? Especially a child?

Apart from my mother.

Except even that wasn't fair, or true, and Heather told herself off in her head for even thinking it. Her mother not being able to love hadn't been the problem. Quite the reverse, really. Even if she *had* left her husband and only child behind because of it, to live with the consequences for ever.

'Exactly,' Cal replied, as if it was the most obvious thing in the world.

Heather chewed her bottom lip as she thought about it. Love wasn't something that could be taught, was it? It was just…natural.

But children—their needs and the way they understood the world—parenting skills and techniques…they were all things a person could take courses in or read books on. *They* could be taught, in a way. She'd studied classroom discipline and how to relate to students, to help and support them, before she'd qualified as a teacher. Although the best lesson was always just standing up in front of a class and having to *do* it…

She smiled. Yes, she could teach Cal from books and studies. But the biggest part of his education would come from spending time with Daisy and Ryan. And *that* was what would help him learn to fall in love with them. She was certain of it.

They might be prickly and difficult, but underneath that spiky outer shell Heather was sure that they were good kids. Ryan was already starting to come out of his shell, and Heather had hopes that Daisy wouldn't be too far behind. Having their uncle spending more time with them could only help with that.

'Okay,' she said, and watched as Cal visibly relaxed. 'We'll start tonight.'

By the time she made it back to the nursery both children had completed the tests she'd set them and were investigating their new computers—and presumably the comprehensive child security software she'd put in place.

'How did you find the tests?' she asked, settling into the window seat as they reluctantly closed their laptops. At least Uncle Cal had already done one thing to win their favour, even if they mostly had to use them for schoolwork.

Daisy shrugged. 'They were boring. But fine.'

'Yeah, easy,' Ryan agreed, shooting his sister a look. But his words didn't sound as sure as Daisy's.

Heather made a mental note to review their scores with them individually. Ryan seemed far more likely to open up to her and speak the truth if his big sister wasn't there.

Summer rain had started to fall outside while they were working, and after their outing that morning

Heather was suddenly reluctant to let them outside the grounds again that day anyway. So instead she pulled a board game down from the shelf, ignoring Daisy's groan of complaint, and they settled down to play it together.

As they played Heather found herself watching them and looking for signs of their father and uncle in them. Hearing Cal echoing Ryan's words about her worrying about them cheating had started her thinking about Cal's own childhood. Hearing him state so baldly that he'd have to be taught how to love the children...well, that only confirmed her suspicions that growing up in Lengroth Castle couldn't have been the warmest of experiences.

But maybe she could help change that for Ryan and Daisy. They'd be half-siblings to her own baby, after all. Which made them family. And Heather believed in family almost more than anything else in this world.

Which was why she had to help Cal see that, too.

After a gloating Daisy won the game, then retreated to her own bedroom with a book, Heather set Ryan up with some vaguely educational games on the laptop, then pulled out her own computer to do some work.

After heading a new document *Lessons in Childcare and Love*, she started to type.

Cal wanted to learn? Then she was more than ready to teach.

Cal was already regretting his request for kid lessons even *before* Heather showed up with a neatly typed syllabus, a reading list and a printout of study findings from the last five years.

'You expect me to do assigned reading?' he asked, incredulous, as he scanned the papers.

'You wanted to learn,' she replied with a shrug.

Rubbing a hand across his aching forehead, Cal

flipped through the syllabus instead. 'What are these?' he asked, pointing to the sections that were colour-coded in green. Of *course* it was colour-coded. He didn't know why he'd expected differently. 'Practical modules?'

'Those are the times you take the kids out and spend time with them.'

'On my *own*?' Cal winced as he heard how high and squeaky his voice had grown on the last word.

Heather shrugged. 'Maybe not to start with. But eventually, yes. You're their *parent* now, remember? The only person they have.'

As if he could forget.

Sighing, he sank down into the same armchair he'd sat in every night since he'd arrived at Lengroth, trying to figure out how to save the place and get it back on its feet before Ryan turned eighteen and took it over. This little sitting room, just off the kitchen, was the warmest room in the house in the winter, but cool and shady in the summer. It had a well-stocked drinks cabinet, a speaker system Ross had installed a couple of years before, and some of his favourite books in the whole castle on its shelves.

If Cal had to stay in Lengroth Castle at least he could use some of the comforts of the place to make it a little more bearable. And since it looked from Heather's syllabus as if he'd be there a long time...

'Maybe we should get a castle dog...' he mused as Heather sat down across from him, in the same chair she'd chosen the night before.

That was nice. They were finding little routines and habits already. Things that might make the summer stretch less dauntingly ahead of him.

Heather rolled her eyes. 'A dog—faithful companion

and lovely pet that it is—can't be a replacement for a parent's time and affection, Cal.'

'I wasn't actually thinking of the children,' Cal admitted with an embarrassed smile. 'Although it might not be a bad idea. We always had dogs here when we were kids, Ross and I.'

They'd been the perfect companions. Friendly, affectionate—and they'd never shared any of the secrets he'd sobbed out to them in the dark of the night, alone in his room.

Heather was studying him again, he realised. 'What?'

'I was just wondering…what was it like, growing up here? With Ross?'

Was she asking because she wanted to know more about his brother? Or because she was trying to figure out what it must be like for Daisy and Ryan? Or maybe… just because she cared?

Cal looked away from those bright green eyes that always seemed to see just a little too much. 'It was… difficult. Our parents had firm ideas about the aristocracy and our place in it, and the obligations that brought with it.'

Heather nodded seriously as she said, 'I imagine they expected a certain standard of behaviour from you both, knowing that the world would be paying more attention to the sons of an earl than to just us normal folk.'

Cal barked out a harsh laugh, one that hurt even his own ears and made Heather wince. 'Sorry. I just… Yes, you're right. To a point.'

'To a point?'

Her head tilted to the left again and he wondered suddenly if she'd purposefully led him down this path to revelations. However they'd got there, he wanted to backtrack.

'We're not here to talk about my childhood. We're here to talk about Daisy and Ryan's.'

'True.' Heather shuffled the stack of paper in her hands—even larger than the binder of clipped pages she'd given him. 'Let's get started, then.'

Cal tried to listen as she talked about recent studies and best practice and a child's need for attention. But his mind wouldn't focus. He felt as if he was drifting back twenty years and her words faded away to a hum at the back of his mind.

Because the rest of him was a child again, trying to survive within the cold and loveless walls of Lengroth Castle.

'The strange thing is, our impulse is to believe that shouting at children, punishing them—giving them negative attention, basically—will drive them away from the behaviour that caused it,' Heather said. 'But actually the opposite is often true. If a child isn't getting high-quality, regular and predictable time and attention from a parent or guardian or whoever, then they'll take whatever attention they can get—however negative. So rewarding bad behaviour with attention of any sort can actually just make the child do it more.'

Rewarding bad behaviour. Was that the problem the Bryce family had? No matter how badly they behaved they only seemed to be rewarded for it—with lands and estates and money and attention in glossy magazines like the one Ross had that bloody contract with.

Except, no. Because those rewards relied on nobody ever finding out about all the scandals and cruelty. Their high station had just made it easier for them to get away with things.

Like Ross had done for so long.

But Ross had to have been a better father than their

own had been, right? Cal felt sure about that much, at least. Ross would never have beaten a child. Would never have threatened to slit his dog's throat in front of him at the dinner table for some imagined or perceived slight against him.

Would he?

Cal swallowed as he remembered the reason he'd never had a pet dog as an adult. Not after what had happened to Cavall, the night of the worst of his father's rages...

'Cal?'

Heather had put her papers down on the table beside her chair. When had she done that? When had she stopped talking? He wasn't sure.

He shook his head. 'Sorry. I was just...remembering.'

'Growing up here?' she asked softly, and he nodded.

She bit her lower lip, a habit he'd noticed last night in the hallway and something that had previously made his pulse kick up a gear just at the sight of it. But tonight his heart was already racing from memories, and Heather's lips couldn't compete with them. *Quite.*

'I think... Cal, I think that if you want to learn how to take care of Daisy and Ryan we need to talk about some other stuff first. Okay?'

Cal reached for the bottle of brandy beside his table. 'There's nothing to talk about.'

'Right. Except...you know...*everything.*' She gave him an apologetic smile. 'Look, if it makes you feel better I'll go first.'

'Go first?'

She shrugged. 'You know... I'll show you my childhood trauma if you show me yours.'

Cal paused halfway through taking the lid off the brandy bottle to pour himself a glass. 'Your childhood trauma?' He couldn't imagine Heather having anything except the kind of perfect, idyllic childhood he'd read about in storybooks before he was old enough to accept the world as it really was.

'We all have one, right? So... Pour me a drink—non-alcoholic, please—and I'll begin.'

Slowly he leaned across to select a second glass, then found the bottle of elderflower cordial. There was no way he intended to share his childhood at Lengroth with anyone. But he wanted to know what kind of childhood had made Heather the way she was. Especially since it couldn't be anything like his own and Ross's.

Maybe then he could learn how to make Daisy and Ryan's better, too.

'Tell me.'

CHAPTER EIGHT

HEATHER'S HANDS SHOOK at the very idea of sharing her past with this man. But if it was the only way to get Cal to open up about his own childhood then it was the right thing to do. For Daisy and for Ryan—and maybe even for Cal himself.

Taking the glass of elderflower cordial from him, Heather allowed herself a small sip before she started talking.

'I grew up in a little Hertfordshire village,' she started. 'You know the sort—where everyone knows everyone else and all their business.'

'Sounds like Lengroth. Well, mostly,' Cal amended.

She wondered what that amendment was for. She could well imagine how difficult it must have been for Cal and Ross, growing up in a small community where everyone would have been watching them even more closely than most young boys, waiting for them to screw up or do something worth reporting back to the Earl—or the newspapers.

'Anyway, my father was leader of the village council, and he ran the post office and corner shop on the high street, and my mother was a teacher at the nearest secondary school.'

They might not have had aristocratic status, but her

parents' jobs and roles in the community had made them more than high-profile enough for Heather's liking.

'So far so idyllic,' Cal commented. 'Go on.'

What came next? The fall from grace, of course. The point where everything had gone wrong. But the words stuck in Heather's throat even as she pushed herself to say them. She'd never needed to tell anyone this story before. Either they already knew it or they had no need ever to hear it.

Until now.

'My mother…she taught the sixth form, mostly. Seventeen- and eighteen-year-olds.' Heather swallowed. 'She fell in love with one of her students—a seventeen-year-old boy. Only seven years older than I was. They started an affair.'

With a wince, Cal topped up her elderflower cordial.

She took another gulp. 'They got caught, of course. In the classroom, in fact, by the head teacher. The news was around the village before she'd even made it home to tell Dad.'

'What happened next?' Cal asked.

She could hear the tension in his words. He obviously knew it wouldn't be good. 'Mum was suspended from her job immediately, of course. His parents talked about pressing charges. But the boy—John, he was called…'

Oh, hell, her eyes were burning now. Could she blame the pregnancy hormones for the tears on her cheeks? Probably not.

'He told everyone who would listen that they were in love. That Mum loved him far more than her husband or me. Mum…she said it wasn't true. That John had made it all up—that it was all a misunderstanding and there was nothing between them.'

'And was it untrue?'

'No. But even after everyone knew she kept on lying. Until…'

Cal's eyes fluttered closed, as if he were feeling her pain. Heather was just glad he wasn't looking at her as she told him the rest of the sordid tale.

'Two nights later they ran away together. Just disappeared in the middle of the night. I… We never heard from Mum again. Not in the last eighteen years.'

Cal's eyes flew open. 'Never? She didn't leave a note or anything?'

Heather shrugged. 'She did. Just a short letter, saying she was sorry, but she loved John and that was more important than anything.'

'How did your dad take it?'

'Badly.' Which might be the biggest understatement of the year. 'He was destroyed. He loved her so much, and it broke him when he realised she loved someone else.'

Broke *her*, too—not that she intended to mention that. Cal already had the pitying look in his eyes that she'd grown so used to seeing from the villagers. Well, the ones who weren't giving her knowing looks and talking behind her back, anyway.

'He started drinking,' she went on. 'Lost his place on the council, his reputation… Almost lost the shop, too. People felt sorry for him, of course, but the scandal was too juicy for them to resist gossiping about it. He grew paranoid, started thinking everyone was talking about him all the time. He'd be walking down the street and he'd hear someone say something, and then he'd be yelling at them, threatening them—all sorts. It was…horrible.'

Another understatement.

'And now?' Cal asked. 'How is he now?'

'Better.' Heather attempted a smile. 'Much better.

Eventually he landed himself in enough trouble that his doctor insisted on counselling, and that helped, I think. But he still can't bear to talk about her, or hear her name. He took down all her photos, but…I look just like her, you see.'

Cal's expression turned stony. 'He took it out on you?'

'No!' Heather's eyes widened. 'No, my dad loves me. It was never… No. Not that. But I don't think it made it any easier for him, having me there as a daily reminder.'

He'd tried so hard never to let on, bless him. But Heather had always known when he got that faraway look in his eye, watching her, that he was thinking of her mother.

'So. Not quite so idyllic, then,' Cal said.

He was watching her carefully, Heather noted as she wiped a stray tear from her cheek. Watching her responses, her reactions. His, however, seemed strangely absent. As if the story that had defined her whole life was more of an amusing anecdote than a tragedy. Apart from when he'd thought her father had hurt her, he'd been emotionless throughout the whole thing.

Heather was almost afraid of what that said about his own story.

She shrugged. 'Not perfect, no. But it could have been worse. My father loves me, and that counts for a lot. He did his best by me once the worst of it was over.' And she did her best by him in return. They were family, after all. They had to stick together. 'Growing up without Mum… that was awful. But it was her choice.'

'But not one you would ever have made?' Cal said quietly.

'No.' Heather's hands went protectively to her stomach. Her baby was barely more than a cluster of cells, and already she couldn't imagine ever leaving it. 'The worst part—well, no, not the worst part, but the part that lingered the longest—was the gossip. The scandal. I'll for ever be the girl whose mother ran off with a student and left her behind. People can't look at me and see past that once they know.'

'I can,' Cal said, and she knew he believed it.

She gave him a small smile. 'Wait and see.'

He looked away. 'I'm sorry that happened to you.'

'People grow up with worse,' Heather replied. She bit her lip and took a chance. 'In fact, I'm almost certain that *you* did.'

He met her gaze with a crooked smile. 'Is that a subtle hint that it's my turn to share my pain?'

'If you want to tell me,' Heather replied, settling back in her chair.

The only problem was, as much as she knew she needed to hear it—for Daisy and Ryan's sake—she wasn't at all sure she wanted to. She already felt too close to this man. Had shared more than she'd meant to. It was as if she could feel the room—hell, the *world*—growing smaller around them, until they were all that mattered.

When she knew his truths, his secrets, how much harder would it be to pull back again? But all the same… She needed to know.

'Tell me,' she repeated.

And Cal began to talk.

'Tell me.'

She'd said it as if it were nothing at all—a story round a campfire. As if there should be marshmallows. As if it wasn't generations of secrets he was letting out.

Why should he tell her? Why not just lie? Make up a slightly awkward childhood filled with minor issues and small hurts? Pretend, the way every member of his family had for hundreds of years, that they were upstanding, respectable people?

But then he met her steady green gaze and knew that he would tell her everything.

What *was* this hold she had over him? It was as if her goodness, her determination to do the right thing, was lashing him to her morals.

Because he wanted so badly to be more like her. To have less of the Bryce blood and darkness in him.

Because he wanted to believe that he could give that to Daisy and Ryan. Make their future brighter than their family's past.

But only if he told the truth now.

'My family...the Bryce family...they've held land and power and influence here for hundreds and hundreds of years. And their reputation has always been...impeccable. No scandal, no mistresses, no illegitimate children.'

Heather winced at that one—understandably.

'No financial difficulties, not even a servant dismissed under suspicious circumstances. Even more recently there's never been a photo of any Bryce falling out of a taxi, drunk at a nightclub, and no Bryce woman has ever worn the wrong thing to a royal wedding. Bryce men fought in all the wars like they were supposed to. Bryce women dutifully gave an heir and a spare to every generation. The family here at Lengroth Castle are purer than pure, whiter than white—the pinnacle of what the aristocracy should be. Looked up to throughout the land.'

'And we need to keep it that way, son,' his father had always told him.

Even now Cal knew he was living the Bryce legacy— keeping Heather here, where she couldn't let on about what his brother had done. Keeping the scandal close so it couldn't get out.

Although, now he knew about her mother, he knew for certain that she'd never tell. She'd never want to bring another scandal down on herself—or her father. And the illegitimate child of an earl who had died under what even Cal now had to admit were suspicious circumstances... that would definitely count as a scandal.

He looked over at her, another wave of guilt crashing over him as he thought about what Ross had done to her. If nothing else, he'd upended her life. And Cal hadn't exactly helped with that, either, forcing her to stay here at Lengroth for the summer.

Heather, meanwhile, looked sympathetic but confused. 'I can see how that level of perfection would be—'

'No,' he interrupted, anger flaring that she should believe it even for a moment. She'd met Ross, after all. She knew more of the truth than most. 'The problem is that it's all a pack of lies.'

'Oh.' Heather gave him a small smile. 'I'll admit I was wondering where Ross fitted into that picture.'

Cal ran his hands through his hair with a chuckle. 'Ironically, Ross was the one I thought was different. I thought he'd broken the Bryce curse. That he had the perfect happy marriage and the perfect happy children. Then I came home after his death and found all of this.'

He cast his hands around him, hoping the movement would encompass both the castle, the kids, the debts, Heather's baby—and that damn contract upstairs in his study.

'How bad is it here?' Heather asked. 'Really? You mentioned that the finances aren't as healthy as you'd like...'

Cal sighed. 'That's just part of it. The next logical step for the whole Bryce legacy, I suppose. Ross has run this place almost into the ground—huge gambling debts, obligations to people and companies he'd obviously made to try and buy himself some more time to get the money together. I can cover the financial stuff myself—one of the benefits of being the younger son has been spending the last decade getting out of the shadow of Lengroth and making my own way in the world. I've had enough success that the money isn't too much of a problem.'

'But you didn't count on the scandal of an extra illegitimate child to throw into the mix,' Heather murmured. 'And we haven't even talked about how we're going to tell Daisy and Ryan the truth about that, when it's time.'

'Or *if* we are.'

That was his Bryce blood rising up again. The instinct to hide from scandal, to pretend none of it had ever happened, wish it away. But he couldn't pretend Heather didn't exist. And, heaven help him, he didn't want to wish her away.

He shoved that thought down. As if the situation wasn't bad enough as it was. The last thing he needed to do was develop *feelings* of any kind for the woman carrying his brother's illegitimate child.

'The thing I learned about scandal from my mother,' Heather said softly, 'is that it always comes out in the end. If she'd told my father the truth up front…managed the situation properly…maybe everything wouldn't have been as awful as it was. But because she lied everything was a hundred times worse.'

It was hard to imagine a teacher and student relationship like that *ever* ending particularly well, but Cal didn't mention it. He knew what she was really saying.

'We'll talk about it,' he promised. 'Add it to the list.'

'Speaking of which… You've told me about Ross as an adult. But what about when you were children? And when you say your family's reputation was all a pack of lies, that's not just Ross, is it? So…what's the truth?'

He looked away before he answered, as if he couldn't meet her eyes while admitting to it. God, how bad was it? She'd known Ross was no saint, but Cal seemed upstanding and respectable—apart from his lack of understanding about love. How bad could the rest of his family have been?

'In every generation Bryce men have cheated, gambled, drunk, caused pain and suffering and humiliation. They're just better at covering it up than most people.'

'Okay…' That sounded bad, obviously. But a lot of people drank too much or spent too much on the horses. Her own father had succumbed for a time. She leaned forward, towards Cal. 'When you say pain and suffering…?'

'I mean it,' Cal said openly. 'My father… Ross used to stand in front of me to protect me from his fists, his belt or just his knife-edged tongue. But he always found a way around eventually—unless he was too drunk to stand up. You know why I can find the kids when none of the nannies can? Because I know every damn hiding place in this castle. I remember cowering in the nook behind that hanging by the main staircase while my father bellowed for me—until he got so mad at my hiding he threw my dog down the stairs in front of me and broke his neck.'

Heather shuddered and reached out towards him, desperate to offer some comfort if she could. But Cal pulled back before she could touch him.

'I still didn't come out from behind that hanging. I slept there until Ross found me—after midnight.'

'Cal, I'm so sorry.'

No wonder he thought he couldn't love the children

like a father. He'd had no example of it, no way to learn—except from the older brother he'd clearly idolised, but who had turned out to be flawed, too.

'Your father sounds…terrible. But that doesn't mean that every man in your family is like that. Ross wasn't—was he? I know he wasn't exactly faithful…'

'He never hit the kids, as far as I know, if that's what you're asking.'

Heather let out a breath of relief. She'd dealt with abused kids before, and hadn't thought that Daisy and Ryan showed any signs of that at least, but as a teacher she knew a person could never be totally sure.

'I only knew Ross for one night, and heaven knows I realise he had failings. But he didn't seem like a cruel or unloving man.'

'He was cheating on his wife and lying to you *and* her about it,' Cal pointed out.

'You have a point,' Heather admitted grimly. 'But his bad behaviour—or your father's—doesn't mean that your whole family is bad.'

Or that Cal was incapable of giving Daisy and Ryan the family they needed—because she was almost certain that was what *Cal* thought.

'You're not listening. It wasn't just Ross, or our father. It's every Bryce man *ever*.' Cal looked up suddenly, his eyes wide and feverish. 'You know that damn ghost that all the nannies claimed to be running from? She was a servant here, a hundred years ago or so. Story is she got into trouble with a stable hand and lost her footing on the stairs trying to run away and elope with him. Crashed her head open on the stone steps.'

Heather winced. 'That's horrible.'

'And it's another lie. My great-great-grandfather knocked her up then denied it. When she threatened to tell people in the village the truth, he pushed her down the stairs.'

Heather fell back into her seat. 'How can you be sure?'

'Because my father used to threaten to do it if Ross ever knocked up any girl out of wedlock.'

'Like me.'

Oh, God. Every generation of Bryce men, Cal had said. But not him. Whatever he thought. He wouldn't do anything to hurt her. She was sure of it.

Cal looked up at her, a wicked glint in his eye. 'You still sure about staying?'

'You wouldn't hurt me,' she said, meeting his gaze head-on, making sure her voice never wavered.

She was rewarded by a sudden vulnerability in his expression. 'How can you *know* that, Heather? How can you know I'm not just like all the rest of them?'

'Because you asked me here tonight to teach you how to love your niece and nephew,' she said softly. 'You're a good man. I don't know what else your father did— or your grandfather and your great-grandfather and so on—to make you think otherwise. But I've only been here two days and I can already see that. So how about you try forgetting about the past and focussing on the future for a change?'

'Like you are?' he asked, his defences back up. 'I know the money I offered you was good, but can you *really* tell me that's the only reason you're staying? That you're not avoiding having to admit to your scandalous pregnancy in your home town?'

Heather looked away. 'I never said that wasn't part of it. My dad doesn't deserve another scandal being brought down on him.'

'And neither do you.'

Reaching between them, Cal took her hand in his, and

Heather glanced up to meet his gaze again. The wicked gleam was gone, and so was the anger and the defensiveness. In its place was an expression Heather couldn't quite identify, but it made her stomach flip-flop all the same.

Was ten weeks too early to feel the baby move? Probably. Which meant this was something else.

And whatever it was, it scared her.

'We'll figure this out, okay? Together.' Cal's voice was rough, as if admitting to his family's past had torn his throat raw.

'Okay,' she whispered back. 'Okay.'

Because she believed him. Even if she had no idea how they could do it.

CHAPTER NINE

CAL WAS SUDDENLY all too aware of the softness of Heather's skin under his fingers and the trusting look in her eyes. God help her, she honestly believed that he was different. That he wasn't just like all the others.

He almost didn't want her to stay long enough to realise she was wrong.

Her copper curls fell around her shoulders and he longed to run his fingers through them. Wanted to reach an arm around her and pull her closer. To brush his hands down her sides, her curves, until they rested at her waist and he could lean in for the inevitable kiss he could feel building...

Except he couldn't.

He could see it in her eyes that if he pressed his lips to hers right now Heather wouldn't pull away. Knew in his bones that she wanted this as much as he did.

Was it the strange closeness that came from knowing each other's secrets? From being with the only other person in the world who knew everything? Or was it something more basic? Primal? A connection between them that came from attraction and lust and nothing more?

Or was it the strange sense of trust she brought out in him—something Cal had thought bred out of him generations ago?

Perhaps the problem was that it was all three. He wanted Heather—but she was beautiful, so that was hardly a surprise. And he could relax with her in a way he couldn't with anyone else, because she knew the truth. Most of all, he trusted her, and that felt wonderful.

But, despite all that, he couldn't have her. Couldn't let himself give in to this moment, however tempting it was.

He might be a Bryce, but Heather had given him a glimmer of hope that he could beat down those genes and actually behave the way the rest of his family pretended they did. She was pregnant with his brother's child. She was scandal enough already—he couldn't make it worse by seducing her.

Especially now he knew what that kind of scandal would do to her, and to her family, if she had to live through it again.

Swallowing hard, Cal pulled back and watched the light in Heather's eyes flicker and fade. But then she gave a small nod and he knew that she understood.

However much they both wanted this, it could never be a good idea. And they were just going to have to live with that.

'I should get back to the children. Check they're actually asleep this time.' Heather was on her feet before she'd finished the sentence. 'Oh, I got in touch with the hospital, by the way. I have a scan booked in two weeks' time.'

'I'll take you,' Cal said automatically.

Heather shook her head. 'You don't need to do that. If you could look after the children while I go, though...'

'Mrs Peterson will take care of them,' Cal insisted. 'You shouldn't be alone for that.'

Whatever else there could or couldn't be between them, Cal knew that going to the scan with Heather was the right thing to do. And Heather always did the right thing for other people. It was time other people started doing the same for her.

'Okay, then,' she said, giving in with a small smile.

'Okay.' He returned it, and their gazes met, and suddenly Cal realised that whole minutes might have passed and he wouldn't have known. He was too lost in her green, green eyes.

That was when he realised he might be in real trouble this time. Some things were just too tempting to resist.

The next few days, after the kiss that never happened, were somehow both awkward and not.

Heather found herself overthinking every tiny interaction she had with Cal. Like the day she stopped by his study with a new book for his reading list that had been delivered, and found him with his head in his hands at the desk. She'd paused in the doorway, uncertain as to whether she should go in, but then he'd looked up, smiled tiredly at her and held out his hand.

What had made her take it, she still didn't know. Knowing Cal, he wouldn't have offered it if he hadn't been so exhausted. But she knew he'd been working long mornings, from the early hours, spending the afternoons with the children after their lessons had finished, and then working again after dinner before heading down to the small sitting room by the kitchen for kid tuition with her before bed.

No wonder he was worn out.

She'd taken his hand and he'd pulled her close, resting his head against her stomach as she stood beside him. And for a moment—just a blink of a second—she had almost believed that it was his baby growing inside her. That they really were in this together, not just muddling through as partners because they had no other choice.

He'd come to his senses pretty quickly, letting her go so fast that she stumbled backwards.

'I'm sorry,' he'd said, but she'd shaken her head.

She wasn't sorry. But she knew they couldn't have anything more than those stolen moments, either.

She'd placed the book on his desk and left.

But most of the time when they were together the children were there, too—walking in the woods, down by the river, or popping into the village to visit the sweet shop. Cal had relaxed a lot around them, which had helped the kids to relax in turn. Heather couldn't help but think that his lessons in children really were paying off.

Even if the lessons themselves were a torment.

Every night they met in that damn sitting room and talked about Daisy and Ryan—how they were getting on with their lessons, how they could both support them, the counsellors Cal had found for them to talk to about their parents' deaths. They discussed techniques for discipline and support, ways to make important days feel special, what to do when Daisy had another one of her nightmares...

They talked about everything, as long as it had to do with the children.

They never talked again about the secrets they'd shared in that room. Or how sure Heather had been that Cal would have kissed her that night if the circumstances had been different. If she hadn't been pregnant with Ross's child.

And still, underneath all their carefully neutral talk, she could hear echoes of it. In the tone of his voice, or in the smallest aside about her appearance or behaviour.

The connection she'd felt that night hadn't gone away, Heather knew. It just simmered under the surface. And that was where they needed to keep it.

So Heather made sure they both always stayed in their chairs during their lessons, across the room from each other. She tried not to let their fingers touch when she passed him a book or a paper. She tried not to meet his gaze when she smiled. Because then she'd have to watch his eyes turn darker and know it was lust she saw.

Some nights she was more successful than others.

'I think it's time for you to take the kids out on your own,' Heather said, looking up from her notebook to see Cal balancing an apple on his head. Where had he even got the apple *from*?

It rolled off and he caught it as he stared at her in alarm. 'On my own? I do that all the time. We went into Lengroth last week.'

'Once,' Heather pointed out. 'And I was thinking somewhere a little further afield.'

'But *why*?' Cal whined, sounding so like his nephew that Heather couldn't help but smile.

'Because that's what we're building up to here, right? You being able to look after them alone after I leave.'

A shadow fell across Cal's face. Heather knew her own smile had slipped, too. She didn't like to think about leaving Lengroth Castle, and not only because it meant that Daisy and Ryan would be heading off to boarding school.

Unless I can convince Cal otherwise.

'But you're still here right now,' Cal argued. 'And I'm still learning, right?'

Heather eyed the apple in his hand disapprovingly. 'Yeah, right. *Lots* of learning going on here tonight. Besides, all the education in the world counts for nothing if you can't put it into practice.'

'I thought I was,' Cal grumbled.

Heather took pity on him. 'Yes, you have been.'

In fact, he'd been doing so well she wasn't sure he'd even noticed that she stepped back from any sort of discipline or emotional management of the kids when he was in the room. He might not realise it, but he was doing everything he needed to already. He just needed to take the next step, and continue it when she wasn't there as a safety net.

'That's why we're taking it up a level.'

'Where would I even take them?' he asked.

Heather shrugged. 'Anywhere. Take them bowling, or to the cinema. Crazy golf. Swimming. Soft play.'

Cal pulled a face. 'I've got a meeting with my lawyer in Edinburgh the day after tomorrow—'

'I was thinking more of something that would be fun for *them*,' Heather interrupted.

Cal rolled his eyes. 'I know that. I was thinking the three of you could come with me for the day. The kids could stay with you while I have my meeting, then I could take them around the city on my own afterwards. We could all meet up for dinner before driving back.'

Heather blinked. 'That's actually a really good idea.'

'Then it's a date,' Cal said with a smirk—one that faded quickly when Heather winced. 'Yeah. Not that. You know what I mean...'

'I know,' Heather said.

She also knew that it was moments like that which were going to drive her insane with the effort of not kissing Cal Bryce.

Cal was starting to think that this was a very bad idea.

Edinburgh was packed with tourists—all in town for the Fringe Festival, he supposed. His meeting with the lawyer had gone even more badly than he'd expected. Heather had skipped off for an afternoon in the city alone *after* feeding the kids ice cream and waffles, so he'd have nothing to bribe them with later unless he wanted them on some sort of almighty sugar high. And it was raining.

None of these things were making his mood any brighter.

'So, what do you want to do?' he asked Daisy and Ryan, as they sheltered in a shop doorway, with the sound of bagpipes blasting through the weather on the Royal Mile.

Daisy shrugged. Ryan widened his eyes and shook his head.

'Really helpful, kids.'

'Well, we don't know what there is *to* do,' Daisy pointed out. 'Whenever we came here with Mum it was to go shopping.'

'We don't want to go shopping,' Ryan clarified quickly.

'Good.' Cal rubbed a hand across his forehead as he tried to think about what *he'd* liked about the city as a child. Being away from Lengroth, mostly.

Then he had a stroke of genius.

'Okay. Follow me, stay close and don't wander off.'

He strode through the rain towards Castle Hill and the hulking shadow of Edinburgh Castle, stark against the cloudy sky.

'You *do* realise that we *live* in a castle,' Daisy pointed out as they got closer. 'You really don't need to take us to another one.'

'But what if this one has functioning dungeons?' Cal asked. Beside him, Ryan gasped, and Cal shook his head. 'We're not going to the castle. Come on.'

They stopped at a building just before the castle and Cal hurried his charges inside, out of the rain.

'World of Illusions?' Daisy asked, sticking her head back outside to check the sign.

'What's a Camera Obscura?' Ryan frowned as he sounded out the word on the leaflets by the door.

'Let's head in and find out.'

In his head Cal had imagined introducing the kids to all the different mirror tricks and plasma balls, the mind-bending illusions, and explaining how they worked. The kids would hang off his every word as he made magic real or demonstrated something properly cool.

As it was, the minute they had their tickets and were through the doors Daisy and Ryan both raced off in different directions, leaving him staring after them dumbly.

He shook his head and prepared to yell.

They're just overexcited.

Great. Now he was hearing Heather's voice in his head.

Ryan raced past him again, so Cal grabbed his sleeve as he passed, held his hand firmly—despite his admonishments that, at eight, he was far too old to hold hands—and headed out to find Daisy.

'Right. Now, here are the rules,' he told them, as the three of them were reunited beside a mirror that stretched them out into giants.

'Set your expectations,' Heather always said. *'Kids like to know what their limits are, even if they go on to test them.'*

With Heather's gentle voice in his head, he forced himself to keep his tone even and calm, rather than just yelling at them. 'We stick together, okay? We can look at everything in here, for as long as you like, but we do it together. And we finish at the Camera Obscura, okay?'

'I still don't know what one of those is,' Ryan grumbled.

'Then let's get exploring,' Cal said, deciding to take their lack of answer as tacit acceptance.

Daisy rolled her eyes, but followed anyway.

To start with, Cal used the kids' fascination with the illusions, the shadow wall and the plasma globes as an opportunity to check his emails. Daisy rolled her eyes at him again, but she and Ryan seemed to be having a nice time so he didn't worry.

When they reached the Ames Room—where an optical illusion meant people appeared to shrink and grow as they moved around—he surrendered his phone to Daisy, so she could take photos of Ryan seemingly much taller than him. Then they reached Bewilderworld, where Cal just concentrated on not feeling dizzy and disorientated as they crossed a metal bridge surrounded by a tunnel of twisting, turning lights.

'Where's Ryan?' he asked Daisy as he stepped off the other end.

'He ran into the mirror maze,' Daisy replied with a shrug. 'I'll go find him.'

She raced off before Cal could stop her. Uncomfortably, he stared into the walls and walls of mirrors and steeled himself to follow.

Apart from flashes of the kids as they ran ahead, their laughter echoing off the glass, all Cal could see was himself, reflected everywhere. A reminder of who he was... who he'd always be. A Bryce, with all the history that brought with it. And, try as he might, he couldn't catch up with Daisy and Ryan, who always seemed just a stretch out of reach.

'This is every parent's worst nightmare,' Cal muttered, before stopping inches away from crashing into another mirror.

Parent. He was the parent—or as close to one as these kids had. And while he might still have a long way to go in learning to take care of them...let alone loving them the way they needed…he was making progress. He was here, in a damn maze, not waiting outside on his phone.

He was here. And that was the first step.

Smiling to himself, he turned confidently left—and walked straight into another mirror pane.

'This way, Uncle Cal!'

He spun to find Ryan waiting behind him.

'Come on!'

This time his nephew grabbed *his* hand and led the way. And Cal couldn't help but admit that it felt strangely right.

CHAPTER TEN

'AND THEN UP in the roof there's this magic camera that lets you see all the streets of Edinburgh right as they're happening, only tiny. And we looked for you but we couldn't see you. But the guy doing the show built a bridge for some other people and they walked right across it and it was brilliant!'

Ryan's epic run-on sentence came to an end and he took a large gulp of the brightly coloured drink he'd ordered from the kids' menu in the restaurant Cal had chosen. Heather was now regretting agreeing to let them have anything they wanted. The E-numbers would keep them awake for a week.

'Magic camera?' she asked Cal, while Ryan was quiet.

'The Camera Obscura,' Cal explained. 'Victorian ingenuity at its finest. Have you ever been?'

Heather shook her head. 'I'll have to go some time.'

Cal opened his mouth—almost as if he were about to say *I'll take you*—then shut it again, so hard she heard his teeth click.

'So you had a good afternoon, then?' she asked, turning to Daisy.

Daisy shrugged. 'It was okay, I suppose.'

Heather gave Cal a small smile. From Daisy, that was high praise indeed. She'd *known* letting them spend the afternoon together was a good idea—and she'd managed to do some much-needed clothes shopping, too. Ordering online could only get a girl so far, especially when it came to maternity bras.

Later, as they drove home into the darkening summer sky, with Ryan passed out in the back and Daisy with her headphones on, Heather asked, 'Was it really a good afternoon?'

Cal's smile was slow, but telling. 'You know...it was. I mean, there's a big difference between a few hours at a tourist attraction and the rest of their lives, but it was good. It's a start, right?'

'A really good one,' Heather said, and tried to ignore the warmth that filled her at his words.

She was *not* falling for her boss. And she was *definitely* not falling for the brother of her baby's father. No matter how gorgeous he was when he smiled. Not happening.

She hoped.

'Daisy did well on her history assignment this week,' Heather said, handing Cal a printout of Daisy's short essay as they sat in the little sitting room by the kitchen a few days later.

Despite Cal's progress he'd insisted on continuing their kid lessons, even if they were mostly just catch-ups on how they'd got on that day.

'Seems she has a real grasp of the blood and guts part of historical conflict.'

'Why am I not surprised?' Cal took it, grinning up at her, and Heather knew it was pride she saw in his gaze.

She couldn't help it; she smiled back. Just as their fingers touched and his eyes turned dark again...

Was this how her mother had felt? Falling for someone she knew she couldn't have? She'd been married, he'd been thirteen years younger than her... Her mother couldn't have thought it was a good idea.

And yet she'd fallen for him anyway. Been so consumed by love and lust that she'd left her whole life behind for him.

Heather, fortunately, wasn't that stupid.

She might not be able to stop the feelings that flooded through her every time she was with Cal, but she could call them what they were. Attraction. Lust. And wildly inappropriate.

She pulled back quickly and turned her attention to her notes. She'd found early on that if she didn't approach each evening with a list of things to discuss with Cal about the children it was too easy to forget everything she'd meant to say when she was with him. Or for the conversation to get distracted, to stray onto forbidden topics.

Like how badly she wanted to kiss him.

It hadn't felt like this with Ross, she realised. Or anyone else ever, actually. This incredible drawn-out anticipation of something that couldn't happen.

With Ross, it had been a stupid idea after one too many cocktails. He'd been gorgeous, oozing confidence, and she'd been having a bad day. He'd wanted her, and she'd wanted cheering up, and that had been enough.

But with Cal... *Want* wasn't a strong enough word to encompass the feeling that flooded through her every time she saw him. It seemed impossible that they'd never even kissed. That her body could hum with need just being in the same room as him, yet she'd never felt his lips on hers or his hands against her bare skin.

And it felt even more impossible that she never would.

'How about Ryan?' Cal asked, clearing his throat first.

Heather forced herself back into the moment. 'Um...

he's doing fine, too. A little distracted this week, actually. I'm not sure why.'

Cal shrugged, as if to say *Why are you asking me?* Heather was about to remind him exactly why this was his problem, too, when his face fell and his eyes grew wide.

'Oh, hell.'

'What?'

'It's his birthday. This weekend.'

Cal looked mortified that he'd forgotten. Heather was just relieved that he'd remembered *now*.

'I need to buy him a present, right? What on earth do I get him?'

Of course he thought this was all about the present. Ryan's first birthday without his parents there to celebrate with him and Cal thought it could be fixed with a remote-control helicopter or something.

Which actually wasn't a bad gift idea, now she thought about it. But it wasn't going to be enough.

Chewing on her lower lip, Heather doodled a helicopter on the notepad in front of her.

'Actually,' she said slowly, 'I've got a good idea.'

Cal wasn't entirely sure how him organising Ryan's birthday celebrations was a *good* idea. In fact, it seemed like a bad one to him. But Heather was adamant.

'It's the perfect opportunity for you to show him that you're here, that he's not parentless, and that you know important things about him.'

'Like when his birthday is?'

'Like what he enjoys and how he'd like to celebrate,' Heather corrected him.

Cal sighed. 'Except that's the point. I *don't* know that stuff.'

'Well, if his birthday is on Saturday you've got three

days to learn. Right? And you did okay in Edinburgh. You'll be fine.'

Not helpful. If he'd remembered that Ryan's birthday was coming up he'd definitely have saved the trip to the World of Illusions for that. Now he was all out of ideas.

As if he didn't have enough to do without a nine-year-old's birthday party to arrange. He'd tried quizzing Daisy on what sort of things they'd done for birthdays before, but that hadn't been as helpful as he'd hoped.

'Mostly we just had a birthday tea here,' she'd said with a shrug. 'Mum would get a cake from the bakery in town, and sometimes we'd invite a friend each, but that was about it.'

Well, cake he could manage. Friends he could not. As far as he'd seen since he'd returned neither child had any—or wanted any. They were happiest in each other's company.

Although, as a book on Heather's reading list had informed him, that was probably because they were the only people who understood what they'd each been through.

A bit like him and Heather, really. They'd both been disillusioned by someone they loved, and both had had to cope with a scandal looming over their heads, waiting to break.

And he absolutely wasn't going to make it worse by kissing her. However much he wanted to. God, he really wanted to.

Except when she landed him with things like organising Ryan's party.

In the end he'd come up with a plan, of sorts—only slightly assisted by Heather on the subject of present ideas. He had no idea if Ryan would have chosen the same things to celebrate turning nine, but at least it showed he was making an effort—he hoped.

This stuff he could do. This kind of thing came with an action list and a basic template. He could follow instructions well enough. It was figuring out how to deal with the stuff that *didn't* come with a manual—like emotions and love—that caused him problems.

Saturday dawned sunny and bright, fortunately for Cal's plans. Mrs Peterson made pancakes for breakfast—much to everyone's delight—and Ryan opened presents from Daisy, Heather, Mrs Peterson and Cal himself.

Heather's presents were books, unsurprisingly, but since they seemed to be about some sort of monsters, and brave young boys capturing and training them, Ryan was thrilled. Daisy had spent some of her pocket money in the sweet shop last time they went to the village, so Ryan now had enough sugary chewy things to rot his teeth for months. Mrs Peterson had bought him a sensible jumper for the Scottish winters. And Cal, on Heather's advice, had bought him a remote-control helicopter.

'This is awesome! Thank you, Uncle Cal!'

Cal shot a grateful smile at Heather. 'I'm glad you like it. How about we take it out for the day and see how it flies?'

'All day?' Ryan asked. 'No lessons first?'

'No lessons on birthdays,' Heather confirmed. 'It's a rule.'

'For me, too?' Daisy asked.

'Absolutely,' Cal told her. 'Go on, you two—go and get ready to head out. We'll meet you at the front door in twenty minutes.'

'So far so good,' Heather murmured as the kids raced off.

'Long way to go yet,' Cal replied.

* * *

This was going well. Against all the odds—and definitely all his expectations—this was going well.

Cal had spent some time thinking about when he'd seen Ryan look happiest, or most relaxed, and had realised that it was whenever they were outside. Ryan was all boy, after all, and constantly moving, so getting him somewhere he could run and jump and yell just made sense.

Especially since they could also fly the new helicopter.

'I swear you're more excited about that thing than he is,' Heather had muttered as Cal and Ryan had planned flights and adventures for it on the drive there.

He'd chosen an area he and Ross had loved exploring as kids, whenever they'd been able to persuade someone to take them. Just past Lengroth Woods, at the edge of their estate, was a valley with a stream running through it, steep hills for rolling down on either side, purple heather and yellow gorse blooming all around, and no people for miles in any direction.

It was perfect for a family walk, a picnic in the sunshine—and for sending the helicopter on its first mission, to find out how good the inbuilt camera that was meant to talk to his smartphone really was.

Pretty good, was the answer. As they all settled down for their birthday lunch Cal and Ryan reviewed the footage together, heads close as they stared at the little screen.

Something tightened in Cal's chest as Ryan's hair brushed against his cheek, and he realised that maybe— *maybe*—this was what he'd been looking for. A connection with these children he didn't know and couldn't understand. There hadn't even been the tension between them that he'd felt in Edinburgh, when they'd still been figuring out how to spend time together at all.

Maybe all those lessons with Heather were paying off.

He looked up, wanting to share the moment with her, only to find her already watching him, with the softest of smiles on her face. She already knew, he realised as he returned the smile.

'Is it time for cake now?' Daisy asked, sounding bored. 'I only really came for the cake.'

Heather rolled her eyes. 'Of course you did. Hang on.'

She pulled a large bakery box from the picnic basket they'd lugged from the car, fiddled around with some candles and matches, then presented it to Ryan as they all chorused a slightly off-key version of 'Happy Birthday'.

Ryan beamed as he bent forward to blow out the candles, and Cal snapped a photo on his phone so he could remember this moment. The day when he'd finally started getting something right.

He just hoped he could keep it up.

Heather thought her heart might burst as she watched Cal and Ryan together as they flew the helicopter back down the valley to the four-by-four.

She and Daisy were walking behind, a little slower, enjoying the last of the sweet summer air blowing off the stream. Even in August it grew a little chilly as the sun started to sink, and they'd stayed much longer than they'd intended since they were having such a lovely day.

Heather couldn't remember the last time she'd lazed around in the sunshine like that. She and Cal had sat in companionable silence as the kids had raced around collecting flowers from the heather and gorse, or paddling in the stream as far as they could go before the current got too strong. For once the tension between them seemed to have faded, and they'd just been able to enjoy the day.

Heather hadn't felt so relaxed, happy and at home since she'd arrived in Lengroth.

'Did you tell him to do all that?' Daisy asked suddenly, and in an instant Heather's shoulders tensed again. 'All the birthday stuff, I mean.'

'Actually, no,' Heather replied honestly. 'He remembered it was Ryan's birthday, and I suggested he did something special, but the actual plan was all his.'

'He asked me about the cake.' Daisy sounded faintly horrified that she might have aided and abetted the plan.

'He wanted to get it right. For Ryan.'

'Why?' Daisy sounded honestly confused by her uncle's efforts. 'He never cared about us before Mum and Dad died—we barely saw him except at Christmas, and not always even then.'

'Things are different now.'

'Like I don't *know* that,' Daisy huffed.

Heather tried to find a different tack. 'He's your guardian now,' she said gently. 'He might not know how to be that just yet, but I reckon nobody does when they start. I mean, think about your parents. They were just handed you one day, and suddenly they were responsible for a whole human being. That's got to be kind of scary.'

'They had nine months to get ready for me,' Daisy said sceptically. 'I *do* know how pregnancy works, you realise.'

Heather noticed almost too late that she had one hand clutched around her middle, as if she were protecting her secret. She tried to drop her arm casually and hoped Daisy didn't know as much as she thought she did. Until she'd had her twelve-week scan she and Cal had agreed it was better not to tell the children she was pregnant.

How they were going to tell them *after* that was a whole different question they hadn't answered yet.

'Even with preparation time it's a huge undertaking, and I don't think it's one you can really prepare for,'

Heather went on, feeling the truth of her words in the weight on her shoulders.

She *definitely* wasn't going to be prepared in six months' time. Right now she didn't even know where she would be living.

'I suppose Uncle Cal didn't have those nine months...' Daisy said thoughtfully.

'Exactly!'

'So this summer...this is sort of like Uncle Cal's pregnancy,' Daisy went on. 'I mean, he's figuring out how to look after us and you're helping him, right?'

'Right. At least, I'm trying to.'

Daisy didn't look at her as she answered. 'I don't think you're doing *too* badly. At least not as bad as some of the others.'

Then she raced forward to catch up to Cal and Ryan without even glancing back.

Heather stopped by the edge of the stream, watching after her, as Daisy swung on Cal's arm and made him drop the picnic basket. She waited, tense, for Cal to complain, or even shout—but instead she heard his laughter, echoing back through the valley.

Ryan had had a good birthday. Daisy had opened up to her a bit. And Cal had laughed.

Maybe she *wasn't* doing too badly after all.

Now she just needed to figure out how to fix things for herself and her own baby before it arrived. Starting with Wednesday's scan.

Heather followed the others towards the setting sun and the car, and hoped that things were on the right track now.

They were all due a little bit of luck, she reckoned.

CHAPTER ELEVEN

TRAFFIC WAS BAD driving into Edinburgh on Wednesday morning. Cal wished he'd put the radio on or something when they'd set out—anything to distract them both from the awkward silence and the thought of what was ahead. But they were nearly at the hospital now, and putting it on at this point would only draw more attention to the awkwardness.

'Are you okay?' Heather asked from the passenger seat, a small line forming between her copper brows.

'I'm pretty sure I'm supposed to be the one asking *you* that,' he pointed out. 'You're the one with a hospital appointment in twenty minutes.'

'It's a scan. I'm not scared.'

Cal shot her a disbelieving look. He could hear the nerves in her voice.

'Much,' she amended, obviously reluctantly. 'I just don't want to be late.'

'We won't be,' Cal promised, silently cursing the traffic ahead.

In the end, they almost were.

Cal wheeled into the hospital approach, a little faster than was probably advisable, and reached across her to open the passenger door. 'Go on. You go in and get registered. I'll park up and meet you in there.'

She nodded, straightened her shoulders and got out of the car.

Cal sped off, risked parking his car somewhere it was almost certainly going to get scraped by passing traffic, because it was the only place left, then raced back to the hospital entrance, spinning through the revolving doors so fast he was half-afraid he'd end up going round twice.

'Whoa!' A man in a nurse's uniform caught him by the shoulder as he stumbled out. 'What's the rush, mate? *Cal?*'

Cal took a hurried step back, scanning the man's face as he tried to place him. 'Harry?'

Harry Malcolm—a classmate from Lengroth Primary, before Cal's father had pulled him out and sent him away to boarding school. His father was the postman in Lengroth, his grandmother the biggest gossip in the whole village. There wasn't anything Enid Malcolm didn't know about what went on in Lengroth.

Including, after this, the news that Cal Bryce had been seen at the hospital in Edinburgh with his nanny. *Perfect.*

Harry beamed. 'That's right! I wasn't sure if you'd remember. My nan says you're practically the Earl up at Lengroth these days. We were all surprised that you'd come back, last time I was down the pub with the old crowd.'

'I'm not the Earl,' Cal corrected him, scanning the lobby for any sign of Heather. Maybe she'd already gone through to wherever it was she was supposed to go. He'd have to ask. Ask anyone except Harry, that was. 'Ryan is. I'm just his guardian.'

'Yeah, but you're responsible for everything that happens up there, right?'

'Unfortunately.' Suddenly Cal spotted a head of copper curls headed their way.

Heather. *Damn.* He'd never thought he'd be unhappy to see her.

He shot her a look across the lobby and she frowned. Resisting the urge to roll his eyes, he jerked his head away from Harry and hoped she'd got the message.

The last thing he needed to do right now was explain to Harry—and by extension to Harry's grandmother and the rest of Lengroth—why he was visiting the maternity unit with his niece and nephew's nanny.

'Look—sorry, mate—but I've got to…' Cal pointed vaguely in the direction of a corridor that he hoped didn't lead to anything embarrassing.

'Sure…right. Well, good to see you!' Harry clapped Cal on the shoulder and wandered off—right past an annoyed-looking Heather.

'Sorry about that.' Cal hurried over to her the moment Harry was gone. 'But, trust me, we did *not* want to be seen here together by him.'

'Right. Whatever… Come on—we're going to be late. It's this way.'

Heather moved away with long strides down another corridor—one with paintings on the wall and motivational quotes in swirly fonts. Cal ignored them and kept his eyes on the copper hair in front of him and the swing of her hips.

She was angry. He could tell that much by the way her hair snaked from side to side as she walked and the force of her step. He could read her body so easily, considering he'd never even touched it.

What he *couldn't* quite figure out, however, was why. Heather wanted to avoid a scandal as much as he did—so she couldn't possibly object to him taking steps to do that, could she?

She'd tell him in her own time, he supposed. And in the meantime they had a scan to get to.

Cal quickened his step to catch her up.

* * *

She shouldn't be annoyed. Heather *knew* she shouldn't be annoyed.

But she was.

However unforeseen the circumstances, she was here for the first scan of her first child—maybe her only child. She was going to see her baby inside her. It was a special, momentous day.

Was it too much to ask for it just to be treated normally—not hidden away and treated as an embarrassment?

Apparently so.

Heather sighed. She knew what Cal had been trying to do. He'd explained about Harry and Harry's grandmother once she'd checked in with Reception and they had been sent to sit in the waiting area. It all made perfect sense—after all, she *didn't* want the whole of Lengroth talking about her and Cal, especially since there *was* no 'her and Cal'.

But another, nagging part of her brain kept reminding her that it was the secrecy and the lies that had been the worst when the truth had come out about her mother's affair. And the lies she'd told after that—the ones that had given her dad hope again and made him defend her mother to strangers. It was the broken trust that had been the hardest thing to fix.

Cal's family had spent generations pretending to be perfect, while behind closed doors they'd behaved however they'd pleased, whomever it had hurt. Was she wrong to be worried that Cal was just carrying on the tradition he'd claimed to hate?

'When are we going to tell Daisy and Ryan?' she asked suddenly, as another couple were led into the scanning room.

Beside her, Cal started, looking up from the *Mother and Baby* magazine he was flicking through.

'Uh... I don't know. I guess it depends what you want to happen in September.'

Of course. By September—just a few weeks away now—she'd be gone from Lengroth. If she didn't want to she'd never have to see Cal or the kids again. They'd never know about their half-brother or sister. She knew for certain that Cal would never tell them if she chose to go.

Nobody would know. The scandal would be contained. Sure, she'd still be an unwed mother, but that was nothing these days. She could even claim she'd chosen it— gone to a sperm bank and picked a donor. One with dark hair and amber eyes.

She could tell whatever lies she wanted. But she knew the truth always came out in the end.

'I want Daisy and Ryan to be part of their half-brother or half-sister's life,' she said firmly. 'And that means telling them the truth.'

How that would work back home in Hertfordshire... Well, maybe it was time to move on, anyway. Move away from home and out of the shadow of her mother's scandal. Her father was doing so well these days—she was sure he'd be fine.

Of course, telling Daisy and Ryan also meant that Cal would be a part of her life, Heather realised. For ever.

She wasn't entirely sure how she felt about that. Half of her was cheering, because she couldn't imagine *not* having him around. The rest of her was wondering how on earth they'd manage it without falling into bed eventually.

But maybe—just maybe—that would be okay. Maybe eventually the risk of scandal would pass and nobody would care. They just had to wait it out.

'I don't want to rush it,' Cal said finally. 'They've been through so much and we're finally making progress. They're relaxing, opening up to me and letting me in. And Daisy hasn't thrown anything out of the window at people in weeks—not since that stupid rubber duck you carried in on your first day.'

Heather smiled at the memory. When she'd seen that duck bobbing along in the moat she'd had no idea where it would lead her.

'I guess I just don't want to ruin all our hard work, right before they leave for school,' Cal said, with a sigh.

'You're still planning on sending them away, then?' Heather asked.

Cal looked at her, surprised. 'Of course. It's the best thing for their education.'

'Right…' But was it the best thing for their lives? Just when she'd thought Cal was making real progress…

'Heather Reid?' a nurse called, and they both stood up.

'Ready for this?' Cal asked, and Heather nodded.

'I think so.'

Suddenly he grabbed her hand. 'Heather… I really am so sorry my brother dragged you into all this. I know this can't be how you dreamed about doing this, with *me* here at your side. But I *am* here, for whatever you need.'

'I know.'

Heather smiled gently as she realised the truth. Maybe this wasn't what she'd planned for her life, and it wasn't what she'd have chosen if she'd been given a choice. But she'd have been wrong.

Because right now there was no one else she wanted with her except Cal. And that terrified her almost as much as the prospect of becoming a mother did.

'Come on. Let's go see this baby.'

'Now, Daddy, if you'd like to come and sit on this side, please?' the technician asked, oblivious to the confusion she'd thrown up inside Cal.

He glanced over at Heather, settling herself on the table and lifting her top to show off smooth white skin. He looked away quickly.

Should he correct the technician? Explain that he wasn't the father, but the uncle. And her employer. Maybe friend…?

But it was too late already. The moment had passed. And besides, surely that would only make a bigger deal of everything? Make them more memorable if someone asked, later, if he'd gone in. Not that they would. Probably.

You never knew with Lengroth people. They were the worst gossips in the world. It was a minor miracle that the Bryce family had never been rumbled before, quite honestly. Or perhaps that was how they'd got so good at hiding the truth.

Maybe he was just discombobulated because of their conversation in the waiting room, Cal decided as he took the indicated seat at last. He'd imagined that come September Heather would walk out of their lives again. That she'd realise she didn't want any part of the Bryce legacy and leave.

The kids would miss her, but they'd be away at school anyway, making new friends, so they'd cope. And he… Well, he hadn't done much thinking about how *he'd* cope without her. Without seeing those bright green eyes every morning, or catching flashes of those coppery curls around the castle.

Hadn't *wanted* to think about it.

But what place was there for her at Lengroth with the children gone? He couldn't very well ask her to stay because he might get lonely. People would talk.

So what if they did?

Cal pushed the errant thought aside. He couldn't make Heather the centre of a scandal, and he couldn't ruin the reputation of Lengroth and the Bryce family for Daisy and Ryan. It was as simple as that.

However much he wanted to.

But if she wanted to stay in their lives… What would that mean, exactly? Visits at Christmas and birthdays? Emails and postcards?

That wasn't enough for him.

Nothing he could have with Heather would be.

Because he'd realised that the truth was he *wanted* to be here at her side today. Not because she was carrying his brother's child. But because he wanted to be part of her life.

That's just lust talking. The good old Bryce desire for whatever is worst for us.

But he needed to be different for Daisy and Ryan. He couldn't give in to it.

The technician smeared jelly over Heather's still-flat stomach and held the wand. 'Are we ready to see our baby?'

Our baby.

Cal swallowed hard as he nodded, not daring to look at Heather's face. He kept his eyes firmly on the screen as a picture started to emerge. A grainy black-and-white picture of nothing that made any sense until the technician suddenly beamed and said, 'There we are! Right there. Can you see the head?'

And suddenly he could. He could see Heather's baby.

His heart thumped too loud in his chest—so loud he was sure Heather must be able to hear it. The whole *hospital* could probably hear it.

He felt like he had when Ryan had bent his head close to his on his birthday, as he'd climbed into his car seat, and whispered, 'This was a brilliant birthday, Uncle Cal.' Like he had when Daisy had stopped by his office yesterday to ask him a question about her maths homework and then stayed and chatted for twenty minutes about nothing and everything.

He felt like he did late at night, when he walked Heather to her bedroom after their tutoring sessions. Which neither of them would give up even though he wasn't sure they were learning anything new. And sometimes, if she was tired enough, she'd lean her forehead against his chest, just for a moment, and he'd feel her warm breath through his shirt.

He'd never had a name for those feelings—the feelings that thrummed through his veins and told him he was truly alive. He'd known they were important, but just getting to experience them had been enough for him. He hadn't wanted to label them in case it scared them away.

But now...

He twisted round to look at Heather and found her staring at the screen in wonder. Then, as if she'd sensed his gaze on her, she turned to smile at him—and there was a whole world in that smile. A whole future.

Cal let himself drink it in, just for a moment.

Then he swallowed and looked away.

Lust. That was all it was. He wanted her because she was the worst person in the world he should desire and he was a Bryce.

He was the Bryce legacy come true all over again, but he was damned if he was going to give in to it.

CHAPTER TWELVE

SOMETHING ODD WAS going on with Cal. Well, odder than normal, anyway.

Ever since they'd got back from the hospital after the scan he'd been going out of his way to avoid her. Heather couldn't decide if it was because of the guy he'd bumped into in the hospital lobby, the conversation they'd had about telling Daisy and Ryan, or the strange expression she'd seen on his face when the technician had shown them the baby, wriggling around on the screen.

She knew how strange this must be for him. He'd gained two children almost from nowhere and now there was a third on the way. But he had to realise that she wouldn't ask him for anything for *her* baby, right? If he wanted to be part of their little family then she would welcome him. But she was just as prepared to go it alone if she had to, as she had been the day she'd arrived at Lengroth.

No. That wasn't quite true. She wasn't the same person she'd been the day she'd first climbed those steps. That woman was gone for ever, and Heather couldn't quite bring herself to miss her.

That woman had been almost without hope. She'd been weighed down by guilt and fear and desperation. And, while the guilt still lingered, she hoped she'd at least gone some way towards making amends by helping the children this summer. As for the fear… She'd been afraid because she hadn't had faith in herself to fix her situation. Now she knew it didn't need fixing—and she had complete confidence that whatever happened next she would be able to handle it.

Even if that meant being a single mother, ostracised by her father and everyone in her village, and hundreds of miles away from Cal, Daisy and Ryan.

Worst-case scenario, Heather. Don't think about it.

'Where's your uncle?' she asked as she sat down to dinner with the children a few days later.

Daisy shrugged. 'I went to call him. He yelled at me to go away.' She was obviously trying to sound nonchalant, but failing.

Heather had been surprised the first time she'd stopped by Cal's office and heard Daisy's voice behind the door. But now it was every bit as everyday an occurrence as Ryan stealing the last piece of toast at breakfast. Heather couldn't entirely explain it—and she knew for a fact that Cal had no idea how it had happened—but Daisy had not just warmed to Cal, but had latched on to him completely.

They talked about everything, Cal had said, from the planets to the environment, from the history of the castle to West End musicals. And somewhere in all that, when she needed to, Daisy would slip in a comment about something that was bothering her and Cal would try to help her. Or, more often, report it to Heather, who would give him advice so he could tackle it the next day.

As far as Heather could tell, his whole relationship with Daisy had more of a big-brother vibe than a parental one, but if that was what Daisy needed then she was happy she had found it.

Or seemed to have until tonight.

'I'm sure he was just very busy,' Heather said soothingly, even as she exchanged a worried glance with Mrs Peterson.

The housekeeper widened her eyes and shrugged, to indicate that she didn't know what was going on, either.

'Whatever…' Daisy mumbled towards her plate. 'I don't care.'

'Shall I go call him again?' Ryan jumped to his feet before he'd even finished his question.

'You stay here and eat,' Heather said quickly. 'If Uncle Cal is busy he probably won't want to come down for dinner. I'll take him up a plate once we've eaten.'

The meal was a mostly silent one. Afterwards, with the kids settled in their bedrooms after baths and toothbrushing, Heather took the dinner tray that Mrs Peterson had put together and carried it carefully towards Cal's study, bracing herself for the response she was likely to get.

Balancing the tray on one hip, she knocked lightly.

'I said I'm not coming down for dinner!'

Heather rolled her eyes and inched the door open. 'That's why dinner has come to you.'

Not waiting for an invitation, she crossed the study, placed the tray on the desk in front of him—handily covering whatever papers had him so work-obsessed this evening—then sat in the chair opposite him.

'Heather, I really don't have time—'

'Then *make* time.'

Something in her voice obviously caught his attention because he looked up, rubbing a hand across the back of his neck.

He looked exhausted, Heather realised. Not just tired, but worn thin and on the edge of everything. The fine lines around his eyes were suddenly more pronounced, and the shadows under them were grey and heavy.

'Cal!'

Heather hopped up again and moved around to the other side of the desk, leaning against it so he had to sit back in his chair to look up at her.

Food could wait. This was more important.

'Tell me. What's going on?'

What was going on? Everything—all at the same time. And he couldn't focus on any of it because he kept seeing the soft smile on Heather's face as she'd looked at her scan picture in the car on the way home, or remembering the way she'd hugged him and whispered 'thank you' in his ear afterwards.

As if that wasn't bad enough, he'd started dreaming about her, too. And those dreams were far less chaste than his memories… Everything he wanted and couldn't have.

'Heather… I can't talk about it.'

How could he tell her how much he wanted her *now*— when this damn reporter was arriving next week and his lawyer had told him there wasn't a thing he could do about it unless he wanted to repay a hell of a lot of money and deal with articles in the magazine speculating on why the Bryce family were so secretive about what was going on at Lengroth Castle these days.

That would only lead them to reinvestigating the circumstances of Ross's death, and Cal wasn't sure any of them wanted to know what they might find out.

He definitely didn't. Which was why he hadn't asked any more questions before now.

Heather's fingers smoothed across his forehead, cool to the touch and instantly calming. Cal took a deeper breath and found himself relaxing against all his instincts.

'I think you need to talk about it,' she said softly. 'Because it's eating you up. I think maybe we've both not talked about things for too long.'

Cal looked up and met her bright green gaze and knew she was right. Ignoring things hadn't got either of them very far up until now.

Apparently she saw something in his expression that gave her encouragement, because she shifted closer—so near that if he just reached out and let go he would have her in his arms in a heartbeat.

'Tell me what you're thinking,' Heather whispered, and Cal felt something open up inside him.

Floodgates, perhaps. Or a door in the walls he'd built up to keep his family's secrets inside. For a moment he felt again as if Heather was standing on those stupid seventeen steps up to the castle door, a rubber duck tucked under her arm, knocking on the ancient wood and asking to come inside.

And, just like last time, he let her in.

'I'm thinking that my whole family is a curse.' Seeing her look, he corrected himself. 'Not the children—although who knows? Give them time... They probably don't have any more chance of avoiding the family legacy of scandal than I do.'

'I think you're doing pretty well,' Heather said.

Cal stared up at her incredulously. 'Are you kidding? I'm sitting here trying to cover up all my brother's misdeeds—just like all the Bryce men before me—and pretending they didn't happen, that people weren't hurt, and that we shouldn't have to pay for our mistakes because we have a castle and some money.'

He looked up at her, flinching at the pity in her eyes. Didn't she realise he was doing exactly the same thing to her?

'Look at you,' he murmured, taking her hand. 'I'm hiding you away in this castle, pretending you're not pregnant by my own brother, letting you help raise his orphaned kids and hiding from anyone who might figure out the truth.'

'So this is about the guy you bumped into at the hospital?'

Harry and his gossipy grandmother. Did she honestly think that was all that was eating him alive from the inside?

Cal shook his head. 'It's not about Harry. It's about this damn castle. It's about Daisy and Ryan. And it's about...' He trailed off. He couldn't say it. He couldn't put that on her. She had more than enough to deal with right now, without bringing his inability to control his libido into the mix.

It's only because I can't have her, he reminded himself. The forbidden was always the most alluring to Bryce men.

But Heather slid a little closer and he couldn't bring himself to look away from her gaze. He felt locked in place, staring into those green eyes, searching them for the same truths he held inside himself.

'It's about...?' she asked, so softly it was barely more than a breath.

'It's about the way I don't think I can make it for another moment without kissing you,' he said, before his brain or his sense of shame could talk him out of it.

Heather bit down on her lower lip and his caution jumped out of the castle window and into the moat. In a heartbeat he had her in his arms, her legs swung over his as he pulled her into his lap.

He'd tried. Really he had. He'd tried to be the one good Bryce man, the one male in the family who'd avoided scandal and stayed away from temptation. He'd tried not giving in to it when temptation had come knocking, with a rubber duck tucked under her arm.

But it was no good. Bad blood won out, and he couldn't fight his genes any longer.

So, with a relief so palpable he could feel his whole body relaxing as the decision was made, Cal kissed Heather, and forgot—just for now—all the reasons that this was the worst idea he'd ever had.

Oh, God, she was kissing Cal Bryce.

The one thing she'd absolutely sworn to herself that she wouldn't do. One of the few things she could do to make her own scandalous situation worse.

And hands down it was the best kiss of her whole damn life.

Heather allowed herself to fall into the kiss, to experience every sensation and luxuriate in them. His hands on her back, firm and warm. His lips against hers, so sure and confident that she had to wonder if he'd been imagining this moment as much as she had.

And the very hard evidence against her hip that told her this wasn't just an accidental or a casual kiss.

He wanted her.

A lot.

And the feeling was very, *very* mutual.

Heather let out a small gasp as Cal deepened the kiss, pulling her into him until she wasn't sure where she ended and he began. She shifted in his lap, trying to free her arm from where it was trapped between them, desperate to use it to touch him, feel him, make this experience last for ever...

Which was, of course, when she unbalanced them completely.

Cal swore as the chair tipped backwards towards the window, reaching out with both hands to grab the desk and stop them falling. Heather, however, no longer tethered by his arms, tumbled back towards the floor, and he let go of the desk to catch her—resulting in them both tipping sideways off the chair and landing on the Persian rug under his desk.

'This was *not* how I intended this to go.'

Cal let his head fall back onto the floor, and Heather patted his arm sympathetically as she rested her cheek against his chest.

'Maybe we'll do better next time,' she said.

Cal's hand, which had been rubbing slow circles against her side, stilled, and she knew she'd said the wrong thing.

'Heather... I shouldn't have done that. I'm sorry.'

Something cold settled in her heart. 'Shouldn't have tipped me onto the floor of your office or shouldn't have kissed me like that?'

Like it meant *everything*.

'I think *you* tipped us,' Cal pointed out. 'And I shouldn't have kissed you. It was...inappropriate.'

'You mean scandalous.' Heather sat up, brushing her unruly hair away from her eyes as she stared down at him.

'You're pregnant with my brother's child,' Cal reminded her—as if she didn't already know. 'And you're my employee.'

'I hoped I was your friend, too.'

'Friends don't kiss friends like *that*,' Cal said, his eyes shut tight, and she knew he'd felt it, too.

Knew that the kiss had meant as much to him as it had to her.

'Cal...' She stared down at him, willing him to open his eyes and look at her.

As if he'd heard her thoughts, he did. 'Heather. We can't.'

'Why? *Why* can't we?'

Yes, yes, she knew the reasons. Had argued them with herself for weeks now. But in the end it came down to basics. Undeniable, irresistible basics. He wanted her. She wanted him. His brother certainly hadn't had such reservations...

Oh. 'Is this because of Ross?'

'Indirectly.' Cal gave a tired sigh and pushed himself up to a seated position, leaning back against the desk. His dinner would have gone cold by now, Heather thought as she watched him. He'd be hungry later. But this was more important.

'Because I slept with him first?' she pressed.

She hadn't thought that Cal was the sort of guy to judge her for her past behaviour, but she supposed it *was* a kind of unusual situation. She couldn't blame him for finding it confusing —she certainly did.

'No! Not because...' He swallowed so hard she could see his throat move. 'It's just...the situation.'

'Yeah...'

She knew what he meant, she thought. After all, hadn't she been stamping down her feelings for Cal for weeks now, for exactly the same reason? All this could lead to was scandal and gossip and talk. The situation was so far from ideal it was laughable. Who got pregnant by an earl who inconveniently died and then fell in love with his brother?

Except...

'Except if it wasn't for this situation I never would have met you,' she said, and the hope in Cal's eyes gave her all the courage she needed to go on. 'Do you think I haven't regretted that night in the bar a million times?' she asked. 'When I found out Ross was married I was physically sick—did I tell you that? I've spent my whole life trying to avoid a situation like this—well, not exactly like this, because I never even imagined that *this* was an option for someone like me—but avoiding scandal and talk. I've tried *so hard* to do the right thing—always. For my dad, yes, but for me, too. Because it *mattered* to me. And then I let my guard down for one night and—'

She broke off, shook her head and started again.

'The point is—yes, I made mistakes. And, yes, I regret them—in a way. Except not completely. Not any more.'

'Why?' Cal's voice was dry and cracked, as if he wasn't sure he could take the answer but felt compelled to ask the question anyway.

'Because if I hadn't met Ross that night I wouldn't have my baby growing inside me right now—a baby that I already love so much. If I hadn't come here to Lengroth to find Ross I'd never have met Daisy and Ryan, whom I adore. And...'

Could she say it? She had to, Heather knew. This had been building for too long, drawing them together while forcing them apart all at the same time.

'And I never would have met you,' she said.

CHAPTER THIRTEEN

CAL STARED UP at Heather's beautiful face, trying to imagine a world in which he didn't know her. Didn't want her.

He couldn't.

If she was just beautiful, or sexy, that would be one thing. He could resist that kind of charm when he wanted to which, to be honest, wasn't all that often. Under these circumstances, it would be easy.

But Heather was more than that. She'd worked her way into his life—and into the castle—so deeply that he couldn't imagine her not being there. She was his *friend*, as well as the most desirable woman he'd ever met. She was good and kind and all the things that Lengroth Castle normally killed.

Daisy and Ryan needed her in their lives. Which meant he couldn't wreck this by giving in to his lust. Except it wasn't just *his* lust they were dealing with here, apparently.

'What is it?'

His face must have given him away, because in a moment she was sitting back down beside him, her expression concerned.

'Heather... I need you to not take this the wrong way.'

'Suggesting that there is a *very* wrong way for me to take it?' Heather said.

Cal resisted the urge to wince. 'Yeah, you might.'

Heather folded her arms across her chest. Cal forced himself not to stare at the neckline of her summer dress, or the wonderful things the action was doing for her breasts.

Are they always that perfectly plump? Or is it the pregnancy?

Maybe he would find out one day. But not until after this damn summer was over.

'I'm listening,' she said, and Cal tried to find his train of thought again.

'As much as I loved kissing you—and, trust me, I really did—we can't do it again.' It was as simple and frustrating as that.

'Because I'm a scandal for sleeping with your brother and getting pregnant or because your family is cursed?'

She didn't seem to be taking this very seriously, Cal noticed. And he was almost certain she was pushing her breasts up on purpose. To torment him.

It was totally working.

Until he remembered the real reason they couldn't do this.

'Both. But also because Ross signed a contract with some awful magazine, promising that a reporter could come and live at the castle for a week at the end of this summer—next week, in fact—and write all about the life of the Earl of Lengroth.'

Heather blinked. Then she sat back, taking those beautiful breasts with her.

'But *Ryan's* the Earl. He can't have some reporter following him around for a week! He's *nine*!'

'Which is why I've spent the last five weeks in legal wrangling with their contracts team.' Cal sighed. 'I can't get us out of it. Trust me, Heather, I've given it everything

I can. But the reporter is coming here next week—unless I hand over an absurd kill fee for the story *and* resign myself to them writing about us anyway, since apparently my brother was incapable of reading a contract.'

Maybe he'd been drunk at the time. Or just really, really desperate.

'Why would Ross have agreed to something like that? I mean, I know he'd have thought it would be *him* the reporter would be following around when he signed up for it, but still… I can't imagine anyone would want their lives being scrutinised that closely.'

Heather shuddered at the very idea. Cal didn't blame her.

'I've been trying to figure out the same thing myself. Ross was in debt, and in trouble with some…unsavoury people—so it could just have been that he needed the cash. Or…'

'Or…?' Heather prompted.

She'd shifted again, so she sat opposite him, cross-legged on the rug, and Cal found his gaze drawn to her stomach. Was that just the tiniest hint of rounding…the start of a baby bump there?

Cal sighed. That baby was coming, whatever happened, and it would be welcomed and loved. There was nothing Ross could do about that now.

'Or because he wanted to put on a show. I think…I think that maybe rumours were starting. That people were beginning to talk about him and his behaviour. The Bryce family rule has always been to keep trouble away from Lengroth, but there were enough people locally that Ross owed money to, or who had seen something. People might have been asking questions…'

'You think he was bringing the reporter here to show

how perfect and scandal-free Lengroth Castle was?' Heather asked incredulously.

Cal shrugged. 'It's the family way. But now...'

'Now this reporter—'

'Anna Jenkins,' Cal supplied helpfully.

'Now Anna Jenkins is going to arrive to find Ross's pregnant one-night stand looking after his orphaned children and carrying on with his brother on the floor of the study.'

'Basically?' Cal flashed her a smile. 'Yes.'

This was awful. This was worse than awful. It was potentially front-page news for all the tabloids and gossip rags in the country. It was basically Heather's worst nightmare—and her father's, too.

And the worst part of all was that it didn't make her want Cal any less.

'So what do we do?' she asked, helplessness filling her.

The expression on Cal's face matched the way she felt. 'I guess we carry on as we were. Pretending that this—' he motioned to the air between them '—isn't there.'

Because that had been working *so* well for them before...

'For ever?'

'Hell, no.' Cal swore, and then crossed the space that had opened up between them and pulled her back into his arms. 'I can't keep my hands off you for that long. Even the next week is going to be a struggle, to be honest.'

Relieved, Heather snuggled into his embrace. 'So once the reporter has gone, then...?'

Cal nodded slightly—a gesture she felt rather than saw, since his chin was tucked over her head. 'Just another week. Well, eight days. Then we'll talk, figure this out together. What we're going to do next and everything.

I… Heather, I don't know what this is between us. But I want to at least give us a chance to find out.'

She nodded. 'Me, too. I mean, if my baby is going to know his half-brother and sister, then we can't screw this up.'

Desperate desire was one thing. But they needed still to be able to be friends when that faded.

If it faded.

That seemed pretty impossible right now.

She clenched her jaw and forced herself to push aside the thoughts that had been crowding her head since Cal had first kissed her. The thoughts that told her she was getting into something far deeper and far more dangerous than just a fling with her boss, or Ross's brother.

She was falling in love.

Heather knew better than to expect too much from Cal in the way of emotion. Lust he understood, clearly, but this was the man who hadn't even known how to love his niece and nephew. Expecting any romantic declarations from him was a disaster waiting to happen.

But even knowing that that wasn't enough to scare her off.

She'd deal with it all later, Heather decided. Her growing feelings for Cal could wait. There were too many other pressing things to worry about right now. Like the baby. Daisy and Ryan. Boarding school. The castle. The world… Not to mention her own future, her dad, her job, her home…

She should be using this time to plan, to figure out what the right thing to do by everybody was. But instead all she could think was *Eight days is too long.*

Far too long.

Pulling back ever so slightly, and feeling Cal's arms tightening around her automatically as she did so, Heather tilted her head to meet his gaze.

'She's not here until Monday?' she asked.

After all, today was only Saturday.

Cal nodded, apparently unable to look away from her eyes.

She knew how he felt. Whatever had brought her to Lengroth Castle in the first place, she knew that it was Cal who was going to keep her there. The thread that joined them now was too strong for her even to imagine it breaking.

'Not until Monday...' Cal repeated, his words barely a whisper.

'Then maybe we don't need to worry about what she or anyone else will think just yet.'

Heather pushed herself up until her lips brushed against Cal's again—the lightest feather touch, just a hint of what they could have.

Cal's eyes fluttered closed as he swallowed. 'You are temptation incarnate.'

'I thought you Bryce men liked that sort of thing?'

His eyes flashed open again, and the depth of lust and want in his amber eyes caught her by surprise.

'Oh, we do,' he said, with a wicked grin.

And then he kissed her again, and Heather decided to stop *thinking* about the right thing to do for a while and just *do* it instead.

Later—much later—Heather kissed Cal's bare shoulder and slipped out of his bed, her whole body still humming with pleasure.

'Where are you going?' Cal asked, his voice muffled by the duvet.

'Back to my room, before the kids wake up and come looking for me.'

Ryan in particular had developed a habit of waking

her up by jumping on the end of her bed in the mornings. Heather quite liked it, really. It showed how comfortable he was with her now. But if she wasn't there when he came looking…

'Okay,' Cal said, pulling her back for another kiss all the same.

'Cal, I need to get back.'

He sighed, resting his forehead against her shoulder. 'I know. I just don't want to let you go when I've just got you here.'

She couldn't help but smile at that.

One last, swift kiss and she was on her way, padding down the stone corridors in bare feet, her shoes dangling from her fingers. The ultimate walk of shame, she supposed.

Suddenly she blinked as a figure appeared at the end of the corridor. Too tall for Daisy or Ryan, she realised quickly.

'Mrs Peterson?' she called, trying to smile.

The old housekeeper would expect an explanation, and Heather wasn't sure she had one just yet. She was a terrible liar, apart from anything else.

But then the figure turned, and although Heather couldn't quite make out her face she knew in her bones that it wasn't Mrs Peterson.

It wasn't anyone living at all.

Then the Lengroth ghost disappeared as quickly as she'd appeared, leaving Heather shivering in the stone-walled passageway of the castle, hoping this wasn't some sort of sign of things to come.

Cal stood at the top of the stone steps, scowling at the woman climbing out of Lengroth's only taxi down by the castle gates. She wasn't even fully on the premises yet and already he found himself hoping that Daisy might throw something at Anna the journalist.

Except no. Because that would look bad in the magazine.

Cal rubbed a hand over the back of his neck, squinted in the early-morning sunshine and tried one last time to think of a way out of this. Or at least to shake his foul mood.

He failed on both counts.

It was even more annoying because he'd been in *such* a good mood yesterday. Even waking up without Heather had been okay, because he'd known he'd have her back in his bed that night. Back in his arms, where she belonged.

Except then he'd remembered about the cursed Anna and her stupid magazine, and realised that he now wouldn't get to touch Heather again until the castle was journalist-free—a week from now.

A whole week.

He wasn't going to make it.

He knew it had been a bad idea to give in to the temptation of Heather's lips, her hands, her body. Because the problem with temptation was that once you'd given in the first time, the second was so much easier…

Cal was so lost in thought, remembering that one perfect night with Heather, that he almost failed to notice that the smart brunette was making her way up the castle steps.

She was dressed in a suit that was worlds away from Heather's sundress and woolly cardigan wardrobe choices, and he couldn't help but think that Anna Jenkins was all wrong for this castle. Maybe she'd have fitted right in when Ross had been the Earl—he'd always been smartly dressed himself, and Janey had had exquisite fashion sense—but now that Ryan was in charge—and by extension Cal—standards had definitely slipped.

Hell, if it was hot enough they were lucky if they got Ryan into more than a pair of boxers some days—especially in the playroom, where the sun streamed through the large windows onto the window seat.

He'd have to remind Heather to try and keep him fully dressed...

'Lord Bryce.' Anna smiled brightly as she made her way up the seventeen stone steps, one tentative high-heeled foot at a time.

'Just Cal, please,' he said, reaching out a hand to her—partly for shaking, partly to make sure she didn't fall into the moat. 'My nephew is the Earl, not me.'

'So what does that make *you*, exactly?'

Anna's smile was shark-white, with every bit as much bite, as she took his hand. Her palm felt cool and dry, despite the morning sun, and it slid away from his almost as soon as they touched.

'It makes me Ryan's uncle.' Cal stepped back into the castle, holding the door open for her.

Already she was angling for the story she wanted to write, he realised. She must have been thrilled when Ross had died. An ordinary earl giving a magazine this kind of access was opportunity enough. But a child aristocrat with only an uncle for support, until recently absent? That was far more interesting.

Well, if she was hoping for resentment and jealousy on his part she was out of luck. He'd never wanted to be the Earl of Lengroth for a moment. He just hoped she didn't find anything more interesting to write about.

'Come on in,' he said, as pleasantly as he could. 'I'll introduce you to our housekeeper, Mrs Peterson. She'll show you around the castle and get you settled in your room.'

At the far end of the castle, away from the children

and Heather by design, even if it put her rather closer to his office than Cal would have liked.

'The housekeeper?' Anna's perfectly curved eyebrows arched just a little higher. 'Really, I'd love it if *you* could show me around yourself, Cal.'

'Unfortunately I have work to be getting on with. But here's Mrs Peterson now.'

Right on cue, the housekeeper arrived, resplendent in her best blue suit and pearls.

'And she'll introduce me to your niece and nephew?' Anna pressed.

Cal shook his head. 'I'm afraid the children are out on a day trip with their nanny. You'll meet them at dinner.'

A look of annoyance flashed across Anna's face.

Cal couldn't really blame her—but that didn't mean he was going to change his tactics. He and Heather had a plan, developed in the dark of night, curled up together in his bed. It was simple. Keep the reporter as far away from the children—and from Heather—for as much of her visit as possible. Mrs Peterson would handle the history of the castle and the family and so on, using the usual sanitised version, and Cal would do a proper interview—enough to keep her happy.

They'd fulfil the letter of the contract, but not the spirit. Because there was no way in hell Cal was allowing his nephew and niece to be exploited in some gossip magazine, however high-class the editor insisted it was.

And he wasn't letting Anna Jenkins find out about Heather and the baby, either.

Not if he could help it.

CHAPTER FOURTEEN

'HOW'S IT GONE TODAY?' Heather asked, slipping into Cal's office late on Thursday night.

His eyes widened. 'You shouldn't be here!'

Dropping into the chair opposite him, Heather rolled her eyes. 'Anna's already gone to bed for the night. Annoyed, according to Mrs Peterson. I do worry that if we frustrate her too much she'll go digging around for a scandal just to get back at us.'

For four days now Heather had kept the kids as far away from the castle as possible. There'd been picnics and day trips and long hikes—even a train ride into the city for the day. Anna had tried to suggest she accompany them on that one, but Cal had put on his best aristocratic voice and said, 'I thought you were here to cover life in the *castle*, Anna?' and that had been that.

Even Heather had been able to sense the journalist's annoyance although, as per the plan, she'd only seen her at breakfast and dinner each day. The children had stayed on their best behaviour for meals, answered Anna's questions in boring monotones, and basically helped create the impression that life at Lengroth Castle was nothing to write home about.

It was working, and Heather was glad.

But that did mean she'd barely seen Cal alone since the

night she'd spent in his bed, and she missed him. More than she'd thought possible given that they were still living in the same castle.

'We just can't risk getting caught now, Heather. Not when we're so close to getting this over and done with.'

'I know,' Heather replied. 'I just…needed to see you.'

'I know the feeling,' Cal said, giving her a wry smile that reassured her he was suffering every bit as much as she was.

'I'll just sit here,' Heather promised. 'With a whole desk between us, getting into no trouble at all. We can talk about the children's educational progress, if you like.'

'Okay.' Cal sat back in his chair, arms folded across his chest. 'What have they learned this week?'

'Basically nothing—because we've been here there and everywhere, staying out of Anna's way.'

'Right. So we're done with that topic, then?'

Heather sighed. 'Cal…'

'I know. I know. I just… If you stay, I'm going to kiss you. I won't be able to help it. You're the ultimate temptation, and you know how bad the men in my family are at resisting that.'

'I do,' Heather agreed. 'But would it *really* be all that bad if you kissed me right now?'

She licked her lips. Her insides felt warmer just thinking about it. As if her blood was heating up inside her veins.

Cal's amber eyes darkened, and she knew he felt the same.

'Maybe not,' he said. 'But I wouldn't be able to stop at kissing you—you know that.'

'No?' Heather smiled dangerously. She knew this was a game they could ill afford to be playing right now, but maybe Cal wasn't the only one who had a problem with temptation. 'What else would you need to do?'

'*Need* is the right word,' Cal said, shifting in his seat.

'Because I need you so much right now, Heather. I need you naked on my desk. I need your skin against mine. I need you in my arms. I need—'

'I need you inside me again,' Heather interrupted, and Cal let out an honest-to-God growl at her words and got to his feet.

'You are going to be the death of me,' he said as he circled the desk and pulled her up out of her chair and into his arms— just where she wanted to be.

'Not just yet,' Heather said with a grin. 'I've got plans for you first.'

'Your room?' Cal asked.

'My room,' Heather confirmed. She was furthest away from Anna, and overwhelming lust hadn't completely dulled her good sense. *'Now.'*

It had just made her ignore it for a little while.

One more day. Tomorrow morning Anna would be on her way and the castle would be theirs again.

Theirs.

Not just his, or Ryan and Daisy's, but Heather's, too. Almost like a home.

When had *that* happened?

Long before he'd first taken Heather to bed, he knew. She belonged here—with them. The 'in his arms' part was purely for *his* benefit. And hers, he thought, smirking as he remembered leaving her breathless in bed that morning as he'd crept back to his own room before the rest of the castle awoke.

Heather might not stay for ever, but for now…she was everything he needed. Until the absurd levels of passion between them cooled he *had* to find a way to keep her at Lengroth. Otherwise he was honestly afraid he might go insane with want and need.

They were risking a lot, he knew. This last week had given him a far greater understanding of his ancestors than he'd ever expected to have. He'd always avoided any kind of personal risk—even the sort of risk Ross had apparently been addicted to as he'd gambled away his inheritance. But now... His whole world could go up in flames and as long as he could have Heather with him he wouldn't care.

He almost didn't recognise the person he'd become in the last six weeks. But that didn't mean he didn't like him.

'You're in a good mood this morning.'

Anna's sharp tones rang through the corridor and Cal looked up suddenly to find her standing in his way.

'It's a beautiful day,' Cal said, before glancing out of the window to see that rain clouds were gathering. Summer in Scotland. He supposed they'd been lucky to get away with as much good weather as they'd had that week. It would make it trickier for Heather to get the kids out of the castle today, though.

Anna followed his gaze to the window. 'I suppose summer means something rather different in Scotland to the rest of the country,' she said scathingly.

'You must be in a good mood, too,' Cal replied, falling into step with her as they headed for the dining room. 'You get to go home tomorrow.'

That was putting *him* in a very good mood, anyway.

'And leave all this splendour?' Anna replied, waving an arm towards the long dining table, loaded with Ryan's favourite sugary cereals and half a *pain au chocolat* left on Daisy's plate.

'Not what you expected from an earl's castle, huh?' Cal asked, hiding a smile.

Anna smiled back, but there was no warmth in it. 'Not exactly. I *would* like to get one last interview with you and the children before I leave, however.'

Cal glanced up to see Heather coming in from the kitchen. Meeting her eye, he knew she'd heard Anna's question. She gave a small, reluctant nod.

'I'm sure that can be arranged,' he told Anna, hoping she hadn't clocked the exchange. 'As long as I'm in the room with the children.'

'Of course.' Anna smiled sweetly, then made her way to a seat at the far end of the table.

Heather, Cal noticed, didn't look at all reassured by her promise.

'So, Heather, what do you and the children have planned for today?'

Heather met his eye before answering. He gave her what he hoped was an encouraging smile, rather than an *I want to ravish you on the breakfast table* smile, but really it could have gone either way.

'Since it looks like it's going to be a soggy day out there, I think we'll work on our history projects in the schoolroom today.'

'They're studying the Second World War,' Cal put in, as Daisy and Ryan both groaned in unison. He silenced them with a glare.

'You take a strong interest in your niece and nephew's education, then?' Anna commented, looking between them.

'Of course,' Cal said, surprised. 'And Miss Reid is excellent at keeping me updated on their progress.'

'I'm sure she is.'

Anna gave Heather a speculative look, and Cal suddenly regretted drawing attention to her. Still, they were nearly out of the woods. Just one more day and then Anna would be back on the early train to London, and he and Heather could sit down and figure out what happened next.

Preferably naked.

* * *

Heather was halfway through gluing a cardboard evacuee's suitcase together, while Ryan held the sides and Daisy found vital things to put in it when it was dry, when Mrs Peterson knocked on the schoolroom door.

'Miss Reid?'

The housekeeper had the same, slightly disapproving look on her face that she'd had ever since Heather had arrived at Lengroth Castle. The only slight consolation was that the look Mrs Peterson gave Anna Jenkins was even more scathing.

'Mr Bryce is looking for you.'

'He is?' Heather got to her feet. 'Keep holding that, Ryan, I'll be back in a moment.'

What on earth could Cal want? They'd agreed that they needed to stay away from each other as much as possible during the day while Anna was roaming the castle. At night it was a different matter. The only person likely to see Heather then was apparently the Lengroth ghost—and even she'd been absent since that first night Heather had spent with Cal.

Heather knocked on the office door lightly, then let herself in.

Cal looked up from his computer screen with surprise. 'Heather! What's wrong? Do you need something?'

'I thought *you* did.' Heather frowned. 'Mrs Peterson said you were looking for me. Which I thought was strange because you knew exactly where I'd be...'

Their eyes met and they both reached the same conclusion at the same time.

'Anna!' they said, in unison.

'Your stupid castle is too big,' Heather muttered as they hurried down the endless stone-walled corridors back to the schoolroom.

'Yes, it's definitely the *castle* that's the problem here,' Cal replied, striding ahead. 'And it's not *my* castle. It's Ryan's.'

Ryan.

Ryan and Daisy—who were probably being cornered by that shark of a reporter right now, being asked heaven only knew what about their lives, their family, their parents' deaths—maybe even Cal and Heather.

Thank goodness they'd held back on telling them about the baby. Heather dreaded to think what Anna would have made of *that*.

Still, Heather's heart pounded as they rounded the final corner to the schoolroom and heard Anna's voice from inside.

'And how do you both feel about being sent away to boarding school by your uncle so soon after your parents' deaths?' she asked, her tone sweet but her words sharp.

Cal pushed past her to get inside, obviously not wanting to hear the answer to that one. But he wasn't as fast as Ryan's mouth.

'We're not going,' Ryan said defiantly. 'Heather would *never* let Uncle Cal send us away from Lengroth.'

Cal froze in front of her and Heather could almost hear his heart beating too fast, too hard, at his nephew's words.

'Do you think your nanny has that sort of influence?' Anna asked. 'I thought she was only here for the summer...'

'Heather's not just the nanny,' Daisy replied, her tone scathing. 'She's pregnant with Daddy's baby. And Uncle Cal is in love with her.'

'So she's going to stay for ever and we'll all be a family again!' Ryan shouted. 'You'll see!'

CHAPTER FIFTEEN

RYAN PUSHED PAST Anna and ran out through the school-room doorway—and barrelled right into Cal, who pulled him into a hug, holding the boy's trembling body against his chest.

Behind him, Heather slumped back against the wall, and he didn't need to look at her to know that she had to be looking as stunned as he felt.

How did they find out about the baby?

A question for later. Once he'd dealt with the enormous problem directly at hand.

'I think it's time you left Lengroth Castle, Miss Jenkins,' he said over Ryan's head, his tone icy.

In one short minute Daisy and Ryan had destroyed generations worth of the careful deceit and lies protecting the Bryce family's reputation. All the work he'd been doing to keep Ross's infidelities and gambling a secret was pointless now.

But, worst of all, they'd exposed Heather to gossip and scandal, too.

'My train isn't until tomorrow,' Anna said.

'It's a long walk to the station,' Cal replied. 'Go. Now.'

Her eyes widened as she looked up at him, and whatever she saw in his expression obviously convinced her, because she scuttled past him down the corridor. He'd have to deal with her again eventually, Cal knew—if only to find out what and when her magazine would be printing in order to do some damage limitation. But that would have to wait.

First he needed to take care of Daisy and Ryan. And Heather.

He glanced over his shoulder, looking for a moment of solidarity with Heather before he dealt with the children, but she was gone. The corridor was empty. And Cal felt a sneaking feeling of dread working its way towards his heart.

'Uncle Cal is in love with her!'

That was what Ryan had said. Obviously that was crazy, but did Heather know that?

'Uncle Cal?' Daisy's voice wobbled as she spoke, and Cal spun back to face her. 'Are we in trouble?'

Time slowed and stilled as his niece's question echoed in his brain. He knew instantly what his father's reaction would have been—and his father's father's. He'd lived it once. Never on this scale, but with an unguarded comment at a dinner party that had resulted in a broken arm, or a conversation with Harry at school that had ended with Cal being thrashed after someone had started asking questions.

He could never know how Ross might have handled this moment with his children. But he knew how *he* wanted to handle it. And he knew why.

He looked between Daisy and Ryan and realised that whatever happened next it had all been worth it. Because right now, in this moment, he found himself reaching for a truth he'd believed would always be beyond him.

He wasn't angry. He didn't want to shout. Even with everything that was at stake his only concern was protecting the children.

Because he loved them.

Against all the odds, he loved them.

'You're not in trouble, either of you.' He held an arm out towards Daisy and pulled her into his embrace along with her brother. 'I want to talk to you about what you both said, but I promise you this—you're not in trouble. I love you both, and nothing either one of you could ever do could possibly change that.'

The force of his words filled him as his niece and nephew clung to his shirt, which was suddenly suspiciously damp in places. Daisy would never admit to crying, but Cal didn't need her to. He'd done what he'd thought was impossible.

He, a Bryce male, had found a way to love his children—*his*, now Ross was gone. And *his* in his heart.

He wouldn't inflict the cycle of lies and secrets upon Daisy and Ryan. They'd spoken the truth—however they'd learned it—or the truth as they saw it. He couldn't be angry with them for that, whatever the consequences.

Heather had been right when she'd told him that it wasn't the scandal and people's actions that hurt the most. It was the secrets and the lies people told to keep their misdeeds from seeing the light of the day.

Which meant that the only way out of this was to tell the truth.

All of it.

However terrifying that was.

But first he needed to take care of Daisy and Ryan.

'Come on,' he said. 'Let's go find some hot chocolate and talk about all this. I have some questions—and I'm sure you both do, too. And questions always go better with chocolate.'

That sounded like something Heather would say. Heather, who had given him all this. Heather, whose smile lit him up from the inside and whose body against his had made everything feel real and right for the first time in his life.

Heather, whom he wanted to protect and care for, just as much as he did the children. Heather, who was carrying another child that he wanted to be a part of their family.

Heather, who…

Oh, hell. Ryan was right.

Except Heather was missing in action right now, so there wasn't anything he could do about his realisation except stamp it down to deal with later. The children came first, and without Heather there to help this was all on him.

For the first time he felt as if he was equal to the challenge.

Heather stared at the rucksack on her bed, filled with only the things she'd brought with her when she'd arrived at Lengroth Castle. She couldn't take any of the things Cal had bought her. Not now.

It looked strangely empty, though.

She should have left already. She should have run the moment that Anna had gone from the castle. How could she stay now all their secrets were out?

Cal had spent a lifetime keeping his family's secrets—and his forebears had been doing it for much longer. And she… She'd worked so hard always to do the right thing, never to make her father worry, never to bring gossip and talk to his door—until this year.

This year she'd thrown caution to the wind—twice—and given up everything she'd fought for since her mother had left in her own cloud of disgrace.

The moment Anna published news of the Lengroth scandal—online or in print—Heather's name would be out there. And so would her misdeeds.

She had to get home to her father and tell him before he heard it from someone else. But she had to talk to Cal first. Which was why she was still standing there, staring at a half-empty rucksack as if it reflected her own half-empty heart.

'The kids are in bed.'

Cal's quiet voice behind her made her jump. She spun to see him standing in the open doorway, leaning against the doorframe, his amber eyes watchful.

'I'm sorry. I should have stayed with you. But I needed to—'

'Pack,' Cal interrupted, his gaze flicking to the rucksack.

'Think,' she corrected. 'And I wasn't going to leave without talking to you first.'

'But you *are* going to leave.' His eyes weren't watchful any longer. They were hard. 'You said you weren't going to do that.'

Heather swallowed. 'My contract with you finishes next week anyway. You're sending the kids away, remember?'

Cursing under his breath, Cal crossed the room and took her hands. 'Do you really think things are the same as they were at the start of this summer? Heather, *everything* has changed.'

'Does that mean you're going to pay me anyway? Even if I leave a few days early?' she joked, but Cal didn't seem to find it funny.

'You can take all the money you want if you're insisting on leaving. I'd hoped… I'd thought we could talk tonight. Come up with a plan for what happens next.'

Heather gave a small bitter laugh. 'We both heard what Ryan and Daisy said to Anna. I think we *know* what happens next. The whole country finds out that I slept with a married man, got knocked up from my one-night stand with him, then came here to seduce his brother and win over his other kids. My father will spiral into despair at my actions, and I will become an absolute outcast and a scandal.'

She'd seen it before. Her mother would have been forced to leave the village in the end—even if she hadn't taken off with her lover. It would have become untenable for her to stay.

Just as it was for Heather now.

'It doesn't have to be that way,' Cal offered.

Heather shook her head. 'You know better than that, Cal. How can I walk into Lengroth with Daisy and Ryan now, with everyone knowing who I am and what I've done?'

'With me at your side,' Cal said, squeezing her hands as he dropped to one knee. 'Heather, stay here and marry me.'

A chill swept through Heather as if the Lengroth ghost had walked right through her. That poor woman who'd been knocked up by the old Earl and murdered when she'd tried to tell the truth about it.

Now here was Cal, offering her everything that any woman could have wanted—and Heather knew she couldn't take it.

'I can't—' Her voice broke on the words.

'Why?' Cal didn't move from his knee. 'We can make this work, Heather you've taught me that. You've taught me that I *can* love, even if my parents never could. I know I can do this now—be a parent to Ryan and Daisy, love them the way they need to be loved. And if I can do that maybe I can even have a happy marriage—as long as it's with *you*. You've shown me that it's not always what we do that hurts others, it's the secrets we keep. So I'm not going to keep secrets any more. I'm going to shout the truth from the turrets of this cursed castle.'

He swallowed so hard she saw his throat bob, then he held her gaze with his own as he spoke.

'I'm going to tell the world that I love you. Starting with you. Heather Reid, I'm in love with you—and I need you to stay.'

Oh, God, his words were arrows through her heart. She knew how much those words must have cost him. How hard he'd fought to be able even to *think* them, let alone say them. And she wasn't even going to try to deny any longer that she was just as much in love with him.

But it didn't matter.

She couldn't live this life.

Couldn't stay here with everyone—even Daisy and Ryan—knowing what sort of a person she was. With her *child* knowing.

'What about Anna?' she asked, her mouth dry.

Cal smiled, obviously taking her question as agreement. 'I've already called Anna's magazine and offered them a proper interview about it all with a different journalist if they don't print Anna's piece. We can announce our engagement, explain our side of the story. It'll all blow over in no time.'

But it wouldn't. People in her village still talked about her mother's misdeeds now, eighteen years or more later. Nobody would forget what she'd done, either—and, most of all, *she* wouldn't forget.

She'd done the wrong thing—sleeping with a married man, falling for Cal, lying about it all.

She didn't deserve a happy-ever-after here.

But her child did.

And she was going to make sure he or she got it.

Even if it broke her heart.

This was all going to work out. All she had to do was say yes and he could fix everything—just as he'd been fixing things ever since he'd returned to Lengroth Castle. With Heather at his side he could do it all.

Except she wasn't saying yes.

'I'm sorry, Cal. I can't marry you.'

He could *see* the pain in her eyes, hear her voice cracking. He knew she wanted this every bit as much as he did. He didn't need her to say the words. He could feel it between them whenever they were together. Hell, she'd probably known he loved her before *he* did. They'd both just pushed everything aside to deal with later.

But she wanted them to be a family. She wanted *him*. So why wouldn't she say yes?

'I'm not doing this because it will avoid a scandal. I'm doing this because I love you.'

It was possibly the first time anyone in his family had *ever* proposed purely for love. Janey had been pregnant when Ross had put a ring on her finger, and Cal was pretty sure he wouldn't have if their father hadn't insisted.

And Heather was turning him down.

'I know. I know. And I love you, too. I tried not to, but...'

There were tears in her eyes, he realised.

Cal pulled himself up to stand, tugging her closer as he did so. 'You love me, Heather. And I love you. So to hell with everyone else. Marry me, make us a real family and let us be happy together.'

She met his gaze, eyes gleaming. 'I want to. But I won't do that to my child. I won't let my child grow up here, where people will always talk about us. Where his or her whole life will be defined by what I did before he or she was even born. I grew up like that, Cal, and I can't do it to my baby. However much I love you, I love my baby more.'

His hands fell away from hers without his permission and he stepped back without planning to. It seemed his body had accepted what she was saying even if his heart hadn't.

'What about Daisy and Ryan? I thought you loved them, too.'

'I do,' she said, her voice pained. 'But they have you—and you have them. I know the three of you can be a happy family together. And it will be easier for you without me and my scandal hanging over you.'

'*Nothing* will be easier without you,' Cal replied, his temper rising.

But Heather only shook her head. As if the matter was out of her hands. But it wasn't. His whole future was in her hands.

'You're running scared,' he accused her. 'I always thought that *I* was the one too scared of repeating the past to risk falling in love, to try to be part of a functioning happy family. But *you're* the one who told me that I could—that kids need love more than perfection. More than *anything* else. Well, the same goes for me. I need your love—not for you to be perfect, or scandal-free.'

'You might not say that when people start talking.'

'I will. I know I will. Because you've made me believe it—made me believe that I can change my family legacy. But you won't even take a chance on changing yours.'

'I *can't*, Cal.'

His heart breaking, Cal tried one last time. 'You say you're doing this for your baby, to make things easier for Daisy and Ryan and even me. But what about *you*? What about what you want?'

With a sad smile Heather picked up the rucksack from her bed. 'I don't deserve what I want.'

And then she walked out of the room, the castle and his life—like the ghost he wasn't even sure existed.

CHAPTER SIXTEEN

THE TRAIN RIDE home was miserable.

Even in summer the sleeper train from Edinburgh to London was freezing, and Heather's coat barely kept her warm enough to stop her shivering. Tears leaked constantly from her eyes, chilling her cheeks, but she couldn't have stopped them if she'd tried.

She'd left her heart, maybe even her soul, in Longroth Castle, and she had no idea if she'd ever get them back again.

But the train wasn't the worst part. The worst part was telling her father everything.

It took her four days to pluck up the courage, but in the end she knew she couldn't wait any longer if she wanted him to hear it from her instead of reading it in some magazine.

It was a miracle the news wasn't out there already—that or the fact that Cal had used the old Bryce magic to keep it hidden for now. But the truth would come out in the end. Even the truth about her feelings for Cal, which she realised now she'd been denying for as long as she'd been feeling them.

Now her father sat opposite her, in the same armchair by the window that had been 'Dad's chair' her whole life, a cup of tea long gone cold at his elbow. She'd wanted to shield him from the worst of her actions, wanted to fudge the truth and skip over certain events.

But she hadn't been able to. She owed him the whole truth, however awful it was.

'And so you came back here?' her dad asked eventually, after she'd finished.

'Yes.'

Her dad reached for a biscuit from the plate on the coffee table.

'I can leave if you want,' Heather said. 'I mean, I know this is going to be a big story. It'll probably make the papers. And I'll totally understand if you want me far away when that happens. I was thinking maybe I could rent a cottage somewhere in Wales—like where we used to go on holiday. Take some time away from everything.'

Before she'd even reached London there had been a full year's wages sitting in her bank account. Cal had been as good as his word—even when she hadn't. He'd given her the means to take time to figure out what to do next, and she could never thank him enough for that.

Maybe she'd send him a postcard from Wales. If he ever wanted to hear from her again, that was.

'Or you could go back to Scotland right now,' her dad said, and Heather started, staring at him in confusion.

'You…you really want me to go?'

She'd said she'd understand it if he did, but when it came to it she'd hoped her father would support her. And why would she run away to *Scotland*, of all places?

Her dad slipped his glasses from his nose, folded them, then placed them on the table next to his cold tea—a gesture so familiar that it made Heather's heart ache for the time before this summer. Before she'd ever met Ross Bryce, when life had been simple, ordered and safe.

'Heather. Sweetheart. I will love you and support you

your whole life—whatever you choose to do, and whatever mistakes you make. And you will always have a home here.'

'Thank you,' Heather whispered, her eyes burning with more tears that wouldn't fall.

'But I'm your father, and it's my job to tell you when I think you're making a mistake. And I don't mean getting pregnant by an earl, or running away and not telling me. I mean leaving Cal and those two children up there in Lengroth.'

Heather blinked. 'I'm sorry…?'

Sighing, her dad reached forward to take her hands—a reassuring gesture that reminded her so much of Cal that her heart ached anew.

'You love that man, *and* those children—even I can see that, just hearing you talking about them. Not to mention how miserable you've been since you arrived home. So you need to go back and be with them.'

'But—'

Her father put up a hand to stop her. 'No buts. Whatever reasons you've dreamed up to keep you apart from them, I guarantee they're not good enough. When your mother left…'

'Dad, you don't have to talk about this.' He never had—not once before. She didn't want to think about how miserable she must look to make him want to talk about it now.

'Yes, I do. Because you need to understand. When she left…she took my heart with her. All the talk, all the gossip…it hurt, of course it did. But not because of what other people thought about me, or my marriage. It was because every single word was a reminder that she didn't love me the way I'd loved her, the way she'd said she did, right until that last day. Worse—it was a reminder that she didn't even love *you* enough to stay. And that was the part I just couldn't make sense of. Because you are the best thing in my life, and I don't understand how anyone could walk away from you.'

'Dad…'

'I'm not finished. Because if your Cal feels about you half the way you feel about him…I imagine he's in a lot of pain right now. Just like I was.'

I need your love—not for you to be perfect, or scandal-free.'

Oh, God, what if he'd really meant that? And what if…what if that was all her baby needed, too?

Two parents who loved him or her. A family to be part of.

Cal might not be her child's biological father, but she knew he'd be his or her dad in his heart, just as he would for Daisy and Ryan.

'I always thought… I thought it was the scandal that broke you. I spent my whole life trying to avoid bringing that kind of talk to your door again.'

Had it all been for nothing? No. Because it had made her the person she was. The person who'd trekked all the way to Lengroth to do 'the right thing'.

The person Cal had fallen in love with.

Cal had loved Ross—loved him still, despite all his flaws. And he loved her, too. Maybe as much as she loved him.

'I can take any words any person throws at me,' her dad said softly. 'But I can't take my only daughter, the love of my life, being unhappy when she doesn't need to be.'

Heather fell to her knees in front of his chair, letting her father wrap his arms around her as she sobbed into his lap. And when at last she was all out of tears, he helped her to her feet and said, 'Grab your bag. I'll take you back to the station.'

'What are you going to do now?'

Cal looked up as Mrs Peterson placed a cup of hot chocolate on the table in front of him, then added a tumbler of brandy beside it. She'd been apologetic and full of guilt ever since she'd realised that Anna had tricked her into getting the children alone so she could interrogate them.

'What *can* I do? I'll call Anna's editor again—manage the story as well as I can now it's out there. I've already paid Heather what I owed her, so that's sorted. Next I'll call the boarding school and—'

'And what?' Daisy's voice rang out from the kitchen door, where she stood with her pale hair hanging around her face and her pyjamas hanging off her slim frame. 'Do we have to go? Now that Heather isn't here?'

Telling the kids she was gone had been awful. Daisy had pretended she didn't care, of course, but Ryan had sobbed, and Cal had known that Daisy was lying, so that wasn't any easier. They couldn't understand why she'd gone if it wasn't because she was cross with them, and Cal hadn't been able to explain because he didn't understand either.

He knew her reasons. But he couldn't understand them.

He'd always assumed that when it came to relationships it would be him who couldn't make it work. Who pulled back for fear of the world learning the truth about his family, or because he really was a product of his gene pool and incapable of true love.

But in the end he'd overcome all that—and it still hadn't been enough.

He'd felt those old walls and old beliefs rising up again that night when Heather had left. But in the morning Daisy and Ryan had been there, a constant reminder of why he had to fight to be more than his own father had been. Why love mattered even when it hurt.

'What do you and Ryan *want* to do?' Cal asked, realising belatedly that he had never asked them. 'Go to Derryford or stay here with me, even if Heather isn't here? You'd have to go to the village school, but I always quite liked it there.'

'Stay at Lengroth,' Daisy said promptly. 'Ryan would be miserable away from Lengroth. And besides, I think you need us.'

Cal smiled. 'I think I do, too. Well, that's decided, then.'

And with that one thing sorted, things began to fall into place.

Anna's editor wasn't exactly accommodating now there were no engagement photos to publish, but eventually they reached an agreement. He refused to let Anna back into the castle, but did submit to a lengthy, open and honest phone interview with one of her colleagues, and agreed that they could use the photos Anna had taken at Lengroth.

People were still going to talk. A lot. But Cal didn't care. The truth was the truth, and lying about it wouldn't change it.

He did have to sit down with Daisy and Ryan and tell them everything, however, in the most age-appropriate way he could manage. Apparently they were far better eavesdroppers than he'd given them credit for—as was Mrs Peterson. And the housekeeper had been far less discreet than he'd hoped.

Which was another uncomfortable conversation he'd have to have...

Cal cornered the housekeeper who'd run Lengroth like clockwork since he was a child as she was making apple pie.

'When you called me the night Ross died you told me they were coming home from a party. But that was a lie, wasn't it?'

She shook the flour from her hands. 'It was.'

'Why?'

'Because that's what we do at Lengroth. We hide the things we don't want other people to see.'

'Not any more,' Cal said firmly. 'Sit down and tell me the truth.'

And she did. She told him about all the women Ross had paraded through the castle, right in front of his wife and children. About the late-night poker games when the attendees had ended up taking home precious heirlooms instead of the money Ross owed them.

'Why didn't you call me? Tell me what was happening?'

Mrs Peterson shrugged. 'He was the Earl.'

'And the night they died?'

'Janey lost her patience—finally. I don't know what it was that did it, but it could have been any one of a hundred things Ross did. She told him she was leaving—packed a bag and everything.'

'She didn't take the kids?'

'I think she knew that Ross wouldn't let her. And as the Earl he had more power. I don't know. I don't think she was thinking straight. They'd both been drinking, I know that.'

'So what happened?'

Mrs Peterson toyed with the apple peeler on the table.

'She got in the car, ready to drive away, but he forced his way into the passenger seat. Told her she couldn't go anywhere without him—people would talk. She drove off anyway. And that was the last time I ever saw them alive.'

Cal shuddered, thankful beyond belief that Janey hadn't tried to take the children. He might have lost everyone in one awful night, and all because Ross hadn't wanted the world to know that his wife was leaving him.

The magazine hit the stands the next day, with the article and photos already up on the website and gaining comments the night before. Cal woke that morning to a throng of reporters gathered around the gates, waiting for a comment.

'What do I do with them?' Mrs Peterson asked.

Cal shrugged. 'Offer them a cup of tea?'

He'd told the truth, answered the questions, and now it was up to others to think what they wanted about it.

Inside Lengroth Castle with Daisy and Ryan, his family, he felt safe and happy. Or as happy as he could be with a hole in his home where Heather should be.

'What are you going to do?' Mrs Peterson called after him.

'Talk to the kids about redecorating their rooms,' Cal answered over his shoulder.

It was time to bring some new life into the castle, he'd decided.

The reporters were still there the next day, too, happily munching the bacon butties Mrs Peterson had made them. Cal ignored them, looking at wallpaper and paint swatches with the kids in the playroom instead.

At least until Ryan looked out of the window and yelled, 'Look!'

Cal crossed to the window seat and looked. And then

he smiled as, down below, Heather walked through the gates of Lengroth Castle, a rubber duck under her arm.

Heather had made it all the way to Scotland before anyone had recognised her from the magazine photos, and even then they hadn't been too hard to put off. But here at Lengroth, with a crowd of reporters thronging around the main gate, there was no pretending to be anyone other than exactly who she was.

The pregnant one-night stand of the late Earl.

Or maybe the fiancée of the new Earl's uncle—if the offer still stood.

Climbing out of the taxi, Heather took a deep breath, adjusted the rubber duck she'd carried all the way from London King's Cross, and grabbed her bag.

'Good luck, Heather.' Harris the taxi driver threw her a grin. 'I reckon you'll all be fine now you're back.'

'I hope so. And thanks.'

Maybe this wouldn't be all bad.

'Heather! Heather!'

The reporters were calling her name before she even reached the gates. Heather ignored them—especially the ones calling out questions that asked her to 'compare and contrast' the two brothers.

Finally, as she opened the gate, she spun to face them. 'Thank you all for your interest,' she said, as they fell silent apart from the click of the odd camera shutter. 'But this is a family matter. And I'd like to get home to my family, please.'

If they'd still have her.

The questions and shouting started up again immediately, but Heather barely heard it. Because when she turned towards the castle again she saw Cal, standing at the top of the seventeen stone steps that led to the front door, waiting for her.

'I'm so sorry,' she said as she reached the first step.

'I thought you were never coming back.' Cal jumped down a few steps to meet her sooner, sweeping her into his arms as soon as she reached the middle step. 'I've never been so happy to be wrong.'

'Me, neither,' Heather admitted. 'I couldn't stay away. And my dad made me see that I shouldn't. I love you—and Daisy and Ryan. I belong here, and so does our baby.'

'Too right.' Cal kissed her, hard and deep, dipping her over his arm as a cheer went up from the reporters at the gate. 'Wait—*our* baby?'

'Our family, really, I thought. If you still want to marry me?'

'In a heartbeat,' Cal answered, and kissed her again.

This time, the cheer that went up was much closer, and Heather opened her eyes to find Daisy and Ryan watching from the doorway.

'You're *really* getting married?' Ryan asked.

'You're *staying* this time?' Daisy added.

Heather and Cal exchanged a glance.

'Yes, to both,' Heather said, smiling widely. 'Want to be bridesmaid?'

Daisy rolled her eyes. 'No. But I'll help you choose the food.'

'Even better.'

'Guess what, Heather!' Ryan grabbed her arm as he spoke. 'We're not going away to school! We're staying here.'

'I'm so glad,' Heather said. 'I'd have missed you too much if you'd gone.'

'We *all* missed *you*,' Cal said. 'So maybe it's best that we just stay together from now on—agreed?'

'A family?' Daisy asked tentatively. 'You two, us, Mrs Peterson and the baby?'

Behind them, Mrs Peterson looked surprised to be included—but Heather was almost certain she saw a tear in the housekeeper's eye.

'All of us,' Heather said firmly. 'Together.'

'Always,' Cal confirmed.

And as he spoke Heather could have sworn she saw another figure—a thin white figure, almost transparent in the late-summer sunshine—behind Mrs Peterson. A ghostly figure that raised a hand in farewell, then disappeared.

Heather lifted her own hand automatically, before realising there was no one there to see it. The Lengroth ghost had moved on at last. Maybe because the Bryce family no longer needed a reminder of the harm their misdeeds could cause, Heather thought with a smile.

Suddenly the whole castle felt lighter. As if years of secrets and lies had been lifted from the stones.

Heather gathered her family close and, with their arms around each other, they all headed into Lengroth Castle.

Together.

EPILOGUE

THE DARK METAL gates of Lengroth Castle were thrown open in the summer sunshine, and crowds of wedding guests were pouring through to celebrate with Heather and Uncle Cal on this glorious July day. Daisy watched them through the playroom window for a while, before deciding she probably had better put on her dress before Heather came looking for her.

It was, Daisy thought, exactly a year to the day since she'd thrown a rubber duck through that same window—the day Heather had arrived at Lengroth. She smiled to herself. Every table at the wedding breakfast had a rubber duck as part of its centrepiece—one wearing a top hat, another dressed as a centurion, a rubber duck sphinx and so on. Daisy didn't know where Heather had found them, but they were pretty funny.

Her dress wasn't too bad, either, Daisy thought as she put it on. Heather had let her choose—and had let her off bridesmaid duties, too, which Daisy was glad about. She didn't want everyone staring at her today. She wanted to sit with Ryan and Heather's dad—who had said to call him Grandpa Bill—and just enjoy it all.

Today, after all the awfulness of last year, they were going to be a family again.

And the new baby was cute. Daisy thought it was nice

that they had someone they could all share, who belonged to all of them together.

Heather and Uncle Cal had called him Will, after her dad. Ryan had pointed out that it wasn't actually the same name. He cried a lot, but he always seemed to stop when Daisy sang him songs. In the end she and Ryan had decided that Will was better than a puppy—but they still kind of wanted a dog, too.

Uncle Cal had said they'd go and pick one after the honeymoon. Heather had given him a big kiss when he'd said that, which was strange, as Daisy hadn't thought Heather was really a dog person.

Checking her reflection in the mirror, Daisy saw a flicker of movement behind her and smiled. She knew who that was.

She turned slowly, so as not to spook the ghost, and then laughed at herself for being silly. Ghosts weren't scared of *people*.

Heather thought the ghost had left the day she'd come back to the castle, but Daisy knew better. Yes, she'd *mostly* gone, but every now and again, on important days, she came back—just to check on them. Daisy liked her. She was the only person she'd had to talk to, apart from Ryan, when her parents had died—and Ryan had been too little and too much of a boy to understand.

'Hello,' Daisy said. 'Have you come to check that we're still all right?'

The ghost nodded.

Daisy sat down on the bed to pull on her shiny silver shoes. 'We're fine. Better than fine, really. Don't tell anyone I said this, but Uncle Cal and Heather are getting really good at this family thing. I still miss Mum and Dad but…we're happy. All of us together. So you don't need to worry any more.'

The ghost smiled. Daisy didn't think she'd seen her do that before.

'Oh, and if you come to visit over the next couple of weeks we won't be here,' Daisy added quickly as the ghost started to fade. 'We're all going on honeymoon together, you see. Uncle Cal says it'll be more fun if we're together. Mrs Peterson is coming, too—to help with the baby.'

And, Daisy suspected, to let Uncle Cal and Heather have some time alone. Really, she was eleven now. She understood more than they thought.

She wondered if maybe their family might grow again soon. That would be okay, she decided. Especially if she got a dog, too.

'Daisy? Are you ready?' Heather appeared in the doorway just as the ghost vanished completely. 'Oh, you look beautiful!'

'You look nice, too,' Daisy said.

It was true—Heather's copper hair was tied up in some complicated plait at the back of her head, and her dress was ivory lace and pearls. But mostly she just looked so happy it shone out of her.

'Shall we go and find the boys?' Heather asked, holding a hand out to Daisy. 'The sooner we get the wedding part over with, the sooner we can get to the dancing.'

Daisy rolled her eyes. Dancing was Heather's favourite thing about getting married, it seemed. 'Might as well.'

As they walked down the stone-floored hallways to the castle chapel Daisy thought she saw the ghost peeping out at them one last time.

'Heather? You'll never leave again, will you?'

When she'd first come back Daisy had asked her that every day—usually in a whisper at bedtime, so she could pretend she hadn't really said it. But now she hadn't asked her in months, she realised. Maybe because she already knew the answer. But it was still nice to hear it.

'Never,' Heather promised. 'Nothing could take me away from you and Ryan, or Will, or Uncle Cal.'

'Good.' Daisy sneaked a look back at the ghost, who smiled again, then disappeared.

Somehow Daisy didn't think she'd be back.

The Bryce family didn't need watching over any more. Not now they had each other.

* * * * *

THE DATING ARRANGEMENT

KERRI CARPENTER

For John, my happy ending

Chapter One

"I'm getting married."

Jack Wright nodded his head in response. Three things had brought him to this conclusion. Number one, she was carrying a stack of bridal magazines. Number two, she was wearing a rock on her ring finger that was so large, he had to wonder if it needed its own zip code.

But the truly telling sign was the fact that she had mentioned it no less than ten times in the five minutes she'd been talking to him in The Wright Drink, his dad's bar.

My bar.

Jack silently admonished himself. He now owned the bar and had to start acting like an entrepreneur. First order of business—dealing with the bride-to-be.

"Ms. Mitchell," he began.

"Soon to be Mrs. Cross," she added brightly, clutching the magazines to her light pink dress. "But please call me Trina."

"Right. Trina. I still don't see how I can help you."

"My fiancé, Nick, and I met here a little over a year ago. Right over there, at the jukebox." She gestured in that direction, with a dreamy expression on her face.

"So you'd like to have your wedding here?"

The look of horror that flashed onto her face was so severe, you would have thought he'd suggested she get married in a maximum-security prison.

"I'd actually like to have my bachelorette party here. And Nick, my fiancé, wants to start his bachelor-party night here, as well."

While he'd attended his fair share of bachelor shindigs, he knew next to nothing about bachelorette parties. Jack pushed a hand through his dark hair and glanced around the gloomy, dank, unappealing bar. The gloomy, dank, unappealing bar that he now owned.

As if reading his mind, Trina blushed. "Although, I hope you don't mind me saying, this place seems a bit, um, different than when Nick and I met here."

What a polite way of saying it was a dump.

He sighed. "Well, my dad recently passed away."

"I'm so sorry," Trina said with true sincerity.

"The bar was left to me and it's hit a rough spot. I'm not sure that hosting a party—of any kind—is the best idea at the moment."

Trina's eyes widened. "Oh please don't say that. How about this? Why don't you think about it? I'll leave my cell number and you can give me a call." She grabbed a napkin from the bar, scribbled her number and handed it over.

Jack took the flimsy paper gingerly. He knew he needed to be frank with her.

"Trina, since you've mentioned it, I know how the bar looks now. I have to wonder why you're still so interested in having these parties here when you could go to a much nicer place."

"Because this place is special to us," she said simply.

Something about the statement clenched at Jack's heart and he had to take a deep, steadying breath. The place meant something to her. Shouldn't he feel the same way?

He couldn't reply, so he nodded his head again. A smile blossomed on Trina's face. "Okay, just think about it. If I don't hear from you in a week, I'll follow up. Plenty of other wedding plans to keep me busy in the meantime."

He'd have to take her word for it, since he was hardly any kind of wedding aficionado.

"Talk to you soon," she said before flouncing out the front door.

Since the bar wasn't open for business yet, Jack flipped the lock. Not that customers would be clambering to get in when he did open the doors for happy hour. Aside from the engaged Ms. Mitchell, soon to be Mrs. Cross, interest in The Wright Drink lay only with a handful of regulars who had been frequenting the place since Jack was a child.

Not for the first time today, his fingers twitched as he reached for the MIA pack of cigarettes he gave up six months ago.

He walked to the back of the room and glanced at the pile of bills spread across the long, wooden bar in front of him. Jack cracked his knuckles. He probably needed reading glasses. Just like his old man had worn.

His old man.

Jack still couldn't believe he was gone. While he knew his dad loved him, they hadn't been particularly close in years. No games of catch in the backyard, after dinner. After all, it was hard to do anything after dinner when you didn't usually sit down for a traditional meal. But that's what came of a dad who owned a bar. He'd spent all of his time at The Wright Drink when Jack was a kid. And the bar had thrived.

If he believed Trina's account, and he had no reason not to, the bar had taken a turn for the worse within the last year. According to several of his dad's friends, that's when his father's health had started to deteriorate. Not surprising for someone who had smoked for well over forty years. Still, no one could ever prepare for the call that their dad had passed away.

Those same friends had also informed Jack that even though his dad's health had been declining, he refused to stop working at the bar. He came in rain or snow, good health or bad. Looking around now, he could see that The Wright Drink had suffered as much as his dad.

After high school graduation, Jack had gone off to college on a baseball scholarship and played in the minors for a couple of years, until a knee injury put an end to that. He'd decided to travel. Backpacked through Europe. Spent some time in both Brazil and Iceland—talk about polar opposites. Eventually he'd settled in Vegas. He'd begun dealing at the blackjack tables at a fancy casino, as a favor to a friend. He'd actually enjoyed interacting with different people every night. He had worked hard and moved up the ranks, until he was a supervisor, overseeing the whole casino floor.

Jack began to pace; his long legs were eating up the distance from behind the bar, through the area of high-top tables and past the cluster of wall-mounted television sets. Another trait he'd inherited from his father.

Still, no amount of walking was going to get him out of this jam. His father had died of a very sudden heart attack, and he'd left the bar and his house to Jack. The Wright Drink had seen better days. It needed a cosmetic overhaul. It also needed a financial miracle. The pile of bills wasn't going to shrink itself.

In their weekly—okay, sometimes more like biweekly—phone calls, James Wright had never let on that he was in trouble. If he had...

Jack stopped pacing. He would have what? Dropped what he was doing and rushed back home to Virginia? Probably not. The painful grasp of guilt wrapped around his heart and squeezed.

His mother had died when he was a freshman in high school. Both he and his dad took her death hard. His dad retreated into himself. As the owner of a business, he'd already spent a ton of time at the bar, but after his mother's death, his dad had managed to devote even more time and attention to work. He'd stopped asking how school was going or putting in appearances at Jack's baseball games.

He'd stopped caring.

Jack and this bar were the only things his father had. Although, only one of them seemed to get any attention from the old man.

Jack tried—mostly unsuccessfully—to shake off the sullen mood. He started to make his way into the small room his dad used as an office, when someone rapped on the front door.

Jack really wanted to tell whoever it was that the bar was still closed, but he was in no position to turn away possible business. He made easy work of crossing the room and opened the door to find his father's lawyer and good friend standing there, holding a large tote bag, a small dog and a big grin.

"Jack, my boy, how's it going?"

Fred Koda had been calling almost every day. Sadly, Jack's answer to his standard greeting never changed.

"Same."

Jack eyed the dog in Fred's arms. He judged him to be about twenty, maybe twenty-five, pounds. He was a very light beige color and had lots of fur; he definitely had to be part poodle. He had a light brown nose, which his little pink tongue darted out to lick. Jack peered closer. The dog had green eyes. Very human-looking green eyes.

"I didn't know you had a dog," Jack said.

"I don't." Fred held the dog out to Jack. "But you do."

Jack froze. "Excuse me?"

Fred pushed the dog into Jack's arms. The dog immediately licked Jack's chin. Fred waltzed into the bar. "This was your dad's dog."

What the what? "My father never mentioned a dog, and I haven't seen any dog-related stuff at my dad's house."

"When James had his heart attack, I went over to the house and collected all of the food, treats, toys and beds I could find. He's been living with me since that day. With you inheriting the bar and losing your dad, I didn't want to bombard you." He scratched the dog's head. "Meet your new roommate, Cosmo."

"Cosmo? What kind of name is Cosmo?" The realization hit him fast and hard. His mother didn't drink much, but when she did, she always had a cosmopolitan.

Jack followed Fred into the bar. "Listen, Fred, I appreciate you taking care of this little guy. He is a guy, right?" Jack held the dog up and looked to his nether regions. "But I can't take a dog."

Fred grinned wider. "He was left to you. You are Cosmo's new owner. But I'm going to miss our man time," he said to the dog. "Cosmo likes to snuggle and watch TV."

Swell. "That's cute and all. But seriously, I can't take this dog."

The ironic part was that Jack used to beg for hours on

end to get a dog when he was a little kid. Now here he was, shunning that boyhood dream.

Cosmo squirmed in Jack's arms until he got comfortable. Then he licked Jack right on the mouth.

"Yuck."

Fred chuckled. "He likes to give kisses." He held up the tote bag before placing it on a nearby table. "Everything you need is in here. Food, toys, files from the vet. Cosmo's a rescue."

"My dad rescued a dog?" It was so strange that he wouldn't mention something like that to Jack.

"Just about a year ago," Fred said. "I think he needed a friend."

Jack let out a long exhale, which did nothing to alleviate the hurt and guilt Fred's comment had lodged in his throat. Intuitively, Cosmo snuggled closer to Jack, wedging his little head under Jack's chin.

"Some other tips," Fred said. "Cosmo is part poodle, but I'm not sure what he's mixed with. So he doesn't shed. He's housebroken. He's also very playful, takes two long walks a day, likes squeaky toys, hates the vacuum. Oh and he's kind of a Velcro dog."

"Velcro dog? What does that mean?"

Fred actually appeared to be a little sheepish. "He's clingy."

Great. Jack sighed. "Fred, Cosmo is really cute." And he was. He would have been exactly the kind of dog he'd wanted when he was little. "But I can't take him. I don't even know if I'm staying in town."

"Why wouldn't you stay here? You have a place to live and you're the new owner of the bar."

"A bar that never gets any customers."

Fred hesitated, then waved his hand as if to dismiss the idea. "Well, I'm sure it will pick up soon."

"I'm still trying to figure out what happened here, Fred. When I was growing up, the place was packed almost every night. Now there's a handful of regulars and that's about it."

The strangest part about this was the fact that The Wright Drink was located on King Street. As one of the busiest streets in the popular Old Town area, King Street generated enough foot traffic to make attracting thirsty customers a breeze. Locals and tourists alike always seemed charmed by Old Town Alexandria, with its quaint cobblestone streets, red brick sidewalks, the history and culture, the close proximity to Washington, DC, the view of the Potomac, and the restaurants and shops.

"I'm not sure what to tell you, kid. I didn't think much of it at the time, but looking back, your dad was acting a little weird for the last year or two."

Jack shifted. "What do you mean?"

"Forgetful. Aloof. Not that he was ever Mr. Personality before."

Maybe something besides the lifelong smoking had been going on with his dad. With his health. His grandfather had had dementia. Perhaps his dad started to get the same thing.

"Do you think that's why most of the regulars haven't paid their tabs? From the receipts and records I've gone through, it seems like my dad hadn't asked them to settle for the last two years."

Fred shrugged. "Could be."

But would asking for money drive them away? Then the bar would truly be empty. Frustrated, Jack gritted his teeth. The only thing he knew about a bar was how to go to one and order a beer.

With a sigh, he said, "Maybe I'm not cut out for this, Fred. I can always try to sell it."

"Nonsense," Fred bellowed. "Your dad wanted you to have The Wright Drink. He told me many times."

"Would have been nice for him to tell me too." He hadn't meant to utter that out loud, but he couldn't take it back now. Fred paused. Finally, he put a hand on Jack's shoulder and squeezed.

"I have to get going. I'm meeting a client near Mount Vernon and I heard the Parkway is backed up."

Panic washed over Jack. "But Cosmo?" he asked helplessly.

Fred laughed as he quickly headed for the door. "You'll be fine."

"He shouldn't even be in here. There are health-code violations. Right?" Were there? He had no idea.

"James had him in here all the time. Cosmo liked to sleep behind the bar."

"Fred, wait…"

But Fred didn't wait. Jack was alone with a little dog— and with his thoughts, which was even worse.

He was in no better place than he was before. He still needed to figure out how to turn the bar around. Or sell. Despite Fred's protests, Jack was considering the idea to be a very viable option.

Ashamed of the thought, he walked to the middle of the bar. In the past, this would be the point where he stepped outside for a smoke. A little stress relief. Since that was no longer an option, Jack decided to have a much-needed tête-à-tête with Cosmo.

He placed the dog on the floor. Cosmo looked up at him with adoring eyes. "Listen, I like dogs. I do. But I'm not the most stable guy on the planet."

Cosmo shifted and then lifted his leg and peed.

Jack sighed again. Loudly. "You really going to do

that in public? In the middle of a bar where people eat and drink?"

Cosmo tilted his head, as if he were considering a reply. He just looked at Jack and walked to another corner of the bar and sat. And stared back at Jack.

"Damn it." Jack ran his hands through his hair. He swore the dog had a look on his face akin to "na-na na-na boo-boo."

Frustrated, he went to the supply closet and retrieved cleaning supplies. "Housebroken, my ass."

He cleaned up the mess and shoved the soiled paper towels into a trash bag. Then he rummaged through Cosmo's luggage and found a blanket and small bed. He stuck them under the bar, and the dog pranced over to them and made himself comfortable.

"Stay," Jack said. "I'm going to throw out this little mess."

He didn't think dogs really smiled, but this one looked to be grinning ear to ear.

"I mean it, Prince Charming. Stay."

He pushed through the back door that led to the alley behind the bar. He threw the black bag into the dumpster. Hard.

March was notorious for unpredictable weather, but today was beautiful. Mild temperature, with a nice breeze. Good day for a walk. Maybe a bit of exercise would help clear his mind. Bring a bit of clarity to his current situation.

He stepped away from the dumpster and glanced up and down the alley. He was unfamiliar with these businesses. He'd have to meander down Prince Street to familiarize himself. He did know there was a seafood restaurant, off to the right, and the door on the left led to…was it a wedding-dress shop? The windows were a little too high to see inside and protected by blinds, in any case.

Jack shook his head. So much had changed in this area

of the city since he'd returned. He was actually rather proud to see Alexandria's expansion.

Then suddenly a movement out of the corner of his eye caught his attention. He turned as a blur of white ruffles began to pour out of the window he'd just been gazing at.

What the hell?

The mass of material made a strangled sound as it continued to shimmy out of the window. A few more inches and a head of curly auburn hair topped with a veil surfaced.

He froze at the sight of a bride climbing out of the window. Either that or a life-size marshmallow had just exploded into the alley.

Yep, that door definitely led to a bridal shop.

"Gotta get out. Gotta get out," the bride chanted breathlessly.

He'd heard of runaway brides, but this was something else. He would have chuckled, but the woman suddenly slipped, leaving her and that massive dress dangling from the windowsill. He assumed her feet were under there somewhere, but it seemed like all of that fluff had swallowed them.

She let out a squeak and Jack rushed over to help. "Hang on, I got you."

Another little yelp sounded and her arms shook right before she fell… Right on top of Jack. He tried to catch her, but with all that dress, he wasn't sure what body part he had managed to grab hold of. All he knew was that he was falling to the hard ground of the alley, with a pile of lace and satin and soft woman covering him.

A friend of his caught the bouquet at a wedding once. Apparently he'd taken it a step further and caught the bride.

Chapter Two

Emerson Dewitt knew two things for sure.

First, she was lying on top of a strange man, in the dirty alley behind her mother's exclusive bridal boutique. And second, she was still wearing the ten-thousand-dollar wedding dress that had given her the urge to flee in the first place.

It was a strapless gown with a ruched bodice, and it had a fit-and-flare style, with an emphasis on the flare part. The bottom half of the dress exploded into layer upon layer of puffy white organza and tulle covered in delicate crystals and ruffled flowers. It was as close to wearing a cloud made out of cotton balls as she would probably get. Although, cotton balls didn't weigh anything. This frilly monstrosity felt like it would clock in at about eighty pounds.

And surely her savior, whoever he was, didn't appreciate having an eighty-pound dress, plus a woman, crash-land on top of him. At least the fall appeared to knock the anxiety attack right out of her—she could feel her pulse returning to normal. She couldn't believe she'd just climbed out of a window. This had to take over the number-one spot on the list of craziest things she'd ever done.

"I'm so sorry," Emerson said, shifting her weight and trying to rearrange herself and the dress. If she'd so much as knocked a crystal loose on this dress, her mother would kill her.

"'t's 'kay," the man mumbled in a deep voice. She could feel him moving under her as he attempted to push the various layers of material out of his way.

"No, it's not. Let me just…" She broke off as she tried to figure out how to get up gracefully. Only, a second later, she realized she'd left grace and all other etiquette behind the moment she'd decided to fling herself out the window.

After a few more moments of rustling about, Emerson and her Good Samaritan had freed themselves and were finally standing again. That's when she got her first look at him.

And *damn*, he was sexy. Tall and muscular, with dark, disheveled hair and dark eyes to match. Eyes that were currently giving her a suspicious once-over as he brushed dirt off his pants.

"Are you okay?" he asked.

"I am, thanks to you," she said, with her voice sounding a little breathier than she'd like. "Emerson Dewitt." She stuck a hand out to shake. He grasped it and she shivered.

"Jack Wright." He looked around the alleyway, eyeing the window to her mother's shop. "Is there somewhere I can take you? Back to the shop?" His gaze fell over her attire. "To a church?"

In spite of everything else, she laughed. "Definitely not to a church. I guess you're probably wondering why a bride would climb out a window."

He nodded gravely but there was a mischievous twinkle in his eye.

"You see, I was trying this dress on and then…well, someone must have sucked all of the air out of the room, and I was seeing black spots in front of my eyes and then…" She sighed, long and hard. "I'll take 'ways to have a panic attack' for five hundred."

Again, he nodded. "I see. Well, marriage is a big step."

She cocked her head. "Marriage?" She felt her nose crinkle. "I'm not…oh of course you would think that." She smoothed down one of the flouncy flowers on the front of the gown. "I'm not getting married." *Blew that chance last year.*

Jack remained still for a moment. Finally, his brows creased. "And you would be in a wedding dress why?"

She sighed. "Funny story."

He crossed his arms over his chest, and the motion stretched the fabric of his T-shirt, so she couldn't help but notice the rippling muscles underneath. *Yum.* She looked up—high up, because Jack Wright was very tall—to see Jack waiting patiently.

He pointed to the door of the wedding shop. "Why don't we get you inside? My dad's—that is, I own The Wright Drink. Looks like you could you use one."

"Right drink, wrong drink, I'll take either. Thanks." She glanced down and happened to notice something. Something very bad. "Ohmigod!"

"What's wrong?"

"I got dirt all over this dress. My mother is going to seriously kill me."

Jack peered at her dress. "Don't worry. I can get that out with a special mixture my dad came up with."

She arched an eyebrow in suspicion.

"You don't own a bar for as long as my dad did without having a great hangover cure and a fail-safe stain remover."

He held the door open and led Emerson through the back of the bar. He gestured for her to take a seat. She took a moment to observe the space. It was nice. The bar, a large, continuous square made of a dark wood, dominated the room. Glasses of various shapes and sizes hung from the shelving above it. And gold fixtures gave the place an old-timey feel, even if the gold needed a good polish. It reminded her of the reruns of the show *Cheers*. All it was missing was Norm and Cliff at one end of the bar.

Jack appeared in front of her, with the bar separating them. He handed her a rag. "Just dab lightly at the dirt. Should come right out."

Miraculously, it did! She was saved, for now.

"Thank you so much," she said gratefully.

"No problem."

She continued to inspect the dress and clean up any imperfections she found. Out of the corner of her eye, she saw movement and jumped out of her chair.

"What is that?"

"Huh?" Jack questioned. "Oh sorry. That's Cosmo, my dad's dog. Apparently."

Emerson clapped her hands together. "A dog!" She crouched down and the poodle-like dog pranced right over to her, with the charms on his collar jingling while he did.

"Aren't you the cutest thing? You are so handsome. Yes, you are." She lost herself in petting the dog, who rolled right over on his back. She obliged by scratching his tummy. "Do you like your belly scratched? Yes, you do." She met Jack's unamused eyes. "He is the sweetest thing."

"Don't be fooled," Jack said dryly. "He peed on the floor ten minutes ago."

"Well, maybe you should have taken him out. It wasn't your fault, cutie-pie. No, it wasn't." She took in Cosmo's adorable little face, with his brown nose. "Are his eyes… green?" she asked Jack.

"Seems like it. I've never seen a dog with eyes like that before. They're very human. I feel like he looks at me and knows things he shouldn't."

Emerson laughed. She picked up the dog and cradled him to her side, the way she would with a baby. Cosmo wrapped his legs around her and seemed quite content.

"I can't believe you're picking him up," Jack said. "Your dress."

Emerson absolutely adored dogs. Her mother had been firmly against them getting a dog, no matter how much Emerson and her sister had begged. Her dad begged too, for that matter. Of course, a dog would not have been good for her mother's antiques and perfect house.

"You better be careful." Jack wagged a finger at her. "I'm not sure if my dad's stain remover can get dog pee out of a wedding dress."

She kissed the top of Cosmo's head. "You won't go potty on me, will you? No, you won't."

"You've been warned. Now, what can I get you?" Jack asked. "Water? Hot tea? Maybe a glass of wine? I have a nice sauvignon blanc."

"A beer would be great, actually. Whatever you have on tap that's seasonal. And Cosmo needs some water."

He blinked, but quickly reached for a mug and pulled on the tab in front of him to fill up the beer. Once the frothy, amber-colored liquid was in front of her, Emerson downed half of it in a single gulp, relishing the malty taste.

A look of surprise, followed by amusement, crossed his face. "Thirsty?" He filled up a bowl with water and placed it on the floor. Emerson let Cosmo down and the dog happily trotted toward the bowl and delicately lapped at the water. Satisfied, he returned to his bed, walked in a circle and then settled into a little ball.

Emerson let out a burp. "Excuse me. My mother would kill me if she could see this." She drank the rest of the drink and held the mug up. "Maybe a water now?"

"Of course." As he grabbed a clean glass and filled it with ice and then water, he eyed her. "Want to talk about it?"

She liked his eyes. They were a dark chocolaty brown. Serious and mysterious, but there was that twinkle after all.

Emerson took a sip of the water and settled in to explain. "My mother owns Dewitt's Bridal, over on Prince Street." She gestured in that direction now. "When she gets new dresses in stock, she asks me and my sister to try them on. She likes to see them on a real person before she recommends them to a customer."

"So you were helping your mom out?"

"Basically." She broke off as she looked down at the dress with an eye roll.

"Go on," he urged, waiting for her to finish her thought.

But Emerson didn't know what to say. What could she say really? The truth? Jack might be nice, and he had provided her with some much-needed alcohol during a trying moment, but he was still a stranger. Did she dare tell him that, as soon as she'd taken one look at herself wearing the wedding dress, in the three-way mirror, the air had whooshed out of her lungs? Her heart had begun beating so fast and so hard that she could practically hear it. The room had started to spin.

She played with the straw in her glass of water.

"Emerson?" Jack asked. "What happened? You seem... upset."

She sighed. "It's stupid, really. I saw myself dressed like this and I freaked. I was being dramatic and unnecessarily emotional." She attempted a smile and shrugged, trying to make light of the situation.

The reality was the last time she'd been wearing a wedding dress, she'd been standing in the back of a church, waiting for her fiancé. But he hadn't shown. Only the note had arrived.

Jack's eyes narrowed. "Climbing out of a window is a bit drastic. But something must have made you feel that way to need to escape so badly."

"Like I said, I overreacted. I'm just not that into weddings."

Jack nodded. "You don't want to get married?"

I did. He didn't.

Not being into weddings and not being into *her* marriage were two very different things. Emerson nodded. She agreed with Jack's presumption because it seemed a lot simpler than going into the whole mess. Let him think she didn't want to get married. It's not like she'd see him again after today.

"That must be hard, since your mom owns a bridal shop."

"Understatement." She sat up straight and put on her best impression of a Southern accent. "Why, Beatrice Dewitt will have both of her daughters married faster than you can say *mint julep.*"

Behind the bar, Jack grinned. Emerson felt lucky to already be sitting down. She was a sucker for a good smile on a handsome face.

"Mama is from Spartanburg, South Carolina."

He met this information with a blank stare.

"She was a deb. You know, a debutante?"

His facial expression didn't change. She was going to have to spell this out.

"Southern women live for weddings. My mama's chosen profession only adds to her wedding-mania. Being surrounded by silk organza gowns, lacy veils and sparkly accessories on a daily basis does nothing to suppress her desire to see me married."

"But you're not engaged right now?"

"I'm not even dating anyone at the moment. But that doesn't stop Mama. My younger and incredibly perfect sister, Amelia, isn't helping matters. She got married six months ago. I'd had a bit of a reprieve while Mama was busy planning her wedding."

She clasped her hands in her lap and studied the bright coral nail polish that was chipping. Her mother had been harping on it earlier.

"So now that your sister's married, your mother is trying to get you married off, even though you're not interested."

Again, she didn't correct his assumption. Mainly because she didn't want to tell him that she had been engaged. She had done the whole song and dance.

"This year is my parents' thirtieth wedding anniversary. They're having a huge party in a month. I think she'd like me to have a date. Or a fiancé. Or a husband." Emerson threw her hands into the air. "It would complete the perfect family image. Amelia did her part."

"Is your sister as pretty as you?"

Emerson sat back and swallowed, feeling her cheeks heat up. "Um, no—I mean yes—I mean… Thank you." She bit her lip. "My sister is gorgeous. But we don't look alike. Except for the hair color." She ran a hand over her curly auburn hair until her fingers tangled with the floor-length veil.

"Amelia is tall and thin and beautiful. She looks like a model. I'm short and curvy and definitely not."

Jack took her in. His gaze swept from the top of her head, over her body, all the way down to the ground. Slowly. Surely. "I think you look just fine."

Emerson fought the urge to fidget. "Again, thank you. You've made me feel a lot better. You must be a really amazing bartender."

Jack's face fell. "I wouldn't exactly call myself a bartender."

She took in the various taps of beer, bottles of liquor stacked neatly on the far wall and rows of pristine glassware. "No?"

"I mean, I own this bar. Now. Recently, that is. My father passed away and left it to me."

The emotions on her new friend's face tugged at her heart. "I'm so sorry. About your father, I mean." She could only imagine if something happened to her mother and she had to take over the bridal shop.

Cosmo made his way to Emerson's chair. Then he let out a sound that sounded very close to a sigh. She picked him up again and placed him on her lap. He snuggled closer to Emerson.

"Poor thing." Emerson rubbed her hands up and down the dog's back, enjoying his soft fur. "I bet you miss your dad, don't you?"

"Yes."

She'd asked the question of the dog, but Jack answered. His word came out so softly, she wondered if he knew he'd said it. By the distant look on his face, she imagined not. She let it go.

"As you can see for yourself, The Wright Drink doesn't exactly have the right appeal."

Emerson took a moment to glance around the space. It needed some light—natural light, preferably. And one hell of a cleaning crew would do wonders. But all in all, she found it charming. Like an old English pub.

"I don't know," she said. "Seems like it just needs some tender loving care. A fresh coat of paint wouldn't hurt either."

"But would new paint bring customers in?"

She wasn't sure if he was really asking her, but she decided to answer anyway. "Probably not. But if you zhuzhed up the inside, spent some time on a social media campaign and planned a couple of enticing events, you could turn things around. I'm an event planner and I've done plenty of grand openings for bars and restaurants, not to mention specialized events like themed nights, New Year's Eve parties, birthday parties, you name it. You'd be surprised what attracts people."

The air hung heavily between them. They locked eyes and it took everything in her power not to squirm from the intensity pouring out of those serious eyes.

She could feel the heat returning to her face and decided to lighten things up. "I mean, there are several ways to get customers interested in a business. I just organized the food truck festival last weekend and I know there—"

"You put that together?" He whistled long and low. "That was amazing. I heard there were two dozen trucks and they maxed out on ticket sales."

She nodded. "The city wanted to focus on local businesses. Every food truck was owned by an Alexandria resident. To be honest, the publicity budget wasn't very large. But word of mouth is a powerful tool. People were excited to support the trucks."

"I got food from at least five or six places," Jack said. "There was such great diversity."

"Fifteen different ethnicities represented," she said proudly. She'd worked extra hard to make sure a variety of diverse foods and cultures were included when she'd begun organizing the festival.

"Sadly, it almost didn't happen. The organizers had wanted to do it for years, but the city kept pushing back. Said it wouldn't bring any interest. There were a lot of things we did to make sure we would pack the festival." She gestured around the bar. "Wouldn't be hard to do the same kind of thing here."

He seemed interested. "Really?"

"Off the top of my head, I would suggest a grand opening. Or a reopening, as the situation would warrant. There are several events you could begin hosting that would help garner interest."

"Like bachelorette parties?" A pained expression crossed his face.

Emerson laughed. "I was thinking more like a weekly trivia night, regular happy-hour specials and maybe even a ladies' night." She didn't even go into the social media opportunities. "You have a lot to work with here."

Jack followed her gaze. "How do you know about all of this?"

"It's part of my job."

Jack leaned back suddenly. "Looks like we both have a problem to solve."

"Trust me, it would be a lot easier to get people into this bar than it would be to get my mother off my back."

Jack rubbed a hand along his jaw. She noticed some dark stubble and could hear a scratching noise as his fingers moved over it. Was it wrong that her mouth watered at the sight?

"How about…" he trailed off.

"What?" she asked.

"Nothing—it's a crazy idea."

"Come on. We've already bonded over my frazzled nerves and your outdated bar."

"Okay then. Why don't I be your boyfriend?"

Yes, please. She coughed. "Excuse me? Why would you pretend to be my boyfriend? I mean, why would any-one do something like that? You don't even know me."

"Because," Jack said patiently, "I need your help too." He gestured to the bar around him. "I don't know if I'm going to keep this place and find someone to manage it for me, or sell it. But no matter what I do, I have to turn it around. And you'd be the perfect person to help me make that happen."

Emerson mulled over his proposal. "So you help me with my family. I help you with the bar."

"You got it."

"You're going to pretend to be my boyfriend?" She couldn't believe she was entertaining this at all. It was nuts. "That's a lot to ask of you."

"It's me being your boyfriend for one night at your parents' party. Believe me, from the looks of it, turning this place around will be the harder part."

She chewed on her lip. "O-okay. So we're going to be a pretend couple. And we'll fix up your bar."

"And no one gets hurt," he finished.

As she considered, a smile began spreading over his handsome face. If it weren't for that damn smile…

"What do you say? Do you want to make a deal?" He held out his hand and Cosmo let out a little *yip*.

She rose, and the wedding dress billowed around her. Then she clasped his offered hand. "I do."

Chapter Three

The last time Emerson had an imaginary boyfriend, she'd been in middle school. Her twelve-year-old sister had announced at Sunday dinner that she was "going with" Jeremy Swanson. So Emerson did what any self-respecting fourteen-year-old would do. She'd invented a boyfriend of her own, claiming he went to a different school and was constantly busy with sports.

That act hadn't lasted long. She'd never been any good at lying, which didn't bode well for what she was about to do with Jack.

He squeezed her hand. "Want me to go in with you?" he asked as they stood outside of her mother's bridal boutique, staring at the black-and-white-striped awning with *Dewitt's Bridal* scrawled across it in a fancy pink script. On his leash, Cosmo stood obediently next to Jack.

Emerson shook her head. "Thank you, but I think it will be better if we wait as long as possible to bring you into the fold." Easier on her, as well. "I'll spring you on them when we get closer to the anniversary party. Plus that will give us time to start work on turning the bar around."

Jack gave her a long once-over, with his face emanating doubt. It looked like he was about to ask a question. But he must have decided against it. "You're the boss," he said simply instead. "Why don't you come over tonight? I can fill you in on the situation with the bar and we can start planning."

"I'll be there. Just text me the address." She paused. "You're not a serial killer or anything, are you?"

He held his hand up in a salute. "Law-abiding citizen, I promise. But if it makes you feel better, we can meet at the bar."

She was probably being silly or overly cautious. She hoped her new pretend boyfriend wasn't a psychopath, but you just never knew these days. "The bar sounds great."

"Done. We can continue to get to know each other better tonight. If we're going to make this work, we'll need details."

Emerson cocked her head. "What do you mean?"

"If we're dating, we need to know essentials. Favorite color, movie, band, food, hobbies. I don't even know your middle name. Or if you have one."

Emerson couldn't believe she was doing this. But desperate times called for desperate measures. Pretending to be dating Jack was a tiny white lie; it wouldn't hurt anyone.

He was really great to suggest this ruse. When was the last time she'd met a decent guy like him? Definitely not any of the men her mother had tried to fix her up with. Certainly not Thad, her ex-fiancé. Thad had barely ever asked how her day had been, so he would never have stepped in to do something as gallant as this.

She eyed Jack now. Damn, he was handsome. No, she

thought. *Handsome* wasn't the right word. More like... *attractive* and *kind*. She only hoped she wasn't taking advantage of him.

She might not know him well yet, but she could tell he wasn't the type to offer something when he didn't want to do it. Besides, it wasn't like Jack was the only one getting something out of this bargain. She was happy to help Jack with his bar. And she would see to it that the place became a success.

"Emerson? You okay?"

"Yes." His question pulled her out of her thoughts. "Sorry. I'll be there tonight and tell you absolutely everything there is to know about me."

Apparently satisfied, Jack nodded. "Okay. Good luck."

Emerson crouched down to say goodbye to Cosmo, and then she rose and took a step toward the shop, anxious to get out of the overbearing wedding gown. She couldn't imagine wearing something like this for her special day.

Before she reached for the door, she turned back, looking over her shoulder. Jack hadn't moved. He was standing on the sidewalk, watching her. He was making sure she really was okay.

"Rose," she said spontaneously.

Jack tilted his head in question.

"My middle name is Rose."

He grinned and her knees felt weak. "See you tonight, Emerson Rose Dewitt. And for the record, I think you make a really beautiful bride."

Their eyes met and she had to work hard to hold back a shiver. Finally, Jack broke the gaze and retreated down the street, with Cosmo trotting alongside him. Emerson placed a hand on her stomach, willing the fluttering to subside.

When she pushed through the front door and entered the shop, she still didn't feel calm. All she could think about was Jack. But a few seconds later, the sound of her mother's voice broke the spell.

"Emerson, finally." Her mother let out a long, exasperated gasp. "Where in the world have you been?" She rushed toward Emerson, wearing a tailored mauve pantsuit; her makeup was absolutely flawless, and every strand of hair was perfectly in place.

"I—I—I mean…"

She struggled to finish the sentence as her younger sister made a mad dash across the store. Amelia's eyes were wide and she was subtly shaking her head. "Hey, Em," she said brightly as she pushed something covertly into her hand. Emerson realized it was her cell phone. "See, Mama, I told you she was just taking a call outside."

Grateful, Emerson let out the breath she wasn't aware she'd been holding. "Right. Sorry. Business call. I didn't mean to worry you."

Her mother's narrowed gaze was almost enough to make her drop the phone and start spilling all of the details of her little alleyway adventure.

"Of course I was worried, Emerson. You're wearing a ten-thousand-dollar dress. What in the hell were you thinking stepping outside in it?"

Or flinging herself out a window. But she decided not to mention that.

"You could have gotten the hemline dirty." Beatrice Dewitt's eagle eye was already examining the dress.

"Looks fine to me," Amelia said.

Emerson took her sister in. She was wearing an elegant lace gown with cap sleeves that was straight and fitted to her flawless body. Just as she'd told Jack earlier, the two of them had the same auburn hair as their mother. But while Emerson did her best to tame her curly, shoulder-length hair, Amelia's trendy layers always seemed to float carelessly, as if someone were following her around with a wind machine.

Amelia was two years younger than Emerson, but she'd surpassed her in height before the age of ten and never looked back. Emerson topped off at a whopping five foot three on a good day, while Amelia was a stately five-nine, without heels.

Emerson had needed braces, while Amelia's teeth had been straight. During middle school, Emerson had become quite familiar with the dermatologist, while Amelia never so much as got a sweat pimple.

Amelia had twenty-twenty vision. Emerson needed glasses and contacts.

Amelia could wear anything off the rack. Emerson paid a good portion of her salary to her tailor.

Amelia had found her Prince Charming and gotten married. Emerson...

Shouldn't it have been the other way around? Didn't the law of archetypes suggest that she was supposed to be the overachiever and her younger sister was destined to be the rebel?

Emerson clutched the cell phone in her hand. The reminder that, despite all of their differences, her sister did have her back. At least that was something. And something that was a constant source of guilt.

It would be so easy to be jealous of her sister, but Amelia—her little Mia—made that next to impossible. For every success Amelia achieved, Emerson seemed to fail at something. Yet, ever since she was born, Amelia looked to her big sister with awe in her eyes, as if Emerson were the one realizing great triumphs.

And here she was, silently bitching about her curly hair and lack of height.

She mouthed *thanks* to her sister and faced their mother. "I'm sorry, Mama. Really. I just needed to take a call."

"From?" her mother asked, after her cursory examination of the wedding dress was complete.

Her palms began to sweat. "Um, just a client."

"Which client?" Her mother put her hands on her hips.

"Well, a new client, as a matter of fact."

"A new client. Way to go, Em," Amelia added. "Your event-planning business is really growing. I knew organizing that food truck festival was going to put you on the map."

She gave another grateful smile to her sister, even if Amelia didn't understand she was lying.

"Food trucks!" Her mother shook her head as her eyes rolled up to the ceiling. "Honestly, who enjoys eating from a dirty truck in the middle of the street?"

"Um, everyone?" Amelia said, with a hint of sarcasm. Emerson stifled a laugh. "Did you see how many people attended the festival? It was epic."

"Thanks, Mia," Emerson said gratefully.

"So, who is this new client?" her mother asked impatiently. Clearly they were done discussing food trucks.

"Um, well…" She almost wiped her hands on the dress until she luckily remembered that sweat stains on a ten-thousand-dollar dress probably wouldn't help her mother sell it.

"Well, what?" her mother said. "Honestly, Emerson, I can't believe you are twenty-eight years old and still stuttering."

I don't stutter. Emerson jutted her chin out. She'd been accused of stuttering since she was a little girl, when in reality she sometimes needed a second.

"My new client is a bar. They want to reinvigorate the place. The Wright Drink, over on King Street," she supplied. If she presented Jack as a client, it wouldn't seem so random when she introduced him to the family as her boyfriend, at the anniversary party.

"Don't we share the alley with that bar?" her mother asked.

Emerson blinked. "The alley? Um, I don't know. Why would I know that?"

"Are you okay?" Amelia asked, with true concern in her eyes.

Emerson's mouth was dry, her heart was beating a mile a minute and she was beginning to feel that same overwhelming feeling that caused her to launch herself out of a window earlier. She didn't know if it was because she was still wearing the dreaded wedding dress or because she hated lying to anyone, let alone her family.

"Yep, great. I'd like to get out of this getup though."

"Let me at least get a look at you two first," her mother said as her keen eye raked over her daughters, no doubt taking in every detail.

Emerson and her sister stood side by side as their mother did a circle. She stopped to dust something off the back of Emerson's dress, and Emerson prayed that she didn't notice the wrinkles from her fall, or any smudges she might've missed. If Jack hadn't been there with his club soda, not to mention being there to catch her in the first place...

She closed her eyes and remembered the feel of his strong arms around her. And the way he smiled at her from behind the bar.

I think you make a really beautiful bride.

"What's that smile about?" Amelia asked.

Emerson snapped to attention. "Uhhh..."

"Emerson, you're all flushed." Beatrice did that universal mother move of pressing her hand to the forehead. "Are you coming down with something?"

"No, just warm in this monstrosity of a dress," she covered. Emerson really hoped she didn't reek of beer or any of the gross alley smells. She took a step back just in case.

"That monstrosity of a dress is going to be a bestseller. I know it." She took another moment to collect her thoughts. "Just as I thought. Amelia, that dress is prefect for a body shape like yours. Plus it comes in white, ivory, and blush. Customers will like that. I wish I could use you in the ad campaign. Everyone would want to wear this."

Emerson couldn't stifle an eye roll.

"And Emerson…"

"I know, I know. I look like a little kid playing dress up." Emerson sighed and steeled herself for the critique.

Her mother scrutinized her for a moment before stepping forward. She pushed a curl behind Emerson's ear. "I know this dress is not your personal style, but I was going to say you look beautiful." She leaned closer and whispered, "Maybe one day you'll realize just how beautiful."

Her throat tightened.

Jack told her she'd looked beautiful, and now her mother had too. But there was one person who had never said that. It was no wonder he'd left her at the altar. Why had she even been surprised?

Stepping back, Beatrice said, "Although, now that you mention it, when you slouch like that, you do look like a nine-year-old. Stand up tall, with your shoulders back. Like your sister."

Once again, discomfort overtook her. She pulled at the dress. "I should change. Amelia, can you help me?" She didn't wait for a response. Instead she pulled her sister through the store, past the racks of tulle, beading, lace, and organza. She ignored the shelves of sparkly tiaras and the glass cases filled with elegant jewelry. She didn't stop until she was locked firmly in the dressing room with her sister.

"I really need to get out of this dress." She began pulling and tugging, trying to figure out how to get it off her.

"Okay, okay, calm down." Amelia was behind her, quickly undoing the buttons.

When she was finally freed from the cumbersome dress, Emerson let out a long sigh. She crumbled down to the chair in her strapless bra and nude panties. For good measure, she took another long inhale of breath.

"Thanks for covering for me out there, Mia," she said to her sister.

"No problem. But, Em, what in the hell happened? Where did you go? What's wrong?"

I hate weddings. I hate wedding dresses. But most of all, I hate that Thad made me hate weddings and wedding dresses.

Emerson wanted to tell her sister. But the words were stuck in her throat.

"Is this because of Thad?" Amelia asked in a quiet voice.

She really should give her sister more credit. Emerson nodded. "Kind of."

Amelia pointed at her. "I knew it. I told Mama not to have you come in today. I told her you weren't ready for this."

"You and Mama talked about me?"

"Of course," she said, as if they talked about her all of the time. "Mama disagreed. She thinks you're ready to start dating again."

Emerson saw her own horrified face reflected back at her in the three-way mirror. It wasn't that she didn't want to date. More, she knew her mother would have a list of suitors lined up, each suckier than the last.

"Maybe you should start getting out there again," Amelia offered. "I mean, your wedding—"

"Nonwedding, you mean," Emerson said.

"Sorry, Em. Your nonwedding was over a year ago. Have you been out with anyone since Thad?"

She shook her head. Amelia's eyes filled with sadness. That look was enough to have Emerson popping up and grabbing her jeans and the red blouse she'd worn when she had first arrived at the shop. She dressed quickly, threw her hair back in a ponytail and faced her sister. "I'm fine. Don't worry."

"But, Em, I, uh, get it. I do. I mean, with me and Charlie…"

She didn't let Amelia finish the thought. It was barely noon and it already felt like the longest day ever. The last thing she wanted to hear about was her sister's perfect husband and even more ideal marriage. Instead she headed toward the front of the store, ready to bid her mother farewell and get back to work. Only, her mother had other ideas.

"Oh Emerson, before you go, I wanted to tell you that my friend Suzette—you remember her, right?" She didn't wait for Emerson's answer. "Suzette is having a dinner party next week and her son will be there. He's just recently moved back from New York. He's a year older than you."

Emerson froze. "Um, I have to work that night."

Beatrice squinted. "I haven't told you what day it is." She waved her hand nonchalantly. "Doesn't matter. Also, Patty Ellington-Ross's nephew is available and I thought it would be nice for you to show him around town. After all, Patty did attend your wedding. Or she tried to."

Emerson didn't know which part of that statement pissed her off the most.

Amelia jumped in. "Mama, I actually have a guy that I think would be perfect for Em. He works with Charlie."

Emerson knew her sister was trying to help her, attempting to get their mother off her back. But she honestly couldn't tell if Amelia really did want to set her up or not.

"I don't need anyone to set me up on dates," she said.

"Of course you do." Her mother waved a hand in a flippant manner. "You haven't been on a date since Thad."

She took a deep breath. "Actually, I'm seeing someone," she shouted.

Her mother and Amelia both paused, with their eyes going wide.

"Why didn't you tell me?" Amelia asked.

At the same time, her mother said, "Who is he? What's his name?"

Now she'd really done it. She had wanted to keep Jack out of this for as long as possible. But it looked like she would have to move up the timeline. At least, she could probably keep her family away from him until the anniversary party. They should be happy enough to simply know of his existence.

"His name is Jack Wright and we haven't been seeing each other very long." She glanced at the time on her cell phone display. A whole hour had passed since she'd landed on top of Jack.

"Jack Wright," her mother rolled the name around on her tongue, the same way her father savored a good bourbon.

"Right. I didn't tell you about him because the whole thing is still so new. You know, I didn't want to jinx anything."

Her mother folded her arms across her chest.

Emerson felt obliged to elaborate. "Plus I was so ridiculously busy planning the food truck festival."

Her mother started tapping her foot. "What does this Jack Wright do?"

Not for the first time in her life, Emerson had to wonder why mothers insisted on putting *this* in front of people's names.

"He owns The Wright Drink, that bar I mentioned."

"A bar?" Her mother's eyebrows shot so high up her forehead, they might as well be across the Potomac River, in the District. "He's a bartender?"

"Yes, but he also owns the bar." Emerson could feel her anger rising. God forbid her boyfriend—or fake boyfriend—wasn't a lawyer, like her father and her perfect brother-in-law.

"Wait," Amelia added. "Didn't you just say that bar was a new client? You're going out with one of your clients?"

Thanks, sis. "That's how we met. He hired me. I know it's not the best idea, but I'll only be working on the bar for a limited time."

Silence fell over them. But the quiet was a mere reprieve, because the rapid-fire questions began almost immediately.

"How old is he? Where's his family from?" her mother asked.

"Is he hot?" Amelia asked.

"Where did he go to school?"

"What's he like?"

Jack was right. They totally needed to get to know each other. And fast.

"Um, um…"

"You need to bring him to dinner," her mother announced. "At the house. We should meet him."

"Why?" she screeched.

"Because it's customary for the family to get to know your boyfriend."

Amelia snorted. "Yeah, maybe in 1950. Mama, you are so old-fashioned."

Beatrice actually appeared shocked by the statement. "No, I'm not. I'm just a concerned mother, taking an interest in her daughter's life."

Amelia rolled her eyes dramatically. "Concerned? More like nosy."

"Fine, fine, I'll stay out of it completely." Beatrice tipped her nose into the air. "I won't ask either of you anything about your lives. I'll just stay on the sidelines, completely quiet."

"Sounds good to me," Emerson said.

Unfortunately, Amelia had a different reply. She put her arm around their mother's shoulders. "Mama, we would never want that."

Emerson shook her head. Her sister would never learn. She fell into their mother's traps every single time.

Seeming appeased, Beatrice said, "Thank you, darling." She kissed Amelia on the forehead. "Besides, *most people* think I'm quite modern, with impeccable taste. You know how in-demand this store is. We rarely have an opening for a fitting."

"Here we go again," Emerson said in a stage whispered to her sister, knowing exactly where this was going. "The reality show."

Beatrice put on an air of shock. "What? It's true. That network did want to film a reality show here. But I didn't want to expose our brides-to-be to that kind of public scrutiny."

Amelia snorted. "You may be on the cutting edge here at the store, but everywhere else in your life, you are so, so…"

"Southern," Emerson finished for her.

"And what is wrong with that? My mama knew every young man who courted me."

She saw Amelia biting her tongue at the use of *courted*.

"But the whole thing is so new," Emerson protested.

"Thursday night at the house. Let's see." Beatrice tapped her finger against her lips. "We'll have a filet and use my mama's china."

"Honestly, Mama, no one does stuff like that. We're eating dinner with some guy Em's dating, not the Queen of England."

"I think it's nice to put a little effort into dinner. Makes a guest feel special."

"I'm gonna throw up," Emerson announced.

Her mother narrowed her eyes. But after a long moment, she acquiesced. "Fine. We'll have chicken and dumplings."

"Yes!" Amelia pumped her fist into the air. Beatrice De-witt truly did make the best chicken and dumplings in town.

"I'll even use our normal, everyday plates. Satisfied?" She arched an eyebrow in Emerson's direction.

"But, Mama, this is all unnecessary."

"However, we are definitely eating in the dining room. I will not compromise on that." Her mother wasn't listening. She was already in full-on planning mode, filling a void left after Amelia's wedding.

"Seven o'clock, Emerson. Tell this Jack to be there. Amelia, come with me." She snapped her fingers, and with a smile to Emerson, Amelia was following their mother. "Did you remember to change the bridesmaids' dresses from pink to lavender for the Theez-Porter wedding?"

Emerson turned toward the door, feeling her heart once again beating much too quickly. She'd really done it now. If it wasn't bad enough that she'd hooked up with a fake boyfriend, she'd gotten her fake boyfriend hooked up with her family.

Chapter Four

"We've been outed."

Jack was behind the bar at The Wright Drink with Oscar, the one other bartender who had been on the payroll. They both looked at Emerson, who stood across the bar from them, wearing an exasperated expression.

"Good evening to you too." He found himself amused by her yet again.

"It's not going to be good for too long, once I tell you what I stupidly did today."

"Didn't I see you not too long ago? How many things could you have done?" He exchanged a few words with Oscar, made sure he would be fine with the five whole customers who'd come in tonight, before he walked around the bar to join Emerson. She was removing her jacket. That's when his mouth went dry.

"What?" she asked, eyeing him.

"Your outfit."

She looked down, running a hand over her cherry-red shirt and fitted jeans. "What's wrong with it?" She fidgeted, and it drew his attention to the sexy boots she had on. Tall, black leather boots that almost reached her knees.

"Nothing. It's just a lot better than the last thing I saw you in." Not to mention, her face wasn't pale and she didn't have that anxious look in her eyes. Instead it had been replaced with a wild, somewhat exasperated look.

"Oh well, anything would be an improvement over that massive white monstrosity, otherwise called a wedding dress. Cosmo, my love. Hello, handsome." At her voice, Cosmo had stirred from his bed under the bar and come out to visit, tail wagging happily. She bent to pet, and lavish attention on, the dog.

Jack had meant what he'd said to her earlier. She had looked beautiful. But she was gorgeous now too. He loved the reddish-brown color of her hair and how one curl fell right over her pretty blue eyes. And he couldn't deny that he really liked her petite, yet curvy, body. Emerson De-witt was a beauty all around.

He swallowed a lump down his overly dry throat. "Thirsty?" Because he sure as hell was.

"Sure."

"We have some iced tea, water, soda, if you're not in the mood for alcohol. Of course, we also have a fully stocked bar."

She had picked up Cosmo again and was snuggling him to her chest. "How about scotch?"

"Seriously?" he said with a laugh. Damn, the woman impressed him.

"After the day I've had, I really need one. And please go with a good one."

"You got it, boss." He gestured to Oscar, who grabbed

two glasses, even as he wore an amused expression. "How do you like it?"

"Neat."

As Oscar poured two Scotches, neat, Jack eyed her. She placed Cosmo onto the floor and scratched behind his ears. Clearly in heaven, the dog closed his eyes as his little pink tongue lolled out of his mouth.

"And I didn't forget about you. No, I didn't," she cooed. After digging in her purse, she produced a rawhide bone. "Is this okay?" she asked Jack.

Not only did Jack have no idea if it was okay for the dog, but he couldn't deny him when Cosmo was now practically doing backflips over the prospect of a treat.

"It's fine."

She made the dog sit before giving him the bone, and Jack was surprised to learn that he actually knew that command. He'd tried most of the afternoon to get the dog to do all manner of tricks. He'd gotten nothing.

He returned his attention to Emerson. "So, what's going on?"

She sighed. "The jig is up. My mother knows about you."

Jack ushered her toward one of the back corner booths. Cosmo trotted along, carrying his bone. The dog jumped up first, making himself at home between the two of them.

"I thought you weren't going to mention me for a couple of weeks?"

She took a long pull of her scotch and closed her eyes as a seductive little sound emanated from her mouth. Despite the sip of scotch he'd just taken, his throat remained dry.

"That was the plan," she said, as her eyes opened

slowly and focused on him. As if she knew where his mind had just been, she smiled slowly. Seductively.

"Anyway," she continued. "I panicked. I'm a horrible liar."

"That should be interesting, considering what we're about to do." He chuckled.

"I don't think you're grasping the severity of the situation." She pulled one leg up under her and draped her arm over the back of the booth, as the glass of scotch dangled from her fingers. It was the sexiest thing he'd ever seen.

Honestly, he'd gone through a myriad of emotions when he'd first stumbled upon her. Or, he should say, when she'd stumbled out of the window and onto him.

Jack had gone from curious to concerned, to amused. Finally, he'd had to admit that he'd also been attracted as hell. He was happy to help her out with this little ploy so that he could get some help in turn on the bar. But even if he weren't getting anything in return, he'd probably still help her. How could he say no to those light blue eyes, that pouty mouth and, okay, that sexy rack.

"Jack, are you listening to me?"

Her voice pulled him out of his musing and he hoped he hadn't been staring at her chest. "Sorry, what now?"

"I said we have to have dinner at my parents' house this Thursday. Amelia and her new husband, Charlie, will be there too."

"That's not so bad. It's just dinner."

She stared at him as if he'd just told her the Earth was flat. "This is going to be torture. You clearly have no idea what a card-carrying, mint-julep-drinking, honest-to-goodness Southern mama is like. I mean, she wanted to use her antique china for dinner."

"Is that bad?"

"It's...not right. And don't get me started on this whole

reality-show delusion she has. I mean, we showed her one episode of *Say Yes to the Dress* and she thinks she's TV-ready."

He was having a hard time keeping up with her. "What's *Say Yes to the Dress*?"

His question seemed to snap her out of her rant. "Never mind." Finally, she took a breath. "Where is your mom, by the way?"

His face fell. Even after all of this time, his heart still ached for his mom. "She died when I started high school."

"Oh Jack."

She reached over and placed her hand over his. The shock of her skin on his was immediate and electric. He'd never experienced anything like this sensation before—not with any woman he'd ever met before. Her fingers curled around his hand and squeezed. He might as well have eaten a big bowl of chicken noodle soup. His entire inside warmed.

"Thanks. It was tough, but it was a long time ago." He knocked back more scotch, anxious to change the subject. "So, I don't understand why this dinner is going to be so terrible." He nudged her leg with his and she smiled.

"We are going to be so grilled about our 'relation-ship'—" she made little quotes with her fingers "—we might as well pierce ourselves with kabob sticks and jump on the barbecue now."

He laughed. "I don't want to be just another charred kabob, so let's tackle this problem one step at a time."

She took three calming breaths, put her scotch on the coffee table and then placed her hands primly on her lap. "First, we need to get to know each other."

That was easy enough, he thought. Plus he'd like to get to know more about the intriguing Emerson Rose Dewitt. "How about a rapid-fire Q and A session? I'll go first," he said, without waiting for her to respond. "I already know your middle name. Mine is Martin, after my grandfather. What's your favorite color?"

"Pink," she said with a nod. Then she jerked forward. "No, purple. Well, it used to be pink, but I really do like purple more. My bedroom's purple. I suppose you would know that if we were really dating and you weren't just my fake boyfriend. Although, you should definitely not tell my father that you know the color of my bedroom."

"Emerson, breathe. There are no right or wrong answers here. If you don't have a favorite color, that's not a big deal. How about favorite movie?"

He waited for her to name a typical chick flick. *The Proposal*, *Love Actually*, something with Ryan Gosling in it.

"*Die Hard*," she said definitively.

He almost choked on his scotch. Instead he got up and retrieved a bowl of pretzels from the bar. She took one and he did the same.

"You?" she asked.

"*Star Wars*, any of the original trilogy. Favorite kind of food?"

"Italian definitely," she said with a mouthful of pretzel.

"Me too," he admitted. "Eggplant parm?"

"Totally," she said, and then licked her lips, drawing his attention there.

He wondered what it would be like to lean over and just take a little nibble. She would taste of scotch and sex, he was sure.

"What about women?"

He snapped to attention. "Excuse me?"

"Women?" She grinned. "You know, the sex that's opposite of yours. Girls? Girlfriends?"

Ah. "You mean did I have a lot of girlfriends?"

Her head tilted back and forth. "More like, has there been anyone special in your life. As your pretend girl-friend, that's something I should probably know."

He began tapping his foot. "There've been some women."

Emerson waited before blowing out a loud whoosh of air. "Please, stop talking. You really are a chatterbox."

Despite himself, he chuckled. "What do you want me to say?"

"I don't know. Who was your last serious girlfriend?"

"Jessica."

Again, he went silent and she waited patiently before finally saying, "Good. Now, what was the deal with Jessica?"

He was getting the idea that Emerson wouldn't let this drop, so he decided he might as well let her in.

"Jess and I dated when I was living in Vegas."

"Ohh, Vegas. Fun. What did you do there?"

"I learned to play cards in my dad's bar as a kid. All kinds of different games. But I had a real talent for poker. At one point, I was hanging out in Europe and met this guy from Vegas. He convinced me to come back to the States with him. We returned to his hometown and I entered my first official poker tournament."

"Did you win?" she asked.

"I won that first tournament and kept winning for a long time." In the meantime, he made a killing and acquired quite the impressive nest egg.

"I liked playing, but I got a little bored after a while. I had gotten to know the owners of different casinos. One of them hired me on. I started as a poker dealer and ended up moving up to this job where I analyzed the workings of the casino and the flow of employees. I tried to build shifts around the busiest times."

"Cool job."

"It was," he agreed. "That's where I met Jess. She was a blackjack dealer. A good one. Very sassy and straightforward."

"How long did you date?"

"About a year." He would have seen her longer, only...

"Why did you break up?" Emerson asked intuitively.

He shrugged. Jack really didn't like talking about breakups. He'd much rather talk about baseball, traveling, beer, the national debt. Anything.

But Emerson nailed him with an expectant stare.

"There was a period where I was working long hours. It didn't leave much time for a social life. But it was a temporary experience. I thought she understood that."

Emerson nodded once, soundly. "She didn't."

Again, he shrugged. "I found her in a compromising position with a guy who worked in guest services."

She frowned. "I'm sorry. It must have been really hard to work together after that."

It would have been. But no way would Jack stick around after that hurt. He'd really liked Jess. Found himself opening up to her in a way he hadn't with any other woman who'd been in his life. She was funny and smart. She could throw a football better than he could and she made a mean chocolate pie.

Then she betrayed him. It stung. Badly.

"I picked up and moved," he said.

"Because of the breakup?"

"Mainly. I headed to Tahoe and found work there."

Emerson cocked her head. It seemed like she wanted to say something. He was actually curious about her thoughts. But in the end, she remained quiet.

They continued going over their likes and dislikes.

Unimpressed and finished with his bone, Cosmo curled up on the booth and went to sleep.

An hour later, Jack ordered a pizza. Normally, there was a cook in the back who made the typical bar foods: nachos, chicken tenders, burgers, mozzarella sticks and the like, but he was on vacation this week. Jack was thrilled when Emerson agreed to a supreme pie with the works. He was even more impressed when he watched her take a big bite into her first slice. Most women he'd met were less voracious in their appetite. At least in front of a man. But he liked to see a woman who could eat.

While he went for a third slice, Emerson told him she liked country music, especially anything by Blake Shelton. In fact, he would venture a guess that Blake Shelton was her big celebrity crush by the way she blushed when she talked about him.

"I stayed in Virginia for college and went to William & Mary." She frowned.

"What's with the look? Didn't like college?"

"Oh no, I loved it. It's just that, well, both of my parents went to Clemson. They weren't thrilled when I picked William & Mary."

Jack sat back. He was impressed she even got into that school and couldn't imagine that her parents weren't too.

"My sister ended up going to Clemson, so that made them happy," she said softly.

"Emerson," he began, leaning forward. "You should be incredibly proud of where you went to school."

Her eyes widened. "Oh I am. It's just that…" She trailed off as she raised her hands and then let them fall into her lap. "It doesn't matter."

But clearly it did. Something about her family dynamic was off and Jack was curious to learn more.

"Anyway," she continued, "After college, I worked for

a large event-planning firm. I really love all of the details and nitty-gritty of planning an event. Eventually I started doing my own events on the side and found that I didn't need a hundred-person office behind me. Plus I had a ton of contacts. So I started my own business. I work with a lot of mom-and-pop businesses, nonprofits and other outfits that need help planning events but don't necessarily have huge checkbooks."

Jack liked the way her face lit up as she discussed her company.

Another thing to be in awe of, in his opinion. She was beautiful, smart, funny, had attended a great school and owned a business. She was a catch and he had to wonder why she wasn't taken already.

"Damn, this pizza's good." She sat back, with a satisfied smile on her face.

"Glad you like it. Tony's is the best. Wish they could serve it here in the bar."

Her eyes lit up. "Why can't they?"

"What do you mean?"

"For the reopening party. I can ask the owner of Tony's if they'd cater. That shouldn't be too hard to organize. Actually, they might even be willing to make a deal with you and deliver you a certain amount of pizzas a night to sell."

He liked the idea. A lot. "So…you could do that?"

"Totally," she said nonchalantly. "I know the owner. I brought some business his way. I planned an office holiday party last year and had them go to Tony's, where they made their own pizzas and had a party. It was really fun."

Emerson dabbed her mouth with her napkin before folding it and placing it on her empty plate. "Now that we've brought up The Wright Drink, we really should discuss the bar a little more." She gestured around the room.

"Ah, the bar…"

It wasn't that he hated the bar. He had some good memories from the place when he was growing up. His mom taking him there to visit his dad, sitting on the barstools and spinning around and around until he got sick, and eating more bar nuts than was probably healthy for a kid.

"Your dad left you the place."

"Surprisingly," he muttered. Her eyebrow lifted. "I didn't expect it."

"He never mentioned it? Consulted with you?"

Jack shook his head. Why hadn't he mentioned it? Or even asked if that was something Jack wanted to do. His father's lack of communication was something that had forever troubled him about their relationship—and was something he'd never be able to go back and fix. He cleared his throat. "Not a word. He also hadn't told me it had fallen on hard times."

"Well, don't worry. We're going to fix that."

Guilt built up. He knew he needed to make sure Emerson understood the full story.

"Listen, Emerson, about the bar..."

"Yes?"

"I might sell it."

Her face fell. "What? Why? That a shame. It's such a great space."

At that moment, Cosmo let out a loud snore. With his eyes firmly shut, he turned over, onto his back, exposing every part of himself to the room.

Emerson glanced at the dog and then turned her big blue eyes on him in shock. "What about Cosmo?"

Jack gulped and shook his head.

"You're not going to keep him?"

"Honestly, I don't know." He scrubbed a hand over his face. "I didn't even know about him until this morning."

He leaned forward, propping his elbows on his thighs. "My life… Well, I don't know what I want to do next. Or where I want to go. Dogs need consistency, routine."

Emerson's eyes were wide and filled with worry.

"I would make sure Cosmo had a good, stable home before I left. I'm not a monster. I'm just not sure that I want to run a bar. That I would even be very good at it."

"I bet you would," she said confidently.

"What makes you say that?"

"I'm not sure. I mean you definitely have the customer-service experience from your time working in casinos. But, more importantly, you grew up watching your dad. That was probably the best preparation."

He never thought of it that way. "I suppose so. But in any case, I want to fix it up. I'm either going to stay and need a good overhaul so I can reclaim some business and get back into the black, or I'll make it attractive enough to interest a potential buyer. It's prime real estate on King Street."

"True."

She seemed sad at this news, so Jack tried to change the subject. "Speaking of King Street and Old Town, so much has changed. There are so many new restaurants and bars and shops."

"When was the last time you were home?"

"Five years… No, more than that." Jack tried to remember. He'd been busy. But doing what? Roaming the world, working in casinos, playing poker, shirking from responsibility of any kind. "I wasn't a very good son."

Whoa. Where had that comment come from? Emerson's eyes locked on to his. Kindness emanated from them.

"Why do you say that?" she asked.

He ran a hand through his hair. "I didn't come home very often. I didn't call as much as I should have."

"I think most people feel that way about their parents."

Agitated, he stood and walked toward one of the front windows. The customers had dwindled down to two, and they were both engrossed in the basketball game on TV.

Emerson had risen, as well, and joined him near the window.

"I was off doing my own thing. Kind of selfish."

The sun had set and shadows fell over King Street. White twinkly lights were strung in all the trees that lined the street. He saw his reflection in the glass, a reflection that showed a mixture of guilt and regret.

"How can you say that?" she asked. "What's selfish about living your life? Doing your own thing? That's what you're supposed to do." She walked closer. "I wish I had done a little more of that," she said quietly.

Jack continued to stare out at the glittering lights and all of the people dashing to different shops and restaurants. "My dad used to make me Shirley Temples," he said suddenly. He hadn't known the name of his favorite drink when he'd been a kid. He'd called them the "cherry drink" because his dad always added extra cherries in his.

"I realize now how sweet those drinks are. But man, to a ten-year-old, they were the best."

He shifted his weight. "Had my first real drink here too. A beer with the old man. He'd seemed proud to give it to me. A real moment, you know? It was after we won the championship in baseball."

Without warning, a feeling so strong and so potent took over. Grief, pure and simple, filled his entire being. The air thickened around him and he placed his head against the cool glass of the window.

Jack didn't know how long he stood there. But at some point, he felt Emerson's arms wind around him. She pressed her body against his, hugging him tightly.

Her scent, which he'd already come to know, enveloped him, wrapping him in a hug that smelled like flowers and spring.

She didn't say anything, and he was grateful. He reached down and squeezed her hands, trying to convey his gratitude. Until tonight, he'd had no one to really let go with. Funny how a runaway bride with family issues could help him gain a little perspective. He wasn't alone. Not anymore. At least, not for the next month.

Thanks to Emerson.

He turned to face her. Her head tilted, and she met his gaze head-on.

There were a lot of things Jack Wright didn't know at the moment. What he would do with the bar, whether he would stay in town or once again go off seeking more adventures, or why his father left him the bar to begin with. But the one thing that he knew for damn sure was that he wanted to kiss Emerson more than anything.

His gaze dropped to her full lips, watched them part in anticipation. Heard her intake of breath. Saw her chest rise and fall as her fingers slowly curled around his hips.

He began to lean toward her, but as he did, his phone rang shrilly. He groaned, and Emerson let out a tentative laugh.

The moment was over.

"I'm sorry," he said, with his voice sounding raspy.

She shook her head and backed up. "No, I'm sorry. We shouldn't… I mean…ah, your phone is still ringing."

He frowned. "Right."

Jack begrudgingly took the call, which turned out to be from his attorney. While he talked, he noticed Emerson walking back to their booth, petting Cosmo, and then gathering her coat and purse. By the time he got Fred off the phone, Emerson was standing by the front door.

"Leaving?"

"I think I have to."

"I'm sorry, Emerson. I think we got carried away back there."

"Listen, Jack, we're already up to our eyeballs in this whole thing. It's probably not a good idea—"

But he couldn't let her finish that thought. "I liked what happened back there."

She blinked. "You did?"

"Didn't you?" he countered. She blushed, and he thought the extra color in her cheeks was adorable. He reached for her hand. "And thank you for listening. It was nice to have someone. To talk to, I mean."

His words seemed to do the trick and got rid of her nerves.

"I'm glad. Your turn to be there for me next, on Thursday night. We have one uncomfortable family dinner to look forward to."

Jack watched Emerson walk out the door and head up the street. He waited until she'd turned the corner. He'd meant what he'd said. He did appreciate her being there for him tonight. In no way had he expected to break down like that.

Of course, there was also that kiss. Or almost-kiss. That had been unexpected, as well.

As Jack walked back into the bar, he had a feeling that the uncomfortable family dinner was going to be a hell of a lot more awkward than he'd bargained for.

Chapter Five

"Are you nervous? Don't be nervous."

Jack tore his eyes away from the large two-story brick mansion to look at Emerson, who was sitting in the front seat of his truck, in a forest-green dress and those same sexy boots she'd worn the other night. Her hair was swept away from her face, drawing his attention to the long column of her neck.

"You look beautiful," he said.

"What? Oh. Well, thank you," she spluttered. The catch of words was better than the nervous chatter he'd been witnessing since he'd picked her up at her townhouse in Old Town, and drove the twenty minutes to her parents' swanky neighborhood, down the George Washington Parkway, near Mount Vernon. She folded her hands in her lap and he noticed her nails were painted a bright red. "You're not nervous?" she asked.

He covered her hands with one of his and squeezed. "Em, I'm not nervous. We're just having dinner with your family." He turned off the truck and looked back at her. "Is it okay for me to call you Em?"

She smiled. "My sister and my best friend call me Em. Maybe we should have cute nicknames for each other. What do you think, schmoopie?"

He stifled an eye roll. "You know, I'm okay with Jack."

She laughed. "You got it, cupcake." Her smile faded, and she pressed a hand to her stomach. "Why am I so anxious?"

"I'm really not sure, honey bear." He was glad to see her lips twitch at that. "We have a solid and semi-true story. You were hired to help me with some events at the bar. We quickly got together. If we get into any trouble, we fall back on the fact that we haven't known each other all that long."

"Well, that part is true enough." She glanced at the house. "Okay, let's do this."

Jack grabbed her hand as they got out of the car and walked toward the door. As soon as their fingers intertwined, he felt that thing again. That electric buzzing that seemed to surface any time he touched her. But he had no time to dwell on it, because the front door opened and a tall man with dark hair that was graying at the temples appeared. He pinned Jack with an overtly assessing stare. But then his gaze fell on Emerson, and a warm and adoring smile broke out on his otherwise serious face.

"Hi, sweetheart." His arms opened, and Emerson walked into them.

"Hi, Daddy." She leaned back and put her hands on his chest, tapping her fingers against the golf shirt that Jack knew was one of the more expensive brands. "You look nice."

"Thank you. Your mother wanted me to stay in my suit."

He rolled his eyes and Jack realized he had the same eyes—and same eye roll—as his daughter.

"I wear a suit to the office all week. Why would I want to wear one for dinner in my own home?"

"Daddy's a lawyer," Emerson explained. Then she made the introductions. "This is Jack Wright. Jack, my father, Walter Dewitt."

"Sir," he said and shook the man's hand.

"Nice to meet you, Jack. Come on in. Your mother has been fussing over everything since you told her about Jack a couple of days ago. But don't tell her I said that." He winked, and Emerson grinned.

Jack stepped into an impressive foyer, complete with a grand staircase that wound its way up both sides of the room, to the second floor. A large crystal chandelier hung from the high ceiling. He noticed a very formal living room to one side and a dining room that probably seated at least twenty on the other. While his dad's house was more about comfort, Emerson's family home appeared to be for show.

"Your house is really nice," he said.

Mr. Dewitt looked around and shrugged. "It's all Beatrice's doing. To be honest, I'd prefer a nice little cabin on a lake. Somewhere I could fish all day and relax on a rocking chair at night."

His preference surprised Jack.

"I've been married for thirty years. The best advice I can give you is to agree. The key to a happy marriage is appeasing the Mrs."

"I'll remember that," Jack said, amused.

"I'm going to find Mama. Daddy, you're in charge of Jack. Make sure he doesn't get lost," Emerson said and then disappeared around the corner.

Mr. Dewitt turned to Jack. "Do you fish, son?"

"I do. I haven't been in a while, which is a shame. I

spent some time up in Canada a couple of years ago. Did a lot of ice fishing."

Mr. Dewitt raised his brow. "No kidding. I'd like to hear more about that."

"Daddy," a woman's voice bellowed from one of the back rooms. "Bring Jack in here so I can meet him."

"Amelia, stop screaming in the house," another female voice said.

"Speaking of the Mrs.," Mr. Dewitt said with a smile. "I think it's time for your inquisition. Are you ready?"

Honestly, the grand foyer threw him off a bit. But he was here for Emerson and he was determined to remain level-headed and calm. "I feel pretty confident."

Mr. Dewitt slapped him on the back. "Good for you." He stopped walking before they could turn the same corner Emerson had rounded. "Before we go back, I just want to say that it's great to see Emerson dating again. After what happened last year, I've been worried about her."

Jack paused. What happened last year? Something fairly serious, if the lines in Mr. Dewitt's face had anything to say about it. He'd have to ask Emerson later.

"Uh, yeah." He treaded lightly.

"Nice to have that twinkle back in her eyes."

"Right. Last year was, well…"

"Exactly," Walter nodded before a shadow fell over his face. "If I ever see that little pri—"

"Walt," a female voice called.

"Coming." Walter's features returned to normal and Jack followed him into the kitchen.

"Smells amazing," Jack said. The distinctive aroma of chicken, veggies and buttery biscuits wafted from the large stovetop and stainless-steel oven.

"Thank you."

Turning, Jack found himself face-to-face with Beatrice

Dewitt. The woman was stunning. She had the same color of hair as Emerson, but hers was pulled back into some kind of twist. She wore a frilly pink-and-white apron over khaki slacks and a crisp white blouse. Despite the casual clothing, everything about her was completely together and pristine. From her manicured nails to her impeccable makeup. But most noticeable was the confidence and self-assurance in the way she carried herself. There was no denying that she was the one in charge in this house.

"For you." Jack offered the bouquet of flowers he'd brought.

"How nice," another woman with auburn hair said. "I'm Amelia, Emerson's sister." They shook hands. "Meet my husband, Charlie." She gestured to the man in the corner, who was preoccupied with his cell phone. "Babe, come meet Em's new boyfriend."

Charlie nodded toward Jack in greeting.

"Babe, get off the phone," Amelia said, with her cheeks blushing red. She turned to Jack but didn't meet his eyes. "Charlie works so hard. It's tough to get him to take a break."

"It's good to have a husband who works hard to provide for his family." Mrs. Dewitt said before she turned her trained eye on Jack. "Speaking of work…"

"Mama, give the man a second to catch his breath before we start with that."

"I simply want to get to know this man who has appeared out of nowhere, into your life. Is that so wrong? We had all known Charlie for years before he started dating Amelia. They had a proper courting."

"Mama, no one says courting in the twenty-first century," Amelia said, with a final glance at her husband, who'd retreated even farther into the shadows.

"Jack, can I get you a drink?" Mr. Dewitt asked.

"Sure, thanks."

"I'll have a beer," Emerson said.

An annoyed sound escaped Mrs. Dewitt. "We don't have any beer. Walt, get her the same wine Amelia is drinking."

"I don't want—"

"How about a tour?" Jack said suddenly, cutting Emerson off. Emerson shot him a grateful smile.

"Babe," Amelia said. "Babe," she repeated louder.

"Leave him," Emerson said and grabbed her sister's hand. "We don't need Charlie to show Jack around. Come on, everyone. The tour leaves from the kitchen. Keep your hands and feet inside the train. No photography please."

"Unless you're from *Southern Living*," Amelia whispered, and Emerson laughed.

As Emerson and her sister gave Jack a tour of the sprawling house, he came to a few conclusions. The first was that he wouldn't be surprised if he did see this house on the pages of *Southern Living*. Each room was practically photo-shoot ready. Pillows were fluffed, tables were polished and vases were overflowing with flowers.

The second thing he noticed about the Dewitt home was that it was clear Amelia had grown up here. He noticed pictures, trophies and other memorabilia. What he did not see was the same attention for Emerson.

They walked into a family room, toward the back of the house. Despite the size of the place, Jack had been feeling somewhat claustrophobic. This was the first room that actually made him feel welcomed. There were also more personal items here.

He stepped up to a large shelf that held trinkets and framed pictures. Jack took in a photo with a little redhead wearing a tiara and holding a huge bouquet of roses. He chuckled. "Who's this? You?" he asked Emerson.

"No, that's me," Amelia said.

"Amelia used to do pageants." Emerson peered at the photo closer. "She was about five in that one."

"Did you do pageants too?" he asked, putting the frame down. "Were you Little Miss Alexandria?"

Amelia let out a very unladylike snort.

"Thanks for that," Emerson said, elbowing her sister. "I tried. And by 'I tried,' I mean Mama had me entered in pageants before I could even eat solid food. But it became clear pretty fast that runways and posing wasn't really my thing."

"How come?"

"Let's just say I wasn't quite as graceful as my sister."

Amelia put an arm around her sister. "She fell off a stage, right onto the judges' table. Mama was horrified."

"Thank God she had a second daughter."

The two sisters were laughing, but Jack sensed something sad underneath the jokes. He eyed another photo of a cheerleader waving pompoms over her head. "Amelia again?" he asked.

"Yep, I cheered all through middle and high school."

Jack quirked an eyebrow at Emerson.

"Nope," she said. "I tried out a couple of times. But I never made the squad." She smiled but it didn't reach her eyes. After turning back to the shelf, she tapped another frame. "And this is Amelia being crowned homecoming queen."

Jack thought he was getting the lay of the land. "Amelia, what do you do now?"

"I work in Mama's store."

Aha. So Amelia, the pageant-winning, cheerleading homecoming queen, worked with her mother, while Emerson, the non-poised, pom-pom-less black sheep, had started her own business. Interesting.

Jack grabbed another frame and studied it. He couldn't contain the smile. Emerson's perfume alerted him to her nearness before he realized she was peering around his shoulder.

"Ugh, don't look at that." She snatched the photo away. "I look so ugly in that one."

Amelia reached for the picture. "No, you don't. You're so hard on yourself, Em." She returned the photo and took another. "This is my favorite picture of Em." She thrust it at Jack.

Jack saw the two sisters. Emerson was wearing a cap and gown, and Amelia had on a flowered dress. Emerson was sticking her tongue out, while Amelia was making a funny face at the camera.

"Your college graduation was so much fun. Remember the party?"

Emerson giggled. "After we dropped off Mama and Daddy at the hotel and claimed we were going to bed."

They both made a weird noise at the exact same time and then did a little dance, clearly reminiscing about some shared memory.

Jack could tell they really loved each other. Beatrice and Walter Dewitt were incredibly lucky their two daughters got along. Jealousy could have easily pervaded their relationship.

"Jack. Girls. Dinner is ready," Mr. Dewitt said from the doorway.

Jack followed everyone into the formal dining room. His mouth watered at the sight of chicken and dumplings, although he had to admit he couldn't remember the last time he'd eaten in a formal dining room, with candles and flowers.

"Jack, want to help me pick some music?" Mr. Dewitt asked.

Jack walked over to the side of the room, where he was surprised to find a record player and a shelf filled with vinyl records. He perused the collection. "Now, this is impressive."

He clapped Jack on the back jovially. "Some people think my selection is old."

"Nothing wrong with oldies," Emerson said before she and her sister started doing a little dance as Amelia sang "Here Comes the Sun."

"No respect for the best music of all time," Mr. Dewitt said. But he was smiling as he watched his girls joking. "I'm telling you, this was music. I can't even categorize what you people listen to now."

Jack and Mr. Dewitt went through the records, while Mrs. Dewitt and her daughters brought the food in. Jack loved seeing the album covers from the Beatles, The Mamas & the Papas, and other groups from the sixties and seventies. They ended up choosing an album of Chicago's music.

"Amelia, where's Charlie?" Mrs. Dewitt asked.

"Oh he said he needed to make one more call. We should go ahead and start though."

Mr. Dewitt said grace and they all dug in. The food was delicious, the wine was amazing and the conversation flowed. Charlie eventually made his way in, but even Jack could tell he wasn't giving anyone his full attention. Charming guy, he thought.

"We're sorry to hear about your father's passing, Jack," Mrs. Dewitt offered. "Emerson explained that it happened recently."

"Yes, and quite suddenly. Thank you for the condolences."

"I understand he left you The Wright Drink. I used to pop in there," Mr. Dewitt added.

"When?" Mrs. Dewitt asked, with eyes narrowed.

"Quite frequently actually. I didn't know your father well, but he was always kind and a great bartender. The bar is only a couple of blocks from my office. It's over on Washington."

Mrs. Dewitt leaned forward. "And what were you doing before you became the owner of a bar?" She said *bar* the way some people might say *serial killer*.

"A lot of different things actually. I traveled quite a bit after college."

Mrs. Dewitt eyed him over the rim of her wineglass, and Jack had the distinct impression that she knew exactly what he'd been doing. Nothing. Floundering as he traveled the world, trying to find himself. Staying away from Alexandria and not helping his father.

Of course, he wouldn't say any of that. "The last place I lived was Tahoe. I was working for one of the casinos. I was a floor manager."

Apparently this career didn't please Mrs. Dewitt. She remained still.

But Amelia popped up. "I adore Tahoe. What a fantastic place."

"You've been?" Jack asked.

She nodded. "A couple of times actually. I've competed in several pageants on the West Coast."

Finally, Mrs. Dewitt smiled. "Amelia was a top competitor on the beauty-pageant circuit. She always placed."

Jack didn't really know what that meant. "And Emerson? What was your thing?"

"Emerson didn't really have a thing," Mrs. Dewitt said.

"I played soccer," Emerson said quietly. "And I was a good student."

Ignoring her daughter, Mrs. Dewitt continued. "Amelia seemed to get all of the performing talent in the family. She probably could have kept competing too. But she opted for college instead. Of course, you enjoyed your time with your sorority sisters, didn't you, sweetie?"

Amelia shifted in her chair. "Um, actually…"

"Emerson didn't get into a sorority."

"That's probably because I didn't even pledge one," Emerson said quietly. "It wasn't my thing."

"It's a shame, that's what it is," Mrs. Dewitt said. "You could have gotten into any sorority you pledged. You would have made a wonderful Kappa."

Emerson rolled her eyes. "I didn't want to be a Kappa. Or a member of any other sorority," she added. "Just like I didn't want to compete in beauty pageants."

"You could have done really well in pageants." Mrs. Dewitt took a delicate sip of her wine.

Emerson, her sister and Mr. Dewitt all exchanged glances before breaking out into laughter.

Mrs. Dewitt tilted her head, and her perfectly straight nose pointed in the air. "So you fell off the stage one time. I would have gotten you a coach. You could have been amazing. With all that curly hair, you would have really stuck out."

Emerson scoffed. "I think I would have stuck out because I was about half a foot shorter than most of the other contestants."

Mrs. Dewitt considered. "True. Amelia did get all of the height between the two of you."

This conversation felt very weighted in Amelia's direction. Jack felt for Emerson. He wanted to squeeze her hand or, hell, wrap her in a massive hug. But she was seated across the table from him. He'd have to try to save her another way.

"Emerson's event-planning business seems to have really taken off," he said. He noticed that Emerson had her eyes trained on her nearly empty plate. "I can't believe she put that food truck festival together single-handedly. People are still raving about it. And it's brought a lot of business to the area." She gave him a grateful look and he winked at her.

Mrs. Dewitt waved a hand. "Yes, yes. But why people want to eat food from a truck is beyond me. I prefer a nice crisp salad."

"There are food trucks that serve salads, Mama," Amelia said.

"Hmm."

"Well, I'm still impressed that Em did the whole festival," Jack said.

Beatrice picked up her wineglass and twirled it in her hand. "Emerson with her business and Amelia married and getting ready to start a family."

Jack practically heard bells and angelic chimes when she said the word *married*. In his opinion, starting a business was a hell of a lot harder than getting married. And continuing to run it alone was even ballsier.

Mr. Dewitt raised his glass. "We have two successful daughters."

Charlie, who finally tore his eyes away from his phone, although it was positioned right next to his plate, decided to weigh in on the conversation. "Totally. And personally, it's better that you and Thad didn't go through with the wedding, Emerson. He used to tell me that he didn't like the idea of you working so much and that after you were married, he would get you to slow down. Who would have managed the food truck festival then?"

It felt as if all of the energy had been zapped from the room. Everyone seemed to be looking anywhere but at each other.

Jack froze. He obviously didn't know the particulars,

but something had him holding his breath. Emerson had almost gotten married? Why didn't he know that? Because the other night he'd been so busy lamenting his relationship with Jess that he'd never asked Emerson about her past relationships.

To his credit, Charlie didn't appear to realize he'd shoved his large designer-clad foot in his mouth. He shoveled chicken and dumplings into his mouth right before he added, "I never really liked Thad. Jack seems way cooler."

Jack snuck a glance at Emerson. Her face was beet-red and her eyes held a shine, as if she were about to…cry?

Emerson's mother coughed. "Everyone stumbles from time to time. What happened last year is over," she said with a head nod.

What in the hell happened last year? Jack wanted to scream the question out. But he didn't have a chance, because Emerson had scooted her chair back, excused herself and quickly rushed from the room.

Oblivious to the awkward moment he'd created, Charlie stood as well. "I need to make a call. Be right back, babe."

Amelia let out a sigh.

Mrs. Dewitt put her wineglass down with a frown. "Maybe I should go talk to Emerson. I don't know why she gets so worked up."

Maybe because you devalue her at every turn. Maybe because she's constantly compared to her sister. Maybe because something painful happened last year and it was just thrown in her face.

But Jack kept that all to himself. Instead he rose, mumbled his excuses and left the room to find his fake girlfriend.

Emerson made her way through the house, to the patio door, and kept walking until she'd wound through her mother's extensive garden and found herself sitting in the gazebo, at the back of the property.

The air was cold and crisp. Even as it felt good on her overheated skin, she shivered, and wished she'd brought her jacket with her. Next thing she knew, someone was draping it over her shoulders.

She looked up to find Jack studying her.

"Hi," he said.

"Hi."

Emerson couldn't say more. She was too embarrassed to really go into anything. Her mother had massively humiliated her in front of Jack. Although, Emerson didn't know what was worse—that her mother had brought up her biggest failure to date or the mere fact that she'd had such a failure to begin with.

Added to that was the fact that her perfect sister hadn't been left at the church on her wedding day.

How could she compete with Amelia? She couldn't.

Jack sat down next to her on the built-in bench.

"Thanks for the coat," she said.

"No problem, schmoopie." He stretched his long legs out in front of them. "And see, you were worried that your family would know we were lying."

"Silly me."

"Are your family dinners always like that? Because, let me tell you, I'd have gotten myself adopted into a new family by now."

She tried to smile but suddenly felt too tired to put in the effort. "I should be used to it by now. It's just that my sister is so amazing."

"She's okay," Jack said. "You're more interesting."

"You don't have to say that."

"I wouldn't say it if it weren't true. Your sister basically spent her youth parading around stages and at football games. Now she works in your mom's bridal shop. And she has a husband who probably wouldn't notice if she sprouted three heads and flew away to Mars."

That got her attention. Emerson faced him. "What are you talking about?"

"Your brother-in-law is kind of a..."

"Perfect husband?" Emerson supplied. "Hard worker, good provider, top attorney?"

"I was going to say douche but sure, we can go with your words."

Emerson's mouth fell open.

"Come on, Em. We've been here for a couple of hours and he's been on his phone for most of that time. He's ignored his wife and been rude to his in-laws. My dad sure as hell would never have let him get away with that."

Charlie had been in her life for years now. Ever since he started working at her dad's firm, while he was still in law school. If she was being honest, she didn't really know much about her sister's husband, despite the fact that he'd been around for years. Jack was right. Charlie *was* a bit absent.

"I guess you're right," she said. "I'm still sorry you had to witness all of that in there." She pointed toward the house.

He scooted closer. "Well, the food was good. The drinks were great. The music was fantastic. Your parents' house is beautiful and fancy. I could have done without the post-dinner let's-make-Emerson-feel-bad conversation."

She let out a long, drawn-out sigh. "I hate disappointing people."

Jack grabbed her shoulders and turned her to face him. "What in the hell are you talking about? You haven't disappointed anyone. How could you? By not being in beauty pageants, cheerleading or a sorority? Come on."

"All of those things are important to my mother. And I was never any good. To top it off, last year…well, I probably achieved my biggest failure yet."

Jack dropped his hands. "I don't know what happened last year, but I can only tell you that I think you're amazing." He pushed an errant curl back behind her ear, and his fingers lingered for a few seconds. Emerson's breath caught in her throat.

She wondered if she should just tell him the truth. All of it. Every dirty detail about what had gone down last year. Surely Jack was curious, after everything that had been said tonight. Only, she really didn't want to talk about it. In fact, she wished she could blink her eyes and erase it from her personal history.

"You know, failing at stuff would be a lot easier if I were an only child. But there's Amelia. She's beautiful."

"You're beautiful."

Emerson shook her head. "She's smart."

Jack gently cupped her cheek with his hand. "You're smart. Really smart." His thumb traced a slow circle along her skin, eliciting shivers.

He'd moved even closer. Or maybe she'd done that. Emerson didn't know. All she could tell at the moment was that she was practically in Jack's arms and she hadn't felt this good in ages.

"Amelia doesn't mess up," she whispered.

"That's not very interesting." He lowered his head. "She's…"

"Not you," he finished. With that, Jack covered her mouth with his.

Emerson let out a surprised gasp but couldn't stop her arms from snaking around his neck. His lips were soft, but urgent, as they moved over hers. He ran his hands through her hair and emitted a satisfied sound.

She could taste the wine on his lips and smell the cologne he'd put on. And those talented lips continued to delight her. He now ran his hands up and down her back, pulling her even closer. She felt safe and warm cocooned in his arms.

While their kiss may have begun gently, even sweetly, it was beginning to pick up steam. Her mouth opened for him and she felt his tongue sweep in to tangle with hers. Her breathing was labored, and her heart rate was sky-high.

"Oops, sorry, guys."

Emerson jumped back, and Jack's eyes darted around at the sound of Amelia's voice.

"I was just making sure you were okay, but I can obviously see that you are. Sorry again."

Emerson snuck a glance at Jack. He seemed as dazed as she was. She stood, with her chest rising and falling rapidly from the exertion of the kiss.

"Um, that's okay," she told her sister, even though the interruption was pretty much as far from okay as it could get. "We should probably get back inside."

Jack looked like going inside was the worst idea ever and she almost laughed out loud. Reluctantly, he followed her as Amelia led them both through the garden.

Maybe her sister's interruption came at the perfect time. Maybe she shouldn't be kissing Jack at all. After all, their whole relationship was fake.

Only, that kiss hadn't felt fake.

Out of all of the things that had gone wrong tonight, Jack's kiss was the only thing that had felt right.

Chapter Six

Emerson had woken up with a headache the size of the National Mall.

It didn't help matters that she had berated herself from the second she got out of bed. Even while showering and getting ready for the day, she couldn't stop being annoyed with herself. The short walk from her townhouse to the local coffee shop had allowed her more time to criticize. Even during her morning meeting with a potential client, she had lost focus and begun mentally scolding herself.

She'd done a lot of irresponsible things throughout her life, but kissing Jack was possibly the dumbest, most irresponsible one of them all.

Well, maybe the second most irresponsible move, after climbing out the window of her mom's shop in that wedding dress.

Even now, as she sat at the desk in her office, all she could do was try to figure out what in the heck she'd been thinking. The two of them were already up to their eye-balls in lies and a complicated relationship. Not to mention the fact that Jack was a short-timer.

She'd certainly been disappointed the other night, when he'd revealed that he might not keep the bar. Even though he said he hadn't completely made up his mind about staying in Alexandria, she had a strong feeling that he would be out of there as soon as he could.

The worst part was that, while she rationally knew that kissing him had been beyond stupid, she couldn't stop remembering how it had felt. He was a damn good kisser. Not that she had oodles of experience, but from what she did know, he was head and shoulders above the rest.

"Hello!"

At the exasperated voice of her best friend, Grace, bellowing over the phone, Emerson finally pulled herself out of her funk.

"Sorry, Grace."

"What's with you today? Are you having second thoughts about not writing up a formal contract? Because this wedding is a really, really big deal, and I know the guest list is reaching seven hundred, and I could really use your help, and I really love you."

Emerson couldn't help but laugh. "How many *really*s did you just use?"

"Too many?"

Emerson could just see her friend now. She would be sitting behind her desk, with her long beautiful black hair perfectly styled. No doubt she was crossing her fingers, waiting on Emerson's reply.

She and Grace had met right out of college, when they had both just been starting out at a large event-planning company in DC. The work had been grueling. They'd worked long days, getting coffee for higher-ups, doing

boring tasks no one else wanted to do and bonding beyond belief. They'd become roommates and the closest
of friends.

Emerson had lasted two years before she moved on to
work for a smaller event firm; Grace had made it a few
months longer. But their friendship had endured through
all of these years. They'd lived together, until last year,
when Emerson had moved into the townhouse she was
supposed to share with her soon-to-be-husband.

After the nonwedding debacle, Thad gave her his share
of the property. He'd acted like he was doing it as a good-
will gesture. Emerson just remembered how terrified
she'd been. She couldn't afford the mortgage on a three-
story townhouse in the heart of Old Town. Not by herself. Especially after just starting a new business. But her
pride hadn't allowed her to admit that to Thad.

After a couple of terrifying weeks of thinking she
was going to have to return to working for other people,
she'd been struck with inspiration. To her delight, Thad
had never moved in, but Grace had. She was living with
Emerson and paying rent.

They'd converted the bottom floor, turning it into of-
fices. Emerson had set up shop on one side of the first
floor, and Grace, who had also started her own business
as a wedding planner, was right across the hall. The two
of them lived on the upper two levels and could boast the
best commute in the city.

Emerson glanced around her office space now. She absolutely adored it. She'd painted the walls a neutral and
calming gray tone. The floors were a light wood, large
windows faced the street and the walls were trimmed
with gorgeous crown molding that had probably been
added in the 1920s. She'd added touches of color with
a turquoise area rug and matching throw pillows on the

chairs and the small couch. She'd installed a glamorous miniature chandelier and had a dozen mirrors in various shapes and sizes on one wall, to pick up the sparkling crystals. The gray-and-turquoise curtains tied everything together. The space was clean but fun. The perfect area to talk about events and parties.

"I'm sorry, Gracie. I have a lot on my mind today."

"Say no more."

With that, the line went dead. Emerson laughed, because she knew exactly what her friend was up to. In fact, she could have timed her.

Ten minutes later, right on the dot, Grace waltzed through the front door of Emerson's office, with two coffees in hand. She handed one to Emerson, then sat in the chair reserved for clients, crossing her graceful legs and smoothing down her hair.

Grace Harris was stunning. She had thick black hair that fell well below her shoulders. Her skin was flawless, which made her gorgeous green eyes stand out. She was tall, with legs for days. She was wearing a lilac-colored wrap dress, with nude heels, and carried a plum-colored tote.

After she handed over Emerson's preferred coffee drink, she produced a white paper bag from their favorite local bakery, out of her Kate Spade tote. "Chocolate croissant?"

"God, yes," Emerson said around a happy sigh.

"I really should hate you, you know." Emerson took a large bite of the croissant. "This is so great."

Grace simply arched a dark eyebrow in response.

"I mean, look at you. You resemble a damn Disney princess. Why are you so perfect at this hour of the morning?"

Finally, Grace sat forward. "As much as I love you

gushing about me, I'm going to go out on a limb and guess that something is bothering you."

Emerson fell back against the chair and sighed. "You're perceptive too."

Grace began tapping her fabulous shoes in a quick staccato against the hardwood floors.

"I kinda did something stupid."

The toe tapping halted, and Grace waited patiently. Emerson told her about the wedding-dress freak-out.

"Wait a minute." Grace flung a finger into the air. "You climbed out of a window and into a dirty alley, wearing the new Pnina Tornai gown?"

"Guilty."

She reached inside her tote, pulled out her iPad and made a quick note. "I have got to get over to your mom's shop to see that dress. I have a bride who is going to do backflips for it."

"It wasn't very comfy."

"Of course it wasn't comfy. It costs ten thousand dollars."

Idly, Emerson wondered what a person would have to shell out for comfort. Fifteen thousand? Twenty?

"What happened next?" Grace asked.

Emerson told her everything as the two of them drank their coffee and ate their chocolate croissants. She filled her best friend in on meeting Jack—well, falling on top of Jack—the bar, the arrangement they made and the dinner at her parents' house. She told her every detail, up until their kiss.

"I can't believe your brother-in-law brought up Thad in front of Jack. Actually, I can believe it. I love your family, but man, Charlie is out of touch." Grace threw away their trash and returned to her seat. "That must have been awful though."

"It was. But then…"

Grace tilted her head. "Then what?"

"Then Jack found me outside, in the garden."

Grace leaned forward, and her eyes were sparkling. "Ohmigod."

"Grace, stop it."

Emerson loved her BFF but she knew that look. Grace was in love with love. She watched romantic comedies, read romance novels nightly and put up Valentine's Day decorations on the same day that she took down her Christmas tree. She was the most romance-loving person on the planet, and any hint of love in the air set her over the edge.

"I can just see it now." Grace's face softened, and she got that dreamy expression that Emerson knew all too well.

"And we've lost her, ladies and gentlemen," Emerson said.

"You were upset. You ran off into the garden and the cool, crisp night. You ended up at the gazebo." She quickly looked up. "The twinkly lights came on."

"There were no twinkly lights."

"There you were, under the glow of the moonlight, which cast a halo-like aura around your fabulous red hair."

"My hair is auburn."

"And then Jack came out and swept you into his arms and kissed you as the orchestra music swelled."

"I think there was a dog barking in the background."

"He did kiss you, didn't he? Tell me you guys kissed."

Emerson crinkled her nose. She wanted to hold out. She desperately wanted to keep the make-out session to herself. If, for no other reason, that she was still trying to justify her actions. But how could she resist Grace's hopeful face. She nodded.

Grace let out a squeal that only that dog from the night before could hear.

"This. Is. So. Exciting." Grace punctuated each word as she did a little dance in her chair.

"Exciting? Are you nuts?"

"You have a boyfriend!"

Emerson shook her head. "I have a pretend boyfriend, and I'm lying to my entire family about him."

"Maybe he's your soul mate. Maybe you're going to marry him. Maybe I'll get to plan your wedding." She finished with another squeal.

"I'm not thinking about marrying him, Grace. Or anyone," she quickly added. "I'm afraid I might be thinking about sleeping with him though. Ugh." She flung her head onto the desk.

"What's wrong with sleeping with him? You're both adults. Is he attractive?"

"Oh good Lord, yes. That's the problem."

"That doesn't sound like a problem to me."

"Every time I'm around him, I just want to…to…jump his bones," she finally finished.

"What's stopping you?" Grace wondered.

I'm scared. She should have been married for a year already. But Thad hadn't only called it off; he'd broken up with her in the most humiliating and public way.

But if Emerson was being honest with herself, she'd had a feeling that something was off. In her profession, growing up helping her mother out at the wedding shop, and even with assisting Grace, she was around brides and weddings constantly. A bride could be stressed out beyond belief, but they still managed to have a certain glow. There was an excitement, an anticipation, that came with being engaged.

Emerson had never felt that. Sure, she'd been happy

when Thad had proposed. They'd been dating for two years. He had given her his mother's cushion-cut diamond ring. They'd taken professional engagement photos. She'd registered for a china pattern that she didn't really like but her mother had insisted was amazing.

Between her business, planning the wedding and buying the townhouse, she hadn't had time to really ask herself if she was in love with him. Well...she hadn't allowed herself that time. If she had, Emerson would have had to admit the truth.

"I don't know if I'm ready to be with a man again," she said to Grace. "In that way or any other way. It's too soon."

Grace reached across the desk and squeezed her hand. "It's been a year, Em. It's time to get back out there."

Suddenly uncomfortable, Emerson started fidgeting in her seat. "I'm happy, you know."

"I know."

"I love my job. I have a great house. Fabulous friends."

Grace smiled. "I know," she repeated. "But did you ever think that you could have more?"

More sounded scary. She'd had more. She'd lost it.

Emerson didn't like the serious feeling that was permeating the air, so she shook her hands in front of them as if she was wiping away the mood. "It doesn't matter anyway, because Jack is in the middle of some major life changes. His dad just passed away. He's been given this bar. And he inherited a dog."

"Ooohh, a dog! Men with dogs are so hot."

"He's really cute too. The dog, I mean. His name is Cosmo and he is just precious." She took a long breath. "But he doesn't really want the bar. He doesn't even know if he's going to stay in the area."

"What do you mean?" Grace looked shocked. "He's not going to live here?"

"Maybe not."

Grace appeared to be deep in thought. "You like him."

"I just met him."

"You like him. I can tell. But if he's going to be leaving soon, you really need to protect yourself. I don't want to see you get hurt again. You've already committed to this lie with him. But try to keep your wits about you. You don't want to get in too much further at this point."

They began talking about the wedding Grace needed help with. Emerson was happy for the topic change.

Still, her friend's words were echoing throughout her mind. She didn't want to get hurt again either. Yet she had the feeling she was already in way too far with Jack.

Jack didn't consider himself an indecisive person. Nor did he scare easily. Yet he'd picked his phone up and considered calling Emerson, before returning it to his pocket, about a hundred times already.

Once again, he unlocked the screen and studied her name. He hadn't heard from her since Thursday night, when they'd had dinner with her parents.

Since you kissed her.

He shoved a hand through his hair. "Christ," he said into the silence of the empty bar. It was only Monday. And she had texted a few times.

But he wanted to talk to her. He really wanted to see her. And he definitely wanted to kiss her again.

He'd spent the weekend mooning over Emerson like some love-crazed teenager, when he should have been thinking about the bar, his dad's house, his life. He had serious decisions to make and all he could do was obsess over a kiss.

The only thing keeping him from going that extra mile and hitting Send on his cell phone was the unknown. Did she regret the kiss? Jack could tell she'd been into it in the moment. And he sure as hell had been too.

She'd been fairly quiet on the drive home from her parents. Hardly surprising, considering the events of the evening. The reminder of her mother's behavior caused him to exhale a long, frustrated breath. How could she not see how amazing Emerson was?

Even more frustrating was Emerson herself. Jack understood respecting the people who raised you, but Emerson's blatant lack of self-respect was troublesome. Why didn't she defend herself?

His earlier worry morphed into anger. Emerson was awesome and he wanted everyone to know that. Especially her.

He snatched his phone from his pocket once more and punched the send button.

"Hey, Jack," Emerson answered, after two rings. "I—"

But he didn't let her finish. "I want to see you."

The line was disturbingly quiet for a long moment. Jack worked hard to calm his breathing.

Finally, she spoke. Jack thought he heard a bit of humor in her short answer.

"Okay."

Okay? That was easy. He was about to say so when the door of the bar swung open and she appeared, looking professional and beautiful in gray pants and a navy blue sweater. Her auburn curls bounced around her face as she stepped into the bar.

"Here I am," she said with a smile.

Instantly, he relaxed. "That was fast."

She laughed and made her way toward him. "Well,

I was actually on my way over here." He stared at her blankly. "You know, to talk about plans for the bar?"

"Oh. Right!" He met her halfway, by coming out from behind the bar.

"Want something to drink?"

She shook her head. "I'm good." She looked around the room. "Where's Cosmo?"

"He's at home. I didn't think keeping a dog here was the most sanitary thing on the planet."

Her face fell. "Oh. Well, I brought him some treats from the doggie bakery down the street."

Jack stared at the bag she offered, covered in little bones. "There are doggie bakeries?"

"Of course. There are doggie gyms and doggie day-cares, not to mention doggie happy hour. Oh," she said excitedly, clapping her hands together. "You should look into doing something like that. People love it."

Jack ran a hand over his face. "I am not serving a four-legged beast a daiquiri," he said stubbornly.

"Maybe the four-legged beast preferred a beer any-way," she said with a smile. "How was your weekend?"

"I was here all weekend."

"Was it busy? A lot of customers?"

Jack groaned. "Hardly. We really need to turn this place around."

"That's why I'm here." She walked to the closest table, placed the bag she was carrying onto it and reached in-side. "I've been working on the bar all weekend."

He sat at the table with her and raised an eyebrow. "Oh really?"

"Yes. Thanks to me, The Wright Drink is now on Facebook, Twitter, Instagram and Snapchat. I also did some upgrading to your website. Thanks for getting me the access to it, by the way."

She pulled her laptop out of a separate bag and pulled up the website. "Until we clean this place up, do a little redecorating and decide on some events, there's not much I can do with the website. We need photos. Videos would be even better."

Emerson showed him each of the social media platforms. He was impressed to see small followings in each place.

"Wow. You did all of this in a couple of days?"

"Well, I took Saturday off completely, if you must know."

His fingers itched. This moment definitely called for one of his banned cigarettes. "This is really great, Em. I'm on Facebook, but none of those other things. I'm not really a social media kind of guy, so I don't really have the expertise to manage them. Or the time."

"Of course not. I hired someone for you."

"You *what*? Who? When? How much does something like that cost?"

"Don't worry. I have a couple of people who I work with on the social media side of things. Katlyn's really good. And she's inexpensive. But she'll have a ton of social media attention in no time. It's the easiest way to advertise, and it can be cost-effective too."

She really had her stuff together. How could her family not see that?

"Happy, shmoopie?" she asked with a wink.

"No."

"No?" Her face fell. She fumbled with the laptop, toggling between pages. "What don't you like? I was just playing around with this banner on Twitter, but we can certainly change it."

Jack had noticed that, all during her social media spiel she hadn't made eye contact with him. That's when he realized that she might be embarrassed about what had happened between them the other night.

So he grabbed her chair and pulled her closer, forcing her to look up at him.

"I don't like that you've been using work to avoid me."

Her cheeks blushed red. "I haven't been avoiding you." She quickly averted her eyes.

With a light finger under her chin, he tilted her head up so she had to meet his gaze. "Emerson."

"I've been working for you." She gestured toward her computer.

"Are you embarrassed about something?" he asked.

"Such as?"

"You tell me," he countered. She was cute when she was annoyed. Her blue eyes took on a bright crystal color.

"My parents? Well, it's probably too late to get adopted into a new family, as you suggested the other night."

He shook his head.

"The awful photos you saw of me at their house?"

He waited patiently.

"What?" she asked.

With his finger still under her chin, he gently pulled her face closer. "That kiss," he said quietly. He moved his other hand to caress the soft skin of her cheek.

"No, I mean, I, well, I…"

"I really liked it," he filled in for her.

Her lips twitched. "Really?"

"Oh yeah. Did you?"

Her tongue poked out to wet her tempting lips. "Um, that would be a definite *yes*."

He gave a hard nod. "Good. That settles that."

"No, it doesn't. Things are complicated between us." She tried to pull away, but he held firm. "We're lying to everyone. We're pretending to date. I'm helping with your bar. To top it off, you said you're probably going to move out of the area in a month or two. I would be crazy to start anything with you. To kiss you again." But she tilted her head as she said the words.

Jack didn't need more invitation than that. He took her lips for a second time.

Instantly, her lips softened, and he took advantage by moving his mouth over hers. Hungrily, greedily.

She moaned as her arms came up to wind around his neck. He pulled her even closer, unable to get enough of her.

The kiss felt amazing, surreal. He ran his hands through her hair, tangling his fingers in those silky curls. His tongue dove into her mouth, taking the kiss even deeper.

Someone made a guttural sound and he had no idea which of them it was. He ripped his mouth from hers and trailed it down the column of her neck. She obliged by throwing her head back.

But he needed more.

He yanked her up and pulled her onto his lap. She met his gaze, with her eyes dark and full of lust. Threading her hands through his hair, she brought her head down for another satisfying, delicious kiss.

"Excuse me?"

They both started and moved to separate, but Jack was seated in one of the chairs and Emerson was on top of him. Realizing they were more entwined than one of the soft pretzels served at the bar, they both turned toward the voice.

"Am I interrupting something?" A man stood right inside the door, wearing a long black coat over a black suit, and he had an amused grin. He walked down the three steps and his grin got even bigger.

"Xander Ryan," Jack said. His best friend from high school was standing there as Emerson jumped off his lap and adjusted her top, her gaze ping-ponging between the two of them.

"I think one of the last times I saw you in high school, you were in a similar position with Lizzie Demarco."

"Ass," Jack uttered as he stood. But he was grinning from ear to ear. He grabbed Xander in a hug. "Good to see you, man."

"Ohmigod," Emerson groaned. "This is *so* embarrassing." Jack turned back and saw Emerson glance down at her sweater and then run a hand through her hair. He didn't think it was wise to point out that her lips were swollen from their make-out session and her face was flushed. He also imagined that the majority of her lipstick was on his face.

"Hi," she said to Xander, extending her hand.

He shook it—maybe too enthusiastically, Jack observed. "Hey there. I'm Xander, this loser's best friend. We went to high school together."

"Emerson Dewitt. I'm helping this loser whip the bar into shape."

"Hey," Jack protested. Before he could say more, Emerson was grabbing her laptop and other supplies from the table.

"Well, I think we can finish discussing this later. I'll let the two of you catch up."

"Em, wait." But she was already at the front door. "When should we talk again?"

"Um, just text me. We'll work it out." With that, she ran out the door.

"Dammit." Jack needed a drink. Ignoring Xander, he walked to the bar.

"Nice business meeting," Xander said, following Jack.

"Shut up."

"No, really. It's not exactly how we do things at the firm, but to each their own."

"Drink?" Jack held up a bottle of whiskey.

"Wouldn't say no."

Jack filled two glasses and pushed one across the counter, finally taking a moment to give Xander a once-over. His formerly rowdy and mischievous best friend was all grown-up, wearing a tailored suit, with his dark hair short and perfectly in place.

The two of them had played baseball together. Not to mention, they'd constantly gotten into trouble together, as well. But Xander had always been able to talk his way out of any jam.

When his mom had died, Xander sat next to him in the funeral home. He never pushed him to talk about it, which Jack appreciated to this day.

"It's really good to see you." Jack saluted him with his glass.

"You too. Sorry about your dad. And I'm really sorry I couldn't be at the funeral. I was across the country, on business."

He'd sent flowers though. And a mountain of food to the house.

"No worries. Thanks for everything you sent." Jack leaned against the bar. "Xander Ryan, Esquire. Can't believe a real live attorney is standing in my bar."

"Can't believe this is your bar. And I'm not just an attorney. I'm *the* top divorce attorney in the state."

Jack cocked an eyebrow. "You come up with that yourself, or are people aware of your awesomeness?"

Even though they hadn't been in the same room in close to ten years, they had stayed in touch over the years. Phone calls, Facebook, text messages. Being in the same room again didn't feel any different from when they'd been teenagers.

"Everyone is aware of me. But I don't want to talk about me. How about you fill me in on that lovely lady who just ran away from you?"

"Emerson," Jack supplied.

"New girlfriend?"

"No. Yes," Jack remembered. "Sort of." He straightened. "How much time do you have?"

Xander responded with an arched eyebrow. He crossed his arms over his chest and waited. Jack told him the whole story.

"Well," Xander said, and then chuckled. "That's quite the situation you've got yourself in."

"You're no help."

"Sorry, dude, this is uncharted territory. I've seen you with lots of girlfriends. But fake girlfriends? That's definitely a new one. At least Emerson seems cool."

She was more than cool.

"Interesting," Xander said.

"What?"

"That dreamy look you just got. You sure this is all fake?"

"Of course. She's helping me with the bar and I'm helping her out with her family. Especially her mom. She seems to put a lot of pressure on her."

"Isn't that kind of common with mothers and daughters?" Xander asked.

"Not like this. I mean, Emerson is one of the smartest people I've ever met. She started her own business, and you should see how she's been building it up. Plus she's beautiful."

"Uh-huh." A grin broke out on Xander's face.

"What's that about?" Jack asked.

"I've heard you call women hot, sexy and a string of other words. But never beautiful."

Jack shrugged.

"Man, you're in deep already."

Jack had no idea what to say to that. He didn't know if he was in deep, but he was completely aware that he was interested in Emerson Dewitt. He wanted to get to know her more. He wanted to kiss her again.

But there were so many unknowns in his life right now. What would he do with the bar? How long would he stay in Alexandria?

The one thing he did know was that he was damn glad he was in that alley the day she fell out of the window.

He looked to his friend. "Any advice?"

"You've already committed to this fake stuff." He pointed to the table where Jack and Emerson had their earlier make out session. "But what I walked in on today was definitely not pretend. In fact, it looked about as real as it comes."

It felt real, as well. And what was he going to do about that?

Chapter Seven

Almost a week had passed since Xander had uttered those unforgettable words to him.

It looked about as real as it comes.

Jack knew Xander was right. Because in that moment with Emerson on his lap, his arms around her, his mouth against hers, there was no other place he'd rather be.

At least things were less awkward between him and Emerson. Possibly because they hadn't talked about that kiss. Either kiss. Avoidance might be the key to their relationship.

She was at the bar today, armed with paint supplies. At her insistence, Jack had closed the bar for a week. Emerson hired professional cleaners to come in and work their magic. She'd also had him order new light fixtures, fix a few odds and ends, and rearrange some of the tables. Minimal changes and already it felt like a brand-new place.

Not to mention that he'd had a chance to go through

inventory and meet with his dad's accountant. The bar wasn't in great financial shape, but it wasn't quite as bad as he'd originally feared either.

"This paint color is really going to pop. Between it and the new lighting, you'll really see a difference. Everything will be brighter and more inviting. But don't worry, it will still retain that old-school pub vibe."

"The way you rearranged the tables already gives the space some new life."

She shrugged as if it were nothing. "Minor detail."

He grabbed her hand as she started to walk away from him. "It is a big deal, Em. You've done a lot."

"Not really."

"Yes, really." He would make her realize how amazing and talented she was if it killed him. "You're really good at what you do."

That brought a big smile to her face, which was followed by a sweet pink blush. "Most of what event planners do is behind the scenes. Trust me, we always hear if something goes wrong. But when everything runs smoothly, it usually goes unnoticed. It's just part of the job."

She started rifling through one of the bags she'd toted in. "Aha, here they are." She produced four black frames with black-and-white photos inside them. She laid them out on one of the tables.

Jack moved closer to take a look. The first photo was of King Street. Only, something seemed different.

"It's a photo from the year your dad opened the bar," Emerson said. "So is this one." She tapped a purple-painted fingernail at the second frame.

The photo was the front of the bar. "Where did you get these?" he asked.

She smiled. "I found them in that box we noticed in

the corner of your dad's office the other day. He'd already blown them up. I just bought the frames."

Jack studied the next two photos and felt something clench inside his chest. One was a picture of his dad behind the bar, wearing a huge grin, with his hand poised on top of the beer tap. It was such a familiar pose. How many times had Jack looked up at the bar as a child, and there was his dad in that exact position?

But it was the last photo that had the air choking up in his throat. His mom sat on a barstool, with her long legs crossed and angled off the side of the chair. She looked like a pinup girl from the fifties. Next to her was a ten-year-old boy with too-skinny legs, wearing too-high socks, ratty sneakers and a ball cap, and he was grasping a baseball glove. A Shirley Temple with extra cherries was on the bar in front of him. His dad was standing behind the bar with a dish towel flung over his shoulder.

"Do you like them?" Emerson asked, with her voice betraying her nerves.

He still couldn't speak. Jack was moved beyond belief. A myriad of emotions floated over him, and for the life of him, Jack didn't know which one to focus on.

He actually felt tears welling up, but he coughed a couple of times and willed himself to come back to reality.

"Jack?" Emerson asked.

Finally, he turned to her. In a soft and emotional voice, he said, "I love these."

Relief saturated her face. She let out a breath. "Yeah, me too. It's special touches like these that make a place extraordinary. After we paint the walls, I think you should hang them over there." She pointed to one side of the room as he suddenly closed the distance between them. "Whatcha doing?" she asked coyly.

His gaze landed on her mouth. "What do you think I'm doing?"

"I think you're about to ask me about paint samples."

"Not exactly."

"You're wondering if I picked up paint rollers?"

"Definitely not."

He reached for her just as his phone rang. He looked down at it, cringed, pressed a button and then shoved the phone back into his pocket.

Emerson let out a little laugh. "Who was that?"

He frowned. "That was the pushiest bride I've ever met."

The moment was over, and Emerson pushed away from the him, all business once again. "You must not have met many brides then. Trust me, the pushiest wouldn't be calling you. She would be in here, talking about Pinterest boards and accent colors. Why is a bride calling you anyway?" She strolled to one of the tables, where she'd dumped about twenty different bags from the local home-renovation store and began rummaging through them.

"She and her fiancé met at this bar. They want to have a joint bachelor/bachelorette party here. I told them no—"

She dropped a paintbrush and spun around to face him. "Are you for real? Of course they can have it here."

"Are *you* for real? We're not ready for something like that." He waved his hand around to the bar, most of which was covered in drop cloths, since they were going to begin painting today.

She sighed. "Not yet. But we will be. And that's the perfect way to get this place back off the ground. Why didn't you tell me about this earlier?"

"They want the whole place to themselves."

"Even better. Do you have any idea how it will look

on social media when I say the bar is closed for a private event? Exclusive. Desirable," she answered for him. "People will be strolling by on the street and hear the noise, see the party through the windows. This is perfect."

He waved his phone in the air. "Perfect is exactly what Trina wants."

Emerson froze again. "Trina Mitchell?"

"How did you know? You have a psychic side business you aren't telling me about?"

"My best friend, Grace, is planning her wedding. And Grace owes me a favor because I'm helping her out with a different event. Not to mention a million other things from over the years. Let me give her a call."

She whipped her phone out, dialed and was already talking in excited tones before Jack could even protest again.

"It's all set," Emerson said five minutes later. "Two Saturdays from now."

Jack paused in the middle of opening up cartons of painter's tape. "Excuse me? Two weeks? There's no way in hell we're going to be able to do that. Look at this place." The Wright Drink was a pretty large space, as far as bars in Old Town went. "It will take the two of us days to paint everything."

"Oh ye of little faith." There was a twinkle in her eye and Jack had to wonder what she was up to.

As if on cue, the front door of the bar swung open and Emerson's parents and sister entered the bar, with big smiles on their faces.

"The cavalry," Emerson explained with a smile. "I asked a couple of people to come help us today."

"Reporting for paint duty," Amelia said. Her face fell. "Charlie couldn't make it. Sorry."

"No problem," Jack said. "I can't believe any of you are here. Not a fun way to spend a Saturday."

Mr. Dewitt slapped a hand on Jack's back. "Anything to help out Emerson's boyfriend."

Guilt lodged in his throat. Not only was he monopolizing the Saturday of good, hardworking people, but he was lying to them in the process.

"Emerson, what's happening with your hair?" Mrs. Dewitt asked, with a perplexed expression on her face.

Jack took notice. He liked her hair today. For some reason, it was extra curly. She had it piled on the top of her head, in a messy ponytail. Some of the curls had escaped to frame her makeup-free face. She looked natural, beautiful.

Emerson's hand flew to her hair. "Who cares about my hair? We're about to start working."

"I think it looks nice, Em," Amelia said. Making herself at home, she peeked into the bags of paint supplies.

Mrs. Dewitt pointed at her husband. "Give Jack the food, Walt."

Before he could realize what was happening, Mr. Dewitt produced two large bags from the local deli across the street. He peeked inside to find a mountain of sandwiches, chips, fruit, and all of the napkins, utensils and condiments they could need.

"For lunchtime," Mr. Dewitt explained. "We figured we didn't need to bring drinks," he said with a laugh.

"I think I've got you covered," Jack said. "Seriously, this is really generous of all of you."

Emerson waved a nonchalant hand. He wondered if she realized how similar it was to a gesture her mother had made.

"I invited my best friend, Grace, too. She's going to

be late though. She's with one of her brides at an emergency dress fitting."

"I told Grace not to trust that store in Fredericksburg. I knew they'd get it wrong," Beatrice said from across the room, where she was surveying the ancient jukebox.

"You can remind her when she shows up," Emerson said.

Mr. Dewitt engulfed Emerson in a big hug. Then he moved to the back of the bar with Mrs. Dewitt and Amelia as the door opened again and Xander strolled through, wearing a Georgetown Law sweatshirt that had definitely seen better days.

"What are you doing here?"

"I got a call from a certain event planner, saying my considerable talents were needed here."

Jack raised an eyebrow. "Since when do you have painting talents?"

"I have talents the world isn't even ready for..."

Jack was about to throw back a very sarcastic reply when the door opened and an incredibly gorgeous woman with thick black hair ran right into Xander's back.

"Oh excuse me," she mumbled.

But when she came around and faced Xander, something passed over her face. Jack didn't quite understand it. However, he noticed that Xander had gone as still as stone.

"You must be Grace," Jack said to break the ice.

She turned her gaze to Jack and a smile blossomed on her face. The woman was striking. She wore a cherry-red pantsuit with matching heels. Over her shoulder was an incredibly large red tote bag. Jack was pretty sure he'd carried something the same size when he had backpacked around Europe for a year.

"And you must be Jack. I'm so sorry I'm late."

"No problem. We haven't even begun yet." Jack gave Xander a pointed stare, waiting for his friend to introduce himself. Or even to stop ogling Grace.

"This would be my friend Xander. He's here to help too."

Grace gulped. Then she thrust her hand forward. "Nice to meet you, Xander."

He accepted her hand and they shook for a moment. A very long moment. "Hi," Xander finally said. "Do you live here in Old Town?"

Grace ripped her hand from his and clutched her gigantic purse. "Yes, I live with Emerson."

"You seem overdressed for painting."

"I came from work. I was with a bride. I'm a wedding planner."

Xander emitted a snicker, followed by an eye roll. "I'm a divorce attorney."

Silence, thicker and more potent than the paint, filled the air.

Jack stepped forward. "You guys seem to have similar professions," he tried to joke. But something had changed on Xander's face. If Jack wasn't mistaken, it seemed a lot like disappointment.

"Yeah," Xander agreed with a snort. "Couples go to you first and then find me when they come to their senses."

Grace's mouth fell open and she looked like she'd just been slapped.

Emerson had joined Jack at his side.

"Should we throw some cold water on them?" he muttered to her, only half joking. They exchanged a glance, neither seemingly wanting to step in between their two best friends.

Finally, Emerson let out an obvious cough. "Gracie,

thanks for coming." She walked up the steps and retrieved her friend, who offered one last hostile look at Xander over her shoulder.

Grace took in the bar. "This place is fabulous. I can see why Trina and Nick want to have their parties here."

"Nice outfit, Grace," Amelia said with a smile.

"I was with a client." She tapped her oversize bag. "I have a change of clothes."

"Grace, how are you? Emerson said you were having trouble with the wedding dress. You know, I told you about that shop." Beatrice ushered Grace toward the bathroom to change.

"Lovely woman," Xander said under his breath to Jack.

"Shh, she's Emerson's best friend."

Emerson clapped her hands together. "Okay, everybody, time to get this painting party started."

Emerson directed everyone to certain areas of the room. They passed out supplies, cranked up the jukebox and got to work.

They were all working in a good groove for about an hour when the music changed, and a slow, romantic song started. Jack recognized it as one of those overplayed, shmaltzy types of songs crooned by a popular singer that everyone played at their wedding.

He was about to make a joke about it when he noticed Emerson's face had paled. In fact, she was holding her paintbrush in midair.

"I'll change it, Em." Amelia rushed to the jukebox. After Amelia had fiddled around for a few moments, a fast-paced country song began.

What in the world?

"You seem confused."

He turned to find Amelia standing close, studying his face.

"Em didn't tell you what happened with Thad last year, did she?" Amelia asked.

"I've heard plenty of references to last year, but no one has filled me in yet."

Amelia glanced around the room. Everyone was once again busy working on their area of the bar. Someone was singing along, off-key.

"Come on, let's get started."

He followed Amelia to one of the walls, and together they laid out a drop cloth and filled their tin with paint.

"Emerson was engaged to this guy, Thad."

Jack dipped his paintbrush into the tin. "I'm assuming by the use of past tense and the grimace you just offered that the engagement didn't end well."

"Hardly. He backed out of the wedding."

Jack tightened the grip around his paintbrush.

"Emerson was devastated. She had just started her business, and he left her with an overpriced townhouse. For a while, she thought she might have to give up the business and go work in a corporate job to pay the bills. She's getting by now though. Em is very resilient."

He agreed with the last part. Emerson was strong. The only problem was that she didn't always see that trait in herself.

"So that's why she freaked out when she was trying on wedding dresses," he said more to himself.

"She told you about that?" Amelia asked.

Jack paused. A little too long, if the curious look on Amelia's face was any indication. "Uh, right. She told me about it." He needed to keep his lies straight. He couldn't very well admit that he'd only met Emerson because she'd pitched herself out of that window, while wearing the wedding dress.

"The song that I just changed was *their* song." She smoothed paint onto the wall. "Not getting married was bad enough," Amelia continued. "But it was so much more than that to Emerson."

"What do you mean?"

"She felt like she was letting everyone down."

That was ridiculous. Her fiancé had broken up with *her*, and she felt like *she* was letting everyone down? He snuck a glance at Emerson. He knew her well enough by now to tell that the smile plastered on her face wasn't quite reaching her eyes. She was still stuck on the song.

Maybe she was also stuck on her fiancé.

He was about to say something to Amelia when he noticed the twinkle in her eyes.

"What?" he asked.

"I know what you're thinking." She shook her head. "Emerson doesn't have feelings for Thad anymore. That's not what that was about." She pointed at the jukebox.

"What was it about then?"

"Em's hard on herself. It doesn't make any sense to me, because I think she's amazing and I really envy...well, she's a great big sister. But not marrying Thad was a failure to her. And this year has been incredibly difficult."

Wouldn't know it to look at her though, Jack mused.

"She hides it well," Amelia said, as if reading his thoughts.

Every day he seemed to learn more about Emerson Rose Dewitt. Each new thing made his respect for her grow even more. He only wished she could see herself through his eyes.

What she needed was a little time to relax and unwind. And that was exactly what he was going to give her.

* * *

"It looks good. Really, really good." Emerson was surveying the room with her hands on her hips and a satisfied smile on her face. A face that currently had a swipe of paint across the cheek.

He'd just finished taking out multiple bags of trash. He had to admit that Emerson's family had really come through. The place really did look amazing. In fact, it reminded him of when his dad had first opened it. All shiny and new looking.

His mother had helped with the decorating back then. She'd been so proud of it.

"We'll give it the proper amount of time to dry. Then we can continue putting the place back together. In the meantime, we need to get things rolling on the bachelor/bachelorette party."

"Go out with me tonight."

The words flew out of his mouth. Emerson's head snapped toward him. He couldn't blame her for the shocked expression on her face. He'd surprised even himself.

"Huh?" she asked.

He took a deep breath. "You heard me. Let's go on a date tonight."

She snapped her fingers in front of his face. "Are the paint fumes getting to you?"

You're getting to me. "I feel fine. I just think that we've been doing a lot of work and it would be nice to take my pretend girlfriend out on a real date. Spend some time just hanging out together. You know, relax a little."

She looked at him for a long moment. "You don't have to do that."

He reached over and placed his thumb against the paint

smudge on her cheek. It was dry now. She would need to wash her face to remove it. "I want to."

"But—"

"Emerson, go home, take a shower and put something nice on so we can enjoy a fancy dinner together. Please." He offered her his most cocky grin.

She slapped his arm. "Fine."

He could only hope that going out tonight would be as relaxing as he'd promised her. Because right now being around Emerson Dewitt had the opposite effect. If she was around, he was anything but relaxed.

Chapter Eight

He picked Emerson up at seven o'clock, on the dot. She was waiting outside her townhouse.

Her long black coat was unbuttoned, and from the illumination of the porch light, he could make out a bright turquoise dress that hugged her curves. Her hair looked as if she had freshly washed and styled it; her curls hung softly around her face.

He noticed she'd chosen high heels with a bunch of different straps twisting around her legs. The heels seemed high, yet it did little to get her even close to his height.

"You look amazing," he said, stepping closer.

She bit her lip seductively and slowly brought her gaze up to his. Jack didn't know if that was something they taught to females in a super-secret class, but it got to him every time. He leaned down and brought his lips very close to hers, hovering for several moments, tormenting them both. Finally, he laid a chaste kiss on her lips.

Her perfume emanated toward him, wrapping around all of his senses. She smelled of lavender and honey. It made her that much more tempting. Jack had to move back a step or he would have devoured her right there on the spot.

When he presented her with the bouquet of daisies, a gorgeous smile blossomed on her face. Even in the dwindling light, he could see the utter delight. Funny what a big reaction a little bunch of flowers could produce.

After she quickly ran inside to put the flowers in a vase, she returned and they were off to The Fisherman's King, a posh seafood restaurant at the bottom of King Street, on the edge of the Potomac River.

The great thing about Old Town was the diversity. There truly was something for everybody. You could eat food from all over the world, including Thai, Italian and even Ethiopian cuisine. You could pay a couple of bucks for a meal or drop an entire paycheck.

Because of the variety it had to offer, Old Town drew in people from every walk of life. Everyone from young couples with toddlers in strollers to older couples walking hand-in-hand to flocks of teenagers and people with their dogs roamed the streets.

On one popular corner near the Town Hall and Market Square, guides dressed in Colonial costumes corralled tourists into groups. They would usher them around the historic streets, telling them ghost stories. They'd stop at locations that had hosted George Washington and other famous men who had helped shaped the country.

With so many options, Jack had experienced an hour of panic trying to find the right place to take Emerson. In the end, he'd called Xander, who had suggested The Fisherman's King. Jack had scoffed at first. It took weeks to get a reservation at the restaurant. Especially on a Saturday night. But Xander apparently had an in. He'd represented the owner in his divorce.

After parking in a local garage, they'd walked the short distance. Even with Xander's assistance, they still had to hang out in the bar area for about forty-five minutes, making idle chitchat over cocktails.

Eventually they were shown to their table, in a corner of the restaurant, right next to the windows, which offered an amazing view of the water. Lights glittered off the Potomac River as boats bobbed along in the docks right outside. The Woodrow Wilson Bridge, the drawbridge connecting Alexandria to Maryland, stood majestically in the near distance.

"This is great. Thank you," Emerson said. Her eyes were trained on the window. "Look at the wheel. How pretty."

He glanced across the river, at National Harbor, a recent development in Maryland. There was a large hotel and convention center, shops, restaurants, a casino, and outlets. The place continued to grow each day.

They had constructed a Ferris wheel that was currently lit up in flashy tones of bright pink and blue. Supposedly, the view of the DC area was magnificent from the top of the wheel. Maybe he could take Emerson there some night.

"I'm glad you suggested this. I really needed a break."

She'd put makeup on and somehow whatever she used on her eyes had made them appear even more blue. But Jack could still see that dark circles remained. Not surprising. She had to be exhausted with as much as she had going on. She was doing so much for him, and he imagined that she had other clients that she had to tend to, as well.

"You do so much," he said.

A funny expression crossed her face. "Did my sister say something to you?"

Damn, she was perceptive. "What makes you ask that?"

"I saw you guys talking while you were painting together."

"Maybe we were discussing a TV show. Or a recent bestseller."

She leaned forward. "But you weren't doing either of those things, were you?"

"No. We were talking about you."

"What did she tell you?"

He considered downplaying the conversation, but she deserved to know the truth. "She told me about Thad."

"Right." Her happy expression seemed to deflate, and the glittery blue of her eyes dulled. "That's why you asked me out tonight, isn't it? You felt sorry for me. Be honest."

Before he could say anything, the waiter arrived with their wine. They went through the song and dance of presenting the bottle, uncorking it, and giving Jack the first sip. He had a pretty good sense of wine, even though he was definitely more of a beer man. So he slid the glass to Emerson, who took a sip and announced that it was "awesomesauce." The waiter cringed as he filled their glasses.

Jack took a sip. Emerson was right. It *was* pretty awesomesauce.

They both took a long drink. Suddenly the atmosphere had lost some of its earlier ease.

Emerson put her glass down and leaned forward. "As I was saying before this overpriced bottle of wine appeared, you asked me out because you found out about my ex-fiancé and felt bad for me."

He met her halfway by also leaning into the table.

"No. Emerson, listen to me. I asked you out tonight because I…well, I…"

"Yes?"

"I wanted to spend more time with you."

She scooted backward into her chair and bit her lip. "Really?"

"Yeah, really. I do feel bad about what happened to you. But I don't…pity you or anything."

She gnawed on her lower lip. "That makes one of us."

"It must have really sucked to have to call off your wedding. What an ass."

She emitted a little laugh. "Pretty much. I mean, standing there in my wedding dress and knowing that there were hundreds of people on the other side of the wall… I don't think I've ever been more embarrassed in my life. I certainly hope I'll never be that embarrassed again."

Jack straightened and focused on her. Had he just heard that right? Emerson hadn't only been dumped by her fiancé; if he was understanding her right, that bastard had stood her up at the altar. Actually, bastard wasn't a strong enough word for the coward who could possibly let a woman as amazing as Emerson down.

Tonight was definitely out of the ordinary for her. She'd been out on plenty of dates. She'd even eaten at this particular restaurant before. After all, with its expensive food, snobby waiters and scenic view of the water, it was one of her parents' favorite places.

However, she'd never been out with her pretend boyfriend before. Maybe because she didn't make a habit of acquiring imaginary beaus.

But here they were. Jack cleaned up nicely. He was wearing black slacks and a great tie with a cream-colored sweater over it. Of course, he still didn't quite fit in with the restaurant crowd. How could he when he'd entered the restaurant wearing his sexy leather jacket and sporting the yummiest dark stubble.

He was all dark and brooding, and just delectable. What she wouldn't give to lean over and take a little bite.

When she glanced up at Jack though, his face had become tense.

"Do you need more time with the menu, or are you ready to order?" The tall, thin waiter asked.

"I'll have the halibut special," Emerson said. Jack ordered the same.

Once the waiter was out of earshot, she asked, "Why are you looking at me like that?"

"Em, are you kidding?"

Huh? "I like halibut."

"No. Not the food. We were talking about Thad. I didn't realize that… I mean, I had no idea that he… Are you telling me that this Thad guy left you at the altar?"

Confused, she cocked her head. "I thought you said you talked to my sister earlier."

"I did. But she said he backed out on your wedding. I didn't realize he actually backed out of the church."

Ah, she understood now. He'd assumed that Thad did the decent thing. And true, it *would* have been great for him to call off the wedding when the wedding wasn't actually in progress.

"I'm not sure he ever showed up at the church, to be honest," she emitted a small, humorless laugh. "Not to worry though. He sent a text."

She could see his fingers curl into fists, creating a stark contrast to the tidy white linens, candles and flowers on the table. "You've gotta be kidding me."

"I wish I were."

Her gaze drifted off as she remembered that day. That

horrible, humiliating day. She'd gotten dressed at her parents' house, but once she and her family had arrived at the church, they'd waited in a back room. Her mother kept fluffing her veil and fixing her dress.

Her sister had been absolutely glowing. Besides the fact that Amelia resembled a high-fashion model in her champagne-colored bridesmaid's dress, Charlie had proposed to her the night before, at the rehearsal dinner. He'd gotten up presumably to give a toast to Emerson and Thad. Instead he'd professed his love for Amelia, gotten down on one knee and asked for her hand in marriage.

Everyone in the room had swooned. But Emerson had been pissed. Not that she hadn't been happy for her sister, but it was supposed to be her time. Her wedding. Her rehearsal dinner. She had finally been doing something that made her mother extraordinarily happy. Only, that had been taken away from her too. Of course, Amelia hadn't known Charlie was going to propose, and given what had happened the next day, it didn't matter anyway. But still, after a lifetime of messing up and not doing things her mother's way, couldn't she have that one night to shine?

As they waited at the church the next day, there was a point when her stomach sank. She knew something was off. When Grace had entered the room, carrying Emerson's cell phone and wearing a grim expression, Emerson knew.

"His text said that his heart wasn't into the marriage. He liked me, but he didn't love me."

She felt the heat from Jack's hand before she even realized he'd covered her own. He squeezed lightly. She met his eyes.

"I'm really sorry, Emerson."

"Thanks." She tried to push down the lump forming in her throat but had difficultly. She took a long sip of water. "In the end, I suppose I should be thankful. Thad and I didn't have a lot in common. Of course, I thought that we were a case of opposites attracting."

"What were you, then?"

"Two people who looked great together on paper. The right families, the right schools, the right credentials."

"I didn't realize things like that still mattered."

"For certain people, they do." She removed her hand from his and clasped her fingers together tightly. "The worst part was how much I let down my family." She cast her gaze at the table.

"How can you say that? What does your marriage have to do with your family?"

"It was important to my mama," she whispered. "Mothers love when their daughters get married, and Southern moms, well, amplify that idea by a million."

"Emerson," he began, but she shook her head to stop him.

"I know it probably doesn't make much sense to you."

"Try to explain it," he encouraged.

"I wanted to give my mama this big, beautiful wedding with the perfect poufy wedding dress and a five-tiered cake. I wanted her to have that mother-of-the-bride moment, with all of her friends present. To dance with my dad to their favorite Beatles song. I wanted the picture-perfect wedding day because I knew how much it would mean to her."

Jack narrowed his eyes. "But why? Why did you want to give her that picture-perfect wedding? And why do it if it didn't mean anything to you?"

"There are so many times in my life when I tried to make Mama happy. Dancing and cheerleading and pageants. A dozen other ways. But I would always mess up somehow. I just wanted one time, one day, one moment, of being in the spotlight for the right reason."

"Hmm." Jack rubbed a hand along his jawline. "Bet your sister didn't make it any easier."

"I love Mia." Emerson heard the defensiveness in her voice.

Jack leaned forward. "Of course you do. It still must have been hard to have your little sister outshine you at every turn."

It felt like someone had just removed their hand from Emerson's mouth and she could finally breathe. "I don't want to seem catty or mean-spirited."

Jack let out a gruff laugh. "Trust me, Em, that's the last thing I would ever say about you. Relationships are complex. It's okay to have multiple feelings about a person."

She considered his words for a very long moment. Then finally, she let loose. "It was hard. It still is. Dammit," she added for emphasis.

"Sometimes I feel so exhausted," Emerson continued. "I have to try extra hard all of the time. Either I do something my mama wants me to do and she thinks I did it wrong, or I do something she doesn't support entirely and thrive without her approval. I can't seem to win."

"Why would you want to?" Jack asked. She could see the sincerity in his eyes. "Look at all of the amazing things you have done in your life."

"They weren't the things that impressed Mama. I was never quite good enough. I wasn't Amelia." She finished with a laugh that had absolutely zero humor to it.

"I mean, sure, Amelia was a cheerleader, but it's not like cheerleading ever won her any scholarships." She pointed at Jack. "Did you know that I received multiple scholarships for both academics and soccer?"

"No kidding."

"Amelia went to the college my parents loved. Big deal. She's working in Mama's store now. Um, she studied marketing. Why isn't she using her degree?"

Emerson knew her sister loved weddings and enjoyed working with brides and their families. But she also knew that Amelia wasn't 100 percent happy with her chosen profession. She'd been hinting at her discontent for a while now.

"Ugh." Emerson felt horrible. She rubbed at her temples.

"What is it?" Jack asked.

"I feel awful, being so critical of my sister."

He studied her for a long moment. "You've been compared to your sister your whole life, and instead of begrudging her, you love her. It's so clear to anyone who sees the two of you together."

"One day I might believe that." How she truly wished she would.

"I hope I'm there to see that day."

Emerson took a long, fortifying drink of wine. "There's something else." She fidgeted in her seat. "I've never told anyone this."

Jack didn't press. He waited patiently.

"I don't think I even loved him very much. I think... maybe it was the idea of him?" She sighed. "He snored. And he was kind of snobby. He refused to go to the movies because he said all movie theaters were dirty. Plus he told his mother that he went to church every Sunday, but I don't think he even knew where the closest church was." She was so upset, she knocked over her wineglass. Bright red liquid spilled across the crisp white linen.

A busboy rushed over to take care of the toppled wineglass.

"Thank you," she said to the busboy. Then she turned

her attention back to Jack. "I mean, who did he think he was? Screw him," she yelled a little louder than she should at a fancy restaurant. "Thad thought he was *so* great and *so* charming. You know what though? He wasn't all that."

The maître d' also made his way toward the table. "Miss, is everything okay?"

"Oh yes," Jack said with a twinkle in his eye. "She's having a long, overdue epiphany."

"As cathartic as that may be, we do have other guests here tonight."

Emerson glanced around the restaurant and found that every pair of eyes was trained on her, watching her outburst. Some sat with their mouths hanging open, while others actually appeared to be amused with her theatrics.

All she could think was how her mother would disown her if she saw this. Particularly because this was one of her favorite restaurants. What would everyone think? And that thought actually made her laugh.

Not just laugh. Hysterical sounds escaped her body as tears ran down her cheeks.

"Sir, I'm very sorry, but I must insist you and your companion settle down."

The maître d' didn't even attempt to address Emerson. Probably thought she'd completely lost it at this point. She couldn't be sure she hadn't. But if this was losing it, it sure did feel good. Another belly laugh rolled through her and ended with a loud snort, which only made her laugh more.

"Sir, please." The maître d's gaze darted from table to table. "If you can't tone down your conversation, we do have a lovely table in a more secluded area of the restaurant."

"More secluded?" Jack asked. He rolled his eyes. "Why don't we just leave then?"

"If that's what you want to do."

Emerson was pretty sure Jack's suggestion had been a hypothetical. Nevertheless, the maître d' had snapped his fingers and the busboy appeared. They began stripping the table.

Jack stood and reached for his wallet, but the maître d' shook his head, seemingly more intent to just get them out of the restaurant and away from the normal patrons.

"Our food?" Jack asked.

"Not to worry. I'll cancel the order. Consider the wine complimentary." He gestured toward the entrance. Or, in this case, the exit. "This way, please."

Emerson thought she'd go to the restaurant tonight and get a great meal. Instead she got something much greater.

A little closure.

Chapter Nine

Since they'd forfeited their four-star dinner—all her fault, Emerson had to admit—Jack asked her what she was in the mood for. So they picked up large, juicy cheeseburgers, with two sides of fries, and then Jack drove them a little ways from Old Town.

She enjoyed being in the car with him. Her window was cracked, and the cool night air felt amazing against her skin. She leaned her head against the glass and searched for stars above the twinkling city lights.

She lost track of where they were heading as she ran over all the things she'd said tonight. All of the things she'd thought.

Jack switched on the radio and found the local country station. One of her favorite songs came on. She smiled.

Her favorite food. Her favorite song. And Jack was very quickly becoming one of her favorite people.

With Jack, everything felt different. She could say things to him that she wouldn't dare utter to another soul.

She gnawed on her lip as she considered the situation. When she was with him, she felt…whole. That wasn't quite right. Maybe it was more that she felt like herself. No explanations. No apologies.

Suddenly it hit her.

When she was around Jack, she felt good enough. She never felt as though she had to make excuses for herself. She just was.

Maybe she could be herself with Jack. Perhaps Emerson Rose Dewitt *was* enough.

He put the car into Park at the top of a hill. There was no one else around. No other cars, people, houses. Nothing. It was dark and secluded and absolutely…romantic.

Perfect.

The radio continued playing softly in the background as Emerson leaned her head back against the seat and closed her eyes.

"Did we just technically get kicked out of a restaurant?"

She heard the rustle of the food bags. The aroma of onions and fries wafted through the confined space of the truck. Jack rolled the windows down about halfway. It was still chilly outside, but with each week the temperature rose higher and higher. Summer would be here before they knew it.

"I believe we did."

She opened her eyes and watched as Jack winked at her and stuck a fry in his mouth. Naturally, it drew her attention to those tempting lips. Those lips that had now been on hers twice. Maybe she wanted them to be on hers again. Maybe she wanted to continue her uncharacteristic behavior and just make out right in this truck. After all, what was one more crazy thing when she'd already done so many this evening?

When she finally ripped her eyes away, she noticed that he was grinning at her. No doubt, he knew exactly what she was thinking.

"What are you thinking?"

He was clearly psychic.

But what was she supposed to say? The truth? That she wanted him? That she was on a high from revealing her past to him tonight and wanted to keep the feeling going by ripping his clothes off?

Instead she unwrapped her burger and took a big, juicy bite. Not as satisfying as biting into Jack, but it would have to do.

"I really appreciated you taking me out tonight. The whole routine—the flowers, getting a reservation at that fancy restaurant."

"But?" he asked.

"But I prefer this—a picnic under the stars, a burger and fries. Fancy and polished is not what I crave now."

His eyes raked over her in one sexy, seductive grin. "Oh yeah? What do you crave?"

You. "Now I crave comfort and ease."

He nodded. "You never cease to surprise me."

Emerson looked out the windshield, taking in the setting. To find a quiet area like this, not far from Old Town, was definitely a hidden gem.

"I used to come here in high school."

"Really? But it's so private...oh." Emerson laughed as she realized just what he'd come here in high school to do. "Was this your secret make-out spot?"

He chuckled. "I may have brought a girl or two here." He ate more of his burger and washed it down with a big swig of soda. "But I also used to come up here to be by myself. Take some time away."

He was looking out the windshield, staring out at the

darkness. Even from the side, she could see he'd clenched his jaw. She reached over and gently touched it.

She threw his question back at him. "What are you thinking?"

He opened his mouth, but no words came out. Instead it was as if he had made a decision. He turned to her with a wry grin. "About how great you were back at the restaurant."

Emerson knew he was lying, but she let it go. For now.

"Great, sure. That's one way to put it."

He laughed. "It was. You were amazing. It was good to see you finally realize how messed up that Thad guy was."

He truly was. She'd spent so much time over the last year blaming herself for the humiliating breakup. Like she'd somehow not been good enough for Thad to go through with their marriage. When in reality, it was ridiculous to blame herself at all. Thad was the scoundrel.

Her phone went off. She dug it out of her purse and cringed.

"Let me guess," Jack said. "Your mother?"

"Oh yeah," she said as she declined the call. Almost immediately, a text message popped up.

Emerson, call me.

With her mom, the shorter the text message was, the more pissed off she was. She showed the screen to Jack.

"You think she found out about your outburst in The Fisherman's King?"

Emerson nodded.

"Who do you think told her?" he asked, stretching his arm across the seats.

"Who knows?" She switched her phone to Silent and threw it back in her purse. "Who cares?"

She considered her burger, but she was no longer hungry. She wrapped it up and nestled it back in the bag.

"I realized something tonight. I spent a year mourning the end of a relationship that wasn't all that great to begin with."

Jack remained quiet. He began to massage her shoulder, offering support. That small gesture meant so much to her.

Some of that defiance from the restaurant began to surface again. "He was lucky to have me."

"Damn straight."

"I'm too good for him. I'm..." She didn't know what else. She only knew one thing. She was so done with Thad and that part of her life.

Jack's hand stilled on her shoulder. She turned to face him.

Other than the music playing on the radio, the only sounds were that of crickets and a light wind blowing through the trees. Moonlight filtered into the truck, highlighting Jack's handsome face, with its strong jawline and angles.

There were things that were up in the air in her life at the moment. Aspects that weren't ideal. None of that mattered at this second though. It didn't seem to matter what she didn't have or what she hadn't done correctly. Right now, it was about her. About want.

And Emerson knew there was one thing she wanted very badly.

Emerson climbed over to his seat, practically sitting in his lap, and framed his face with her hands. He met her gaze full on as she leaned in to kiss him.

Finally.

It took less than a second for Jack's arms to encircle her, pulling her closer. She heard one of the food bags fall to the floor.

She opened her mouth, welcoming his tongue as it mingled with hers.

Emerson had no idea how long they kissed. It could have been a couple of minutes or a couple of hours. She only knew that she wanted it to last forever.

Finally, they separated. Jack ran his thumb over her bottom lip. When his hand fell to the seat, she licked her lips and delighted when his gaze flew to that spot.

She giggled. "You have to add me to the list of girls you've made out with here."

He ran a hand over her hair, twisting one of her curls around his finger. "You are at the top of the list."

"Because I'm the most recent?"

His jaw ticked as his eyes darkened. He'd grown serious and the air in the truck felt heavy with an emotion she didn't quite understand. Or maybe, she just wasn't ready to acknowledge it. He shook his head at her question.

Jack sat back and rolled his window all the way down. A breeze whistled through the trees, entered the cab of the truck and shifted her hair around her head. The temperature was still a bit cool. She loved how the crispness of the air felt against her cheeks.

The radio began playing a slow, melodic song. She turned up the volume, closed her eyes, and began swaying back and forth.

"Come on." Jack's voice was gruff and sexy as hell.

She opened her eyes languidly to find that Jack had slid out of the truck. Then he reached back in and pulled her outside. Instantly, she was in his arms. His strong arms cocooned her as he brought her body against his.

She didn't care if the moment was like something out

of a movie. Because Emerson was falling for it. She was falling for *him*.

For real.

He swayed from side to side, moving her body with his, around the grassy field, as the song played from the truck.

"You're a good dancer," she commented. "You probably did this with all of those hundreds of girls in high school."

He raised his eyebrows. "Hundreds, huh? Maybe only like ninety-nine."

She hit him lightly on the chest. He covered her hand with his and held it there. Over his heart.

They continued to move together to the music, gazing into each other's eyes. One song rolled into another.

She didn't know when, but at some point they began to kiss. Lightly, so lightly, at first. Her arms wound around his neck. His lips trailed along her jawline and she shivered.

"Cold?" he asked, with his voice already sounding husky.

How could she be anything but blazing hot when she was in his arms?

"No," she replied. Feeling bold from everything that had happened that night, she said, "Touch me, Jack."

Instantly, his hands traveled down her sides, and back up again. They brushed past her breasts and she shivered. His lips came to hers again, sweeping her away into the passion of the kiss.

"Em, is this something you want to do? I mean, is this okay?"

How cute was he? Big, bad Jack Wright had just gotten tongue-tied. Over her. Because of her.

"I want you, Jack. Now. Here."

"You're sure?"

She nodded. "Oh yes."

He quickly made his way to the truck and rummaged in the back seat. After returning with a plaid blanket, he fluffed it out and spread it on the ground.

Emerson glanced around. They'd been in this spot for at least a half hour, with no other signs of life. Still, they were outdoors. In public. Never in her life had she made love in such an open environment. The thought was both scary and empowering.

In any case, she wanted Jack far too badly to even think about climbing back into the truck and driving to one of their houses. She needed him right now.

He knelt on the blanket and reached out a hand to her. The gesture was so romantic that she almost started to cry. Instead she stepped to him and took his hand, noticing how his large hand dwarfed hers.

Standing over him, she leaned down and kissed him. Her hair fell, curtaining his face. Then she joined him in a kneeling position.

They were on even ground.

She could feel moisture under the blanket. An owl hooted in one of the nearby trees. The wind continued to lightly blow around them.

He framed her face with his hands and forced her to meet his gaze. "You are so beautiful, Emerson. Inside and out."

His words humbled her. "Oh Jack."

"Shh." He pressed a finger to her lips. "I want to look at you."

"You've been doing that all night."

He shook his head. "This is different. This is just us. For us."

Another gust of wind, stronger this time, blew around

them. She felt her nipples harden in response. Or maybe that was due to Jack's intense stare. He continued to take her in, as if she were the only woman on Earth. The only woman he'd ever seen. Like she was special. Like she was enough.

"Kiss me," she said.

He did and she melted into it. When his tongue found its way into her mouth, she scooted even closer to him.

Her hands began to run over his strong chest. He was so hard, so masculine. She delighted in feeling all of his muscles and knowing he had the strength to hold her up.

She ripped her lips from his and pressed sweet kisses to his neck, before lightly nibbling his earlobe. A sound of pure delight escaped his lips and she smiled against his skin.

Feeling powerful and bold, she leaned back and reached for the bottom of her dress. She bit her lip as she considered for one second. But this was right. Everything about this moment felt real.

She inched the dress up and over her head until she was kneeling in front of him in nothing but the matching blue lacy bra and panties she'd chosen to wear that night. His dark eyes dimmed to practically black as they trailed up and down her body.

She attempted to take off her heels, but she got stuck. She told herself it was due to all of the intertwining straps and not the fact that she'd suddenly gotten a case of nerves. In the end, she decided to just leave them on.

Jack reached out and trailed a finger over the top of her bra. Her chest was rising and falling rapidly, causing the cups of her bra to overflow with her breasts.

But she wasn't done yet. She yanked his sweater over his head and loosened his tie until she could remove that, as well. Then she began undoing the buttons of his shirt, thrilled to see that her fingers were calm and steady. This was what she wanted.

When she pushed his shirt off his broad shoulders and to the ground, she inhaled sharply. Damn, he was gorgeous.

She couldn't wait. She pressed her hands against his pecs and ran them down to the waistband of his pants. He sucked in a breath.

Their eyes met. A moment passed between them. Then, completely in sync, they grabbed for each other.

Hands were everywhere. Their mouths fused and then explored every inch they could get to. Nothing was off-limits.

Jack cupped her breasts before leaning down to take her nipple into his mouth. The combination of his hot mouth, the cold wind and the lace against her sensitive skin was delightfully unbearable. Her head fell back and she moaned. He unhooked her bra and covered her naked breast with his mouth, his tongue, his teeth.

As he gave the same attention to her other breast, her hand went on its own adventure over his abs and to the zipper of his pants. She pulled it down and snuck her hand inside. Finding what she wanted, she cupped the length of him.

Jack shivered, and a very raw, primal sound slipped out of his mouth.

"Emerson," he said, with a raspy, desperate voice.

"I know, Jack, I know."

He laid her down on the blanket, cupping her head as he did so. The blanket wasn't the softest in the world. It was scratchy and stiff. Some kind of bird or night creature was making a very strange noise. But none of that mattered, because Jack removed his boxer briefs and then her panties. When he covered her body with his, the only thought in her head was of him.

He kissed her deeply. Their tongues entwined in a seductive dance. She grabbed for him, attempting to pull him even closer. She was more than ready for him, wanted him.

"Yes?" he asked.

"Oh yes," she whispered.

Jack reared back, reaching for his discarded pants. He fumbled in the pocket until he pulled out a foil packet. After quickly sheathing himself, he returned to her. Braced on his arms, he towered over her, his eyes serious.

He positioned himself between her legs, pausing to kiss her again. Kissed her long and hard. It felt like he was pouring everything of himself into it. She was so enthralled by it that she almost didn't realize he was entering her at the same time.

He filled her completely as their lips stayed fused together. He captured her gasp of pleasure with his mouth His arms shook as he pushed in even farther.

Her legs opened wider for him and her arms circled his back, holding on for dear life as he began to move inside her.

This was what it was to be connected to another person. To be intimate. To be adored.

Their bodies moved together as if they had done this countless times. As if they were made for each other.

His arms came around her as he began to move faster, harder. She didn't hear the radio or the night noises, because the only sound filling her ears was Jack's voice, saying her name.

She knew he was getting closer to the ultimate release and could feel her body readying for the same thing. Their hold on each other tightened as stars began to shine behind her eyes. And right there, on the ground in a secluded field, they came together, as one, at the same time.

They stayed just like that for a long time. Wrapped tightly around each other, breathing heavily.

Jack kissed her. Once. Twice. And then another soul-pouring kiss as they stayed connected in the most primal of ways.

Vulnerable. She felt utterly and completely exposed. Not only because of their current state of undress. She felt naked from the inside too.

They held each other, just like that, at the top of a hill, in the darkness, and Emerson knew that nothing in her life would ever be the same.

Chapter Ten

"I am beat," Emerson said to the empty room as she collapsed onto the couch.

It had been a long two weeks. She was up to her eyeballs in events. Two new clients signed on this week. She would be busy through the rest of the year. Between signing contracts, meeting with customers, inspecting event spaces and working on those events she already had in the works, she'd been putting in extremely long days.

She'd never been so grateful for her short commute. Although, after a day like today, the walk from the first floor to her upstairs apartment, had felt like climbing Everest.

She hated to complain about work. Ever since she started her company, she decided that she would be grateful for any work that came her way. Still, it might be time to bring someone else on. At least a part-time employee would help.

"I bet you're tired."

She jumped at the sound of Grace's voice. "I didn't realize you were home."

"Maybe because you haven't been here much this week."

There was nothing accusatory in Grace's tone, yet Emerson felt guilty nonetheless. She'd been spending long hours working. Besides preparing Jack's bar for the upcoming bachelor/bachelorette extravaganza, she was spending a lot of time with Jack.

If the sun was up, she was in complete event-planner mode.

But when the sun went down and the stars came out, that's when she forgot about everything work-related and finally came alive.

It was all thanks to Jack.

They'd spent a lot of time at his house. Sometimes he cooked her dinner, and other times they ordered in. She really didn't have a preference, so long as the night ended in his bed.

Or on the living room floor, as it happened just last night, she thought with a smile.

"What's that grin for?" Grace plopped down next to her on the couch. "You look…hmm…satisfied."

Emerson hit her with a throw pillow. "I'm sorry I haven't been around much lately. Work has been nutso. But all good stuff. Lots of new clients and events."

Grace grabbed the pillow and stuck it behind her head. She scooted down and threw her legs onto the oversize ottoman they used as a coffee table.

"It's okay. I've been busy with work myself. Did you get my email about the bachelor/bachelorette party this weekend?"

Emerson nodded. "Sure did. I replied right before I

came up tonight. Don't worry. Everything is going to be perfect."

"What about with you?" Grace asked. "Is everything perfect?"

Pretty close.

Emerson sat up straight. The silent admission surprised her. Perfection. After a life of never getting close to even being mediocre, this was new and unchartered territory.

She turned to Grace, whom she was surprised to see frowning.

"Jack makes you happy," Grace said matter-of-factly.

Emerson's face grew hot; she knew she was blushing. "I believe someone in this room told me to go for it."

"I was just thinking like maybe a fun little fling. Not spending every day together."

"We don't spend *every* day together." Did they? They'd definitely had a lot to do at the bar, preparing it for the reopening, which would kick off with the bachelor/bachelorette party.

Her phone went off. She could see it on the ottoman, next to Grace's glittery purple-painted toenails. It was a text from Jack.

Apparently Grace noticed, as well. She lifted a perfectly shaped eyebrow in a very what-did-I-just-tell-you arch.

Emerson sighed. "I thought you would be happier. You love romance and happy endings and all that."

"True." Grace dragged out the word and tapped a finger to her lips. "It's just that I'm worried there won't be a happy ending in this case. That there can't be one."

Emerson swallowed a lump the size of the Capitol dome. Her friend was right. She'd been so busy the last couple of weeks that she forgot about the big picture.

She'd been having way too much fun enjoying the small picture, which involved working a fulfilling job during the day, and being in Jack's arms and bed at night.

Jack was only in her life because…well, because they'd made a deal, an arrangement. They weren't even dating.

Although, it sure did feel like they were. She definitely wasn't pretending when she was with him, and she would bet her own life that he wasn't either.

Even if they hadn't talked about it lately, Jack's future was up in the air. He'd been honest and up-front about that since day one. They were preparing the bar to look good for business. Or for a new owner.

The latter choice meant Jack would leave town. Leave *her*.

Purposefully, she avoided Grace's gaze.

"Oh Em, don't be upset." Grace grabbed her hands and squeezed. "I'm sorry."

"You have nothing to be sorry for. You're speaking the truth and we both know it. I've backed myself into a corner." The words tasted coppery as they rolled off her tongue.

Grace wore her heart on her sleeve and Emerson could tell that her friend knew she'd upset her. She tried to offer a smile, but knew it wasn't enough.

"What can I do?" Grace asked. "I didn't mean to rain on your parade. I have to fix this."

"How about some wine? And popcorn? And a really funny movie, so we don't have to think about anything but laughing."

Grace gave her one last once-over. Apparently appeased, she grinned. "Yes to all of the above. I'll get the wine and make the popcorn. You pick the movie."

"And don't forget about the comfy clothes," Emerson called to her friend's retreating back. "Yoga pants are essential."

"You don't have to tell me twice," Grace yelled from the kitchen.

But she knew that comfy yoga pants and some popcorn weren't going to settle her restless mind. Emerson berated herself. Just when she'd let her guard down and had really begun to feel good with a man, reality came charging back in to step on her popcorn.

Now she had to deal with the possibility that had always been around. She'd just thrown a blanket over it.

Although, maybe Jack wouldn't leave. Maybe he would change his mind. After all, they'd been working so hard on the bar. If he saw how great the party went and how much potential there was in the bar, he might be persuaded to stick around.

She would just have to make sure that every single thing went as smoothly as possible. Not just for the bar.

But for her heart, as well.

Jack hadn't been this nervous since he'd stepped out to bat during his first minor league game. Just like then, his palms were sweating, his pulse was racing and he could feel the adrenaline coursing through his veins.

He paced the floor of the bar, trying to release some of his nervous energy. A lot was riding on tonight. He'd never thrown any kind of event like this party, and all he could do now was hope and pray everything went as smoothly as Emerson promised it would.

It was almost 'go time.' The happy couple and one hundred of their closest friends would be here any minute.

He hoped they had enough of everything. He'd hired some new bartenders and waiters since his father's payroll had been mostly empty, except for Oscar. Speaking of Oscar, he'd been a huge help when it came to the nitty-gritty of supply and food ordering.

But maybe there was something else they hadn't thought of. Maybe Trina and Nick would hate what they had done with the place. This whole thing would be a lot easier to deal with if he'd gotten more shut-eye. He'd had a hell of a time sleeping the night before.

He wasn't sure he wanted to admit that the insomnia may have had something to do with his missing bed companion. They'd worked hard on decorating the bar until about eleven o'clock, the night before. Then Emerson opted to sleep in her own bed.

He'd said he didn't have any problem with that.

He may have been lying.

The truth was he missed her. He missed the way she smiled at him. He missed the way she looked when she was all curled up next to him, with moonlight falling across her face.

Moonlight? "Christ," he mumbled while scrubbing a hand over his face.

He took stock of the bar. It really did look amazing. Emerson insisted The Wright Drink display the proper amount of local DC-area pride. She claimed it would make patrons feel more at home. She'd hung pennants and other signage for the local sports teams. Not to mention, she'd gotten ahold of a signed jersey from one of the Nationals players. It was now proudly being displayed in a glass case, with an accompanying autographed baseball next to it.

Besides the new paint, better lighting, and rearranging most of the furniture, Emerson had gone to town decorating for the party. There were balloons in every corner and signs with the couples' names. She'd brought in even more lighting in the form of centerpieces; intricate candle displays added a romantic ambience. Plus, she'd had a friend of hers build a small stage in one of the back corners. She'd set up a karaoke machine for tonight, and encouraged Jack to keep it around for future celebrations.

Now he just needed to see Emerson. He needed her to help calm his anxiety over tonight's event.

He realized something at that moment. He was nervous because this bar meant something to him. He was also coming to realize that a certain auburn-haired event planner had snuck into his heart.

Huh. Something to consider.

Just then she waltzed into the room, holding her phone between her raised shoulder and her ear. She was carrying her iPad, and her eyes were scanning the screen.

"Fine, fine. I have to run." With that, she removed the phone, sighed and flipped the lid of her iPad shut.

"You look frustrated," Jack observed. "Who was that?"

Emerson tucked her phone back into the pocket of her black pants. "That was one Beatrice Carlyle Dewitt."

Ah. "Your mom. Wishing us well tonight?"

Emerson snorted. "Not exactly. She wanted to ask me what I was wearing to the anniversary gala." She used air quotes when she said gala.

"It's a gala now?" he asked, amused.

"Everything at my mother's house is a gala." She said. "Are you planning it for her?"

She looked like he'd just thrown her drink in her face. "Are you serious? Do I look like I have a death wish?"

He laughed. He did that a lot around her. It was nice to be able to relax with someone.

"Was she happy with your outfit choice?"

"Have you met my mother? Has she ever not had an opinion that she simply must share with me." She coughed and stuck her nose up in the air as she took on her mother's Southern accent. "Emerson Rose, you simply cannot wear that dress to this party. It's far too audacious. You really should wear something black. Simple. Sophisticated." She stuck her tongue out. "Blah. I wear black when I work events. Not when I'm being social. *Bor-ing.*"

Again, he laughed. "I'm sure you'll put your own spin on it." He clapped his hands together. "On to more exciting things, like the kick-ass event you planned for *me*. I made the specialty cocktails you suggested, ordered all the food on your list. What else can I do?"

She did a little spin and narrowed her eyes as she took in every inch of the bar. She walked to some of the tables, straightening chairs that were already perfectly straight.

When she returned to him, she grinned. "I think we're ready."

"Not quite," he said. "Aren't we missing a certain wedding planner?"

"Grace has been texting me every couple of minutes, for the last two hours." She took out her phone to show him. "We just went over everything this morning. I've got this. Anyway, she's working a wedding tonight. She often helps set up bridal showers and bachelorette parties for her clients. Unless it's something really big or extreme, she doesn't usually show up. At least, not for the whole thing."

Jack tapped her phone. "And yet she keeps texting you."

"She's not here, but she cares about her bride and groom. She just wants to make sure everything is going well." Emerson glanced up when the bell she'd added above the door chimed. "Showtime." The door opened and a parade of people entered.

"Oh it looks fabulous." Trina Mitchell jumped up and down excitedly. "Even better than the day we met." With that, she jumped up on a man—presumably the fiancé—and planted her lips on his. Jack hadn't met the guy yet. Emerson had handled all of the meetings.

"Look at the sign, babe. Just for us." Trina was now darting around the bar, taking in all of the details, as a barrage of men and women paraded in. Many of the women wore sashes and tiaras, while the men were dressed for a night on the town.

"Ooohhh look at these tiny cocktail napkins with our names. Ohmigod, our names are being projected on the walls and floors. I love that. Whose idea was that? And look, look. Sweetie pie, it's a specialty cocktail." Trina made a noise and Jack wasn't sure if it was a squeal or a scream.

Emerson leaned in and whispered. "See, snookums, I told you that would be a big hit."

"You do have skills, baby cakes."

It seemed to take no time at all for the music to start blasting out of the jukebox, people to get out on the dance floor and the specialty cocktail to start flowing. Jack barely had a moment to take in the scene. Between watching his two bartenders serving up drinks and the waitstaff replenishing food, he almost missed Emerson running around, taking care of every other little detail.

Of course, he was having a hard time keeping his eyes off her. She was wearing tapered black pants and a loose-fitting black blouse. Her hair was pulled back, showing off her sparkly earrings and a pretty little silver necklace with a heart pendant. Nothing about her outfit should make a man's heart stop, and yet… Something about her made him do a double take every time she flew by.

When he did get a moment to really observe her in action, he was impressed. She was fast, efficient and pleasant. She kept to the edges of the room, but was always there when someone needed something. The waiters, bartenders and partygoers all seemed to enjoy speaking with her. She had a way about her that got her point across, while being cheerful and approachable.

He certainly wasn't an expert, but Jack would guess that Emerson was one heck of an event planner.

"Bye, cupcake."

Jack turned in time to see Nick kiss his fiancée. He knew the guys were taking off for a cigar bar. But the ladies were sticking around all night. While Jack was definitely happy to see The Wright Drink hopping again, he was happy to get a bit of a reprieve, with half of the guest list leaving.

Trina launched herself at Nick, as if he'd just told her he was heading to Mars and wouldn't be back for ten years. "I'll miss you, lovey." She plastered his face with kisses. Despite the men in the room making catcalls and throw-up sounds, Nick seemed perfectly content to let Trina shower him with affection.

Once the men were out the door, the ladies filled up their drinks again and hit the dance floor. Jack found himself laughing as he watched the shenanigans.

"Quite the party," Xander said. He'd arrived right as the other men had been departing.

"Yeah. Emerson did an amazing job. Look at this place."

Xander perused the scene. "Are you turning The Wright Drink into an all-female bar? Because I could be down with that."

Jack threw a penis straw that had been abandoned on the bar at him. Xander picked it up, studied it and then quickly threw it back. "Ugh."

"Would you like a specialty cocktail?" Jack asked with a twinkle in his eye.

"Tempting, but how about a beer?"

"Suit yourself."

"And where is Miss Emerson?"

"Right here." Emerson came up behind Xander and wrapped her arms around his waist, squeezing tightly.

"Not that I mind, but what was that for?" Xander asked.

"You helped us paint this place. That means that you helped this whole party happen, and I appreciate it."

Xander wrapped his arm around her shoulders and brought her to his side. He placed a kiss on the top of her head.

Even though the kiss was short and chaste and completely friendly, Jack felt his heart rate rising. He didn't like seeing Emerson with another guy. Even Xander.

He came out from behind the bar.

"Hey, all he did was paint for a couple of hours." He jerked a thumb at Xander. "I painted, cleaned, moved furniture, changed lights."

"Poor baby," Emerson said with a laugh in her voice. She broke away from Xander and went up on tiptoe so she could press a kiss to one of his cheeks and then the other. "You did an amazing job too. Thank you."

"That was all I asked." He motioned to one of his bartenders. "Hey, Scott, you guys good back there?"

"Absolutely. Take a load off. We got this."

"Drink?" he asked Emerson. "I think you deserve a break too."

"Sure. Sounds good. I might as well try this cocktail everyone is raving about."

"She says with pride." Jack winked at her before dashing behind the bar. He grabbed a beer for himself and a cocktail for Emerson. With Xander, they moved to a corner away from the dancefloor, taking over one of the high cocktail tables Emerson had insisted he needed in order to create levels. Now that he saw them, he had to agree with her. It added dimension to the bar.

The three of them enjoyed their drinks as much as they could over the volume of the music. Eventually, Emerson pushed her cocktail toward the center of the table. "Well, I should be getting back to work."

"Back to what?" Xander asked. "Isn't the party in full swing?"

She smiled. "Yes, but there are always details to check and double-check. How's it going in the kitchen? Are the bartenders okay?" she said, ticking the items off her fingers. "Not to mention that we arranged transportation for the end of the night, and I want to give the car company one last call to confirm."

"You make me tired, Emerson Dewitt," Xander said jovially. "But I have to admit that I've been in here a million times and it has never looked quite this good. You did a really amazing job."

She reached across the table and squeezed his hand. "Thank you. That means a lot." Emerson stood up and both men followed suit. "However, my work is never done."

"Hey," Jack said, joining in. "I've worked hard too. This is my bar after all."

Xander scoffed.

"What?" Jack asked.

Xander threw his arm around Jack's shoulder. "Oh yeah, it's *his* bar until he hightails it out of here again."

Jack laughed at first. But then he noticed Emerson, who seemed to deflate right in front of his eyes. Her shoulders sank, her face fell and her gaze suddenly found the ground incredibly interesting.

He felt like a world-class heel.

They'd just spent almost every day together, over the last couple of weeks. He didn't want to assume anything, but he was fairly confident that Emerson had feelings for him. After all, he'd developed them for her.

The realization struck him right in the gut. He didn't know why he was even surprised. He never would have slept with her if he hadn't felt something for her. And he never would have even asked to take her out if he hadn't.

Actually, it probably went back even further than that. Wasn't that strange? He was completely besotted with Emerson, and it must have started from the very beginning. Something about her called to him in a way that no other woman ever had.

The sadness on her face was like a sucker punch to his gut. She didn't want him to sell the bar. The truth was he didn't know yet what he was going to do. He could only confirm that it was still a possibility. He had to try to explain that to her.

"It's just that I…" he began.

She took a breath, seemingly to center herself. "I know."

Did she? She couldn't possibly understand something that he didn't. "We've been so busy getting ready for this. We haven't had time to talk about my plans." He gestured with his arm to indicate the party.

"I only thought that once you saw how hard I worked— I mean, how great the bar turned out and all of the potential it had…"

"It's amazing and you worked magic here, beyond my expectations."

"Still, you've made up your mind. You're definitely going to sell the bar and move away?"

She bit her lip, and if he wasn't mistaken, she was holding her breath. Jack's heart soared at the idea of his presence affecting someone so much. When was the last time anyone had cared if he stayed or went?

Xander said something under his breath that sounded very much like, "Jack always leaves." But Jack ignored it. Instead he touched a hand to Emerson's shoulder.

"Hey, I haven't decided anything yet."

"But you're leaning more toward going." She lowered her voice. "Aren't you?"

"I..." he began. Only, he couldn't finish the sentence. If she had asked him this same question a few weeks earlier, his answer would have been a resounding yes. Now...he simply didn't know.

She was waiting, and her eyes were becoming huge blue saucers. He wished he could tell her what she wanted to hear. But he wouldn't lie to her.

He closed his mouth. She nodded and abruptly turned and walked away.

Damn. A different, harsher oath tore out from his lips.

"What's wrong with you?" Xander asked, oblivious.

He eyed his friend long and hard.

"What?" Xander asked.

"Did you have to say that? In front of her?"

"Say what?" Xander took a long swig of beer. His gaze followed Emerson as she crossed the room and met with Trina. The two exchanged some words. It looked like Trina tried to entice Emerson to the dance floor, but Emerson shook her head. "About you leaving?"

"Yes, that."

"So what?" Xander asked. "What's the big deal?" He stepped back and cocked his head. "Wait a minute." He pointed his finger at Jack and then in the general direction of Emerson and then back to Jack. "This thing between you is fake. Right? It's a pretend relationship."

Jack swallowed. Hard. "Of course. We're pretending for her parents, and she helped me spruce up the bar."

Again, Xander looked from him to Emerson and back again. His hands fell to his side as he squeezed his eyes shut. "Damn. I'm sorry, man. I didn't realize."

"Realize what?"

"That while you and Emerson were so busy pretending to like each other, you actually started to *like* each other."

Jack shuffled backward a few steps. "No, we didn't do that."

All Xander had to respond with was a raised eyebrow.

Jack slumped back into his chair. Xander followed, sitting in the chair next to him, which Emerson had abandoned.

"Yeah, okay, I like her. A lot."

"Dude, this became complicated."

"I don't think I've ever done complicated." He shrugged. "Never wanted to." *Until now. Until Emerson.*

What did that mean? Because, despite admitting his feelings, he still didn't know what to do about the bar. Was liking a woman enough to make him stay in one place? To stop flitting from location to location, trying to figure out where he wanted to be?

He didn't know the answers.

"I upset her just now."

Xander grimaced. "Actually, I think I did. I'm an idiot," he uttered softly.

"Well, we already knew that," Jack said with a grin. But his smile quickly faded. "I don't know what to say to her at this point."

"Do you want to stay here in Virginia?"

Jack ran a hand over his face. "I'm not sure."

"So you want to sell the bar and leave?"

He rubbed the back of his neck. "Not sure about that either."

Xander leaned back in his chair. "One thing is for sure. You need to erase that frown from her face." He jutted his chin toward Emerson, who was on her cell phone, at the other end of the bar.

His friend was right. Without saying so, Jack rose. He watched Emerson end the call and put her cell back into her pocket. Then he quickly crossed the room in eager strides.

"Em, listen, I want to say something."

She looked up, crossing her arms over her chest. Her body language spoke volumes. She was closing herself off to him.

"About before, what Xander said." He shook his head. "No, about what I said. The thing is, I'm a bit in limbo right now."

"You don't owe me any explanations, Jack."

"Yes, I do." How to explain to her when he couldn't make sense of it himself? "My dad's passing was extremely unexpected. I never imagined that one phone call would have me rushing back here and taking over a business that I'm not exactly qualified to run."

Something knowing sparkled in her eyes and she actually smiled.

"What?" he asked.

"I wish you could see yourself the way I've seen you the last couple of weeks."

Her words mirrored what he so often thought about her. He desperately wanted her to view herself the way he did, but never did he expect her to turn that sentiment back on him.

"You're a natural at this." She gestured around the bar.

He snorted. "Oh yeah. I didn't even know how much vodka to order."

She rolled her eyes. "Don't be ridiculous. You handled it. You handled every detail and decision in reopening this place. When you didn't know the answer, you asked the appropriate person. You made this night happen."

He shook his head vigorously. "No, you made this night happen."

She emitted a humorless laugh. "I planned a party. You ran a bar."

Well, huh. She held such conviction in her eyes that it actually stopped him in his tracks. Was she right? Was this true? He had to admit that he'd been enjoying himself where the bar was concerned. One of the best parts of his jobs out in Vegas and Reno was interacting with people. Just like the bar.

She was looking at him with such big, beautiful eyes. And those pouty, tempting lips. He couldn't resist. No man could.

Jack leaned toward her and pressed his lips to hers. The action elicited a small moan from her and Jack took the opportunity to draw her farther into his arms.

The kiss turned steamy fast, and he was sure that was his doing. Kissing Emerson had become as essential to him, in the last couple of weeks, as air.

All of the sounds of the bar—the music, the laughter, the clinking of glasses—simply faded away. Nothing mattered. Only Emerson and her succulent mouth.

"Come home with me," he mumbled against her mouth. A mouth that turned up into a lazy smile.

Her eyes opened. She ran her hands through the hair at the base of his neck. "You may have noticed that you have a bar full of people at the moment."

Oh. Right. "They won't notice."

"Jack," she said, exasperated. "This is a big night for you."

"And I would like to celebrate it with someone who is incredibly special to me."

She swallowed hard. "Me?"

He nipped her bottom lip. "You."

"Okay."

"Hey—will you come home with me?"

"At the end of the night. Yes. Now I have to get back to the party."

She began walking away, but he quickly reached for her hand and grabbed hold. She peeked over her shoulder.

"We're good, right?"

She hesitated, for a brief moment. "We're fine."

Only, there was something in her eyes. A certain shadow that led him to believe that fine was the opposite of what they were.

Because he was falling hard for Emerson Dewitt and he suspected his feelings were reciprocated. Which meant, Xander had been right. This had gotten complicated.

And if he wasn't careful, they were both in very real danger of getting hurt.

Chapter Eleven

Emerson was bone-tired.

Jack pulled his truck into the driveway, and they slowly made their way up the path and into the house through the front door. He turned on a small lamp on the console table next to the door.

Cosmo came barreling out of the living room, with his tail wagging at a hundred miles an hour.

"Cosmo," Emerson squealed and leaned down to pet and rub and fawn. "Hello, handsome boy."

Jack laughed.

"I wish you were more animated with my dog," he said sarcastically.

Emerson straightened. She stared at Jack until he questioned her.

"What?"

"You just referred to Cosmo as your dog. Not your dad's dog."

As if conveying his own excitement at this development, Cosmo jumped up on Jack, placing his two front paws on his thighs and attempting to lick his crotch. Jack laughed and pushed the dog down. Then he crouched and rubbed Cosmo's belly.

Jack coughed. "Well, the little guy has been growing on me."

Emerson grinned from ear to ear. Watching Jack with the dog was melting her heart. She sighed.

All of the adrenaline of the day was crashing around her, and she knew she could curl up right here on the floor of the foyer and sleep for twelve straight hours. Thank God tomorrow was Sunday and she didn't have any pressing events coming up. In fact, she could sleep all day, if she wanted. Probably, she would.

It was always like this after a big event. For some unknown reason, she actually thrived on the feeling.

Spending days, weeks or months planning every scenario, every angle of an event. When the execution day arrived, she lived on nerves and coffee, running from one to-do item to the next. She darted between crises, put out fires and made sure that no one was the wiser.

But a point always came when all of that energy faded. For the Mitchell-Cross party, that point had arrived. It was three o'clock in the morning and she'd been awake for almost twenty-four hours straight.

She stopped in the middle of the floor and let out a long, tired yawn.

"You must be beyond beat," Jack said. He came up behind her and removed her coat. Then he took her purse and the large tote bag she'd used and put them away.

"Come on." He urged her to a bench at the base of the stairs. Forcing her to sit, he knelt in front of her and removed her boots. One at a time.

The heels on her boots were miniscule, since she had

known that it would be a long day on her feet. Still, she wouldn't be surprised if her feet didn't let out a full-blown cheer as they were freed from the shoes.

"Give me one sec. I want to let Cosmo out back and make sure he has food and water. Don't go anywhere."

As if she could go somewhere, even if she wanted. That would involve moving, and she definitely didn't have the energy for that. Emerson leaned back and closed her eyes.

She wasn't sure how much time had passed, but she sensed Jack's presence again. "Where's Cosmo?"

"He went out back and did his business. Now he's having a nice late-night snack." He peered down at her. "Have I thanked you for everything you did yet?"

"You don't have to thank me. It's my job."

"I didn't pay you."

"I love doing it and, besides, you're paying me back. And the currency you're using is much more precious than dollar bills. After all, you still have to spend more time with Beatrice and Walter Dewitt. My parents' anniversary party is next Friday."

"It will be fine, Em."

She shook her head, too tired to elaborate on it. "I can't even think about that now."

Her eyes fluttered closed as the remaining energy left her body. But they flew open again when she was hoisted into the air. Jack had hooked one arm under her legs and the other behind her back. He carried her as if she weighed nothing.

"Jack," she said.

He pressed a soft kiss to her lips. "Shh. I got you."

He walked them up the stairs, down the hallway and into the bedroom he was using. Gently, he placed her on the bed.

The room was dark, and besides the sound of a light rain that had started falling while they drove home, the house was silent. It was so different out where Jack lived than it was where she lived, in Old Town. Even though Jack's house was a quick drive away, in the Del Ray neighborhood, sometimes it felt like they were far away in the country.

It was nice. Calming. Relaxing, even, to be away from the hustle of the heart of the city.

Jack didn't turn any lights on. She heard him removing his shoes, but she couldn't even lift her tired head from the pillow. The mattress shifted when he joined her.

She reached for him. Wanted to feel that he really was right next to her.

Tonight had brought a lot of unexpected emotions. She'd worked hard on this party. Put her whole self into making it perfect. She'd wanted it to be perfect for him. Wanted him to see the possibilities.

But there was that very real moment that had threatened to crush her heart. Jack's future was unknown. This was something that didn't come as a surprise, yet she'd been so busy falling for him that she'd allowed herself to forget about it and push it from her mind.

She needed to protect herself. There was a very real possibility of getting hurt again. Thinking about how much her breakup with Thad had affected her was one thing. With Jack, she already felt more for him than she had for her ex-fiancé. She didn't even want to imagine the pain of actually watching him walk away. So she definitely needed to guard her heart.

But at the moment, she was too tired to fight it. When Jack rolled over, propping himself so he could gaze down at her, she didn't move.

Usually the passion was so explosive between them.

When he leaned over and softly pressed a kiss to one of her eyelids, then the other, then the tip of her nose, and finally to her lips, she realized tonight was going to be different.

He kissed her for a long time, moving his lips warmly and gently over hers. She reached up to cup the back of his head. He deepened the kiss and she sighed, welcoming him in.

Moving his lips to her jawline, he showered her with soft, gentle kisses. He ran his lips down her neck, stopping only to nip her earlobe.

His every movement was relaxing her beyond anything she'd ever felt before. Her limbs were starting to feel heavy, even as her heartbeat began racing.

Jack was running his lips, his tongue, his teeth, along her collarbone and following the neckline of her blouse. When she made to move, Jack reared back and shook his head.

"No?" she asked, surprised.

"Tonight is all about you. It's for you."

Her heart soared. His face was so serious and his eyes full of hazy lust. Maybe this really could be something. Whatever this thing was between them. This thing that had begun as a bargain to help each other out. This thing that had clearly taken on a life of its own.

She'd done her very best to live up to what she thought he wanted tonight, at the bar. And now he was rewarding her. Did that mean he'd stay in town?

Because if their relationship really only was a bargain, half of it was over. After her parents' anniversary party, they wouldn't have any reason to stay together.

Then Jack was removing her blouse, and any deep thinking ceased. With her shirt off and thrown to the floor, he ran his hands up and down her sides. A small giggle escaped her lips when he brushed over her ticklish spot. He grinned before leaning down and licking that very spot. Emerson sucked in a breath.

His clever mouth was warming every inch of her body. She wasn't even self-conscious about her bra. She always wore a more-supportive and less-sexy bra when she was working. But Jack didn't seem to notice or care. He simply unhooked it and immediately covered one nipple with his warm mouth and sucked gently. She reached for him and held him tightly.

He was showering her with attention and, dare she think it, love? Not one area of her body was neglected as he pulled her pants and black satin panties down her legs. His hands, his mouth and his tongue explored every bit of her.

When he moved to the end of the bed and reached for her foot, she opened her eyes and realized he was still fully clothed, while she was naked and bare before him. Normally she would feel self-conscious, but she didn't with Jack. It was as simple as that. When she was with him, she was completely and irrevocably herself.

He sucked her big toe into his mouth and she squirmed.

"Jack, my feet are horrible." She desperately needed a pedicure, and her feet were completely gross after the long winter. Not to mention standing on them all day long.

He tilted his head and studied her. "Your feet are beautiful, just like the rest of your body."

To prove it, he dragged a lazy hand up from her foot, over her calf and thigh, her stomach, her breasts, until he reached her head. He cupped it as he lay on top of her. Then he kissed her so deeply and so very passionately. She was being pulled under big-time, and she was sure she'd never be able to find her way back up to the surface again.

That might just be okay. Did she really need to return to reality when it felt this good to be with him?

Finally, he ended the kiss and stood. Seemingly in no hurry, he took her in. His eyes traveled over every inch of her, from her aching toes to the top of her head. Then back down again. A slow, sexy smile spread across his face.

"What's that for?"

"You have no idea what it's doing to me to see you like that."

She snorted. "What? Lying here like a big old lump?"

He licked his lips and his eyes narrowed in on her. It was as if he were the hungriest man on the planet and she was a big, juicy steak. He looked like he was about to salivate.

"You haven't had your fill yet?" she asked.

"Sweetheart, with you, I don't think I'll ever have enough."

Her heart flipped over. She gulped.

"Then why don't you get over here and start making a dent in that appetite."

He grinned. Then he shed his clothes and opened the drawer of the nightstand on the side of the bed. She knew that's where he kept his protection.

After he returned to her, he hovered over her, stroking her cheek with one of his fingers. Then he kissed her again, slowly, deeply. His hands roamed over her skin again, caressing her breasts, teasing her, setting her insides on fire. But he never stopped kissing her.

"Jack," she murmured against his lips.

"Mmm?"

She nipped at his bottom lip. "I want you."

He pushed a strand of hair back from her face. "Now?"

"Please."

He framed her face in his hands and kissed her one

more time. Then he pushed inside her. They both moaned. The pleasure was absolutely exquisite.

They moved together, completely in concert. They'd been together enough times now for their bodies to understand each other.

Jack reached for her hands and brought them to the pillow, next to her ears. They clasped fingers. Their eyes locked on to each other.

They were joined in every way possible. Their bodies, their eyes, their hands. Their hearts?

It was the most sensual moment of her life. She held on tightly as Jack's movements became faster and harder. As she went right over the edge, with him following right behind.

And then they collapsed into each other, completely sated, as the rain continued to fall.

The rain had picked up. It was drumming a fast *tat, tat, tat* against the roof of the house. The wind was roaring through the trees, and a loose branch was scratching the window.

She and Jack were lying in bed, tangled up in the sheets and each other's limbs as they listened to the sounds of the storm. Cosmo had found his way upstairs and made himself at home at the bottom of the bed. He was curled up in a little ball, seemingly fast asleep. But every once in a while, he would perk up, lick one of their toes and then return to his slumber.

Emerson still felt exhausted, only she now also felt rejuvenated, energized, sated. It was a strange sensation.

"Two weeks ago, we did this for the first time," Jack said.

It was a rare moment of reflection for him. She ran a hand over his bare chest.

"I made love to you under the stars. I felt bad that we were on the hard, cold ground."

"I liked being outside." She had. She remembered thinking that they couldn't possibly do *that* outside. But then they had, and she'd felt empowered. She'd also felt sexy as hell.

"We could go in the backyard now, if you want," he said with a wry smile.

"Nah. It's raining."

"I thought rain was romantic."

"It is. But it can be from inside, as well." She shifted her body against a certain part of his as a reminder of just how sexy rain could be.

He grinned and nuzzled her neck. "Are you okay? Do you need anything?"

"Funny, but I am feeling quite reenergized. Although, some water would be great." She made to move but he stopped her by pushing her back against the pillows. He tucked the blankets around her and kissed her forehead.

"I got it. Be right back."

She watched him rise, in all of his naked glory. She would never tire of looking at this man's naked body. Sadly, he pulled on his boxer briefs before leaving the room.

Cosmo let out a little harrumph at the disturbance. Then he made his way up the bed and made himself comfortable in a ball on Jack's pillow. Emerson laughed and ran a hand over his soft fur.

Jack returned a few minutes later with two glasses of water. She sat up in bed and drank almost the entire glass. Cosmo lifted his head with mild interest and took in the scene. Then he rose, circled around a couple of times before returning to his cute little ball position.

"Seriously, dog? On my pillow?"

"I think it's a sign of love," Emerson suggested with a laugh.

"When you're not here, he lays on your pillow."

Her pillow. How domestic. A little thrill ran through her.

Jack climbed back into bed and sat up against a mound of pillows. He gathered Cosmo up and nestled him on his stomach. She placed her glass on the nightstand and curled up next to him, laying her head on his chest. His fingers ran lazy circles over her back, and her eyes began to close.

Suddenly, Jack said, "I think my dad would have liked the party tonight."

Her eyes flew open. She wasn't sure how to respond. Luckily, she didn't have to.

"He really liked when the bar was full. He enjoyed people having fun, laughing, relaxing. The more bodies that crammed into The Wright Drink, the bigger his smile got."

"Then I'm sure he would have been entertained by tonight. All that dancing and karaoke."

He chuckled. "I'll never hear 'Baby Got Back' quite the same way again."

Emerson bit her lip as she contemplated asking him a question. But it was something that she'd been wondering about since she had met him. "Jack, can I ask you something?"

"Of course."

"The way you talk about your dad… Did you not get along?" She twisted her head so she could see his face, his reaction.

He shrugged and readjusted, sitting back against the headboard. "We did. But he got along with the bar more."

"Must have been tough on both of you," she said, more

to herself than him. "By nature, a bar is open on week-ends and at night. That must have been hard on him."

"Before my mom passed away, we would actually go have dinner at the bar most nights. This guy, Larry, was the cook then. He would always make sure to have kid-friendly options for me. Grilled cheese sandwiches, chicken nug-gets—that kind of stuff."

He was relaxing. He was opening up. Emerson wanted to punch a fist in the air in triumph, but she also wanted to hear his memories. Understand him better. So she didn't move, except to pet the dog. Only listened.

"My mom insisted I get vegetables too. So Larry would always include carrots or asparagus." He rolled his eyes but was still smiling. "There was always a salad waiting for my mom. My dad used to say that she was half rabbit because she ate so much salad.

"Dad bought the pinball machine, the *Pac-Man* game and the air-hockey table for me. Someone was always willing to take me on. Thought they could win over a kid." His eyes were practically sparkling with what were clearly happy memories. "But I was good."

"Oh really?"

"Well, I was there every day. I was a little swindler really."

"Sounds like a fun way to grow up."

"It was. At least it was interesting."

She reached for his hand and was happy when he let her take it. He began running his thumb over her skin, and the small gesture sent shockwaves through her body.

"I can't tell you how many times my mom would end up behind the bar, helping out. Then someone would play a slow song on the jukebox. My dad would scoop her up in his arms and they would dance together."

"That sounds so sweet."

He nodded. "Even the people waiting for their drinks or food didn't seem to mind. They would just watch my parents dance together behind the bar."

His fingers tightened around hers.

"Then one day I came home from school, and both of my parents were waiting for me in the living room. My mom had been to the doctor. She had an aggressive form of cancer."

Emerson swallowed a large gulp on a very dry throat.

"She died only two months later."

She wanted to say something. Anything that would bring him some comfort. But what could you say to someone who lost a parent at such an impressionable age?

"After that, my dad was always at the bar. The house was empty, cold. Lonely. Things changed."

Emerson stifled a sigh. It sounded like his dad had probably spent the same amount of time at the bar after his mother's death as he had before. Only, without his mother around, his perspective shifted and everything felt different.

"I stopped dropping by the bar," Jack continued. "At first, I had no way to get there. I couldn't drive yet," he explained. "Then I was pretty active in high school. Baseball, girls…" He offered a grin, but it didn't quite reach his eyes.

"I wanted to talk to my dad about my mom. I missed her," he said softly.

Emerson shifted slightly. "He didn't talk about her?"

Jack shook his head. "Never. To be honest, he barely spoke to me about anything after her death. He would make sure I had done my homework. He would always ask if I ate. Tell me to clean up my room. The essential stuff. But we never had a long conversation again. Even later in life, speaking over the phone was like pulling teeth."

No wonder he hadn't wanted to return home.

"I wanted to talk about her," he repeated.

Emerson's heart clenched at the raw desperation in his voice.

"Needed to talk about her. I would come home from school to an empty house. My dad was already at the bar. Her perfume lingered in the house. Her clothes were in the laundry room for I don't know how long. And I just wanted to talk about her and remember everything."

Emerson gulped. "Did your mom work?"

"Yeah, she was a teacher in the local elementary school."

His dad had to make up for an extra income. They went from being a two-income household to one.

So, there was a father and son, both grieving the loss of a very special woman, while they went on with life. Lives that would never be the same again.

A realization struck Emerson at that point. Jack wasn't considering leaving Virginia because of his father. He was running away from his mother. From her memory and from the pain that memory brought forth.

She closed her eyes as the thought washed over her. Jack was still grieving for the mom he'd lost way too young. He'd probably never really allowed himself to say goodbye. Because his dad had seemed to shut down after his wife's death, Jack had never gotten the closure he needed. That's why he ran from place to place. That's the reason he didn't settle somewhere and put down roots.

That was probably why he wouldn't stay now.

She wanted him to stay because she loved him. But he was going to leave because he couldn't bring himself to stay in a place where the memory of his mother would haunt him.

How could she ever ask him to?

Chapter Twelve

Even though they were right on time for her parents' anniversary party, Emerson and Jack had to circle the block a couple of times before they found a parking space. It seemed like everyone in Northern Virginia had come out to help the Dewitts celebrate.

Thirty years of marriage.

Despite any hard feelings with her mother, she couldn't help but be happy for them. Getting to the pearl anniversary was no easy feat.

Sometimes it seemed like Beatrice and Walter were so very different. Her dad was so much more laid-back than her mom. He would be content to live in a one-bedroom cabin on a lake, fishing, reading mystery novels and watching World War II documentaries, while her mom delighted in things like flower arrangements, china patterns and hosting tea parties.

Yet they were one unit. A strongly bonded couple that

had raised two daughters, while starting their own businesses.

"What are you thinking?"

She glanced at Jack as they walked from their parking space at the end of the street. He looked so handsome tonight in a black suit and silver tie. He'd left his stubble though, and the contrast with the suit was absolutely mouthwatering.

"About my parents."

"Thirty years is amazing," he replied. "You know what else is amazing?"

She stopped and waited for his reply.

"You in that dress."

She felt a grin spread across her face.

Her mother had strongly suggested she wear a tasteful black dress to the event tonight. Being the good daughter she was, Emerson had complied. But with Jack's idea to make it her own. She was wearing a midi-length black dress with a conservative neckline that was classic and sophisticated. From the front. When she turned around, the big reveal was a low cut back. For an extra splash of whimsy, she'd pinned a bejeweled turquoise flower in her curls.

Tasteful black, without losing herself.

"I feel good." She didn't know where the statement came from. But it was true. She did feel good. Strong. Like herself. When was the last time she could claim that?

Tonight, she felt strong and confident. Even though her mother was sure to dislike her outfit choice, and everyone inside the party would no doubt fawn all over her sister, Emerson didn't care.

She had a growing business that she'd started all on her own. She adored her friends. Over the last couple of weeks, she'd had a strong, handsome, fun, interesting man by her side. It may have started off as a pretend re-lationship, but she knew that was no longer the case. Her feelings wouldn't lie. Her heart couldn't lie. And the way Jack held her in his arms definitely wasn't a lie.

Jack stepped toward her. He had that look on his face she'd come to know so well. His eyes darkened and he was about to kiss her. She held her breath in anticipation.

His lips brushed over hers, once, twice, before delving into a much deeper, passionate kiss. Right there, in the middle of the street, as cars whizzed by, searching for parking spaces, and guests walked toward her parents' house.

She could care less that they were in the middle of a crowd. Her hands came up to frame his face. To keep him anchored to her as she took and took.

When they broke apart, he ran a finger over her cheek so lightly. It was a move that he did with her more and more often. Her stomach flipped. The lightest touch from him seemed to set her soul on fire.

No words passed between them. Rather, he reached for her hand, interlacing their fingers as they continued toward the house.

"Looks great," Jack commented with a head tilt.

Emerson had to agree. The outside of her parents' house looked even more perfect than usual. And that was saying something. The whole place was glowing. She wouldn't put it past her mother to have hired someone to power wash each and every brick. The glass in the windows was sparkling, the beige trim impeccable.

Wreaths hung from the windows. Lights were on inside, which illuminated the outline of people talking and laughing. For such a large house, there was a homey quality.

The front yard had been spruced up after the winter.

New flowers had been planted and surrounded by mulch. The driveway and sidewalk glimmered, thanks to a rainstorm that happened the night before.

Along with two couples she recognized from her dad's law firm, they entered the house. Music was playing softly through the hidden speakers her parents had installed throughout the house. Yummy aromas wafted from room to room. She knew her mother had hired her favorite caterer and servers were passing all kinds of different appetizers. The furniture had been rearranged to make cozy sitting corners and places to invite conversations.

They made their way through the crowd. When they passed the patio doors, she could see that her mother had made sure the outside was also party-ready. Lanterns and twinkly lights illuminated the patio. Heat lamps lined the perimeter, and a bar was set up on one side.

"Your parents sure do have a lot of friends," Jack said.

He seemed to be surveying the space as they searched for her parents.

"Daddy started his own firm decades ago. Between colleagues and clients, he knows a lot of people. And Mama…" She whistled. "I can't even begin to describe the amount of people in her life."

Jack jutted his chin toward the left. "There's Charlie." He waved. "Hey, buddy."

Despite having spent hours together at dinner, Charlie seemed temporarily confused as to who Jack was. He took in Emerson and his jaw worked back and forth.

"Hi, Emerson. Hi…" His phone went off. Immediately, he put it to his ear and walked away.

"Always good chatting with you," Jack called to his retreating back.

Emerson laughed.

"God, I love that man," Jack said, and had her laughter turn into a snort.

"I don't know where my parents are."

"Let's get a drink to fortify the search efforts," he said, smiling at her.

They found another bar in the dining room and got two whiskeys, neat. Sipping their drinks, they stood against the wall. Emerson waved to the occasional person and exchanged greetings with some of her mother's friends.

Everyone she chatted with seemed quite taken with Jack. She knew that, in the looks department, he was quite different from the men she'd dated in the past. With his stubble, dark looks and mischievous grin, Jack was attracting a lot of attention. In fact, people—particularly the female guests—were so charmed by him that they didn't even harp on the fact that Emerson had a new boyfriend as she'd expected.

Amelia entered the room, wearing a navy wrap dress with a gorgeous diamond necklace. Emerson knew the necklace had been a wedding present from their parents. Her hair was off her face, highlighting her long neck. Emerson peered at her sister. Her makeup looked fabulous, as always, but she knew Mia. Emerson worried her lip.

"What's wrong?" Jack asked.

"I'm not sure. Something seems off with my sister."

Jack's gaze sought out Amelia. He studied her before returning his attention to Emerson. "Everyone seems excited to see her."

The room did come alive when Amelia entered, as if a spotlight shone directly on her. Conversations stopped and everyone wanted a turn to say hi.

The feeling Emerson had didn't subside though. In fact, as she watched her sister interacting with the party-goers, it only increased.

Amelia, you look amazing. As always.

How's married life treating you?

Still working at your mom's shop? Well, as soon as you start having babies, you won't have to do that anymore.

Where's that handsome husband of yours?

With each question, Amelia appeared to withdraw more into herself. Her face continued to fall, and as she neared their side of the room, Emerson could actually see dark circles under her eyes. Of course, Amelia had expertly covered them with makeup, but she knew her sister like the back of her hand.

Finally, Amelia reached her and Jack.

"Hey, Mia. Love your dress. When did you get that?"

Amelia looked down at the dress as if she had forgotten she was even wearing it. "Oh. I think I got it when I went with Charlie on one of his business trips. I needed something to do."

What a weird comment. Emerson opened her mouth, but Jack beat her to it. He drew Amelia into a big hug, which actually seemed to calm her. When they pulled back, she asked about the bachelor/bachelorette party. They exchanged words, and then Amelia pointed at Emerson's glass.

"What are you drinking?"

She reached for the glass and had it to her lips so fast that Emerson almost didn't get out, "Wait, it's scotch." But Amelia took a long drink.

"I need some of this."

"You don't like scotch," Emerson pointed out.

"Would you like me to get you something?" Jack asked.

"Get her a glass of wine. Rosé," Emerson said.

Once Jack was out of earshot, she turned to her sister. "What is up with you tonight?"

Amelia shrugged.

Emerson held her ground. She crossed her arms over her chest and waited.

Amelia sighed. "I thought everyone would be over asking me about being married. You're the one with the new boyfriend. They should be peppering you with intrusive questions."

"They're all too gaga over Jack's hotness to care about me." Emerson giggled but noticed that her sister remained stoic.

"Your wedding was only six months ago. Sorry, sis, you're still a hot topic." She tugged on Mia's hair, something she used to do when they were little. "What's the problem anyway? Since when do you shy away from attention?"

"Since I feel...embarrassed about my answers."

What? "Embarrassed? What in the world do you have to be embarrassed about?"

Amelia opened her mouth, about to answer, but Jack returned with her glass of wine. She downed half a glass in one gulp. She looked directly at Emerson. But Emerson got the distinct feeling that she wasn't really seeing her.

"Where's Grace? I thought she was coming tonight," she asked distractedly.

"Where else?" Emerson said. "It's Saturday. She had a wedding. But she'll be by later."

Amelia nodded. "I need to find Charlie," she said abruptly.

Jack watched her walk away. "Is she okay?"

"I'm honestly not sure."

"Emerson, Jack." Beatrice's voice echoed across the room.

Emerson took in her mother, wearing a gorgeous cranberry-colored dress with silver heels. Her dad looked handsome in one of his crisp black suits. They made such a picturesque couple. Her dad paused to press a kiss to his wife's forehead. Despite everything, her parents truly loved each other.

"It's go time," Jack whispered in her ear.

"You look beautiful, Mama."

Beatrice ran a hand over Emerson's hair, pausing on her jeweled clip. "I see you wore black."

"As you suggested."

She coughed lightly. "You look lovely."

Emerson's mouth fell open. Had her mother just complimented her? And about her clothes? When was the last time that happened? Had it ever happened?

Jack jumped in. "She does look great, doesn't she."

Emerson finally recovered. "It doesn't matter what I'm wearing. Everyone is here to see you."

She surprised both herself and her mother when she pulled her in for a tight hug. Then she whispered in her ear, "You look absolutely stunning, Mama. As usual."

Pulling back, Beatrice studied her carefully, with a small tilt of the head. "Something is different about you tonight, Emerson."

Emerson twirled around.

"Seriously, Emerson Rose?" her mother said.

She actually giggled. She'd forgotten about the low back of her dress.

"There are elderly people here tonight."

That just made Emerson laugh more.

Beatrice tapped a French-manicured finger against her lips. "Still, something is different. You seem…"

"Happy?" Emerson couldn't keep the smile from blossoming.

Her mother's gaze scooted over to Jack, who was listening to one of her dad's joke, and then back to her. "In love," her mother said firmly, knowingly, in that way only mothers had.

She had two options. She could deny it, or she could own it. Maybe it was being at her parents' thirtieth wedding anniversary. Maybe it was the fact that every time she looked over at Jack, she got a certain tingle in her stomach. Or maybe it was because she was sick of lying about something that was no longer a lie.

In any case, it was finally time for a little truth.

She met her mother's stare head-on.

"Yes, I am."

Jack was enjoying himself. Maybe a little too much.

He'd been talking and laughing with Emerson's father for the last fifteen minutes. Emerson was deep in conversation with her mother, except for when another guest would interrupt them to offer congratulations and well wishes.

He was introduced to person after person as Emerson's new boyfriend. Mr. Dewitt bragged about Jack's bar, telling colleagues and friends that they had to stop by next time they were in Old Town.

Even Mrs. Dewitt had seemed to come around to the fact that he owned a bar. She was boasting about her painting job in The Wright Drink. She actually winked at him as one of her friends asked him questions about owning a bar.

Jack was feeling like a part of the family.

He grabbed another drink and took a moment to get some fresh air. He stepped outside, onto the patio, and found a quiet corner.

Part of the Dewitt family. Part of Emerson's life. He wasn't sure how to take that idea, because his head was telling him it was a dangerous place to go. But his heart really liked the thought of having people to support him. Of being part of a family again. Of being there to support the woman in his life, every day.

It felt good to be part of such a momentous event. Thirty years of marriage. He couldn't help but think about his parents. No doubt if his mom had survived the cancer, they would have stayed together. They had adored each other.

It was little things with his parents. Small shows of affection. His mom always brought his dad coffee in bed, fixed just the way he liked it. His dad left little notes for his mom around the house. He brought her flowers all the time too. Daisies.

The same flowers he'd given to Emerson when they had gone out on their first date.

Wow. He hadn't even realized. It was like his father's gesture had seeped into his subconscious.

His parents were a unit. They were home for each other.

Jack had been all over the world. Experienced everything, from jumping out of a plane in Hungary to seeing the Leaning Tower of Pisa to hiking a volcano in Hawaii. Yet he'd mostly been alone on those adventures.

Mr. Dewitt seemed interested in his stories. It was nice to have someone to share them with. He'd told a couple to Emerson and had enjoyed watching her eyes widen as he had detailed walking along the Great Wall of China and snorkeling along the Barrier Reef.

He was starting to realize that it would have been nice to have these same conversations with his dad, whom he'd basically denied a relationship with him.

"Someone is deep in thought."

Clearly he had been, since he hadn't even heard Xander creep up on him.

"What are you doing here?" he asked as Xander squeezed a lime into a gin and tonic before taking a sip.

"My firm does a lot of work with Mr. Dewitt's. I've actually known your pretend girlfriend's dad for a couple of years now. Speaking of your pretend girlfriend, where is she?"

Jack pushed a hand through his hair. "Actually, I wouldn't say we're all that pretend anymore."

"Nooo." Xander overexaggerated the word and put a hand to his chest like he was in shock.

Jack answered by way of a finger of choice in Xander's direction. For his part, Xander simply chuckled.

"Give me all the fingers you want. But the truth is the truth."

Jack loosened his tie. "And what exactly is the truth here?"

"That you've fallen hard for Emerson and it's been clear to anyone with half an eye that the two of you are wild for each other."

"Interesting, since I didn't even know that."

"Well, you've always been on the slow side."

Jack punched him in the arm, and Xander feigned being hurt.

"So, you think this thing with Emerson is a good thing?"

Xander's jovial expression slowly faded. He studied the contents of his glass and swirled it around before finally talking. "You know me, dude. I can't get on board with any relationship."

"Why is that again?"

"It's what I believe. They don't work. They're not right. I see the results every day, in my work." He paused, glancing up. "But I do like seeing you happy, and if Emerson makes you happy, then great. As it turns out, I have something else that is going to make you happy."

Intrigued, Jack waited.

"I was finishing up some business with one of my clients today when he mentioned that he was looking to open a restaurant and bar. Asked if I knew of any locations."

For some reason, the hair on the back of Jack's neck stood up on high alert.

"I told the guy all about The Wright Drink. He was really into the location. Wants to know if he can come see it this week."

What should have been a happy development had the result of making Jack's stomach sink. Wasn't this what he wanted?

He took a long, deep breath.

"What?" Xander asked. "I thought this is what you wanted."

"It's definitely one possibility. I'm just not... I don't know."

Xander nodded knowingly, just as Emerson sidled up to them.

"There you are," she said.

He instinctively put his arm around her. She just felt so right up against his side.

"Needed some air," he said.

She laughed lightly. "Are you calling my parents' friends stuffy?"

"Oh no," Xander joined in. "They're all great. Barrels of fun."

"Shut up. When you two are my parents' age, you'll be having the same kinds of parties, talking to the same kinds of people."

Xander responded to that with a joke, but Jack didn't

really pay attention. He was too busy thinking about what Emerson had just said.

Would he and Xander still be friends in thirty years? Would they even be in the same place? If he sold the bar and left town, would they stay in touch? They had last time, but they were getting older.

"Jack."

He shook his head as Emerson pinned him with a look. "Sorry, what?"

"I asked what you guys were talking about before I walked up."

Jack looked to Xander, but his friend's lips were sealed shut. He'd clearly learned his lesson after the party in the bar.

But Jack didn't want to lie to Emerson.

"Xander has found a possible buyer for The Wright Drink."

He could feel the tension ratchet up between him and Emerson, as if someone were building a wall right between them.

He reached down and grabbed her hand, interlocking their fingers. He leaned over and whispered in her ear. "I haven't made any decisions yet."

"But you'll need to soon."

Unclear of how to respond, he simply nodded.

He didn't like the lines forming on her forehead or the way her lips were turned down in a frown. He wanted to tell her he would stay. But Jack just couldn't do that. Something was holding him back.

"Emerson—" But he was cut off as the patio doors opened and scores of party guests spilled out into the crisp night air.

"I think my parents are going to give a toast."

The interruption was probably better. He truly wasn't sure what he had been about to say back there.

People gathered in every available inch of space. Luckily, the Dewitt's had a spacious backyard and patio area.

Mr. and Mrs. Dewitt were the last people to step outside. They took up a spot under one of the porch lights, as if a spotlight were shining right on them. A microphone appeared from somewhere. Obviously this was not the first large party that had happened here.

They thanked everyone for being there. Then Mr. Dewitt kissed his wife's hand, and she handed him the microphone.

"Thirty years," he said as he turned his gaze on to his wife. The crowd broke out into applause and whistles.

"Thirty wonderful years," he amended, making Mrs. Dewitt laugh.

"What's the secret?" someone called out from the crowd.

Mr. Dewitt appeared thoughtful. "Well, I'll tell you what the secret is not. Perfection. People enter marriage thinking that their life will be perfect now that they've met their spouse."

Out of the corner of his eye, Jack noticed Amelia's husband, Charlie, walk away, leaving Amelia standing all alone, in the shadows beyond the patio. Emerson gestured for her sister to come stand by her and Jack, but Amelia shook her head.

"The thing is," Mr. Dewitt continued, "marriage is not a perfect union. There are often more hard times than good. Those are the times that define you.

"When Beatrice and I first married, I was offered an amazing new job. It was everything I had worked for, everything I wanted."

"But it was up here in Alexandria," Mrs. Dewitt chimed in.

"And that was scary for two people who had spent their lives in Spartanburg, South Carolina. But she followed me up here. Left her friends and family and everything she knew and made the move."

Once again, Mrs. Dewitt took the microphone. "I didn't understand the need to move to Northern Virginia, but I supported him anyway. Just like I dare say Walt didn't understand my need to open a wedding-dress boutique." Laughter spread throughout the crowd. "But he supported me every step of the way."

They leaned together for a quick kiss. The crowd clapped and cheered.

"I must be remiss to point out that it's not just about supporting the one you love. Equally essential is to be selfish from time to time. Be kind to yourself."

The speech went on and he heard plenty of "oohs" and "aahs" from the guests. But Jack had stopped listening. He was too concerned with the auburn-haired beauty next to him.

The one who had stopped holding his hand.

Chapter Thirteen

Emerson couldn't explain what had just happened.

All she knew was that she'd been listening to her parents' speech and something inside her had shifted. It felt like a weight she'd been carrying around for most of her life had been lifted.

Suddenly, she realized she was good enough. And not only because she was with Jack. She was enough on her own.

Her mother had spoken of being selfish and kind to yourself. Those words made something click in her mind.

She did support Jack. She understood his issues and the decision he had to make with his father's bar. She got—maybe more than he did himself—his hang-ups with his mother.

But dammit, where did *she* factor into the equation? It seemed like she was giving a lot more than he was.

Emerson didn't want to compete with a bar. Nor did

she want to be completely dismissed because of issues that Jack hadn't yet dealt with.

She was good enough and she wanted to be recognized. She wanted more than what she had right now.

As her parents' guests cheered and offered their congratulations, she backed away. Jack faced her.

"Em?" he asked, with curiosity and confusion in that one word.

Without warning, words exploded out of her mouth. "Are you going to stay here?"

Jack's eyes darkened, a contrast to the pallor his face had just taken on. She knew it was a ridiculous question. He'd just told her minutes ago that he hadn't made any decisions. But dammit, that was the point. Why was this so hard for him?

He reached for her hand, the hand she'd removed from his moments before. She took another step back.

His jaw was working, as if he wanted to say something. The problem was that she wasn't sure she wanted to hear it. So she turned and walked away, heading through the garden, away from the crowd.

She knew he was following her. Could feel his presence as she ended up at the same gazebo where they'd shared their first kiss.

"We're back here," he said, obviously referring to the gazebo.

"We've never left," she replied, speaking of something entirely different.

"What's going on, Em?"

She knew she needed to be straight with him. He deserved that. And she deserved some answers, as well. Even if the thought of him leaving town left her with a cold feeling in the pit of her stomach.

What she knew of Jack was that he didn't stay in one

place for long. Even though she'd realized a while ago that his wanderlust probably had to do with the loss of his mother, it didn't help her feel any more settled.

They'd started off as strangers who had made a deal to help each other, and then their fake relationship had evolved. For her, it wasn't pretend anymore. It hadn't been for quite some time. She didn't know when the change had occurred. Didn't really care.

Emerson realized that she felt more for Jack than she had for any other man in her life, including her former fiancé. How could that happen in such a short period of time?

All of those words her parents had spoken during their toast were real. They were true. They were the way she felt about Jack.

When he entered a room, her heart rate increased. When he wasn't around, her thoughts drifted to him. When he touched her, kissed her, made love to her, she thought of nothing else.

But that needed to change. It was time to start thinking of herself.

She leveled a serious stare at him. "Jack, I need to know if you're going to stick around. I deserve to know."

"Emerson," he began, throwing his palms up in front of him.

She shook her head. "No, don't do that. Don't evade the question." She took a long, deep breath. "We're not having a fake relationship anymore."

Silence hung between them. She could hear the other party guests talking and laughing near the house.

Finally, he said, "No, we're not."

She gestured back and forth between them. "This is real between us."

"Yes."

"Then you need to tell me your plans."

"Emerson, I don't know yet. I've been honest about that."

"I'm not saying you haven't been honest."

"Then, what are you saying?"

She fought the urge to rub her temples. A headache had begun to form. "I'm saying that if this is a real relationship between us, then I should be a part of your decision. I'm saying that, well, I'm worthy of a little respect."

He cocked his head. "Worthy? Of course you're worthy. You deserve respect and admiration. And...love."

"So why aren't you giving me any?"

It was the most empowering statement she'd ever made. She wished she'd said it earlier in her life. To her mother, her sister, her ex-fiance. Instead she was saying it to the one person who had made her realize she could say it at all.

She wanted Jack. More than she could even believe. There was so much she would be willing to give up for him.

There was just one thing she valued higher than him. One thing she absolutely could not do without.

Herself.

Jack was flummoxed. Even though there was space—too much space—between them, he felt like she'd just reached into his chest and squeezed his heart until he couldn't breathe.

Emerson didn't think he was respecting her. Even though he tended to keep women and relationships in his life at arm's length, he'd always shown kindness and respect to any female in his life.

Still, she had a point. He'd been stringing her along because he couldn't make a decision. If he wasn't so hurt over her accusation, he would be proud of her. She was finally standing up for herself. Much to his detriment.

"Emerson, I never meant to—"

She quickly cut him off. "Even if you want to leave Alexandria because you don't want to own a bar or, hell, there's just some place you'd rather live, you are keeping me in the dark. If we're in a real relationship, you should be consulting me. Did it ever occur to you that I might want to come with you?"

He felt his mouth drop open. She would want to leave her life, her family and her business to go with him?

His earlier longing to be part of a family unit returned. How different his life would have been if Emerson had been by his side: traveling the world, experiencing all of the different adventures he'd had.

She was shaking her head, with disappointment written all over her face. "No, it hasn't occurred to you to talk to me about any of this. I guess you also haven't realized just how much I care about you. Or maybe the problem is that you don't care that much about me."

Now he did step toward her. He grabbed her upper arms and shook her lightly. "How in the hell can you say that?"

But he knew. It wasn't like he'd told her.

He released her arms and took her hands gently in his. Looking deep into her beautiful blue eyes, he said, "I care so much about you, Em. You've come to mean so much to me."

"Not enough."

He dropped her hands. She'd realized her power over him, and now she was running with it. He found himself growing irritated.

"I don't see what my feelings for you have to do with

my decision. It's mine to make. The consequences will be something I have to deal with. We only met a month ago."

Her eyes widened. For a second, he thought she might tear up. But she didn't. Instead she started to turn away, and that small action had his blood shooting to boil. He grabbed her arm and spun her back around to face him.

"What are you doing—?"

"No," he said, cutting her off. "What are *you* doing? Running away? Again."

"What is that supposed to mean?"

"It's what you do, isn't it? Things get heated and you climb out of a window."

Her mouth fell open and then quickly shut. He'd hit way below the belt and he knew it. The hurt in her eyes was the equivalent of a sucker punch to his gut.

"That's so not fair. That was one, and only one, time. Besides, it's laughable coming from you. You're the undisputed king of running when things get tough."

A truer statement had never been uttered. She knew it was true, and she knew that he knew it was true. Still, he couldn't admit that. Not to her. Not to anyone.

"When was the last time you were in town, Jack? How long did you stay away from Alexandria?" She shoved a hand through her hair, dislodging the pretty sparkly flower she'd anchored in her curls.

"You know I have regrets about that," he said.

"And yet you kept running. What happened when things didn't go right on a job? You'd run. You ran and ran and ran."

"Emerson, damn it. At least I did things for myself. At least I wasn't afraid to go after what I wanted, no matter what anyone thought. I never cared if I was disappointing my family. I did things for me."

She jutted a stubborn chin out. "And look where that got you. All alone."

"Better than being overly dependent on my mother's opinions of me."

She let out a sound of annoyance. "You know what? I don't need this kind of BS right now. Especially not from you."

She was right. She already got enough grief from her mother. And she'd been through a really tough year.

He relented. "Your mother loves you, even if she stresses you out by being so…overprotective, shall we say? You know that you are amazing. Tonight, you stuck up for yourself with me. But now it's time for you to stand up to your mother."

Silence descended on them. It was as if the party had ceased. Even the creatures of the night stopped making their natural sounds. It was as if the whole universe had been shocked by his words. Jack knew the feeling. He held his breath, waiting on Emerson's reply to his request.

Tentatively, he glanced at Emerson. Her face expressed a dozen different emotions—most noticeably surprise—in a very short span of time.

"I'm sorry," they both said at the same time.

It was his turn to shove a hand through his hair. "What are you sorry for?"

She shook her head slowly. "I'm sorry that I've drawn you into this circus. Into the inner workings of my family."

She took a few steps to the right and then back to the left. "I'm sorry we ever lied about being in a relationship. I'm sorry I couldn't handle this party by myself."

"Em—"

She continued as if he hadn't said anything. "I'm sorry you don't want to stay here in Alexandria. I'm sorry that you don't enjoy having your dad's bar and house, and cute little Cosmo."

"Now, that's not entirely—"

She placed a hand on his chest to stop him and drew in a big breath. Then she looked directly into his eyes. "I'm sorry your dad wasn't there for you after your mother's death. And...I'm sorry that you truly don't see how much losing your mother has affected everything in your life."

His mother's death had happened almost two decades ago. He was over it.

Wasn't he?

He stepped back and Emerson's hand dropped.

Of course he wasn't over it. How did you ever get over the loss of a parent?

But, dammit, that wasn't controlling his life. He didn't let her death permeate other areas.

He turned on Emerson. "You don't know what you're talking about." Anger emphasized each word. How dare she say that?

Emerson didn't back down. "Actually, the problem is that I really do." She started walking away but paused and then spun back around. "Talking about your mother with me isn't what you need, Jack."

"You're an expert on what I need? Enlighten me."

"You need closure. I don't know what you need to do to get it. But I can't help you with that."

The nerve of her. Just because he had revealed a bit of his past to her the other night didn't make her some kind of expert on what he needed. "We're done here."

She nodded slowly. "I know."

"No, I mean we're done completely. This relationship is over."

She glanced down at the ground, then back up to him, and her eyes were shimmering, not just with tears, but with understanding. "I know," she repeated. "I've hurt you. It's time for you to run."

With that, she shoved past him and headed back toward the house.

I've hurt you. It's time for you to run.

What the hell did that mean? More importantly, was it true?

Jack had no idea. All he did know at the moment was that Emerson hadn't merely hurt him. She'd ripped his heart out and stomped all over it.

Without her, he had nothing left here. It truly was time to go.

Chapter Fourteen

The next morning, Jack and Xander were at The Wright Drink, bright and early, doing inventory. Correction—Jack was doing inventory. Xander was sitting around, recounting some story about a woman he'd met at the Dewitt party the night before.

Jack should be tired. He'd barely slept the night before. After making sure Grace could give Emerson a ride home, he said his goodbyes to Mr. and Mrs. Dewitt, who'd given him odd stares. Obviously, he and Emerson should have left together.

Whatever. There was no more him and Emerson.

"She was a knockout," Xander was saying. "Blond hair, big blue eyes and incredibly intelligent."

"Uh-huh."

"We were having the best conversation about Europe too, until Emerson's annoying friend stopped by."

Jack looked up. "Who, Grace?"

"Grace." Xander ground out her name between a clenched jaw. "That woman drives me nuts."

"I think she's sweet."

"What do you know?"

"A lot more than you, obviously." He'd meant it lightly, but it apparently hadn't come out that way. Xander faced him.

"Where's Cosmo?"

Customers were constantly asking about the dog. The guy who delivered the beer had questioned Jack about Cosmo's absence. Now Xander was asking about him. Apparently, his dad had often brought him into the bar. Jack had to admit it had been nice to return to his empty, lonely house, after things had ended with Emerson, to find the mutt excitedly waiting for him. As if he knew Jack had a crappy night, he'd snuggled extra-close to him in bed. Which Jack had to admit was nice. Still, he didn't belong in a bar.

"There are health codes."

Xander shrugged. "Your dad always had him in here."

Jack slammed his clipboard down just a touch too hard. "I'm not my dad."

Xander nodded slowly. "I was going to let it slide, but now my curiosity is piqued. You've been in a foul mood all morning. What gives?"

"You're supposed to be helping me with this inventory, and instead you're sitting on those boxes, waxing poetic about some blonde you met and telling me how much you hate Emerson's best friend."

Xander wagged a finger in his general direction. "Hey, did I say hate? I never said hate. *Hate* is a very strong word. Let's go with *strongly dislike*."

"Whatever," Jack muttered under his breath.

"Emerson is really cool and laid-back. Weird that she

would be friends with someone so high-strung. And annoying."

Jack really didn't want to think about Emerson right now. But unfortunately she was all he was thinking about.

He and Emerson had made an arrangement. They had lied in order to help each other. Maybe they'd taken it to the next level, but they were both healthy, consenting adults. There was nothing to feel guilty about.

So why did he feel so guilty?

He shook his head, wishing the pangs of conscience would fall right out of his head. There was no reason to feel this way. Emerson was now in a better place with her family. She just didn't see it yet.

She was on the path to standing up for herself.

Not to mention that she had a successful business and a townhouse and friends. She was fine. She *would* be fine.

He was the one who wasn't okay. He was the one hiding in a dark, dank storage room in the back of a bar.

He leaned against the shelf and closed his eyes.

"You know, hiding isn't going to help this situation," Xander said.

Jack's jaw ticked. "What situation is that?"

"The one where you messed stuff up with Emerson."

Jack opened his eyes in time to see Xander lean against the opposite shelf and cross his arms over his chest. He was dressed casually, yet still carried that aura of supreme confidence.

"You want to talk about it?"

"Not really." Jack didn't want to talk about it. None of it. And yet he found himself opening up. "We fought. Bad."

"About what?"

"I don't even know how it started." That wasn't true.

It had started because he couldn't open up to her. Because she had totally called him out on his crap. In one month, Emerson had figured him out better than pretty much anyone else in his life.

When he felt hurt, he ran.

"I was telling her about my mom—"

"Whoa. You talked about your mom with Emerson?"

"So?"

"I've known you since we were in kindergarten. You've barely talked to *me* about your mom and I was there when it…happened." Xander grabbed a bottle of water he'd brought with him and took a long swig. "She must be really special."

Jack shrugged.

"Listen, dude, you know my stance on relationships."

"Yeah, it's brilliant. Don't get into one." He turned and counted the bottles of tonic on the shelf. "Real or fake relationships. Both suck. I should have listened to you."

He heard Xander let out a long exhale. He turned to see his friend frowning. "What?"

"I'm only going to say this once and I will deny it if you ever bring it up." Xander gave a long, dramatic pause. "Sometimes I'm wrong."

Jack almost laughed. But he knew his friend was serious. "Oh yeah? And what have you been wrong about lately?"

"Relationships. Sometimes they're good. Damn good."

"You're full of crap."

"Nope. I'm not. But you are if you let Emerson get away."

"I don't want to talk about her anymore."

"You're such an idiot."

Jack shoved his shoulder as he passed him and pretended to study another shelf of inventory.

"Emerson is amazing. She's beautiful and smart and funny. You're in love with her."

Jack froze. Xander had no idea what he was talking about. He wasn't in love with Emerson or anyone else. He'd never been in love. He wouldn't let himself fall in love.

Loving a person was far too dangerous. Loving someone opened up the possibility of loss and heartache. He'd been through enough of that for a lifetime.

"Like I said, I don't want to talk about Emerson. I'm going to sell the bar."

"Jack—"

"I made up my mind. Can you call my dad's lawyer, Fred? I'd like you to be there too."

"Jack," Xander began again. "Please think about this."

He had.

Jack usually felt better after he made a decision. Right or wrong, it was empowering to simply commit to doing something.

He was going to sell The Wright Drink. It was settled.

And yet he didn't feel settled. He felt moody and indecisive. Xander had finally gotten sick of his bad mood and left the bar. Jack finished inventory, made sure his staff members were all set and took the night off.

On the drive to his dad's house, Jack found his car veering down different streets than his usual route. When he threw the car into Park outside the cemetery, he wasn't particularly surprised.

He hadn't been to visit his father's grave yet. It had been raining the day of the funeral, so instead of holding the interment graveside, they'd stayed in the mausoleum, where it had been warm and dry.

But as he walked along the winding path that would

lead him to the double plot, Jack knew that visiting his dad wasn't why he was here.

It was a nice place, as far as cemeteries went. The grass was well-kept and large oak trees lined the narrow road that wove throughout the plots and headstones.

There was a small fountain in the middle of a roundabout. The white marble attracted birds, who delighted in splashing in the water.

His mother had liked that statue. He remembered her saying so when they had visited the cemetery when he had been young. Ironically, the statue now acted as marker to her grave.

Jack turned to the right and walked a short distance, reaching the slate-gray headstone, with their names etched in the stone. When his mother had died, his father had bought his plot and the double headstone. Jack remembered thinking how morbid that was. Although, it had greatly helped him when he'd returned for his father's death.

He knelt in front of the headstone. The ground was damp. He could feel it through his jeans. But Jack didn't care.

His dad's date of death hadn't even been engraved yet. Suddenly, guilt overwhelmed him. He should have come here sooner. Or at all. In the late spring, near Memorial Day, he should plant some flowers. Geraniums. His mother always did that with her departed relatives. And she switched those flowers throughout the year. Brought wreaths at the holidays.

Of course, that would require Jack to stick around. As it were, he wouldn't be here around Memorial Day. As soon as he sold his dad's house, he wouldn't be here at all.

Sorry, Dad, he thought to himself. Jack thought his dad would understand though.

He reached a hand out and traced his father's name with his finger. Then, finally, he looked at his mother's side of the headstone. He didn't expect the quick inhale of breath or the lump that formed in his throat.

"Hi, Mom." He said it quietly, even though there was no one else in the area. He bowed his head. "I should have come sooner."

But he hadn't wanted to. Because he didn't want his mother to be here, buried in the cold, hard ground. He wanted her to be alive, bright and vibrant, with him.

Jack dropped his head into his hand. "Dammit, Mom. I miss you." Thinking of the fact that he would never see her alive again made him feel restless, annoyed, irritated.

Devastated.

The urge to take off running was overwhelming. To stand up and turn around and jog toward the front gate. To keep going through Alexandria, through Old Town, away from his father's bar and his house and everything in Virginia.

If his mother had been there, she would have given him *that* look. The mother of looks. The one that froze him in place. In fact, he felt like she was looking down on him now. He couldn't move, even though every bone in his body wanted him to.

"Well, I'm not running. Not right now. I'm here." His voice was laced with defensiveness.

"It's not like Dad and I didn't get along." He looked at his father's name again. He did love his father, and he knew his dad loved him.

"It's just that when you died, everything changed. I don't know. Maybe it would have anyway." His mother died when he was fifteen. It didn't escape Jack's notice that he'd entered adolescence.

His knees were aching from kneeling. "Hell with it."

He plopped down on the grass, feeling the dampness seep into his pants.

"It didn't feel like home without you. Nothing did," he whispered. "Not the house, not the bar, not Dad."

I was all alone.

Jack had felt so lonely and isolated during that time. That's why he ran. Ran away to college and kept going. The further he ran, the further away the pain was.

It was a heady realization, and he didn't know what to do with it. Emerson had called him out on it the night before. She had claimed he ran to escape hurt. He'd thought she was full of it. But now he had to agree.

"I'm okay though, Mom. You don't have to worry about me. You should see the bar now. It looks really good. Emerson came in and worked her magic."

He thought of Emerson and that glittery clip she'd worn in her hair. "You'd like Emerson. A lot. I do."

It struck him that Emerson and his mom had a lot in common. They both laughed at his stupid jokes. They both rolled their eyes when he was being stupid. They both loved him in spite of everything else.

Emerson brought a sparkle back into his life. A sparkle that had dimmed the day his mother had died.

Xander was right. He was in love with Emerson.

His phone let out a sound, alerting him to a text message. He pulled it out of his pocket and saw Xander's name.

Fred Koda and I will be at the bar Monday morning, at 10:00 a.m., for you to sign all of the paperwork. Less than forty-eight hours as a bar owner. Celebrate your freedom...

He frowned and stowed his phone. For someone who was about to get "freedom," Jack certainly didn't feel light and easygoing. In fact, he felt rather encumbered and stressed.

Jack vividly remembered that summer after high school graduation. He'd left for college early to report for training. As he'd driven away from Alexandria, he'd felt like a million bucks. The world had been at his feet and he had finally been able to breathe.

He had felt about the exact opposite of how he was feeling at the moment.

When he'd left at eighteen, he hadn't felt like he was leaving home. Instead he felt like he was finally out, searching for it. But somehow that journey brought him back to where it had all started. And the place that had made him feel so alone suddenly was the only place where he wanted to stay.

Because this is where Emerson was.

Emerson challenged him. She constantly surprised him. And she'd reminded him that he wasn't in this world alone.

She was home for him now.

Jack didn't quite know what to do with this newfound revelation. He was selling the bar in two days and putting his dad's house up for sale. What about Emerson?

She had fallen out of a window and had landed in his heart.

Chapter Fifteen

Emerson felt like crap.

She spent most of the weekend snuggled up in her bed, watching mindless TV shows and eating food with way too many calories. It was easy to get lost in the problems of the Real Housewives while shoving cold pizza in her mouth. That way she didn't have to think about what was actually bothering her.

Jack Wright.

Falling out of that window had turned out to be the best thing she'd ever done. Even if Jack really left town, her life was better for having him in it for that short time. She felt stronger around him. More confident. She felt like herself.

Still, these recent revelations didn't keep the heartache at bay. And she was suffering.

Usually Mondays were a light workday for her. She caught up on paperwork and reviewed files for her coming events. She'd been looking forward to the mindless work. It would require her attention just enough to keep it from drifting back to Jack.

But her mother had called early that morning and asked—more like demanded—her presence at Dewitt's Bridal. Something about new dresses and inventory and help with the computer system. Whatever. The last place Emerson wanted to go was her mother's bridal shop.

Try saying no to Beatrice Dewitt. A near-to-impossible task.

She and Jack had left her parents' party separately, something that had definitely drawn the attention of her parents. For once in her life, though, they hadn't badgered her with questions. Something told her she wouldn't be so lucky this morning. No way could she escape the questions when she was alone with her mother.

So at exactly nine thirty in the morning, she made her way into the shop begrudgingly. The weather mirrored her mood. It was gray and overcast, with a harsh wind whipping the curls around her face.

Since the shop was closed at the moment, she dug through her purse for her set of spare keys. The bells situated over the door signaled her arrival. Her mother immediately came out of her office.

"Emerson, there you are."

"It's nine thirty. I'm not late," she said, with irritation coating each word. "You said to get here at nine thirty."

It was a rare outburst for her, and her mother responded to it with narrowed eyes. Strangely, she didn't comment or reprimand her.

"Well, come in then. Do you want anything to drink? Coffee? Tea?"

"I'm not one of your brides, Mama. I know where all

of the drinks are kept. If I want something, I'll go get it for myself."

Beatrice arched one perfectly plucked brow but still remained silent.

Emerson shimmied out of her coat and threw it onto a chair. "I'm here. What do you need? I do have a job of my own. Besides, I don't understand why your actual employee isn't here. You know, my sister."

"That's three sassy comments in a row. You've reached your limit."

No matter how infuriating her mother could be, no matter how much she drove Emerson nuts, she was still her mother. And deep down, she didn't like to disappoint her. To make her angry or upset.

But glancing at her now, Emerson didn't see anger or hurt on her face. Instead it was pure concern. And that was her undoing.

She sunk down to the chair she'd just thrown her coat. Tears threatened but Emerson took a deep breath to hold them in. Next thing she knew, a finger was under her chin, forcing her head up.

"What is it, Emerson?"

As if she was still ten years old, she launched herself into her mother's arms. When was the last time she'd done that?

"Oh Mama, it's over between me and Jack," she muttered against her mother's gorgeous blue cashmere sweater. She leaned back. "I'm sorry I'm crying all over your sweater."

"That doesn't matter."

"It does. I've messed everything up. Just like I always do."

"Oh honey, what are you talking about?"

"How I've always screwed up. My whole life. No wonder you're always disappointed in me."

Her mother shook her gently. "Disappointed? Emerson Rose, this is ridiculous. Stop it right now."

"But I never did anything right. Not in elementary school. Or what about how I wasn't homecoming queen or a cheerleader? I didn't go to the college you wanted me to go to. And—and I didn't get married."

Beatrice's face paled. "Emerson, have you been under the impression that you've disappointed me somehow?"

"Of course."

Her mother opened and closed her mouth. Not that she would ever point it out, Emerson saw a line form in the middle of her mother's forehead. She knew that line. Her mother was thinking. After a few silent moments, Beatrice nodded firmly.

"It has been said that I am not the warmest of women."

It was Emerson's turn to drop her mouth open.

Beatrice smiled. "But I can admit when I'm wrong. I probably have given you the impression I'm unhappy with you."

Emerson shuffled her feet and glanced down at the recently vacuumed rug. "You've kinda given me that impression most of my life."

Beatrice sighed and closed her eyes. When she opened them, her gaze was determined. "I'm your mother. It is my job to be hard on you." She reached forward and tucked a curl behind Emerson's ear. "Perhaps I've done my job a little too well. Maybe I should have eased up on you a tad."

"Uh—uh…," Emerson stuttered and then finally dropped back into the chair.

"You are a forward-thinking, independent woman, Emerson. You always have been. I never worried about your activities or college. In fact, your father and I were ecstatic that you got accepted into such a good university. And you did all of the applications and admission work yourself. Then you started your own business. You didn't even ask either of us for help. Even though we would have loved nothing more."

"Really?"

"Of course. My goodness, Emerson. You've accomplished so much in your life."

"Professionally. But not personally."

Beatrice tapped a finger to her lip as she considered her. "What does that mean?"

"I'm not married like Amelia is. I mean I was almost… I mean I know that it was embarrassing when Thad left me at the altar."

"Naturally." Beatrice froze. "Wait a minute. Are you saying it was embarrassing for me? For your father?"

Emerson nodded and felt a lump forming in her throat.

"Oh sweetheart, the only embarrassing thing about that situation is that I didn't go find that little weasel and punch him in the face."

"Mama!"

"Well, it's true. He was a scoundrel for what he did to you. A coward and a liar and a real piece of sh—"

"Mama. Ohmigod." The giggle that burst from her lips actually felt good. But only for a moment. "Still, what happened with me and Thad was bad."

"You were engaged, Emerson. It didn't work out. That's not the end of the world. He did you a favor. You don't want to be married to someone like that."

Beatrice crouched down in front of her. She reached for her hands and Emerson willingly linked fingers with her mom.

"Is there anything else bothering you?"

Emerson couldn't believe how much she'd said to her mother already. Even more surprising was how well her mother was taking everything. At this point, she might as well keep going.

Isn't that what Jack would tell her? To stick up for herself?

"My whole life I've felt like I'm not good enough. I never measured up to Amelia. She was the golden child and I was a big screwup."

Pain, pure and simple, flashed on Beatrice's face. "You don't have to compete with your sister. Not ever." She squeezed Emerson's hands tightly. "Why would you want to, honestly?"

"Excuse me?"

"Amelia's not happy. I wouldn't be either if Charlie were my husband."

She felt like she'd just fallen down the rabbit hole. What the what? "Mama! I can't believe you just said that."

"She's right though."

Emerson and her mother both turned in shock to find Amelia standing there. She'd come in through the back door. They both jumped up.

"Mia," Emerson said on an exhale. "Ohmigod. I'm so sorry you heard that."

"Sweetheart," Beatrice began walking toward her daughter.

Amelia held her hand up to stop both of them. "Don't be sorry. Charlie is a horrible husband. To be honest, he's not even that great a person."

There must be something in the air today. Emerson chewed on a nail as she studied her sister, waiting for her to say she was kidding. But that didn't happen. Amelia's face was calm and her demeanor steady.

"Did something happen between you and Charlie?" she asked.

"Nothing happened. That's kind of the point. Charlie is absent. He's disinterested. He's boring. I follow him around when he travels for work, but he never makes time for me. I know he likes showing me off to his friends and colleagues. I feel like a glorified lawn ornament."

"An absolutely gorgeous lawn ornament," Emerson said loyally.

Mia chuckled, then grew serious again. "I feel like I don't have any interests of my own. I don't really have a life to be proud of." A tear escaped her eye. "I don't have a life at all. Not like you." She looked at Emerson.

Emerson's heart broke for her little sister.

"Don't pity me, Em. It's my own fault." She swiped at the solitary tear. "I just kinda always went with the flow. I never attempted to branch out and do anything on my own. But you know what? I'm done."

"What does that mean exactly?" Beatrice asked.

"I know I want more out of life. I'm not sure where to start, so the first thing I'm going to do is file for divorce. My marriage is over."

Emerson watched her sister, expecting tears and shaking. Instead of seeing sadness though, what she noticed was an overwhelming sense of relief.

Beatrice crossed to Amelia. She paused and then grabbed her daughter in a fierce hug. "About time."

They broke apart and Amelia actually laughed. "About time? We've only been married six months."

"Six months too long, if you ask me. What do you think, Emerson?"

"Totally."

"If you both felt this way, why did you never say anything?"

Beatrice sighed. "Because you were so intent on marrying him. I know how stubborn you can be when your mind is set on something."

Well, how about that, Emerson thought. She definitely didn't give her mother enough credit. Apparently she was attuned to everything going on with her daughters.

"You know what we need right now?" Beatrice said, clapping her hands together. She didn't answer right away. Instead she ran to her office and returned with a bottle of bourbon. "Something to take the edge off."

"Mama," Emerson said as Amelia's mouth dropped open. "You keep a bottle of bourbon in your office?"

"Scotch, wine and a little gin too." She winked. "How do you think I get through dealing with some of those tough bridezillas?"

Emerson's whole world was turning upside down. To be honest, she kind of liked the view from this side.

"Who wants some?" Beatrice waved the bottle.

"We need glasses," Amelia said.

"Says who? The bourbon police?"

Yep, the world was on its head.

"What happened to our prim and proper mama?" Amelia asked, tentatively accepting the bottle.

"Girls, the world is not black-and-white. There are all types of gray. You can be polite and have good manners without being a stodgy, boring dud. Speaking of gray..." She tapped her finger against her mouth.

"What?" Emerson tilted her head. She followed her mother's gaze to the other side of the store. Her eyes raked over the mounds of dresses, but she didn't see anything out of order.

Beatrice pointed at Amelia. "The silver dress. It just came in a couple of weeks ago. You know the one?"

"Very 1920s-inspired. With the beading?"

"That's the one."

She rushed off to the other side of the store and returned carrying a gorgeous sleeveless silver gown. It was covered in beading, had a V-shaped neckline and hung straight down to the ground. It was a modern version of a gown that could have been in *The Great Gatsby*.

"That's gorgeous," Emerson said, unable to hold in the wistful sigh.

And it was. Different. Unique. Unlike so many of the cookie-cutter gowns that cluttered the store.

"I think this would look exquisite on you."

Amelia began clapping her hands together. "Yes. You have to try this on, Em." Amelia came to her and squeezed her hands.

Emerson broke away and backed up. "No, no, no." She threw her hands up in front of her.

"Yes, yes, yes." Beatrice also stepped forward. "Time to fully let go of your past and all of your hang-ups about weddings and wedding dresses."

"Mama," she groaned. "I can't."

Beatrice stepped forward and framed her face with her hands. "Yes, you can. You are my strong Emerson."

She didn't know how it happened, but ten minutes later she was standing in front of the three-way mirrors, wearing the gorgeous silver dress, which fit her to a tee. Except for the length, it almost didn't even need an alteration.

"This is amazing," she whispered reverently.

"It really, truly is," Amelia agreed.

Emerson turned to her mother and almost fell off the pedestal. Beatrice Dewitt had tears in her eyes.

She exhaled. "That's simply perfect." She coughed and dabbed at her eyes. "You need a headpiece. I'll be back."

Emerson exchanged a glance with her sister. "Wow. Didn't see that coming."

"I did. You look amazing. This is the dress you need to wear when you get married."

Emerson sighed. "If that even happens."

"Of course it's going to happen. You're young and beautiful. Plus you have that hottie boyfriend."

"Yeah, well, I may have messed that up royally."

Amelia shook her head back and forth. "I don't know. Have you seen the way that man looks at you?"

"You've mentioned that."

"Thad never even compared to him, you know."

Emerson went sentimental. "I'm over Thad. I really am. In fact, I don't think I loved him at all."

"You think?"

"I know."

"How do you know?" Amelia asked.

"Because I didn't get *that* feeling with Thad. You know, that kind of tingly feeling. The one that makes your head all fuzzy and your knees weak."

"I've never experienced anything close to that kind of feeling with Charlie. Or with any of my boyfriends, really."

"I have. With Jack," she whispered.

Beatrice came back in, carrying two different veils. She took a turn holding each up to Emerson. Then shook her head. "Nope, neither of these work with the dress."

"I don't think she should wear a veil at all. Maybe just something sparkly, like a headband or something," Amelia offered.

Emerson started playing with her hair, pulling the curls up into a loose ponytail. "Maybe something like this. Then some kind of headband or clip here." Her mother grinned. "What?"

"See, wedding dresses aren't so bad."

Emerson let her hair fall back down. She ran a hand down the column of the dress. It really was stunning. And she truly loved how it looked on her.

She could see herself standing at an altar. Not in a church, but maybe at a vineyard. Something that had a nice room that opened onto a patio. Under some kind of gazebo. With twinkly lights strung from wall to wall.

Her sister would be there, and her parents, of course. But the crowd wouldn't be too large. Just immediate family and close friends. Grace and Amelia would be her bridesmaids.

A white cake would sit off in one corner of the room. Cascading flowers decked out in glitter to match her dress would tumble down one side of it.

She closed her eyes. She could almost smell the flowers, taste the wine on her tongue, hear the sounds of the string quartet. Her eyes opened and she took another peek at herself in the mirror.

The dress was perfect. The vision was perfect.

Jack was perfect.

She shook her head. Jack wasn't perfect. He was just perfect for her.

And he was leaving. Her eyes widened and she hiccupped to hold in a tear.

Her mother stepped up onto the pedestal. "What is it, Emerson?"

"Jack's leaving me." Her voice wavered as she said those three horrible words out loud.

"Oh Em." Amelia joined them, as well.

"I don't want him to go."

Beatrice pushed a curl behind her ear. "What do you want?"

"I want him to stay. I want him to keep the bar, because I think it means more to him than he'll admit. I want him to realize how much he needs Cosmo in his life, because he's such a good doggy dad. And I want... I want him to be with me."

"Does he know that?" Amelia asked.

Sadly, she shook her head.

"I didn't say anything when you were dating Thad," Her mother said. She looked at Amelia. "And I haven't said anything about you and Charlie. Well, that stops now. I'm butting in." She took Emerson by the shoulders. "Don't let Jack get away."

"But our whole relationship has been a lie. We started out playing pretend." Her hand flew to her mouth as soon as the words were out.

Her mother and sister stared at her. So she told them everything. When she was done, she waited for the disappointment. What she didn't expect was for her mother to seem skeptical.

"I absolutely don't like that you and Jack lied to all of us. And climbing out of that window in the Pnina dress— I could just strangle you. However, we've all seen you together. You may have started out playing pretend, but trust me, the two of you evolved into a very real couple. There's just one question left."

She tilted her head. "What's that?"

"What are you going to do about it?"

Her mother stepped back and yanked on Amelia's hand to bring her with her. That left Emerson alone on the pedestal.

"You want Jack Wright? Go get him."

"I...uh, I..." Emerson bit her lip. She took another look at her reflection. She made a beautiful bride. Jack had told her that when this had all begun. He was right. The only thing missing was her groom.

A smile blossomed on her face. She turned to her mother and sister and offered a strong nod. "You're right. You're so freaking right. I love Jack. And it's about time he knows it."

She jumped down and frantically searched for her shoes. She slipped her feet into the loafers and wondered where her coat was. Realizing she was wasting time, she gave up the search and started for the door.

"Em, what are you doing? Where are you going?"

"To see Jack."

As suddenly as the urge to run to her pretend boyfriend filled her, the excitement dissipated. Emerson froze and then slowly turned back to her mother and sister. She shook her head.

"No. Nope. I'm not going to run to him."

"And why is that?" Beatrice asked, with a knowing twinkle in her eye.

"Because if Jack really wants to be with me, then he needs to realize that. He needs to come to me. I'm good enough just the way I am."

Her mother enfolded her into a fierce hug. "About time you realize what the rest of us already see."

Emerson smiled on the outside. She felt lighter and more confident. But as she walked to the window at the back of the dressing room—the window she'd climbed out of not that long ago—she was still hurting on the inside. She wanted Jack.

But there was now something she wanted just as much. Happiness for herself.

Chapter Sixteen

"You're sure about this?"

Jack nodded at Fred Koda's question. He didn't even need to take the time to think on his decision. It may not please everyone, but in his heart, he knew it was right.

Time to take a new step in life.

"Given everything that's happened over the last couple of weeks, I want to make sure you're thinking clearly. Are you positive you know what you're doing here?"

Jack offered his oldest friend a wry grin. Then he clasped Xander on the back. "I thought you would agree with my decision." He knew where Xander stood on the matter.

As if offering his support, Cosmo let out a little yip. Jack leaned down and rubbed a hand over the dog's head.

"I think Cosmo agrees with me," Jack said.

"And I thought you were so strict about not bringing him into the bar," Xander said, with one eyebrow arching in question.

"Well, it's a big day. I thought my new roommate would want in on it."

Jack rolled Xander's fancy pen over and over in his hands. Why anyone thought to spend such an absurd amount of money on a writing utensil was beyond him. He handed it back over to Xander.

Fred shuffled through the papers on the table where the three of them were sitting. "Looks like all the right lines have been signed." He reached over and clasped Jack's hand firmly. Silently, they shook hands.

Xander said, "I think we're all done here."

The three of them stood. Anticipating activity, Cosmo popped up as well, with his tail wagging.

Jack grinned. "Well...not quite." He turned to Xander. "Do me a favor and man the bar?"

Xander straightened the tie that complemented what had to be a very expensive business suit. "For how long? I'm not exactly dressed for the occasion."

"I'm not sure. If I'm back in a couple of minutes, you'll know it didn't go well."

"Fine. Can Mr. Cosmo stay with me?"

"No way. I need him for moral support. Plus who can say no to his face?"

He didn't give Xander another chance to speak, because he was already leashing Cosmo up and heading toward the door. Sensing something exciting was happening, Cosmo was extra animated.

It would have taken Jack a minute to walk around the block, but the dog had other ideas. "Must you pee on every blade of grass?" he asked Cosmo. The dog just lifted his leg one more time.

Finally, he reached the bridal boutique. "This is it, Cosmo. Wish me luck." Taking a huge breath, he pulled

the door open and stepped inside to a land of white puffi-
ness and sparkles and all things bridal.

He walked through the store for a few minutes before
he heard voices coming from the dressing rooms. Jack
picked up Cosmo and headed in that direction.

He rapped his knuckles on the open door before stepping inside. Mrs. Dewitt and Amelia both turned in his
direction. Shock initially registered on their faces. But
then Amelia grinned and Mrs. Dewitt narrowed her eyes.

He gulped. But then he looked to the right and saw
her. Emerson was at the window, peering out.

She was an absolute vision. Her auburn hair a curly
mess around her face. And she was wearing the most
beautiful silver dress. Jack had never seen anything so
beautiful in his entire life.

"Emerson," he said.

She whipped around and stumbled. He darted across
the room and grabbed her arm to steady her. But then
she stepped back.

"Climbing out another window?" he asked, going for
light and humorous. But feeling the room, he quickly
realized it wasn't the time for that. "I have some things
to say."

He turned and handed Cosmo to Mrs. Dewitt.

"If this dog pees or chews on one single thing in this
store, I will skin you alive," she said to Jack. Then she
looked down at Cosmo, who stuck his little tongue out
and licked her chin. Her face softened. "Aren't you such
a cutie? How sweet."

"He won't damage anything," Jack tried to assure her.

"The same cannot be said for me." She kissed Cosmo
on the head and then stared Jack down with such intensity that he started considering climbing out the window himself.

"I do not appreciate being lied to. While I understand you were helping my daughter—"

"Mama," Amelia interrupted. "I want to hear what he has to say. Let's hold off on grilling him for a second."

"Thanks, Amelia," Jack said gratefully. "Would you two mind if we had a little privacy?"

Neither of them moved.

"I would like to talk to Emerson in private," he tried again.

"No," Mrs. Dewitt said.

He could argue, but Jack had a feeling he wouldn't come close to winning. Instead he turned back to Emerson, who hadn't uttered a peep since he'd barged in.

"Em, I just met with Xander and Fred Koda, my dad's lawyer."

Emerson's face fell and it seemed like her entire body deflated. "Oh. You did it then?"

"Yeah," he said. His voice was husky and there was nothing he could do to stop it. Just seeing her standing there in that dress was forcing his heart to beat in a staccato rhythm. It was hard to keep up with it.

"You're really leaving then?"

What? He closed his eyes. He was doing this all wrong.

Jack crossed back to Emerson and took her hands in his. "I didn't sell the bar."

Amelia gasped behind him, but Emerson remained still. She wasn't going to make this easy on him. But he deserved that.

"I didn't sell," he tried again. "In fact, I made a decision. I'm going to stay here with Cosmo and run it myself. My dad's bar. Well, now it's my bar."

"What made you change your mind?" she asked cautiously.

After Jack had visited his mom in the cemetery, he'd

returned home to another sleepless night. He realized he was in love with Emerson. He knew he wanted to spend his life with her.

Still, comprehending these new feelings hadn't come easily. Years of running away threatened to overtake him.

But he'd spent all day Sunday trying to imagine what his life without Emerson would be like. Maybe he would meet someone new. But he knew that wouldn't do. There would never be anyone else like her.

She was his everything.

"You did. You made me change my mind, Emerson."

"And why is that?" Mrs. Dewitt asked from behind him. He turned and winked at her.

"Because I'm in love with you, Emerson Rose Dewitt. I know we haven't known each other that long and we've been lying to everyone for most of that time."

"Which is wrong and we will be discussing later," Mrs. Dewitt added.

"Mama, shush," Amelia said.

"I'm so crazy in love with you. I can't imagine my life without you in it. Before I met you, everything was dull and dark. But then you climbed out of a window and all of a sudden, the lights turned on. You bring a sparkle to my life that I haven't felt since my mother was alive."

As he watched her eyes widen and her mouth fall open, he couldn't think of any other words to say. Instead he pulled her to him and crushed his mouth to hers.

The kiss was a total-mind-and-body experience. He poured everything into it. Every feeling, fear and desire. Emerson met him at every turn.

When they parted, her eyes slowly opened and met his.

"I love you too," she whispered.

"You do?"

She nodded. "Oh yeah."

"Good, because...well..." He looked back at Mrs. De-witt, who, if he wasn't mistaken, was wiping a tear from her eyes. "I'm not exactly doing this right."

She waved a hand at him. "No, no, it's perfect. Keep going."

He chuckled and turned back to the love of his life. Jack squeezed her hands and then got down on one knee.

"Ohmigod," Amelia screeched.

"Emerson," he began. "I have nothing to offer you."

She bent over and kissed him. "You have everything because you're my everything."

"Please marry me."

It was probably only a second, but to Jack, it felt like a lifetime. A huge smile broke out on her face before she said, "Yes, yes, of course I'll marry you."

He flew up and kissed her again. Cosmo ran over and started jumping around them. They broke apart and laughed.

He knew with every ounce of his being that she was the most right decision he'd ever made in his life. Everything—all the running and all the hiding—was worth it because it eventually brought him to her.

Jack kissed the tip of her nose. "You make the most beautiful bride."

"I seem to have heard that before."

He reached down and scooped up Cosmo. One arm around Emerson and one holding his dog. A perfect little family. "Do you believe me this time?"

She nodded.

"Do you also believe that I love you and that I want to spend the rest of my life with you?"

"Depends," she said, brushing a hand over his cheek. "Do you believe that I love you too and that I can't wait to start spending the rest of my life with you?"

Together, completely in sync, they said, "I do."

Amelia gasped. "Wait, this isn't right! The groom isn't supposed to see the bride in her dress before the wedding. It's bad luck."

Beatrice smiled. "I think, in this case, it won't matter at all."

"Cheers to Emerson and Jack!"

"Thanks, Mia." Emerson touched her champagne flute to her sister's, then repeated the gesture with her parents and Xander. Finally, she turned to Jack. Their eyes met and held.

"To the future Mrs. Wright," Jack said quietly, as he wrapped an arm around her.

"To our future," she said and kissed him.

She couldn't believe it. She was engaged. To her once-fake boyfriend—the man she truly loved. But more than that, she was so happy that Jack was putting down roots in his hometown. He was keeping his dad's bar. He told her about visiting his parents' graves, and somehow, he seemed more at ease than she'd ever seen him before. He'd made peace.

Cosmo jumped up on her leg, making his presence known. "And cheers to you too," she said, reaching down to scratch behind his ears. His tail wagged excitedly and his little pink tongue lolled out of the side of his mouth.

They were gathered in the alley behind The Wright Drink. She and Jack thought it was the appropriate place to celebrate their engagement. Of course, they had to relay the story of how they met again.

They'd waited until the evening, so her dad could join them after work. When Walter arrived, Jack had pulled him aside, apologizing for not asking for his blessing before proposing. Her dad was all smiles though.

"I asked Beatrice to marry me in a similar way. I just blurted it out."

"And here we are thirty years later," Beatrice added.

Emerson let out a huge sigh of relief. For the first time in her entire life, everything felt absolutely right. She'd dared to wish for more than what she had, and shockingly, she got it all.

"Should we go inside for more champagne?" Amelia asked.

"Yes, though it has been charming standing out in this dirty alley with the enticing aroma of trash," Beatrice said, with one perfectly raised eyebrow.

Emerson laughed. Her mother had not been too keen on coming out here in the first place. But after their talk this morning, she knew that her mother supported her. And loved her. And thought she was fine just as she was.

It was more than she could have ever wanted.

She reached for her mother's hand and led the way back inside The Wright Drink, where the music was going on the jukebox, the TVs above the bar were set to a variety of sports and news channels and the drinks and food were flowing. It looked inviting and fun. Just as she'd envisioned.

The family and Xander congregated on one side of the bar. Oscar broke out another bottle of champagne and Jack announced that everyone in the bar was getting a drink on him.

The chimes above the front door sounded and Emerson turned to see her best friend enter.

"Emerson," Grace screamed. "O-M-G! You're engaged." She raced down the steps, dashed through the room, and practically ran Emerson over in her excitement. Grace hugged her so tightly Emerson thought a rib or two may have cracked.

Happy tears pooled in Grace's eyes. "I am so freaking happy for you."

"I couldn't tell at all," Jack said with a big grin.

"Shut up," Grace said and launched herself at him for another big hug. "Congratulations. You're getting the best woman on the planet."

"I agree," Jack said.

As Grace continued her animated delight, Xander returned from the restroom. Grace's enthusiasm died and her smile faded.

"Xander," she said dryly.

"Grace," he replied with the same amount of irritation.

"Isn't it nice when two people get engaged? Don't you just love celebrating love?" she asked him.

Xander rolled his eyes. "It's what I live for."

Jack snorted. "Okay, you two. No sniping today. Only celebrating."

Grace turned from Xander and her smile returned. "In that case, I'll need a glass of that champagne."

As Oscar passed another flute across the bar, the front door opened again and a huge group of girls—at least a dozen—waltzed in the front door. They were talking excitedly amongst themselves until they stopped and looked around the bar. Emerson held her breath. She hoped they were impressed with what they saw.

"This place is so cute," one of them said.

"Has it always been here?" another asked.

She gave Jack a little nudge. "Go," she whispered.

While Jack welcomed the group and got them set up at a long table, Emerson took a moment to glance around the bar. For a Monday, there was actually quite a crowd. Besides the table of women and her family, most of the seats around the bar were occupied. She'd helped Jack work on happy hour specials, and she was happy to see people taking advantage.

Cosmo was happily prancing around the bar, going from table to table to greet the patrons. Everyone seemed delighted to meet him. He received more belly rubs and scratches than ever.

"You did this." Jack had come up behind her and wrapped his arms around her waist.

She turned in his arms, so she could look into his eyes. "We did this."

"Together," he said. He nipped her earlobe. "I have something for you. Come here a moment." He led her back through the bar and out into the alley once again.

"What are we doing out here?" she asked.

Jack pulled a small box from his pocket. "I thought I should give you this in the same spot where we met."

He opened the lid, and she gasped. "Ohmigod, Jack, that is stunning."

The ring was gorgeous. It was an antique platinum ring with a vibrant ruby in the center, surrounded by tiny diamonds.

"It was my mother's," Jack said, his gruff voice revealing deep emotions. "If you don't like it, or you want to add something to it, we can do that."

"Are you kidding? I couldn't love anything more. I'm honored to wear your mother's ring."

"She would have loved you." He slipped the ring on her finger.

"It's a perfect fit," she said, wiggling her fingers so she could watch the ring sparkle.

"So are we," Jack said. Then he reached down, put one arm under her legs and other behind her back, and lifted her into his arms. "This is more how we met."

She laughed. "Without the cumbersome wedding gown."

"But you were such a beautiful bride."

She tilted her head and met his lips for a long, sultry kiss. "And I will be again."

"But this time you'll be my bride," Jack said, his eyes darkening.

"And you'll be my groom."

The sun began to set as they kissed again, sealing their arrangement—for real this time.

* * * * *